BODYLINE

SIMON RAE

D1439801

NINE
ELMS
BOOKS

Bodyline

First published in 2015 by
Nine Elms Books
An imprint of Bene Factum Publishing Ltd
PO Box 58122
London
SW8 5WZ
Email: inquiries@bene-factum.co.uk
www.bene-factum.co.uk

ISBN: 978-1-910533-03-1

A CIP catalogue record of this is available from the British Library.

Cover design by Henry Rivers, thatcover.com
Book design by Bene Factum Publishing

Set in Borgia Pro
Printed and bound in the UK

Simon Rae is a poet, prose writer and broadcaster.

For many years he wrote topical poems for the *Guardian* and was for a time presenter of Radio 4's Poetry Please! In 1998 he published the definitive biography of W.G. Grace. He won the National Poetry Competition in 1999. His most recent collection of poems is *Gift Horses* (Enitharmon, 2006). Other books include *It's Not Cricket* (Faber, 2001), and the children's novels *Unplayable* (Top Edge Press, 2009), *Keras* (David Fickling Books, 2013) and *Medusa's Butterfly* (Corgi, 2014).

He has taught a creative writing evening class at Cherwell College, Oxford, led an informal writing group for a number of years, and had two stints as a Royal Literary Fund Fellow, at Warwick University and Oxford Brookes.

He lives in Little Tew, near Chipping Norton, Oxfordshire.

To Michael

Always a live wire at the wicket

PROLOGUE

'Is that you, Ted?'

The front door slammed. Footsteps approached across the hall and the door to the drawing room opened.

'No, it's the village serial killer,' Ted Roper said, coming up behind the sofa where his wife was watching television. 'I've come to strangle you with your own silk stockings,' he added, glancing at the popular detective who was grilling a suspect. He leant down and kissed her on the cheek.

Margot Roper pushed her husband away. 'The village idiot, more like,' she said, pressing the pause button. 'And if you think strangulation's a way of spicing up our sex life, you've got another think coming. Though after last night, I'd be within my rights if I strangled you.'

'Sorry about that,' Ted said, sitting down heavily in the armchair opposite the sofa and dropping his attaché case beside him. 'Shouldn't have had that second brandy.'

They both revisited – briefly – their failed sexual encounter from the previous evening, during which Ted had fallen asleep in the act and Margot had had to push her way out from under him as though from under a beached whale.

She looked at him sternly over her reading glasses. 'Good meeting?'

There was a note of asperity in the question. A glance at the clock showed it was after nine. How long could half a dozen grown men possibly spend talking about cricket, for God's sake? And, not for the first time, she thought she detected scent through the nicotine and beer fumes that had engulfed her when he'd kissed her.

'Yes, yes. The usual rot about the mower, the parking, the sightscreen, the wicket, the pavilion roof; but other than that, all tickety-boo. Oh, and look what I've got!' Out of the attaché case he produced a large brown envelope. Opening it, he drew out a shiny gloss photograph and passed it across the coffee table.

Margot looked at it without enthusiasm. The annual team photo, two rows of cricketers, the front row seating, with Ted in the middle, legs spread, hands on thighs, the broad grin of proprietorship spread across his jowly face.

Ye gods, she thought. Has it come to this?

'All the usual suspects,' Ted remarked complacently.

'So I see. Though you seem to be the only one smiling.'

'Well, you can't have everything. At least none of the rogues at the back are exposing themselves.'

'None of the rogues at the back *is* exposing *himself*,' Margot corrected.

'Oh, and who got a first in English at Cambridge?' Ted said with a moue.

'Well you read *something* at Cambridge. Anyway, why would anyone want to expose themselves in a team photo?'

'Oh, you know, bit of a lark, that kind of thing. There was a case a few seasons back when one of the county boys did it. I think it got printed in the members' handbook.'

'No pun intended?'

Ted was beginning to enjoy this unexpected repartee – until she added, 'I suppose we ought to be grateful they're not all baring the blades of their daggers like the conspirators in Julius Caesar.'

Ted frowned. 'It's not that bad, Margot. For goodness sake, can't we just forget things for an evening?'

'If you say so, darling. But you have spent the last few months right royally pissing off virtually every man jack of them. I'd watch my back – if I were you.' She flicked the team photo across the table.

Ted Roper let it lie there, staring at it morosely.

Margot Roper reached for the remote and resumed watching her programme.

Less than ten miles from the Ropers' comfortable drawing room, the same team photograph was the object of scrutiny in a very different environment. It had been pinned incongruously to the dartboard of the Poacher's Arms, a low dive buried in deep woodland and accessed by a single-track road.

Amidst gleeful laughter a rough voice said, 'A pint for the closest to his lordship.'

There was silence and then a cheer as the first dart zapped into the photo. It pinned the figure sitting next to Ted Roper through the heart.

'Vice captain, not bad,' said the original voice amongst more laughter.

The second dart was closer to its target, just missing the left ear.

'He'd have felt that all right,' a wag called out from the back.

'Close, but no cigar! My turn. Winner takes all.'

An intense silence fell, followed suddenly by a short, sharp thud. There was a gasp of astonishment as all eyes stared at the dartboard. Instead of a dart, a clasp-knife was sticking out from between the two previous darts – it had split Ted Roper's smiling face in two.

'Think I deserve a whisky chaser for that, don't you lads?'

Outside in the woods, perhaps disturbed by the gusts of laughter and applause that came roaring from the pub, a fox barked testily into the dark.

ONE

'Dalliance.'

Although he'd uttered his name with a pre-emptive sigh, Detective Chief Inspector Dalliance could hardly claim to have been interrupted in the middle of anything important. He glanced around at the Sunday papers, then looked at the clock on the mantelpiece. 4.38 p.m.

'What is it?' He reached for his pad and a pen, ready to jot down the details of a crime someone thought it worthwhile interrupting his Sunday afternoon for.

But then he stiffened.

'Murder? At a cricket match? Are they sure?' He paused to hear more details. 'Sounds more like a heart attack… Okay. So obviously it's not a heart attack. Where? Lower Bolton – I know it. Played there myself once. Pretty little ground. Last place I'd expect a crime scene… You'd better send Riley over for me now then.'

'Right up your street, sir.' Riley glanced across as he manoeuvred onto the main road. 'Nice afternoon's cricket match.'

'Except they'll have stopped playing. I assume...' Dalliance said, stroking his moustache. 'I can't honestly believe someone would be murdered at a cricket match – though I've known some umpires I wouldn't have minded seeing the back of. Do you know any of the details?'

'He'd apparently just caught a slip catch. Everybody gathered round to slap him on the back, and then he collapsed. Everyone assumed it was a heart attack and rang for an ambulance. The guys in the green fatigues pronounced him dead, but didn't buy the heart attack.'

'Because of this puncture in the lower back?'

'Yes, sir.'

'Hence our Sunday afternoon going down the chute. What are we looking at – poison?'

'You'd have thought. Obviously we won't know till the lab's checked it out. But no dagger sticking out of his back, no magic bullet from the nearby book depository...'

'So it's been secured as a crime scene?'

'I assume so, sir. I only got the call half an hour ago.'

'Well, we'll see. Left here – we can cut across through Mapplethorpe.'

A sign to Lower Bolton stuck out of an uncut hedge at an angle. Dalliance remembered his match there. The ground was cradled in an unspoilt valley about half a mile out of the village. A small pavilion, cars parked up on the bank. Quite a decent pitch for a village, though the ball that Dalliance had edged to slip had deviated just enough off the seam.

He wondered if it would prove the same man. He remembered a large, confident chap, captain as though by right, who stood at first slip throughout the innings, however freely the runs flowed. And for all the air of insouciance, a very safe pair of hands.

It had been a while back. He hadn't played a game for five years. He wondered how he'd used all those free Sundays. Not much to show for them. But at least he avoided the humiliation of hobbling into work on the Monday, aching in every limb.

It took him a moment to get his bearings when they reached Lower Bolton, but then he remembered. 'Left after the store, and up that lane.'

After a bumpy quarter of a mile, Riley swung the car through a gateway and was immediately flagged down by a uniformed officer, who waved them through. Dalliance was looking attentively about.

'If it is a crime scene, why are there people milling about round the pavilion? God damn it!' he fumed, leaping out of the car almost before it had stopped. 'Who's in charge?' he asked the man nearest him.

'Mitchell's waiting to brief you, sir.'

When Riley caught up with Dalliance, he found his boss giving Mitchell a sharp ticking off.

'It's a crime scene, man. We can't have people wandering around as though they were at a jumble sale. You!' He turned on a boy who was standing by the door to the pavilion. 'Was that you coming out of there? What were you doing?'

'Sorry, sir,' the boy said, looking guilty and dropping his head. 'I just... I just needed—'

'Well you could have gone in the hedge. And that applies to all of you.' Dalliance raised his voice and looked around the group of cricketers, some of whom were still wearing their whites, while some had changed back into their every-day clothes. 'I am sorry about the disruption to your after-noon's entertainment,' Dalliance went on, slightly modify-ing his tone. 'But there has been a very unfortunate incident, which we are now treating as suspicious.'

He had their attention now.

'We thought he'd just – you know – collapsed...' the man nearest Dalliance said.

'As I say, we're treating his death as suspicious, which means this is now a crime scene, which means that no one goes into that pavilion until I say so.'

'I've got to get back for milking,' a voice said.

More voices chimed in, claiming various urgent commitments.

Dalliance raised his arms.

'You must have expected the game to go on till well after seven. You wouldn't even have started the last twenty overs if you were still playing.' In response to the looks he received, Dalliance went on. 'Yes, I speak cricket. In fact I played here once. Decent track and a very nice tea. On that occasion we managed to complete the game without anything more suspicious than a dodgy LBW decision.'

There was a ripple of laughter, and the atmosphere perceptibly lightened.

'I do understand your predicament, gentlemen; but you will, I'm sure, understand where I'm coming from. Crime tends to be inconvenient – especially for the victims.' Dalliance left a pause and the mood sobered once more. 'We will need to interview you all to get an idea of what happened – and to eliminate as many of you as possible from our enquiries. Detective Sergeant Riley and I will do the preliminary interviews now. So can we have the two teams separated – Lower Bolton over there...'

Ten men moved slightly shiftily to form a huddle to Dalliance's left. Most were in whites, but two of them had changed.

'I see you two have been back in the changing room since the match ended,' Dalliance said.

'We didn't mean any harm—'

'I'm sure. Anyway, if you weren't told...' Here he gave the hapless Sergeant Mitchell a glare.

'To be fair, they got changed before the coppers even arrived.' A small man pushed forward. Despite his age, he radiated energy, and his sun-stained skin suggested a healthy life spent in the open air.

'I know you!' Dalliance laughed in recognition. 'You're the scorer! Though I'm blessed if I can remember your name.'

'Ebby Melksham. And very good to see you again, sir, albeit in less than ideal circumstances.' The nut-brown man came forward, extending his hand. Dalliance shook it warmly. In a low voice, the scorer added, 'I seen most things in my time, but I never seen a man killed out on the square, if that's what happened. And it'll be the first time I writes "Murder Stopped Play" at the bottom of the scorebook.'

Dalliance pursed his lips, and his expression darkened. 'I can see you're going to be an invaluable witness. Who were you playing today?'

'Tilsby. 78 for 2 they were. Ted 'ad just caught the number three, then the next thing we knew, he was down on the ground. Thought he'd had a heart attack to be honest with you.'

'What happened exactly?'

'It's hard to say. They all rushed in to congratulate him.'

'All?'

'Yes – all. I don't approve myself, sir. In the old days the odd slap on the back was enough. But they see it on the telly, so they all do it. Anyway, as they broke up and started going back to their fielding positions, Ted just keeled over.'

'I see,' Dalliance said, glancing out to the square and trying to picture the scene. 'I'll talk to you later, but first we need to do the basics. Okay,' he said, speaking to the whole group now. 'First we're going to need the names and contact details of everybody in the Tilsby team. My sergeant will see to that.'

He indicated Riley, who had already got his notebook out.

'Take a note of the two who were batting, especially the man who was out,' he muttered to his subordinate. 'Ask each of them if they saw anything strange, out of the ordinary.'

Riley nodded.

'Tell you what,' Dalliance added as an afterthought. 'For neatness' sake, do it in batting order. I'll do the home team.' He reached into his pocket for his own notebook.

'I can help you with that,' the scorer said, producing a scrap of paper with a list of names from one to eleven.

'Thank you, most helpful,' Dalliance said. He looked up. 'Mitchell.'

'Yes, sir?'

'You can redeem yourself – a little – by getting everybody else's details.' There was a third group, some men, and two or three women huddled unhappily by the side of the pavilion.

'Tea ladies and spectators,' said the scorer.

Dalliance nodded. 'Right, gentlemen,' he said, turning to the Lower Bolton team.

'I didn't see anything' – 'He just went down like a' – 'I couldn't believe me eyes—'

Dalliance raised his hand to quieten the random voices. 'All in good time. First I want your names and contact details.'

Several started talking at the same time. Dalliance again quelled the hubbub.

'One at a time. As I said, let's stick to the batting order. ' He looked at the list in his hand. 'David Henderson.'

A tall, slightly shy-looking man raised his hand. Mid- to late-thirties; thin, sandy hair; closely shaven. He gave his address and the two numbers of his landline and mobile in what Dalliance identified as a neutral, educated voice.

'Barney Grover.'

'Aye-aye,' called out a shorter man – shorter, but robustly muscular. He had a full weekend's growth of stubble and sported an elaborate tattoo on his right forearm. 'No need to guess who gets the runs out of us two,' he said with an amiable grin.

'Excepting when you gets out slogging,' said another voice, to a murmur of amusement.

'Number three – Rees Jones.'

An athletic youth in his twenties mumbled his details. He was one of the two that had changed out of his cricket clothes already, and Dalliance looked him over carefully. Although he spoke in the local accent, his ironed jeans and smart shirt suggested upward mobility.

'And what made you change so quickly?' Dalliance asked him. Rees Jones went slightly red and a wave of suppressed mirth, punctuated by a mocking wolf whistle, rippled through the group.

Dalliance had his answer. 'All right, all right,' he cautioned. 'The sooner we get through this, the sooner we can all get back to those we want to spend our evening with. Four – Norman Standing.'

'Yes,' came the reply. Standing was the other man who'd changed. Medium build, and dapper in his cavalry twill trousers and very smart jacket – a near certainty for the Aston Martin pulled up at a rakish angle near the pavilion, Dalliance thought. He had three telephone numbers: home, work and a mobile, and a London address in Kensington. 'And honestly, Inspector, if we could get on with it. I've got to get back to Town.'

Ted Roper was the next name on the list, but the scorer had put a line through it in black ink. So the victim was the mainstay of the middle order, Dalliance thought, looking up at the group as they waited for the next name.

'Number six – Steve Royce.'

A big man stood twisting a faded baseball cap in his hands, without saying anything. There was a groundswell of laughter.

'Can't remember his own phone number!' someone quipped. Another shouted out, 'Give him the Three Horseshoes' number, Roller!'

Dalliance again raised his hand for silence.

'Nearest we've got to Freddie Flintoff,' the scorer said. Judging by his massive frame, Royce looked capable of bowling at some speed. Dalliance was glad he hadn't been around on his last visit to Lower Bolton.

'Do you have a mobile?' he prompted gently.

'I do, but I can never remember the number. But like Barney said, you'll find me in the Shoes.'

'Or the Poachers,' another voice sang out.

Dalliance moved on to the next player. 'Seven – Ben Cowper.'

A short man with long, unkempt hair and a Mexican bandit's moustache lifted his finger, the one eager to get back to his cows. Dalliance imagined the same slightly raised finger bidding at any number of cattle auctions over the years.

'*Coo*-per,' the man said. 'It's pronounced *Coo*-per.'

'Like the poet,' Dalliance replied, not surprised to see the eyes tighten in incomprehension. 'Never mind. Contact details?'

'Harbledown Farm.'

'Tumbledown Farm, more like,' someone said *sotto voce*.

Cowper ignored the comment and gave his phone numbers, adding, 'An' I really do have to get back for milking.'

Dalliance acknowledged his request with a nod, but went on methodically. 'Eight – Daniel Pottinger.' This was the school kid he had told off for going into the pavilion to relieve himself.

'I'm at school, sir.'

'I'm glad to hear it,' Dalliance said, to a few snickers of amusement.

'Boarding school,' the boy clarified. 'I'm a weekly boarder at Stonybrooks. Got to get back tonight.' Stonybrooks was a middling public school about twenty miles away.

'So how do we contact you? Your parents live locally?'

'My mother does, yes, sir. My father's dead.'

'I'm sorry,' Dalliance said.

'Mum'll be coming to pick me up – that's her driving up now actually.'

Dalliance looked over to the gate where a modest hybrid was being held up. He waved to the uniform on duty to let it through, wondering idly why the boy's mother should continue to keep him boarding after her husband had died. You'd have thought she'd want his company.

'Okay, we'll get you on the road as soon as we can.'

'And the rest of us, I hope, Inspector!'

This was Standing, who was jangling the keys to his Aston Martin impatiently. Dalliance found he had already taken quite a dislike to him. 'Chief Inspector,' he corrected. 'Number nine – Jez Jones?'

One glance showed Jez and Rees were brothers, Jez seemingly the elder by no more than a year or two. He was a large-boned fellow, with a sly, cynical look and a natural slouch. He had clearly not been tempted to emulate his upwardly mobile brother.

'Jez was bowling when it happened,' the scorer said quietly at his side.

Dalliance nodded and took down his details. 'Number ten – D. Tucker?'

'Desmond Tucker, at your service – a complete local taxi service, railway station and airports a speciality.' A round little man had stepped forward, smiling confidently and offering Dalliance his card. Dalliance took it without responding to the smile.

'Thank you. And finally, number eleven – E. Phelps.'

Ernie Phelps was not much to look at with his sloping shoulders and dark pink bald patch. Dalliance suspected he was the one making up the numbers, turning his arm over for a short spell of declaration bowling when required. He jotted the man's address and telephone number down and closed his notebook.

'Right, gentlemen,' he called out to both teams. 'This is how it's going to work. DS Riley is going to sit in the away changing room and the Tilsby team are going to go in one at a time, show him their kit bags, answer any questions he decides to ask, and, as is fitting on a Sunday evening, depart in peace. Meanwhile, I will be in the home changing room where we'll do exactly the same thing, though for obvious reasons, my questions may take a little longer. I will start with Mr Cowper so that he can get off to his cows—'

'Bugger his cows. They can't tell the time. I'm the one who has to drive to London.'

'Ladies present, Mr Standing,' Dalliance said, turning to the woman who had come to the edge of the group. 'Mrs Pottinger?'

She was an attractive woman, and she knew it, Dalliance thought. Even though she was wearing the most casual clothes, she had taken the trouble to put make-up on.

'Yes – oh this is so awful. I couldn't believe it when I heard. He can't really have been…' She looked at Dalliance, then at the sergeant beside him, then out to the pitch where the SOCO team in their white head-to-toe overalls were busy erecting a tent over the wicket where Ted Roper had died. She moved over to Daniel, reaching for his hand. 'Are you all right, darling?'

The boy withdrew his hand – tactfully, Dalliance thought.

'Of course I am. But I won't be if you don't get me back in time for Chapel.'

'What about the religious observances of the rest of us?' Standing chipped in.

'You'll be third, Mr Standing,' Dalliance reassured him, without enthusiasm. 'Mitchell!' he called out. 'You can let your lot go, once you've got everything I could possibly want. Then come and supervise here.'

'All right for some,' Standing muttered, glancing over to the soon-to-be released group gathered around Mitchell.

'As far as I'm aware,' Dalliance said, 'none of the spectators was nearer than sixty yards from the wicket, whereas everybody here' – he looked around the circle of faces; no one was smiling now – 'was a great deal closer.'

'I was at mid-on.'

Dalliance was slightly surprised to find it was Phelps, the unassuming eleventh man, who had spoken.

'We'll go into the details of where everybody was as I conduct the interviews,' he said sharply.

The expression 'herding cats' wormed its way, uninvited, into his head.

TWO

Before going into the pavilion both detectives climbed into white overalls. Anderson, the senior Scene of Crime Officer, walked over from the tent and accompanied them into the changing rooms.

Dalliance looked around him, taking in the familiar untidiness – bats, pads, helmets on every surface, the floor and table taken up with the ugly and space-consuming coffins that had replaced old-fashioned cricket bags. Out of these spilled jerseys, spare socks, vests – the usual jumble sale of male clothing. He breathed in, savouring the old familiar scents of stale sweat and liniment. It had been a while since he'd retired. He still missed it.

'Mr Cowper,' he called.

Ben Cowper didn't exactly sidle in, but neither did he walk through the door four-square.

'Right, Cowper, which is your pile?'

The farmer indicated a nest in the corner. A pair of ancient-looking boots stood splayed with a couple of socks trailing out. Looking around, Dalliance saw a number of other pairs of boots and sighed. Pretty much everyone had changed their footwear. It was the most contaminated crime scene he could remember. Anyone wanting to conceal or remove something would have found it laughably easy.

Still, even the most cunning murderer could slip up, and although the chances were small, he would insist on the most thorough application of forensic good practice on the off-chance of finding something. It would help if he had the first idea what that 'something' might be.

'So that's your corner?'

'Has been for twenty-five year or more,' Cowper said, lunging forward as though to gather up his bag.

'What are you doing?'

'Getting my stuff – what does it look like?'

Dalliance shook his head. 'Your stuff stays here – as does everybody else's. Until my team have checked it out.'

'Checked it out for what?' Cowper stood with his arms sulkily akimbo.

'And we're going to need the clothes as well.'

'Clothes?'

'Everything everybody was wearing at the time of the incident on the site of the crime scene. Maybe it hasn't sunk in, Mr Cowper, but you – all of you – were present at a highly suspicious death that was almost certainly murder, so we need to check everything that might give us a clue as to what happened and who was responsible.'

'Well, it weren't me, I can tell you that much. And anyway, what was he meant to have died of? I didn't see anything sticking out of his shirt – nor seen anybody stabbing him neither.'

'That's because there was no knife, Mr Cowper. But everybody was clustered round him, and the natural inference is that somebody – one of your teammates – introduced something into his system that killed him.'

'Why didn' they just take 'im out with a twelve-bore while he was strolling about the estate like the lord of the bleedin' manor? Christ knows I've been tempted myself.'

'Would you like to tell me why, Mr Cowper?'

Cowper scowled. Then he spat and wiped his thin lips with the back of his hand. 'Well, it'll come out soon enough when you start prying around, so I may as well tell you. I 'ated the bastard. And, given the way he treated me, he liked me just as much in return.'

'And what was the cause of this mutual antagonism?'

Cowper looked levelly at Dalliance.

'You wouldn't understand – you townies. You buys and sells your 'ouses, move from one place to another, and never give it another thought. My land and my farm's been in my family for two 'undred years – and I don' take kindly to some Johnny-come-lately trying to rob me of any part of it – not a damn square foot of it. I'd kill him first – and you'll find folks that'll say they heard me say as much, so I'll tell it to you straight myself. But I didn' kill him on a Sunday afternoon playing cricket, and nor would I 'ave neither. Twelve-bore – both barrels. And buried 'im deep. That's my style. And now if you've finished with me, perhaps I can go and see to my milking.' He gave a terrific hitch to his belt and glowered at Dalliance.

Mindful of the other impatient souls waiting to be seen, Dalliance gave a slight nod of the head to dismiss him.

'Almost tantamount to a confession,' Anderson said, as he shook out a large plastic bag and started to pile Cowper's clothing and kit into it. 'What is it we're looking for exactly?'

'If only I knew,' Dalliance said with a sigh, before calling out, 'Danie Pottinger!'

The boy put his head shyly round the door frame.

'Come in, Daniel. Don't worry, this won't take a moment. We'll soon have you on your way.'

Daniel walked uncertainly into the changing room.

'Oh, I'm so grateful to you, Inspector.'

A woman's voice, and Dalliance noticed another head in the doorway. He mustered a weary smile.

'Mrs Pottinger, I'm afraid I really need to talk to Daniel on his own. It won't take a minute, just a preliminary interview, to help us get a handle on what happened. He's not under caution, and I promise I won't try to trap him into a damning confession.'

Mrs Pottinger's handsome face showed a moment of concern, but then broke into a relieved smile before disappearing behind the closing door.

Dalliance's own smile broadened – reassuringly, he hoped. 'Now, Daniel. Let's get on with it.'

The boy had identified his kit – the newest and most pristine of the coffins – and relatively neatly folded whites and shirts. He seemed alarmed at not being allowed to take his possessions away with him.

'I know it's inconvenient,' Dalliance said, 'but we do have to unleash forensics on this lot.' Seeing the boy's crestfallen face, he asked, 'Is there a problem?'

'There's a house match on Wednesday.'

'You must have a spare set of kit,' Dalliance said. 'And you can borrow pads and gloves, can't you?'

Dalliance peered into the boy's coffin, and saw the jock-strap with its pouch for the all-important plastic box. 'Abdominal protector' it had been called in his day, an item of special significance, source of much changing room humour, and not an easy item to negotiate the loan of. He caught the boy's eye, and took pity on him.

'Go on then – but don't tell anyone else.'

Daniel reached into the coffin and put the jock-strap with its contents into his trouser pocket, going slightly pink in the process.

'Thank you, sir.'

'That's all right,' Dalliance said. 'Now, if you could just tell me all you can remember about the – incident.'

'There's not much to say really, sir. I mean, Ted – Mr Roper – caught the catch. And we all crowded round –

and then moments later he suddenly collapsed. Everybody thought he'd had a heart attack. No one thought – I mean I still can't believe—'

'No, it's hard to get your head round it. But that's what the science is telling us. And that's what we have to go by. Do you like science?' Dalliance asked by way of keeping the exchange conversational.

'More design,' the boy said.

'An arts man myself – literature, drama,' Dalliance said. 'But I'm governed by the chaps in lab coats. Where were you fielding by the way?'

'Fine leg.'

'So you'd have had a pretty good view.'

'I suppose so. But as I say, it was all pretty routine – Jez came in and bowled – good line, good length – their guy lunged forward, and nicked off to Ted.'

Dalliance suppressed a wince at the expression. 'Go on,' was all he said.

'Ted doesn't – didn't – miss many. He snapped it up.'

Dalliance nodded, remembering his own efficient dismissal ten years previously. 'And then what – everybody ran up and—?'

'The usual huddle. High-fives, slapping him on the back – you know.'

Dalliance did. It was getting as bad as football. 'And you came in, did you?'

'Oh yes, I ran up. I wanted to congratulate Jez as much as anything. He was bowling really well.'

'Did you touch Mr Roper?'

'I may have done. It was all a bit of a scrum, to be honest.'

'But you didn't see anything – of note?'

The boy shook his head. 'Just everybody milling around, excited. It was a good wicket. We'd been under the cosh for the first hour, so getting Mills out cheaply was good.'

'Mills?'

'Their number three. Very good bat. Took a ton off us last year.'

'So everyone was relieved to see the back of him?'

The boy nodded.

'And you saw nothing suspicious – no one acting oddly?'

'Ben – Ben Cowper—'

'What about him?'

'Well, he wasn't exactly turning cartwheels. But then that's not his style.'

'But he was in the group around Roper?'

'Oh yes. Definitely.'

Dalliance scribbled something in his notebook. He often did this as much for effect as anything else. There'd be far more detail in the formal statements, which he would go through line by line.

'All right, young man. Thank you. You've been very helpful. Good luck in your house match.'

'Thank you, sir,' the boy said politely, giving Dalliance a shy smile of gratitude for sparing him embarrassment over his box.

'Mitchell,' Dalliance called out through the door as he left. 'Send Mr Standing in.'

Norman Standing didn't need any ushering. He strode into the changing room, looking impatiently at his watch. At Dalliance's prompting he identified his kit – of considerably better quality than anyone else's and with an MCC sweater hanging prominently over the side of his coffin. There was also an old-fashioned hooped cap in black and light blue.

'Cambridge Crusaders?' Dalliance asked, nodding at it.

Standing seemed rather taken aback.

'Spot on,' he said. 'Had hoped to get a Blue, but my rival for the number five slot ran me out against Essex and went on to score a ton and got my place. Had to make do with the Crusaders-Tics match.'

Dalliance nodded. He had played in the fixture himself, though a few years earlier, and for the Dark Blues. 'Bad luck,' he said, with an attempt at sympathy.

'Didn't do me any harm, long-term,' Standing said. 'I was too nice, in those days. Disappointment can toughen you up. That was the last time anyone ever ran me out. And I derived enormous satisfaction from making my rival bankrupt a decade later.'

Dalliance looked at him sharply, and found a level gaze directed back at him.

'Power, Inspector – the greatest motivational driver. Far more potent than greed, lust, envy, revenge, and all the rest of them. Because, of course, when you have power you can satisfy them all.' He smiled briefly. 'But I can assure you, I didn't assassinate poor old Ted to take over the captaincy of Lower Bolton Cricket Club. This is not Richard II.'

'I didn't suppose for a moment that it was, Mr Standing,' Dalliance said. 'I was thinking more of Julius Caesar.'

'Yes, I suppose so,' Standing replied, with a half-laugh. 'But no *et tu, Brute*, I'm afraid. Whoever did it wanted to remain very much a part of the crowd. If that's really what happened, which I for one find hard to credit.'

'It would certainly take meticulous planning – someone very clever, and utterly ruthless, Mr Standing.'

Standing threw his arms wide. 'Banged to rights.' He smiled broadly. 'Very clever – and utterly ruthless.'

He put his hands together as though offering them to Dalliance for the cuffs. Dalliance ignored the play-acting.

'Could you tell me a bit about your relations with Mr Roper?' he asked levelly.

Standing dropped his arms to his sides. 'Ted and I go – went, sorry – back a long way: chums at Cambridge, messing about on punts together, chasing the prettiest girls. Actually he got the prettiest girl. But before you ask, no, that didn't sour our friendship. For once losing had its compensations.'

Dalliance raised an enquiring eyebrow.

'I just never got around to settling down. Too busy making pots and pots of money, thanks to deregulation. Women were throwing themselves at me – as were the banks. It seemed rude to disappoint them.'

'And did you remain friends?'

'Ted and I stayed pals, yes. I won't say there wasn't a cooling off period when he married Margot, but we got together again. At her suggestion, actually. They invited me for dinner – rather shabby flat in Islington at the time – and she basically told Ted to give me all his money – so that I could make them rich.'

'And you did?'

'Of course. Which is why for the last twenty years Ted has been lording it around the Boltons as to the manor born.'

'And what is you do exactly, Mr Standing?'

'Alchemy, turning base metal into gold. I'm very sharp; I'm very well connected; but above all, I'm not frightened of noughts. In fact, I like them. The more the merrier – except when I'm batting of course.' He gave a dry laugh. 'Naturally everyone thinks I'm the devil incarnate doing wicked things with people's pension funds in the city; but they're all happy to take a drink off me in the pub after a match, and one or two have tapped me up for a discreet loan now and then. The devil can be an awfully useful drinking companion.'

'And Mr Roper – how had your dealings with him progressed?'

'Ah…' Standing frowned, and rubbed his chin, as though trying to make his mind up over something. 'Well, Inspector,' he said, having obviously made his decision. 'You'll hear about it sooner rather than later, so I may as well come out with it. Just recently things have not been good. No, that's not right – things have been bloody awful. I put together a rather elaborate investment – won't bore you with the details – but suffice it to say it was complicated, high risk, but potentially an absolute goldmine. Ted was all over me to come in on it. I pointed out the high risk but he wouldn't listen. Nothing else we'd ever done together had failed. Why should this? Well, of course, in the world as it is at the moment, nothing's guaranteed, and as I always tell my clients, don't invest what you can't afford to lose.' He sighed. 'Well, you can guess the rest.'

'It failed?' Dalliance suggested.

'Big time,' Standing confirmed. 'I got out as quick as I could. But we took a hit.'

'How big?'

Standing expelled breath from between pursed lips. 'Enough.'

'Ballpark? Number of noughts?' Dalliance urged.

'Six,' Standing replied, looking him straight in the eye. 'Each.'

'I see,' said Dalliance. 'Which didn't put you in Mr Roper's good books?'

'Which didn't put Ted in *my* good books,' Standing riposted.

Dalliance raised an eyebrow.

'I'd leant Ted the money. And of course, he didn't have it.'

'Ouch,' said Dalliance, softly.

'Too bloody right,' Standing agreed. 'Look, there's no point in trying to hide it – we were furious with each other. As the rest of the guys out there will no doubt delight in telling you, we had a blazing row at the end of the match about a month back.'

'And what specifically was the row about, Mr Standing?'

'I told Ted he was going to have to sell the house to cover his debt.'

Dalliance nodded slowly. 'Were you going to force it?'

'I'm not a charity, Inspector. Sorry, Chief Inspector. I'm wealthy, but you don't get wealthy without a very deep respect for money. And a sum like that commands a lot of respect.'

'So tempers were lost – things said…?'

'Tempers were lost and things were said. Possibly even: "I'm going to kill you, you bastard!" But I didn't, Inspector. It's extremely bad business killing your creditors.'

'But despite the bust-up, you still continued to play cricket with him.'

'Inspector, you're a cricketer. It's a team game. You don't let your team down.'

'Even when they think you're the devil incarnate.'

'Satan was a team-player – remember your Paradise Lost, Inspector? Anyway, I love it here – I've had a cottage in the village for the last fifteen years. It's a great stress decompression chamber. But now I have other duty calls, and would very much like to get on the road.'

'For evensong,' Dalliance murmured.

'We all have our particular forms of worship, Inspector. I am keen not to delay mine any longer than is absolutely necessary.'

Dalliance explained that the kit and cricket clothing would have to remain. Standing seemed unconcerned.

'I don't suppose forensics will put them through the wash when they finished?'

'You can go, Mr Standing. Please drive carefully, and watch your speed. We may need to be in touch.'

'I await your call, Inspector. Who knows, we might find time for a little chat about your pension.'

'What, when he's just lost his chum a fortune? I don't think so!' Anderson exclaimed after Standing had left the changing room.

'He's just winding me up,' Dalliance said. Though whether purely out of habit or with a deeper motive, he wasn't sure.

'Sir?'

It was Riley, putting his head round the door from the showers which were located between the two changing rooms and accessible from both.

'We're finished through here. Can I let them go?'

'Anything useful?'

'Not really. Obviously most of them were sat on the veranda watching the cricket or reading the papers. Two more were out there umpiring, and then there were the two batsmen. The guy who was out—'

'Mills?' Dalliance interjected.

'Yup, Mills – well, he just walked straight off to the pavilion. His partner stayed up at the bowler's end and talked to the guy who was umpiring. The other guy who was umpiring out in the outfield—'

'At square leg, Riley. This case is going to require you to brush up on your cricket terminology. What about him?'

'Well, he was going to have to put his pads on, so he started walking towards the pavilion too.'

'So he must have passed pretty close to the Bolton team milling around Roper. Did he see anything?'

Riley shook his head. 'He was more concerned with attracting someone's attention to relieve him. Useless really.'

Dalliance shook his head. 'But you've noted him and the others who were actually out there at the time?'

'Yes, sir. SOCO want to know if we need to keep their clothes and stuff?'

'No, I don't think so. Let them take it away. It'll be easier to do a proper search without the clutter.'

'Okay, sir. I'll tell them.'

'Then come back in here. See if we can't get through the rest of the Bolton lot within the hour. I wouldn't mind some of my Sunday to myself. Not that I hold out much hope of uncovering anything particularly useful,' he added glumly.

And so it proved. Each man came in, identified his case and his clothing, and gave the same account of what happened, adding their own twist to the same event.

'I practically kissed the man,' Barney Grover said. 'I remember what Mills did to us last year. He's a serious batter, that boy. Shouldn't be playing at this level to be honest with you. So when Ted snaffled the catch I was well chuffed.'

Jez Jones, the gangling bowler of the wicket-taking ball dwelt on the quality of the delivery. 'He'd played and missed at a couple, and that one – just nipped away a fraction.' His hand cut through the air to indicate the ball's movement. Then he clapped his hands together. 'Ted never dropped those.' But apart from running down the pitch to take part in the celebrations, Jez had nothing of significance to contribute.

Steve Royce had run in from cover. 'Bloody marvellous catch,' he said, his face breaking into a broad smile. 'Getting old Millsy cheap – well, less than a ton anyway – bloody miracle. I had bruises on my hands for a week after the drubbing he dished out last year.'

Dalliance looked at the very large hand that was held up for his inspection. How easy would it have been to conceal something in that capacious palm, he thought. But what? And why?

'Did you like Mr Roper?' he suddenly found himself prompted to ask.

The smile vanished from Royce's face, to be replaced by a frown of concentration.

'No, I didn't, if I'm honest with you,' he said with a note of defiance in his voice.

'I hope you will be honest with me,' said Dalliance. 'Why didn't you like him?'

'Ted was a bastard.'

Dalliance noticed the huge right hand tightening into a fist. A blow in anger from that would be like being hit by a sledgehammer, he thought.

'Thank you, Mr Royce.'

'That all, then?' He was about to leave but stopped. Looking down into his cricket bag, he said, 'Sorry about the state of my clothes. Washing machine's been broke for the last month. I'd keep your rubber gloves on, if I were you.' With that the smile returned and he clumped out of the changing room.

David Henderson, the neat and self-effacing opening batsman, had little to contribute. He had been fielding at mid-off and could confirm what Jez had said about the ball deviating slightly off the seam. He had joined the congratulatory huddle around bowler and catcher, and thought he'd probably touched some part of his captain's upper body, but hadn't seen anyone doing anything suspicious.

On his personal relations with Ted Roper he would only say that as neighbours they had had 'issues'. When Dalliance pushed him as to what they were, he responded, 'Ted seemed to think he owned the village and could do anything he liked with it. He'd decided he wanted a carp lake, but the only possible source of water was a spring on my land.'

'You denied him the use of it?' Dalliance asked.

'Too right I did. People think the environment will take whatever punishment you dish out to it; but it won't. I said no, very firmly.'

'And was that the end of it?'

'Sadly not. The bloody man had the nerve to start tunnelling for it – under my land, with a view to diverting my spring.'

'Which you understandably took exception to.'

'I was livid. Never felt more strongly about anything in my life. If he wanted to get hold of my spring, it would have been over my dead body.'

'Not his?'

Henderson gave a watery smile. 'We're a law-abiding community here, Inspector. At least, that goes for most of us.

I have a perfectly competent solicitor who'd been instructed to draw up a letter telling Ted to desist. I shall cancel that instruction in the morning.'

'No love lost there,' Dalliance muttered as Henderson left the changing room.

'Not much of a murderer though,' Riley replied.

'Crippen was a very self-contained, nondescript little man, Riley. Try not to pre-judge anything.'

Rees Jones had been at gulley, so had been the next closest fielder to Ted Roper. He had run to his brother first, but conceded that, when the two men met halfway up the pitch, he probably had clapped his captain on the back. When asked whether he had liked the dead man, there was a perceptible pause.

'Ted was all right.'

'Meaning?' said Riley, slightly aggressively.

'Come on. What am I meant to say? We weren't best mates. Who could expect us to be? He was rich – and posh—'

'And stuck up?' Riley suggested.

'If you like. I mean, we played cricket together. That was it. Our paths never crossed otherwise – why would they?'

'You can still like – or dislike – someone you don't have much in common with,' Dalliance suggested, adding, 'It doesn't sound as though you liked Mr Roper that much.'

'Not many people did, if you want the honest answer. Bought his way into the village and set himself up like the bloody squire. Thought he could do anything he wanted – have anything he wanted. And because he had money, he got away with it. But that didn't make him popular. You'll see – as you ask around. Buy you a pint down the Horseshoes for everyone who says they liked him.' He suddenly looked rather self-conscious, as though wishing he hadn't spoken so freely. 'I've got an evening league match Thursday. Any chance of having my kit back by then?'

'We'll do our best,' Dalliance told him before calling out for the next man.

Ernie Phelps was one of life's natural number elevens, Dalliance thought. You would hardly notice him in an empty room. He confirmed Dalliance's suspicion that he bowled a few overs of spin. And almost always fielded at mid-on.

'Didn't really see much,' he said. 'To be perfectly honest, I wasn't really concentrating if you know what I mean. I mean, we'd been out there over an hour, and it was hot. Very hot.'

Dalliance nodded sympathetically. Phelps stood rather pathetically, fidgeting with his hands.

'Is that all?' he asked eventually.

'We'll be in touch,' Riley said.

'Send in Mr Tucker,' Dalliance said as he left the room.

Des Tucker was the opposite of Ernie Phelps: an urgently energetic little man, with quick eyes, always on the lookout for an opening, constantly scanning your face for a reaction.

'Well, this is a turn-up and no mistake,' was his opening gambit. 'Come out for a gentle game of cricket and end up being given the third degree by the local CID.'

'We're just asking a few preliminary questions,' Dalliance pointed out patiently.

'We haven't had a murder in the village for over thirty years,' Tucker went on, undeterred. 'Charlie Coldfield. Got his head bashed in. Didn't take the police long to solve that one, mind. He'd been giving his best mate's missus more than was good for her and his best mate gave him one back. Bit harder than he'd meant in fact. Come to think of it, it wasn't murder. They let it go at manslaughter.' Tucker smiled at both detectives, as though expecting them to applaud. 'Still goes on today, mind.'

'What does, Mr Tucker?' Dalliance asked.

'Oh, you know.' Tucker tapped his nose. 'The same old story – people seeing people they shouldn't.'

'Really? Anything we ought to know about?'

'I'm not one for talking out of school, but I gets to hear a fair bit in my line of business. Everyone talks to the taxi-man, don't they? Not that it's exactly top secret that young Rees' intended's a bit of a looker.'

'Are you suggesting there was anything between her and Roper?' Riley asked sharply.

'Nooo, nooo,' Tucker said, obviously pleased to have drawn the response. 'But,' he added, 'it's often as not not what *is* happening but what people suspect might be happening that causes all the trouble. But as I say, I'm not saying anything.'

Dalliance looked at his watch. He loathed witnesses like Tucker – smart-arses who wasted your time and laid red her-rings for the fun of it. On the other hand, a man in Tucker's position would know a lot about the village. He was worth keeping on side. He explained about the impounding of all the gear.

Tucker looked at his kit. 'S'all yours. Just give it a rinse when you're done with it.'

Dalliance sighed, leaning back against the changing room wall with his eyes shut.

'It seems like just about every member of the team hated his guts,' Riley murmured.

'Which is something our murderer must have been counting on. Clever. Okay, Riley, that's it for today. Might as well enjoy what's left of the weekend – it's going to be full-on from Monday morning.'

They climbed out of their white overalls and, after a few words with Anderson, headed back to the car. Dalliance settled himself in the passenger seat and gazed out over the cricket ground, but said nothing. He remained silent for the whole journey back to his house.

Riley knew better than to interrupt his boss' meditation. Even his 'See you in the morning, sir' elicited no response. Dalliance simply slammed the car door and trudged up the garden path to his front door.

THREE

'Oi! You – Inspector, whatever your name is!'

Dalliance was only a few paces from his car when he was so brusquely hailed. He wheeled round to be confronted by an irate man sporting extravagant sideburns and a very fierce frown.

'How long's that bloody stupid thing going to be there in the middle of my square?'

Dalliance looked at SOCO's white tent. He had to admit, it did look rather ridiculous. And if he was honest, it really wasn't doing much good. They'd already gone over every square inch of the playing surface like old pros giving a test wicket the once-over. Predictably, they'd found nothing more exciting than a stud that had worked its way loose from somebody's boot.

'I'm sorry, Mr—?'

'Hancock. And don't start. I've heard every Hancock gag there is going. But I'll tell this for nothing – it takes a bloody lot longer than half a bloody hour to prepare a cricket pitch. We've got a match on Sunday, rain forecast for Wednesday, and I need to get the mower on the new strip pronto. And a good go with the roller an' all.'

'It's a fine square, Mr Hancock.'

'It should be given the time I give to it. But it's a good cricket wicket. Just enough for the bowler if he puts the work in.' He paused, slightly mollified by Dalliance's appreciation of his labours. 'I'm thinking I could maybe use the same one again, seeing as they didn't get a full game in yesterday.'

The groundsman looked at Dalliance, letting his frown fade.

'I know I shouldn't be stressing about a cricket pitch when poor old Ted's dead.' He shook his head. 'Are you lot really sure about this suspicious death business? I mean, really? I've had blood spilt on my pitches; I've had ribs broke too. And one chap lost most of his teeth before they all wore helmets. Christ, that was a mess. But that's battlewounds – bad luck, but no hard feelings, you know? Murder though? In the middle of the wicket – with everybody crowding round? I mean, why?'

'Why did someone want to kill him, or why did they kill him on your cricket pitch?'

'Yes, that – why out here on my wicket? There's any number of people who would've happily killed him. They had the whole bloody parish to do it in – and they had to choose just back of a length on my best track. And now I've got some sort of bloody scout tent in the middle of my bloody square and my preparations for next Sunday hanging by a thread.'

Dalliance suppressed a smile.

'As I said to both teams yesterday, crime tends to cause inconvenience. Where were you yesterday by the way?'

'Hove. Daughter's down there. Went for the day with the missus to see the grandchildren. Marked out the pitch at half-eight. Thought I could leave them to stick the stumps in the ground and put the bails on by themselves. Get in to the Horseshoes for a night-cap and find all hell's broke loose. Turn my back on them for a day and they bump off the club captain.'

'I'm interested to hear you say there are any number of people who might have killed him. Could you suggest some names?'

Hancock looked at him and spat deliberately. Then, wiping his mouth with the back of his hand, he said, 'There are enough gossips in this village to give you all the leads you need, and keep the press boys in clover to boot.'

Dalliance looked around the cricket ground. There would be no way of stopping the press photographers snapping away at the crime scene. Perhaps without the focal point of the SOCO tent it would look less dramatic.

'I'll tell you what, Mr Hancock; I'll get the tent removed by lunchtime, and I'll tell the man on the gate you're free to come and work on the wicket. Pavilion's still out of bounds till we've been through everything in the changing room but—'

'That's all right,' Hancock said with a wave of his arm. 'Don't need to go in there. Got me own shed – with its own key.' He held up a key-ring with a few keys dangling from it.

'Would anyone else have had access to it yesterday?

'Well, there are one or two with keys – 'cause they help with the mowing. But no one would have needed to go in there yesterday.'

'All the same,' Dalliance said. 'I'd like one of my chaps to have a look.'

'What for?'

'We don't know yet. But we have to explore every avenue.'

Chiding himself for the cliché, Dalliance pushed through the flaps of the tent and knelt down to inspect the bare, scuffed earth of Mr Hancock's pride and joy. There were dozens of indentations from the players' studs, but of the drama that had taken place a mere metre or so above the surface, there was not a trace. He got heavily to his feet, and stroked his moustache. The killer, whoever he was, was a cunning one.

*   *   *

Dalliance walked down the lane to the village. There were a few modern houses on the outskirts and, he knew, a small estate hidden away out of sight and out of mind on the other side of the low hill. But for the most part Lower Bolton hadn't changed much since the nineteenth century. Old houses, one or two of them quite grand, and smaller cottages huddled round the Norman church, and at the heart of the village was a duck pond.

The sun was shining, birds called to each other from the branches of the few ancient trees standing around the green like village elders. Dalliance let himself down onto a convenient bench, and breathed in deeply, savouring the smells wafted on the slight breeze from the neighbouring gardens. A bee hummed companionably by. It was about as close to the rural English idyll as you could get.

He felt his hand reaching towards his jacket pocket – but the only thing that could make the moment absolutely perfect was not available; the familiar cardboard packet was missing. He let out a long, unpolluted sigh of regret. A young mother with her toddler approached the pond. Suddenly all the ducks noticed them and made for the shore to fight for the stale bread that the little figure jerked onto the water for them.

How in this protected world of innocence could someone plan to take a life – and plan so cold-bloodedly? Sudden spurts of anger leading to unforeseen consequences he could understand, almost sympathise with. But this – so breathtaking in its simplicity, so clinical – was something else entirely.

The bee buzzed past again.

Dalliance stopped his train of thought. What if there were a natural explanation – some people had extreme allergic reactions to insect stings. He must remember to ask whether anyone had been aware of bees or wasps around the pitch.

He looked up at the church clock. Nearly eleven. Riley would be arriving soon, bringing news of the tox report.

35

A fatal allergy would make them look a bit stupid, but he could live with that. They wouldn't look as daft as the firearms unit called in to surround what turned out to be an outsized stuffed tiger that someone had mischievously placed in a field near a housing estate a year or so back. Better safe than sorry, even if you did end up a laughing stock.

The toddler had worked through the bag of crusts and was now being led back across the green. The church clock began to chime the hour, and there was Riley coming round the corner by the pub, dead on time.

'What have we got?' Dalliance asked him as he got out of the car. 'It occurred to me that we might be looking at natural causes after all – bee sting allergy?'

'No such luck, sir. They're still working on what it was exactly, but there's no doubt it was a very fast-working poison administered externally. One small puncture' – here Riley patted his lower back – 'I'm afraid we are looking for a murderer.'

Riley handed over a large brown envelope. Dalliance looked at the photographs: Roper stretched out in the morgue, a middle-aged man gone to fat – about the same dimensions as Dalliance himself, he thought with a pang. And there, in a separate print, the tiny puncture mark low on the back – above the waistline of the trousers.

'Any indication how it got into him?'

Riley shook his head. 'Something sharp and inconspicuous – obviously.'

'Obviously,' Dalliance agreed. You could hardly plunge a hypodermic needle into someone's back unnoticed.

'But although they don't know what it was, it's clearly deadly. You wouldn't need much,' Riley said.

'If I gall him slightly, it may be death,' Dalliance murmured to himself. Clever, very clever. But where did the murderer get the poison? In Shakespeare's day there could have been a convenient mountebank selling deadly unctions down any dark alley you chose to explore. Not so easy nowadays. He held his right hand out and placed his left forefinger in its palm, shook his head, and moved the finger up to the base of his right middle finger.

'Bugger!' he suddenly exclaimed.

'Sir?'

'Rings. How many of them were wearing rings?'

'I don't know, sir. I didn't think to check.'

'No, and neither did I. Stupid, stupid, stupid!' He started working his own signet ring loose. It was comfortably embedded in the flesh of his little finger, but with a gasp of pain he managed to dislodge it and held it out for inspection. 'There, you see – that bit's hollow.' He pointed to the gap beneath the shield. 'Plenty of room there.'

Riley nodded appreciatively. 'Bit risky, though. What if you accidently caught yourself?'

'Hoist with your own petard, yes. And how would you field properly with some sort of needle or proboscis sticking out of your ring? And how would you know when Roper was going to get a catch – or indeed that he was going to catch it when – or if – he did get one?'

'Assuming Roper was the intended victim.'

'Sorry, Riley; I don't follow.'

'Well, we're assuming the murderer was out to get Roper.'

'A safe assumption as virtually everyone in the team turns out to have hated him.'

'But what if the killer just wanted to kill someone – you know, a psycho. The fact that he chose the most unpopular man in the village was just his good luck.'

Dalliance nodded. 'Well done, Riley. Impeccable logic. I just don't happen to believe it. If it turns out to be the case, the drinks are on me.'

He frowned again. Even though on closer inspection the ring idea threw up more problems than it solved, he was still annoyed with himself that he hadn't thought to check the previous day.

But if the means of application were problematic, so was disposal. SOCO had gone over the pitch, the outfield and beyond with a fine-tooth comb, but of course the perpetrator, though eager to get rid of the murder weapon, would not have discarded it anywhere it was likely to be stumbled upon. Even if the early suspicions of the paramedics meant the cricket ground had been locked down as a crime scene surprisingly quickly, there had still been plenty of time when anyone or everyone could have roamed about wherever they pleased. Reconstructing the movements of the entire team during that period was going to be time-consuming and frustrating. He had to hope the locals who had come along to watch were of an observant disposition, but even so, how easy it would have been for the murderer to slip away and jettison his lethal delivery system over the fence. Tracking it down really would be like looking for a needle in a haystack.

Dalliance felt an uncomfortable prickling at the back of his neck. It was as though the murderer was looking on, enjoying his frustration. He swore under his breath and his large right hand began to clench.

Still, at least it would give the interviews some substance. More often than not, interviewing suspects – 'to eliminate them from our enquiries' – felt like sitting there waiting for someone to confess. Which, unsurprisingly, they seldom did.

'Got the names?'

'Still in batting order, sir,' Riley said, presenting him with a typed-up list with addresses and contact numbers.

'Okay, let's start with the openers. Give Henderson a ring. He works from home.'

*　*　*

Five minutes later they drove down a neatly gravelled drive to a modestly substantial house set in well-kept grounds. Dalliance noted a couple of ponies in a paddock, a gleaming four-by-four drawn up by the front door, and a smaller vehicle to the side of the building. Money, Dalliance thought. Not in the same league as Norman Standing, but the Hendersons were clearly comfortably off. Henderson had come across as a typically successful professional type who had presumably started in London and moved out to the shires on the wave of one property boom or another.

They stood on the portico and Riley rang the bell. It sent a jangling peel ringing through the house. Nothing happened for a moment, and then the door was flung open and they were confronted by a handsome woman in jodhpurs.

'Good morning, Chief Inspector – sorry I didn't quite catch the name?'

'Dalliance, and this is Detective Sergeant Riley.'

'Dalliance? H'm.' She smiled appraisingly. 'I'm Jennifer Henderson – but do please feel free to call me Jenny. Everybody does. Come in, gentlemen. David's in his office. Due to some administrative oversight, we do not appear to have a butler, so I'll take you to him.'

She gave a peeling laugh over her shoulder, reminiscent, Dalliance thought, of the door bell. If Henderson was self-effacing and restrained, his wife more than made up for him. She led the way across an expansive hallway, skirted the bottom of the staircase and down a corridor.

'And ironically,' she went on, 'David seems to have ended up in the butler's pantry.'

At the end of the corridor there was an internal window through which they could see a small room with crowded shelves and a figure sitting at a desk bowed over a laptop.

'They're here, darling,' she said, flinging open the door – something of a personal speciality, Dalliance decided. 'Assuming they don't drag you off in chains, could you be a sweetie and put the oven on at twelve. I'm just taking Poppy for a gallop.' Then with a wide smile that took in both Dalliance and Riley, she ushered them into the room, turned on her heel and strode off down the corridor again.

Henderson had stood up, but remained focused on his screen. He made a couple of keystrokes and gently lowered the lid. 'Sorry,' he said vaguely, though whether he was apologising for his exuberant wife or the fact that they had found him working wasn't clear. 'Is here all right or—?'

'Fine,' said Dalliance. He liked to see a man in his everyday habitat when possible. People tended to be more at ease, less on the defensive. The seating options were limited to an ancient armchair and what looked like a discarded dining room chair. Riley made for the latter and Dalliance settled in the former.

'How long is this going to take?' Henderson asked, sitting down again in his well-worn swivel chair. 'I've got a busy day.'

'It's good of you to see us at such short notice,' Dalliance said politely. 'And what is your line of business, Mr Henderson?'

'Garden design,' Henderson replied, before adding 'High-end' with just a hint of self-satisfaction.

'That would account for your own nicely presented estate.' Dalliance believed in a few easy balls to build up confidence, which could so easily lead to complacency.

Henderson gave a thin smile of acknowledgement. 'Jenny does most of the work on the home front actually. Best way of keeping an eye on an estate, trotting out on a horse every day.'

'She gave the impression of an energetic woman.'

Again, a thin-lipped smile in response.

Dalliance tried him with a bouncer. 'What did she mean about your being dragged away in chains?'

Henderson's response was almost comic. 'I can't say – I mean, I'm sure she didn't mean anything – she just says things like that. Drama runs in her veins.'

'I see,' Dalliance said. 'But you did admit yesterday that there was no love lost between you and Mr Roper.'

'None at all,' Henderson said, his face drawn into a stony coldness. 'I'm not going to hide the fact that I disliked Ted intensely – his style, his personality, the way he pushed people around. I simply abhorred the way he wanted to impose his ham-fisted vision on the village. I would have been dead against that, even if he'd been the most charming, cultured and sensitive man alive.'

'Thank you for being so honest. It does save a great deal of time.'

'And talking of time,' Riley broke in. 'We're very concerned to get an accurate timeline for the period between the – between Mr Roper's death – and the police arriving. We'd like you to remember everything in as much detail as possible.'

Henderson seemed relieved at the new turn the interview had taken.

'I suppose we were all in a state of shock. I mean, one minute Ted was there, full of vulgar life as usual, being clapped on the back by the whole team. And next, he was lying on the floor, dead. But if that was a shock, what happened next was an even bigger one.'

'What do you mean?'

'Well, the ambulance arrived, of course – we were expecting that. But we hadn't expected the police car showing up not long after. And we certainly didn't expect the policeman to tell us that the death might be suspicious and that we were all going to have to wait while he got back-up. So in the space of about half an hour we'd moved from being cricketers enjoying a Sunday afternoon friendly to a group of potential murder suspects.'

'But you saw nothing suspicious at the time of Mr Roper's collapse?'

'No.' Henderson shook his head. 'There he was one minute, clutching the ball in triumph and running up the wicket to congratulate Jez with everybody all over him—'

'You included?' Dalliance interrupted.

'Oh yes. I may not have liked Ted, but I was mighty pleased to see the back of Mills. It's a team game and we leave the personal stuff – where it exists – in the pavilion.'

'That's exactly what someone didn't do – if he was murdered. But carry on.'

'Well, next minute, down he went clutching his chest. It was like someone going over the top in an am-dram tragedy.' He paused, as though regretting the analogy. 'Sorry – Jenny's a mainstay of our little local group. I've seen enough overacting to last a life time.'

Dalliance smiled sympathetically. In his mind's eye he pictured Jennifer Henderson clasping the asp to her heaving breast, draped heavily over the arm of some local surveyor.

'So what happened – immediately after he collapsed?' Riley had his notebook out, his pen poised.

'Some people stayed out; others crowded in.'

'What did you do?' Dalliance asked.

'I stayed away. I don't know anything about first aid. Frankly, the responsibility scares me. Leave it to those who know what they're doing.'

'And did anybody – know what they were doing?' Riley prompted.

'Barney Grover had a go – you know, got Ted on his back and started doing that awful pressing on the chest business. The assumption was he'd had a heart attack. I mean what else could it be? Anyway, it soon became clear that he wasn't coming round, despite Barney's best efforts.'

'Had someone called for an ambulance?'

'Oh, I think so.'

'Who was that?' Riley asked.

'Rees Jones. He fairly sprinted off – straight into the changing room to get his phone. Mind you, by then one of the umpires had fished his out, so it was a wasted journey.'

Without showing his interest, Dalliance asked casually, 'Didn't anyone call Rees back – I mean if there was a 999 call already being made?'

'You'd have thought – but it was pretty chaotic. People running around, telling each other what to do. You can imagine.'

Dalliance nodded. He could indeed. 'Make a note to check those calls, Riley,' he said, before continuing. 'And in the period after those 999 calls were made and you were waiting for the ambulance – what happened then?'

Henderson sighed. 'Well, some people stayed with Ted... The rest of us drifted back towards the pavilion.'

'And went into the changing room?'

'Yes – why ever not? People changed out of their cricket boots, got their cigarettes, went to the loo.'

'What did you do?'

'Hung around outside for a bit – there was a lot of chat as you can imagine. I mean, the big question was what we were going to do about the game. Some people said that Ted would have wanted us to go on with it. Other people said, no, we should abandon it out of a sense of respect. Then there was the question of tea.'

Ah, tea, Dalliance thought: the ritual around which Sunday afternoon cricket revolved.

'Betty was quite distraught – Betty Marsden – she's in charge. I mean there's a rota, but Betty's there most Sundays. The Bolton teas are a bit of a by-word. Too many clubs nowadays just put out some sandwiches and some biscuits and cakes bought from the supermarket on the way to the ground. Not Betty.'

Dalliance remembered the quality of teas from ten years ago. 'So what did Betty say?'

'She didn't want her tea to go in the bin, but the urn takes a while to heat up, so we decided to wait for that. But then the ambulance arrived and the police started taking an interest, and it wasn't that long before you two arrived.'

'And during that time, did you see anybody acting suspiciously – out of the ordinary?'

'We were all acting out of the ordinary, I suppose. I mean, it's not every day you're present at a murder.'

'Fair point. But what were people actually doing?'

'Most people got their phones out. I certainly phoned Jenny, and I guess everyone phoned home.'

'Did someone ring Mrs Roper?'

'Norman. She was round in about five minutes.'

'How did she take it?'

'How do you think she took it? They'd been together for twenty-five years – at least. She'd seen him off after lunch for another gentle afternoon's game of cricket and then gets the call two hours later to say he's dead. She was distraught! And that was before your lot started suggesting the death was suspicious.'

'I do assure you, we have the strongest forensic evidence that Mr Roper was unlawfully killed.' Dalliance stirred in his chair. 'Okay, Mr Henderson, you've been very helpful – and you'll be relieved to hear we're not going to arrest you for murder, so you will be able to put the oven on as per instructions.'

Henderson gave him a humourless smile. The three of them stood up and made their way out into the corridor.

'Oh, did you ring your solicitor to cancel that letter to Mr Roper?' Dalliance asked over his shoulder as they were walking back towards the hall.

'He'd already done it. Went into the office yesterday – above and beyond the call of duty. Ironically it was probably being made redundant even as he was writing it.'

Dalliance turned as they reached the hall. 'I think I'd like to see it, as it exists.'

Henderson looked at him questioningly. 'You don't really think our *contretemps* has anything to do with Ted's death?'

'Almost certainly not; but it will help us with our profile – give us an insight into his *modus operandi*.'

'Oh, it'll do that all right,' Henderson said with a shrug.

'So, if you can get your solicitor to email it across to me?' Dalliance held out his card. Henderson took it and put it in his pocket, then reached for the large brass doorknob and pulled open the front door.

'Thank you, Mr Henderson. Don't forget the oven.'

'Well?' said Dalliance as Riley drove back down the drive.

'Wouldn't hurt a fly. I mean not a pushover – he was obviously standing up to Roper. But through the correct channels. I think we can cross him off the list, sir.'

There was a cry and a sharp tap on the roof. As Riley made a rather startled stop, Dalliance was suddenly aware of the passenger window being blocked by a horse's flank and a shapely leg. He let down the window.

'So he's still a free man, is he, Inspector?' Jenny Henderson leant down in the saddle, her face flushed from her ride. 'I don't suppose he remembered to put the oven on?'

'We reminded him as we left.'

'Thank you. No wonder our police force is the envy of the world. Do come back if you need to check his alibi. Any time!' With that she turned her horse and started to canter down the drive towards the house. Dalliance watched her full but well proportioned figure in the wing mirror.

'Now that one, on the other hand…'

Riley darted him a look as he put the car in first gear. 'I think someone would have mentioned it if she'd been on the pitch at the time, sir.'

'Yes, Riley,' Dalliance said, impatiently. 'But that doesn't mean she couldn't have exerted an influence. I'm not saying she's a suspect; but we mustn't get sucked into thinking that only members of the cricket team could be responsible. Now, who are we seeing next?'

David Henderson was laying the table when he heard his wife's entrance from the back of the house. The door banged, and he listened to the sound of her riding boots approaching over the old flagstones. She breezed into the kitchen and, seeing the knife in his hand, struck a pose.

'Come, thick night,
And pall thee in the dunnest smoke of hell,
That my keen knife sees not the wound it makes,
Nor heaven peep through the blanket of the dark,
To cry "Hold, hold!"'

She was by his side now, her hand clasped around his, holding up the harmless, round-ended knife.

'But you didn't murder him, did you, my worthy and rather timid thane?'

She rubbed up against him, looking fiercely into his eyes. She was breathing hard and, he noticed, the top three buttons of her shirt were undone.

'Pity. I'd have rather respected you if you'd screwed your courage to the sticking place.' She gave his trousers a playful squeeze, accompanied by a little predatory growl.

Then the performance was over. She let go of the hand that held the knife, and walked over to the fridge to get herself a drink.

Henderson placed the knife on the table, saying over his shoulder, 'Really, darling, you shouldn't let the visit of a young police officer over-excite you.'

'It wasn't the young one I was interested in,' she said. 'It was the Inspector. Dalliance. What a provocative name. I'm sure I remember it from somewhere…'

He turned and saw her leaning back against the work surface, staring into the depths of a large glass of Pinot Grigio. He felt a fleeting sympathy for Macbeth. He was confident Chief Inspector Dalliance was old enough and wise enough to look after himself.

Then the timer pinged.

'That'll be the quiche, dear.'

'It will indeed, darling. It will indeed.'

FOUR

'Barney Grover Heating & Plumbing: No job too small' announced the van pulled up in the drive of a nondescript bungalow on the new estate. Barney himself met them at the door. He was dressed in a boiler suit and had a smear of oil across his forehead.

'Bit of a bastard,' he said without anger, flicking his head back to indicate the job behind him in the house. He rubbed his face with his hand. 'Tried everything, and the bloody thing still won't fire.' He patted the sides of his overalls, the tell-tale sign of a man about to produce a packet of cigarettes. Riley noticed Dalliance watching him closely, reflecting that life had been so much easier when the boss still smoked.

Dalliance was in fact checking for rings, but once he'd seen that Barney didn't wear any – at least, at work – he continued to watch the cigarette-producing process.

Barney eventually located his packet, but before he could offer them round, Riley whipped in, 'We gather you attempted to resuscitate Mr Roper when he collapsed.'

The plumber withdrew his hand with the packet of cigarettes in it and took a pace backwards. 'Keep it social, lad,' he said, shaking a cigarette out and placing it in his mouth. 'I did try to resuscitate him. That's true. But it's not a crime to try to save someone's life, is it?' He put the packet away and got his lighter out.

Riley noted Dalliance watching as the flame speared up and the whitish-grey smoke plumed into the still air.

'No, of course not, Mr Grover,' Dalliance said, although Riley could see that ninety percent of his boss' attention was on the smoke, not the question.

'We just wondered why you took it upon yourself?' Riley asked, taking up the baton.

Barney exhaled long and lingeringly. Dalliance looked away, fixing his eyes on the satellite dish of the house opposite.

'Well,' he said, once the last hint of smoke had slipped from his nostril, 'I done the course – seemed the right thing to do, with my line of work. Never found anyone laid out with carbon monoxide poisoning, but it seemed sensible to know what to do if I did, if you catch my meaning.'

'We do,' Dalliance said. He was now taking a very close interest in the grass at his feet. 'You acted commendably, Mr Grover. We're just trying to establish what happened – who did what when, that sort of thing.'

Barney took another draw on his cigarette. 'I knew if I didn't do something no one else would. First few seconds are vital. That's what they told us.'

'Absolutely.' Dalliance remembered his long-distant encounters with the clammy rubber dummy.

'So I gets him on his back – no easy task, I'm telling you; like trying to move a stranded whale – and I started to pump at his chest.'

'And you didn't notice anything – anything suspicious?'

'I thought he was dying of a heart attack. Why would I be looking for anything suspicious?'

'You didn't find anything or see anything on his clothing when you turned him over – anything on the back of his shirt?'

'What? Like a twelve-inch commando blade sticking out? No, 'fraid not.'

'Mr Grover, this is a murder enquiry,' Dalliance said.

'Yeah, and I wasn't born yesterday. What was the most likely – Ted was having a heart attack, or someone'd decided to do him in in the middle of the pitch? Foul play never crossed my mind – or anyone's so far as I can tell.'

'Well, it crossed someone's mind, Mr Grover,' Riley said, monitoring the progress of the cigarette. 'Any idea who might have wanted to kill him?'

'Take your pick. They could form an orderly queue.' The cigarette fell to the ground to be crushed into the grass with a heavy rubber sole. Riley sensed his boss relaxing.

'What about you, Mr Grover?' Dalliance asked with a perceptible lightening of tone.

'Me? I'd have been right at the front.'

'Really?'

'Well, there'd be a bit of pushing and shoving, but I don't suppose there was anyone he made madder than me.'

'That's very interesting. Would you care to tell us why?'

'Because he was an out-and-out bastard, that's why.'

Riley noticed the plumber's hand moving towards his overalls pocket again. Please don't light up another cigarette, he prayed to no particular deity.

'And how did that manifest itself?' Dalliance asked, as his eyes watched the roving hand.

'My mum – my dear old seventy-three-year-old mum – has lived in the same cottage for fifty years. Ever since she was married. Had me there; had my sisters there. Has the grandchildren round to play in the garden. Nursed my dad there; kept him there till the end, though they wanted to take him into a hospice. And all she wants' – Grover's hand was well away from his pocket now, waving around for emphasis – 'all she bloody wants is to be left in peace there for the remaining years of her life. And then suddenly, out of the bloody blue, she gets a letter from Ted's bloody solicitor saying she's got to go.'

'So Mr Roper owned the cottage?'

'That's what I'm saying, isn't it?'

'But he can't have owned it fifty years ago. My under-standing is he'd only been in the village about twenty years.'

'That's right. And I curse the day he did come in, too.'

'Why's that?'

Grover sighed. 'I suppose we couldn't have expected things to stay the same forever. The Old Man was getting frailer by the year. We hoped the estate would stay in the family, but it didn't. They couldn't agree amongst them-selves and it all got messy and ended up in the courts.' Bar-ney remembered his cigarettes and shook another out of the packet, but didn't light it. 'Damn stupid way of wasting a for-tune. Anyway, in the end they had to settle and that meant it all being sold off piecemeal to a lot of outsiders, flashing their money around like lottery winners. And the man who had most to flash was Ted. Oh it was all hail-fellow-well-met and let-me-fill-your-glass-up-for-you to begin with, but that changed over the years. He stopped ingratiating him-self; just started pushing his weight around, giving orders, behaving like he was the squire.' Barney spat onto the asphalt garden path. 'He was no more squire than I was.'

'And he'd bought your mother's cottage,' Dalliance reminded him.

'That's right. It was just one of the properties in one of the lots in the auction. If they'd sold it off separate I might have got it. I wanted to; but they bundled it up with one or two barns and a couple of acres of grazing land, so it was out of my range. Anyway, it didn't really matter. Ted soon found out my mother lived in it and called me over to the Horseshoes one evening and gave me all the reassurances I could possibly ask for. Even offered to do some repairs – he re-thatched the roof. Which at the time I thought was very decent of him.'

'So he was in some ways a model landlord?'

'You could say that,' Barney said with a frown. He looked at the cigarette as though wondering how it had got into his hand.

'And then?' Dalliance prompted, his eyes glued to the cigarette.

'Everything was fine. For years. And then the bloody letter came. I rang him up straight away.'

'What did he say?'

'He said circumstances had changed. Of course, we could have first bagsy, as the sitting tenant. But of course the value's gone through the roof since he first bought it, and there was no way we could afford it.'

'But your mother must have had a protected tenancy.'

Barney looked at him and slowly shook his head. 'Do you think his lawyers couldn't find a way round that? Tenancy agreements are a double-edged sword, anyway. Landlord has his rights, and if he decides the property needs a total refurb, then he could put you out till the job's done – and that could be weeks, months even. And then of course when it's finished, hey presto, the rent's sky high – to reflect the improvements. He had us over a barrel. The bottom line was Ma would have to go. I couldn't fight it. But I hated him for it, I don't mind admitting it.'

'But you still tried to save his life.'

'Well you would, wouldn't you? Just 'cause I hated him didn't mean I wanted him dead – let alone thought about killing him – and certainly not murdering him in the middle of a bloody cricket match. Leastways, not before I'd batted.' He laughed and finally lit his cigarette.

Dalliance had somehow got himself downwind, and Riley could see the look of guilty pleasure creeping across his face as he postponed saying goodbye for as long as possible.

'Thank you, Mr Grover,' he said at last. 'You've been very helpful – and honest. We might,' he added, 'take a look at that letter, if you've still got it. I'll send someone round for it, if you can look it out.'

'Right you are,' Barney Grover said, taking another pull at his cigarette.

But by then Dalliance was striding back to the car, Riley in his wake.

'You can get patches,' Riley said as he eased the car away from the curb.

'Patches! I don't need patches,' Dalliance said, pulling his jacket irritably out from under his seatbelt.

'Or chewing gum?' Riley offered.

'I'm not a football manager, Riley,' Dalliance snorted. 'Anyway, have you ever tried that stuff? It's abominable. I have decided to give them up, and when I decide to give something up, I give it up. Now, if it interfered in any way with my work – or, heaven forefend – made me tetchy, irritable, irrational and difficult to work with, then I might welcome some suggestions as to how best to alleviate the cravings. But as I have none, I'll thank you to keep your mind on the job, which right now is driving through a built-up area in which the speed limit is thirty miles per hour, not thirty-five.'

'Sorry, sir,' Riley said, easing his foot up and working hard to suppress a grin. He could think of one or two people who would enjoy his account of the exchange back at the station.

'What time are we seeing the widow?' Dalliance asked staring ahead.

'Two-thirty, sir.'

'Well, it's after one now, so we probably can't fit anyone else in. Let's stop by at the pub.'

*   *   *

The Three Horseshoes was a low-slung building set at an odd angle to the green. It sported slightly tired bunting and a blackboard boasting 'Good Homemade Food'.

Dalliance checked his watch as they walked across the road. 'How long to the Roper pile?'

'Five minutes tops, sir.'

Dalliance nodded and ushered his subordinate through the pub door. Inside there was quite a long bar with tables at which one or two customers were having a light meal. There was a further room which looked more like a restaurant for Friday nights and Sunday lunches. More striking than the seating arrangements was the very pretty young woman who greeted them from behind the pump handles.

'Good afternoon, gentlemen – what can I get you?'

Riley got to the bar first and leant his elbow on it in a familiar fashion. 'Let me see – what have you got?'

'What my driver means,' said Dalliance, coming up alongside, 'is what have you got which doesn't contain any alcohol?'

Riley stood away from the bar. There were moments when Dalliance made him feel about fifteen again.

'You won't sell nothing to them – they're coppers. But don't worry, Haze. I'll keep your right arm pumping, love.'

The voice sounded familiar, and Dalliance turned to find Steve Royce staring from the far end of the bar.

'You caught him yet, Inspector? I was just telling this gentleman here we had the county's finest on the case. Results expected soon, eh?'

Dalliance's heart sank as he answered Royce with a wintry smile. His remark might have been couched as a pleasantry but there was an undertow of contempt. As for the man standing next to him – and no doubt standing him as many pints as he wanted – he was so clearly Press he could have been supplied by Central Casting.

'Don't worry, Haze, darling. If they come for your Rees, I'll say I did it. Proud to. With me bare hands. Malicious, fucking stuck-up snob. Sorry – I know. Don't talk bad of the dead. I do know that. But – well, he was, wasn't he?' Here Royce leant on the bar and waved his finger at the barmaid. 'He was giving you the eye, girl, and don't you deny it, 'cause you can't.'

'That big mouth'll get you into trouble, Steve Royce, one of these days,' the girl answered with a frown.

'There's some kinds of trouble a man might welcome, girl, and that's no lie,' Royce replied with a laugh. ''Nother pint of Miller when you've finished serving lemonade to the rozzers.'

'Sorry about that,' she said, with just a hint of colour along her neckline. 'A couple of pints and the handbrake's off. And he's had more than a couple already.'

Dalliance and Riley withdrew to a table with their orange juices.

'That's all we need – some tabloid shark scribbling down village gossip as dictated by the village malcontent,' Dalliance said, moodily ripping into his packet of peanuts.

'Interesting though,' Riley said.

'What is?' Dalliance chomped through a mouthful of dry-roasted peanuts.

'Roper having his eye on Rees' girl.'

Dalliance snorted. 'I should think every man in the village had his eye on her. You haven't taken your eye off her since we walked in here.'

Riley suddenly found the interior of his crisps packet of surprising interest.

Dalliance relented. 'No, you're right. If young Rees happened to be subject to the green-eyed monster, he'd certainly have cause for concern. It's a motive; no two ways about it. The trouble is we've got too many people with motives already. The whole damn lot of them seem to have hated him.'

'That was the beer talking just now, wasn't it?' Riley jerked his head to indicate Royce.

'He wasn't drunk yesterday, and he didn't exactly come across as Roper's biggest admirer. Probably find there was an oil well on an old paddock of his grandfather's and Roper cheated him out of it. Oh God!'

Riley looked up and saw the journalist making his way down the bar towards them.

'Inspector – sorry to interrupt your hard-earned lunch break' – Dalliance flicked his empty peanut packet across the table in irritation – 'but I just wondered whether I might ask you a few questions?'

'What, when you've got a bottomless mine of village gossip for the price of a few beers? Why spoil a good story with the sober truth.'

'Which is?'

'Which is, as our press statement clearly stated, Mr Roper died yesterday whilst playing cricket for his village, Lower Bolton, and the police are treating the death as suspicious.'

'And how is the enquiry going? I see you're relaxed enough to stop in at the local hostelry for refreshment.'

It was going very well indeed until it was brought to a grinding halt by some red-top ambulance-chaser asking me damn stupid questions which he knows damn well I am not going to answer, Dalliance thought.

'Absolutely fine, thank you,' was what he actually said, adding, 'I will be giving a statement later in the day.'

The man nodded. At least he'd tried.

Dalliance exchanged glances with Riley and they both stood up.

'You off? Thank you very much.' Hazel gave them a broad smile from the bar. At the same time the journalist held up his smart phone and took her photo.

'Thanks, gents,' he said, with a knowing leer as they headed for the door. Dalliance bridled, but Riley put a hand on his arm and guided him away from possible confrontation. He was still seething when the car started up.

'He'd have snapped her anyway,' Riley said.

'But he wouldn't have got that response from her. That'll be a candidate for the front page of whatever horrible apology for a rag he works for. And that'll mean the rest of them will be down here trying to trump it.'

They drove the rest of the way in silence.

The Grange was a neo-Palladian pile, far grander than the Hendersons' but lacking something. Architectural integrity, Dalliance decided, regarding the enormous extension some nineteenth-century nabob had thrown up to display his newly acquired wealth. There were all the accoutrements of success – stables, a detached cottage, tennis court, and no doubt somewhere on the premises, a swimming pool. Ted Roper had obviously not stinted.

Dalliance tried not to anticipate the woman they were coming to interview. But whatever he had been expecting, he was surprised when the door opened at the first touch of the bell, and a slim, quietly dressed woman stood in the doorway to greet them. Mrs Roper must have been in her early fifties, and was still good-looking. As a young woman she must have been very attractive indeed. But although there was a quiet style about her dress sense, there were no outward signs of riches. She wore stud earrings, a modest pearl necklace, and a couple of undemonstrative rings.

Dalliance introduced himself, and followed her across a palatial hall with a grand staircase unfurling from the gallery above. He glanced up at the crystal chandelier above them, and took in some impressive-looking portraits hanging on the walls.

'Do excuse the faux grandeur,' Margot Roper said. 'It came with the house and we couldn't think of anything to replace it with. Come through.' She ushered them into a sunny day room. 'More human proportions in here. Tea?' she asked, and immediately disappeared to put the kettle on.

Dalliance and Riley sat on a comfortable sofa, taking in the view of the impressive gardens.

'The thing is,' their hostess said when she returned with the tea tray, 'we're not grand or posh at all. We just got very rich very quickly and – you know – it was fun – buying this slightly ridiculous pile in the country, inviting our friends down, me playing Lady Bountiful in the village, Ted becoming captain of the cricket team, et cetera, et cetera.' She stopped suddenly. 'And now one of them's killed him. Do you suppose they hated us from day one, Inspector?'

'I'm sure they didn't, Mrs Roper.'

'Margot, please. Well, I hope you're right; it would make the last twenty-five years an awful shame if they had, wouldn't it? Until yesterday afternoon, I'd have said they'd been very happy years.'

'And what about you and Mr Roper – were you happy together?' Dalliance asked gently.

'As you well know, wealth does not guarantee happiness. As I say, it was enormous fun – at first. You can see what a marvellous place this was to bring up children.' Her eye fell on a table crowded with framed photographs. 'Charlie and Fiona loved every minute of it. Horses, tennis, the swimming pool. They had their friends to stay; our friends came with their children. It was just a hell of a lot of fun – all the more as we hadn't expected it. Neither of us came from money – neither had expectations of any sort – beyond the usual graduate careers.'

'So what happened?'

'Norman. That's what happened. You'll have met Norman, presumably. I don't know how much he told you. Anyway, he and I were an item at Cambridge. We met Ted at some do and ended up spending a summer punting down the Cam with a picnic hamper. I suppose we must have written the odd essay – and the boys would have been playing cricket. But I remember it as an absolute idyll. And at the end of it I discovered that I was completely in love with Ted. It was a bugger, but there it was.'

'How did Norman take it?'

'Well, he wasn't happy. But if you think he went away and sulked for thirty years, biding his time to take his revenge on Ted, you're barking up completely the wrong tree. Obviously our little trio – "The Three Basketeers" we were known as, on account of the picnic basket – broke up. Ted still saw a bit of Norman at cricket; but Norman was a lot better – he was pushing for a blue – and oh, I don't know. The three years simply sped past, and in no time at all we were thrown out at the end of it and found ourselves in a dank little flat in London wondering what the hell was going to happen next.'

'What did happen next, Mrs Roper?' Riley asked.

'Oh, the usual stuff. I got a job on a fashion magazine. Ted had decided that a history degree qualified him to become an estate agent. We were doing all right – earning enough to pay the mortgage – despite the incredible interest rates they charged back then. And our lives would have travelled along the tramlines of respectable, middle-class graduate lives.'

'Except?'

'Well, as Norman must have told you yesterday, he came back into our lives.'

'At your suggestion?'

'At my suggestion. We hadn't invited him to the wedding – for obvious reasons – but we still sent him Christmas cards. And then one weekend we realised we really missed him. So I said, let's invite him to dinner. If he doesn't come, we're no worse off, but if he does – well, he came, and the rest, as they say – is history.'

'The history being?'

'Norman's a genius, Inspector. A magician – at least with money. You really could make a fortune in those days. Of course you could also lose one; but Norman was very canny. Of course, he got his fingers burnt, but he learnt – and got cannier. And he was also generous – terribly, terribly generous. At least to us.'

'At least to you?'

'Well, maybe – though he genuinely liked Ted – I mean until very recently. They were probably best friends – I'm sure they'd have thought of each other like that.'

'So Norman helped you to get rich…'

'Fabulously rich.' She waved an arm airily out towards the grounds. 'It was almost laughable – scheme after scheme came up trumps, and with every new scheme we had more money to invest from the last one. Property, shares, all sorts of things which I never pretended to understand and which Ted didn't try terribly hard to pretend to understand. It just kept flowing into the coffers. We moved up the property ladder in London – a licence to print in itself – and then when Norman tipped us the wink that the time had come to consolidate, we made the move out here. Ted got wind of this place through an estate agent friend, we rocked up one sunny Sunday afternoon, took one look at the green, another look at the cricket ground, and decided we'd buy the place, whatever it was like. Which was exactly what we did.'

'Joined by Norman – ushering in a period of unbroken peace and prosperity?'

'I wouldn't go that far. The first ten years or so were marvellous – as I say, bringing the children up here was a joy. But life was not all one unbroken wave of pleasure.'

Dalliance raised an eyebrow. Margot Roper paused and seemed to debate with herself before looking straight back at him.

'Ted was a shit. An out-and-out shit. I might as well come out with it because you'll find enough people in the village to say it if I don't.'

'In what way was he a shit?'

'Anyway you like, Inspector; I'm afraid wealth went to his head. It spoilt him. He was brash, bullying, manipulative – and, before you ask, unfaithful.'

'Unfaithful?'

'Not at first: I honestly think we were as happy – as content with each other as any couple could be for the first half-dozen years. I know it's a cliché, the seven-year itch; but as many people have observed, things only become a cliché because they're true. I didn't even blame him particularly at first. Once the children came I was pretty exhausted, and quite possibly not at my absolute best twenty-four-seven. When the big money started coming in, he spent quite a lot of time away, and must have had countless affairs. Still, I preferred that to him creeping about the house in the small hours bonking the au pairs.'

'Did you never challenge him about it?'

'Of course I did. He said: "Divorce me". And I realised I didn't want to – not just because of the house and the money. But actually I still loved him. He was a shit, but he was my shit. And I'm going to miss him.'

Suddenly her chest was heaving and she was fumbling for a handkerchief. She blew her nose noisily. 'Damn. I swore I wasn't going to do that. I'm so sorry.'

Dalliance gave her time to compose herself. 'We won't keep you very much longer,' he said, 'but we do have to ask you about the falling out between your husband and Mr Standing. Mr Standing said something about a very large debt that was going to force the sale of the house.'

'Yes – after all these years – after all the successes, even Norman's luck ran out. I don't know what it was, this latest scheme. I'd lost interest. We had everything we needed. But

Ted kept saying we needed more – for the children – though we'd paid for them both to go to university, and Charlie was quite happy working his way round Australia, and Fiona's very happy with her fellow in Hong Kong, so it was nonsense. But Ted had become a little deranged in recent years – started believing his own publicity, I think the expression goes. He called it "Thinking Big" – but it seemed to involve treading on people's toes and making himself incredibly unpopular. Like the wretched fishing lake he'd set his heart on.'

'We've spoken to Mr Henderson.'

'David was rightly up in arms against it – and absolutely apoplectic when he found out Ted was planning to tunnel under his ground to divert his spring water. Especially as...' She paused.

'Especially as...?' Dalliance prompted.

'Well, we were friends as well as neighbours. And David helped us so much in the early days. He designed most of that.' Again she pointed out over the estate. 'He's a lovely man. I have to say I'm not a member of the Jenny fan club – I don't know whether you met her...?'

Dalliance nodded.

'Well, you'll know what I mean when I say she's most at home dressed up in something revealing, pretending to be some great romantic figure on stage. I dare say she didn't take to me either – people don't like being seen through, do they? But I think she set her cap at Ted. Give credit where credit's due, I don't think he encouraged her.'

'And would you say the same regarding Rees Jones' girl-friend?'

'Hazel? I didn't know she'd shown any interest in Ted.'

'There's no evidence she has; but what about him?'

'I really can't be expected to give you an up-to-date report on Ted's relations with every female in the village.'

'We do have to ask these questions.'

'I'm sorry. Of course you do. Hazel? Well it's not impossible; she's a lovely girl, of course. All I can say is that I had no wind of it; but then I'd be the last person to hear, wouldn't I?'

Dalliance murmured his assent. Riley was taking notes, but Margot Roper didn't seem to notice. He hated these violations of privacy; but it was a painful necessity. He coughed, almost to signal a new line of questioning. 'Another sensitive subject, I'm afraid. Can you tell us where things had got *vis-à-vis* Ted's debt to Mr Standing for the investment that went wrong?'

'Oh, it was frightful. Ted was furious – went lumbering around the house calling Norman every name under the sun. I tried to get him to calm down and eventually he stopped shouting long enough for me to discover the awful truth – which was that he'd borrowed the money for this doomed gamble from Norman. I'd just assumed he'd put together a war chest and that we'd have to take the hit and tighten our belts for a while. It was a shock to find that we actually owed Norman nearly a million pounds.'

'So what happened then?'

'Well, we had an enormous row of course.'

'You were jointly liable for the debt?'

'Oh yes, in up to the hilt. I'll still have to sell the house.'

'Mr Standing would force that on you?'

'Well, not in so many words. I spoke to him last night and he was wonderfully sympathetic. He said I could take my time, but that—'

'Nearly a million *is* nearly a million?'

'He can't afford to just write it off. I mean he lost a lot himself – and so, I gather, did a number of clients, including some rather unamused Russians. I didn't push him on that, but it's quite clear he needs the loan back. And he'll get it. Actually, I don't mind having to sell. I'd probably have done it anyway. It's too big for me on my own. And it's full of memories – memories of the good times.'

'Did Standing come round to see you last night?' Dalliance asked, remembering the man's impatience to be off.

'No. No, he drove back to Town. He's – well, he's rather involved at the moment. You obviously don't read the popular press, but he's cropping up in the society pages a lot these days, accompanied by a very lovely Russian girl.'

'I'll put my sergeant onto it,' Dalliance said. 'But he phoned you?'

'Yes. After I got back from the hospital. Which was quite late. I somehow felt I had to stick around. Completely pointless of course. Ted was gone and there was nothing they could do to bring him back. After a while I realised I needed a drink and should probably make some calls, so back I came. It was pretty bleak. Norman's call was the one gleam in the gloom.'

'So he wasn't ringing about the debt?'

'Good God, no. No, no. He was full of sympathy and offers of support. It was me that brought the subject up, and he just said I could take my time and got back to practical things like digging out Ted's will and so on.'

'Do you have it – Mr Roper's will?'

'I haven't felt strong enough to look for it, but I know what it says. It'll be in his filing cabinet under "W", I'd imagine.'

'We are going to need to look through his papers, check his emails and so on.'

'I'm sure we've all seen enough crime series to know what your job entails. I'll show you his den.'

It was a larger room than David Henderson's butler's pantry, and far, far less tidy. The aggressively large desk overflowed with papers; shelves were crammed with books and box files, subjected to no obvious organisational principle.

'I know,' his widow said, as though reading his thoughts. 'He did have a secretary for a while, but she seemed to spend more time filing her nails than filing Ted's papers, and when they started going off on business trips that involved overnights at spa hotels, I put my foot down.'

'Name?'

'Cynthia. Cynthia West.'

Riley's notebook was out again. 'Was she local?'

'I presume so. As you'll imagine, I regarded the woman as a blight. I didn't care where she came from as long as she went back there pretty pronto. More tea?'

Dalliance accepted the offer and then took off his jacket. Ted's den was going to prove a challenge.

Two hours later they left with their haul. Riley had box files up to his chin; Dalliance carried a clear plastic bag containing Ted's laptop and various notebooks.

'And you're going to want this too, I imagine.'

Dalliance took the smart phone Margot Roper was holding out to him as they stood in the doorway.

'Thank you. You've been very helpful.'

'Not at all. If there's anything else you need, just let me know.'

'This lot'll keep us going for a while, won't it, Riley?' Dalliance said, adding, 'If there's anything we can do for you…?'

'Any idea when I can have him back for the funeral?'

Dalliance pursed his lips and shook his head. 'As soon as we can release the body, we will – but as I'm sure you've been told, the men in the lab coats haven't identified what killed him yet.' He took a step down, but felt there was something else he should say. 'Are your children coming home?'

'Of course. They're both in the air as we speak. Des Tucker's picking Fiona up at some ungodly hour tonight, and Charlie'll blow in some time tomorrow. You have to keep together as a family at a time like this.'

With suitable murmurs of sympathy the two detectives took their leave and climbed back into their car.

Margot Roper watched as they gained speed along the drive and finally disappeared round the bend. She gave it another minute, in case they thought of one last question they had to come back and ask, then went back into the house.

She cleared the mugs from her husband's den and deposited them in the kitchen, before going upstairs to a little private dressing room. Here she removed a key from her jewellery box and went over to the Ile-de-Ré chest of drawers by the window. A moment later she was hurrying back downstairs with a bundle of envelopes clutched to her chest.

Stopping only to pick up a box of matches from the kitchen, she stepped out a side door and walked across an extensive patio towards a little shanty town of sheds and greenhouses. She stopped by an ancient, fire-blackened oil drum – used for burning the more intractable garden waste – and started removing the letters from their envelopes, setting fire to them one by one before casting them in. She didn't stop to read them, but she did glance at each one as she held it to the match:

'*My darling, darling Margot…*'

'*Margot, my goddess…*'

'*Margot, my love, how could you think we could be separated…*'

Page after page flamed and curled as she worked methodically through the pile. She never wavered; she never paused to read more than a line or two. When she'd finished, she pulled a tissue out of her pocket and dabbed her eyes, before letting it too fall into the blackening nest of love letters.

FIVE

'Put up with a lot, didn't she?' Riley said, as he drove them round to the other side of the village.

'Women do, Riley, women do. Who are we seeing now?'

'Jez Jones. His brother Rees is at a sales conference all day, but Jez should be around.'

'What does he do?'

'Repairs motorbikes. Well, not just bikes. Anything with a motor, I gather – lawnmowers, farm equipment. But bikes are his passion.'

Jez operated out of a corrugated barn down a rutted lane. He greeted them with a surly stare, standing beside a stripped-down bike. He wiped his hands with a rag, but didn't offer to shake hands. Dalliance noted a silver death's head ring on his left hand, and asked to see it. Jez pulled it off reluctantly. Dalliance inspected it and then passed it on to Riley.

'We'll need to run it past forensics,' he explained as the sergeant wrote out the label for the specimen bag.

Jez glowered at them. He remained tight-lipped throughout the interview, begrudging every detail, however clearly established. Yes, he'd been bowling when Mills nicked the ball to slip. Yes, he'd been as pleased as anyone that Ted had caught it. Yes, he had carried on down the pitch to join the celebrations.

'That don't mean I killed him, does it? Everybody else was doing the same thing.'

'Everybody?' It was like being repeatedly punched on a bruised shoulder, this constant reminder that the entire team had crowded round their doomed captain.

Jez bridled, as though his integrity had been challenged. 'I dunno – seemed like everybody. I didn't exactly take a roll-call, did I? How was I to know he was just about to keel over in the middle of the pitch?'

Dalliance noted the harsh tone. No love lost there.

Riley read out the names from his notebook. 'David Henderson, Barney Grover, Norman Standing, Steve Royce—'

'I know my own team,' Jez spat scornfully.

'How about your own brother, Rees?'

'Rees came in – course he did. It was partly his wicket.'

'How d'you mean?'

'When I got the opener out, Rees came up and gave me a bit of advice.'

'Which was?' Dalliance took over the questioning. No point leaving cricketing points to Riley.

'Give him some short stuff. Try to keep him on the back foot. Then tempt him outside the off-stump.'

'And it worked?'

'A treat. And say what you like about Ted – he could still bloody catch.'

'So did Rees come to you or to Ted?'

Jez was on the defensive again. 'I don't know – Jesus. It all happened so quick. One minute we were huddling round – next minute he was collapsing at our feet. I don't remember.'

'Try.' Riley again.

'Look, I'd run on through my follow-up. Ted came up from slip. Mills was walking off, and everybody else was steaming in.'

'Where was Rees fielding?'

'Cover. He's our best fielder. No one takes liberties with him.'

'Did you get to Ted before Rees got to you?'

'Yeah – I guess.'

'And what did you do when you reached Ted?'

Jez shrugged. 'High-fived him?'

'And then what happened?'

'Well, everyone else piled in.'

'And Rees?'

'Like I said, he came in too. I think he slapped me on the back. And then—'

'Yes?'

'That's right – I remember now. He sort of got his arm round Ted.'

There was a moment's silence. A wood pigeon gave its throaty call in a copse a couple of fields away.

Jez was looking black. 'But that don't mean he did anything. You may think you're very clever trapping me into saying stuff, but Rees did not kill Ted.'

'No one's saying he did. We're just trying to establish all the facts.'

Jez threw his rag down on the seat of the bike and rummaged in his jeans pocket. Oh no, Riley thought – not another smoker. But it wasn't cigarettes, it was gum. He peeled a white pellet out of its wrapping and popped it in his mouth, dropping the paper to the ground at his feet. 'That it, then?'

Dalliance looked him in the eye. The shutters were down. They wouldn't get anything else out of him. But it was worth one last question. 'How would you describe your relationship with Mr Roper?'

'My relationship?' Jez gave a short bark of a laugh. 'Can't say I had one. I mean, he was the captain, I was the fast bowler. He'd stand at slip all afternoon, while I bowled my bloody socks off.'

'And off the field?'

'Same difference. He lived in a bloody great mansion, and I – well, this is where I work.' He cast an eye around the shelves of spare parts and oil cans. 'Relationship,' he snorted. 'What sort of relationship were you thinking of?'

'What about landlord and tenant?'

'Who told you that?' Jez asked suspiciously.

'We've been going through Mr Roper's papers. He had a number of tenants around the village – including you.'

'So?'

'I'd just like to know if there was any friction between the two of you.'

'Nothing I'd need to kill him for, I'll tell you that for nothing.' When it looked as though Dalliance was about to ask another question, Jez put his hands on his hips. 'Look, my life may seem pretty shit to you, but it suits me fine. I like bikes and engines. I like my own company. I like it here. Rees may want to get up at sparrow fart, put a suit and tie on and drive around all day in his company car – that's his choice, and I hope it works out for him. But it's not for me. I've chosen my path, and I'm happy with it. When I've put that chain back on and unblocked that lawnmower engine, I'm going to lock up for the day, and I'll be sitting outside the Shoes with a pint in my hand at half-five or quarter to six at the latest. It's a simple life – but it suits me.'

With that he reached for a spanner, indicating that his willing participation in the interview was over.

As they were driving back up the lane, Riley said, 'Got a lot of time for thinking down there on his own all day – Zen and the Art of Motorcycle Maintenance.'

'Indeed,' Dalliance said, rather impressed by his sergeant's reference to a cult classic of his youth.

'Where to next, sir?'

'Let's drop in at the ground. That daft tent should be down by now. I'd like to walk it all through on the square.'

*   *   *

Back at the pitch Dalliance told Riley to park the car near the gate next to his own. 'We'll walk across from here,' he said, pushing the car door shut. He looked around, rather like an incoming batsman adjusting his eyes to the light. The tent had indeed gone, giving an unimpeded view of the pavilion and the groundsman's shed with a small motorised tractor standing outside it. The ground was set in rolling countryside with fields of wheat and barley lapping at the perimeter fence. There was a clump of trees behind the bowler's arm at one end; the other was bare apart from the sightscreen.

The two detectives stood in the middle of the wicket. There was a faint outline chalked on the ground where Ted Roper had fallen. Dalliance blew out his cheeks and shook his head.

Riley read his thoughts. 'How – ? What are we looking for?'

Dalliance sighed. 'Some sort of delivery system for the poison. Something the murderer could have on him without it being noticed, that wouldn't draw attention to itself, and which could be activated by some sort of pressure from the finger or the palm. There's no point in looking for it out here. They've scoured every inch of the pitch – but it's a hundred per cent certain the killer got it off the field undetected and disposed of it in the window before the first uniform showed up.'

He sighed again, then roused himself to action.

'Right,' he said. 'Jez was coming in from there' – he indicated the treeless end – 'so Ted would have been around here.' He paced back a few yards in the other direction, walking towards the copse of trees at the bottom end of the ground. 'Very helpful,' he exclaimed, pointing out a rough scoring in the grass. 'That'll be Ben Cowper's mark.'

He saw Riley's blank look.

'The wicketkeeper needs to establish where he's going to stand and that's down to how fast the bowling is and how quickly it's coming off the pitch. Jez may have been the team's fast bowler, but judging by this he wasn't breaking any speed limits. And slip' – he took another pace or two – 'would be a couple of yards or so further back still.'

He beckoned Riley to him and pointed down. There was a discernible flattening of the area at his feet. 'Good. So, I'm standing here' – he put his legs apart and leant forward with his hands out – 'and you – off you go. You're Jez.'

Riley looked uncomfortable.

'I don't mean you've got to actually bowl. Just go back to the far crease and run down the wicket, throwing you arms up in triumph as I take the catch.'

Riley trudged back up the wicket as he was told.

'Come on then!' Dalliance called out, and Riley trotted self-consciously down the wicket.

'Owzat!' Dalliance threw up an imaginary ball and charged up to meet him. 'Well bowled, Jezzer!' he exclaimed, offering his hands for a high-five. Riley reluctantly met his palms with his own. 'Come on, Riley. It's not as though we roll around on the grass kissing each other like you do on a Sunday morning when you score a goal.'

Riley opened his mouth, but thought better of it.

'Actually,' Dalliance went on, 'we ought to get a bit more close up and personal. Put your arm round here...' He took his subordinate's arm and forced it round to his lower back. That was where the tiny puncture in the dead man's skin had been. 'Okay, push.'

'How hard?'

'Just hard enough to force a needle through the skin and squeeze the poison out.'

Dalliance felt half-hearted pressure on his lower back.

'Not exactly throwing yourself into it, are you? Go out into the covers. For goodness sake, that way.' Dalliance pushed him in the right direction. 'A few more yards. Yep, that's about right. So, you're Rees now. I'm going to go back to my position, and when I take the catch and run up to meet Jez, you come steaming in, high-five your brother, and then see how easy it would be to get a hand in the same place on my back.'

Again without much enthusiasm, Riley did what he was told.

'Interesting,' Dalliance said.

Riley looked questioningly at him.

'Coming in from cover and getting to the right spot with your right hand was a no-no. It would have had to be the left hand. That probably applies to anybody coming in from the off side – mid-off, gulley, extra-cover. Unless they moved round the pack. We need fielding positions for everyone, and everybody's recollection of what everyone else was doing. Good. Let's go and see what SOCO have turned up for us.'

Anderson and his team were out on the pavilion veranda. As Dalliance and Riley approached they broke out into mock applause. Dalliance played up to it, but Riley skulked behind him, and stayed out on the balcony while the Inspector went into the changing room with Anderson.

'Do you often come out into the wide open spaces for a bit of man-love with your boss?'

Sally Walker looked pretty even in her white Teletubby suit. Riley had met her a few times, and had been impressed at how bubbly she always seemed, however gruesome the crime scene. Her bright eyes were fixed on his, and a light smile played around her lips.

'Better than rummaging through a laundry bag of jock-straps,' was the best he could come up with.

'Oh, I don't know about that – think about it the other way round – a murder in a women's hockey team.' She laughed at his obvious discomfort.

'Did you find anything?' he asked, willing the warm glow rising from his collar not to turn into a fully fledged blush.

'I don't think so. Didn't really know what we were looking for to be quite honest. We certainly didn't find a needle and a bottle marked poison.'

'I'd better go in and see what you did find then,' Riley said, pushing through the home changing room door.

Everything was considerably tidier than it had been the previous evening. They may not have washed the home team's clothes, but they had certainly folded them up neatly. Some items were bagged up in evidence pouches: spare studs, tubes of Deep Heat, sunglasses, a penknife. Dalliance was shaking his head as Anderson talked him through them.

'Come on, Riley, inspire me,' he said, acknowledging his subordinate's presence.

Riley looked around searching for inspiration. He found it a yard or two away from him, hanging on the changing room wall.

'Sir?' he said. There was something in his tone that made Dalliance look up sharply. 'That's Jez, isn't it – in the team photo. And look what he's wearing.'

'Wristbands!' Dalliance almost shouted. 'Just like Dennis Lillee. Brilliant, Riley. First class. Which is Jez's bag?' he asked Anderson urgently.

'Jez?'

'Jones. Jez Jones.' Dalliance turned to the coffin and flung back the lid.

'I don't remember any wristbands,' Anderson was saying, consulting his list and shaking his head.

Dalliance was rummaging through Jez's kit like a dog after a buried bone, muttering, 'Wristbands – of course – brilliant. Brilliant!'

'But they're not there, sir,' Riley pointed out.

'Exactly, Riley, exactly!' He stood up, almost quivering with excitement. 'You concoct the most ingenious plan –

probably in cahoots with your brother – you come onto the field of play with the most perfect murder weapon – inconspicuous, everyday, standard kit. You use it, and then what do you do with it, Riley? Imagine it was a dagger, or one of our beloved blunt instruments? Would you leave it in your kit bag at the scene of the crime? Or would you find an opportunity to sneak it out to your car to destroy it at your leisure?'

'We don't know he was wearing wristbands, sir,' Riley pointed out.

'True. But at least we're on the right lines. Some inconspicuous way of getting the lethal substance onto the pitch and then delivering it, unseen, in full view of the entire team. And wristbands seem an entirely plausible candidate. We'll ask Rees whether his brother was wearing them when we see him this evening.'

Dalliance rose on the balls of his feet. Riley was relieved – this was always a good sign.

'What else would fall into that category?' Dalliance went on. He frowned in thought, then – 'Gloves! Wicketkeeping gloves. Where are Cowper's gloves?'

Anderson pulled them out and presented them. They were well used, the leather split in places, and the great rubber palms showing extensive wear and tear. 'Checked them inside and out,' Anderson said. 'Nothing…'

Dalliance nodded. Taking the right glove and putting it on, he said, 'No, that would be too easy, wouldn't it? A little sachet of venom secreted in one of the fingers, and' – moving up to Riley and giving him a firm slap in the lower back – 'bingo: Dead, dead for a ducat.'

Riley never knew what possessed him, but playing along, he stumbled over and lay breathing his last. He was inspecting the stud-chewed grain on the changing room floor when an entirely unexpected voice broke in, a familiar – female – voice: 'O me, what hast thou done? O what a rash and bloody deed is this?'

The black riding boots that stood astride him in the doorway gave him the clue.

'Mrs Henderson!' Dalliance's voice sounded shocked.

'Jenny, please,' she said, adding as an aside to Riley as he made to get up: 'You're dead, remember – called to a certain convocation of politic worms.' For emphasis she placed one of her boots on his back.

Anderson moved forward. 'This is a crime scene, madam. I must ask you to leave immediately.'

Ignoring him, Jenny Henderson addressed Dalliance directly. 'I've looked you up. I knew I knew the name. You played the Dane for OUDs in—'

'That was a long time ago,' Dalliance said brusquely. 'Now, I really must ask you to leave. We are in the middle of a murder investigation,' he insisted, only to have another line quoted at him.

'What have I done that thou dar'st wag thy tongue in noise so rude against me?'

Riley had escaped from under the riding boot by now and scrambled to his feet, dusting down his trousers, but Mrs Henderson was still not done.

'Imagine walking in on one of my favourite scenes in all of Shakespeare – performed by one of the great lost talents of English theatre! Your reviews were magnificent. If only I'd had my chance with you; we'd have made a fine pair. Instead I had to make do with a spotty youth besotted with his Ophelia, who got the part because of her looks not her brains.'

'You shouldn't be here,' Dalliance said firmly, pointing towards the door. 'We really must ask you to leave.'

'O, speak to me no more. These words like daggers enter in my ears. No more, sweet Hamlet.' Then with a gruesomely playful smile, she raised her hand and said, 'We'll get you back on the boards, Inspector. I promise you. We're looking at The Tempest for next year's village festival. How would you fancy Prospero?'

With that she disappeared, Anderson following in close attendance.

'I didn't know you—' Riley started.

'Don't,' Dalliance said in a tone that blocked further conversation on the topic. At that moment Anderson came back in.

'Sorry about that.'

'I should think so,' Dalliance said. 'Couldn't one of your team have headed her off?'

'She came across the fields – on her horse. Just climbed over the fence at the back and—'

'Well, embarrassment seldom kills you,' Dalliance growled, not meeting Riley's eye. As they left the changing room Riley heard him mutter, 'No wonder I gave up acting.'

'Of course,' Anderson was saying as they re-assembled on the pavilion's veranda, 'it's a very exposed spot. You can't stop people coming along and gawping over the fence – or taking photos.'

Dalliance sighed. 'Many?'

'Not many,' Anderson said, but his intonation suggested more than he thought Dalliance would be comfortable with. 'Mainly locals – they seemed fascinated with our tent.'

'Well, at least that's down now. Any press?'

'A couple maybe. Hard to say.'

'I saw someone slinking about under those trees.' Sally Walker pointed in the direction of the sightscreen. 'I think they might have climbed into one of them actually.'

Dalliance rolled his eyes. Riley hoped there hadn't been anyone in the trees while they had been grappling with each other on the wicket. Something about Sally's smile suggested she was hoping just the opposite. And where, he wondered, had she been when Mrs Henderson decided to make her dramatic entry?

As though answering him, she said, 'I did a last check in the shed.'

'Anything?' Dalliance asked.

'Nothing, I'm afraid, sir.'

'Okay. Thank you,' he said, before turning to Anderson and adding, 'You'll let us have results as soon as you can?'

'Something on your desk tomorrow, I'd hope,' Anderson replied. 'But I don't expect to learn much more than you know already.'

'And what's that?'

'Men running around in the sun tend to sweat a lot.'

'Meaning?' Dalliance asked.

'The shirt we're really interested in is the victim's – but don't hold your breath. We know that most, if not all members of the team made contact with him. Even failure to find a DNA trace won't prove that someone didn't. But we'll run the tests anyway.'

'Right you are. Keep me posted. Come on, Riley, we must be off. But before we go—' Dalliance suddenly disappeared into the home team changing room. He emerged a moment later bearing the team photo. 'Got anything we can slip this into?'

Sally produced a large brown envelope, into which Dalliance slipped the picture, before leading the way towards the cars with it under his arm.

'I'll bring mine into the village,' he called to Riley. 'See you at the green.' He acknowledged the salute from the uniform on the gate and jolted away down the lane, Riley following in his rear-view mirror.

He liked being driven around by Riley, but he also needed time on his own – especially after an episode like that. Surely he could quote half a line of Hamlet without some lunatic luvvy bursting in on him pretending to be Gertrude. He felt a twinge of sympathy for David Henderson. Perhaps he coped by being as boring as possible and keeping to his butler's pantry.

*   *   *

'Who's next?' he asked as he climbed into the passenger seat beside Riley after parking his own car.

'We're seeing Rees Jones at seven. That should leave us plenty of time to do the other three.'

'Three?'

'The three remaining locals: Ben Cowper, Ernie Phelps and Des Tucker. We'll have to make time to interview Standing and the boy.'

'We should talk to Daniel's mother,' said Dalliance, adding in response to Riley's questioning look, 'Just a bit of background – find out about her husband – when he died, what of, whether they were part of the Ropers' social circle. It beats me why she should still be sending the boy to boarding school. You'd have thought she'd want him at home with her. Perhaps she's honouring her husband's last wishes. Who knows? Anyway, fix up an interview tomorrow. We can drive over to the school to see Daniel any time. He'll probably thank us for half an hour out of history or whatever it is. Standing's going to be a day-trip to the big city. I'll let you drive.'

'Thank you, sir.'

'Don't mention it. By the way, you've left one out.'

'Who?'

'Steve Royce.'

'Thought we'd sort of done him at lunchtime, sir.'

'We saw a side of him, Riley, but only a side of him. I'd like to talk to him on his home turf – without half a dozen pints inside of him. Have we got an address?'

'Of a sort, sir.'

Dalliance looked enquiringly at him.

'Seems he broke up with his missus, sir. Now living in temporary accommodation.'

'Do we know where?'

'In a caravan down a lane, sir.'

'Another bloody lane,' Dalliance said, 'Well, who's it to be? Ben Cowper's probably doing something unspeakable with cows. Let's go and get that over with.'

Six

They became aware of Ben Cowper's herd long before they saw them. First there was the cacophonous lowing, and then, as they turned down a concreted lane at the sign announcing Harbledown Farm, the smell.

'Gordon Bennett,' Dalliance exclaimed, as they got out onto a cobbled courtyard which clearly doubled as a cow toilet.

'Don't like the smell of shit – don't come to a farm.'

Ben Cowper wasn't exactly grinning from ear to ear, but he was clearly enjoying their discomfort. The grimace of a smile apart, however, he gave off waves of hostility and suspicion.

If you don't like the sight of coppers – don't place yourself at the centre of a major crime scene, Dalliance thought, as he looked around him. There was a low-slung shed to his left with a few hairy, pink noses sticking out through the bars of a pen. Next to the shed a ramshackle barn housed an ancient tractor and the leftovers of the winter's hay bales. On the other side of the yard was a run-down farmhouse.

As if following his train of thought, Cowper said, 'We don't all run around in Mercedes subsidised by the EU. It's bloody hard work for shit rewards, if you want the honest truth.'

'Why do it?' Riley asked.

Cowper gave him a withering look. 'Take milk in your tea, do you? Like a fresh egg for your breakfast? Have the odd slice of toast? It doesn't start life all wrapped up in plastic on a supermarket shelf. It starts out here with blokes like me working their bollocks off. And we could do without townies looking down their noses at us.'

'I wasn't—'

Riley's apology was interrupted by a shout. 'Ben – where the bloody 'ell are you?' A short, weather-beaten woman in muddy jodhpurs emerged from behind the cattle shed with a bucket swinging at her side. 'Sorry,' she said with a change of tone on seeing the new arrivals. 'Didn't know you had company.'

'Police,' Cowper said, as though making an important distinction. 'They're not staying long. I'll be with you in a minute.'

The woman gave a nod and stomped off across the yard.

'Nancy,' he explained. 'And yes, she is, and no, we're not, and no, she doesn't.'

Dalliance looked slightly askance.

Cowper elaborated: 'Girlfriend; married; live here – all right?'

'Any particular reason why she doesn't live here?' Dalliance asked. As though on cue, an upper window of the farmhouse opened and a white-haired head appeared.

'Benjamin – where's my tea? My tea's late. And I've lost the remote. Someone's taken the remote. I've got that poncy antiques show on and I don't like it.'

'I'll be up in a minute, Ma,' Cowper shouted.

'You mind you are – gabbing away in the yard, you idle sod.'

The window slammed shut. Dalliance noticed a muscle working along Cowper's jaw. But all he said was, 'You can see why I wake up every morning with a song in my heart.'

'We won't keep you. But we do have to ask you some routine questions.'

'No, I didn't; not that I can remember; you'd have to ask them; and no, I didn't again.'

Dalliance waited for the exegesis, thinking that if all interviews were conducted on this basis they would take very much less time – and probably send him into a lunatic asylum.

'No I didn't see anything unusual; no, no one didn't come in to slap Ted on the back; you'd have to ask the rest of the team why they might want Ted dead; and no, I didn't kill him. Are we done?'

Nancy came back into the yard, her bucket replenished. 'You going to be all day?' she said, as she splashed past. The herd set up a terrific noise. It reminded Riley of the home supporters when the opposition team ran out at the start of a match.

'The one question you didn't answer was what were your relations with Mr Roper like?' Dalliance had to raise his voice to make himself heard.

Cowper's reply came back at an even higher volume: 'I hated the bastard.'

'Was that because he was your landlord?'

'No – because he was a—' The last word was drowned out by the herd, whose excitement at the approaching bucket reached a crescendo, but you didn't have to be a trained lip-reader to make it out.

Dalliance nodded to the car, and they beat a not entirely dignified retreat.

'Welcome to Cold Comfort Farm,' Riley said as he raced back up the lane.

'Think of Ben Cowper when you're working your way through a pile of boring paperwork in your nice warm office on a raw February afternoon.'

'Do you think there's anyone in the cricket team who didn't hate Roper enough to want to kill him?'

'I don't know, Riley; only one way to find out.'

*   *   *

Ernie Phelps lived in a modest two-bedroom house on the other side of the village. He kept it tidy, self-effacingly so. There were no photographs, no souvenirs, nothing personal. The place seemed almost to deny its own existence. Just like the man himself, Dalliance thought.

'I was wondering when you'd be looking in,' Phelps said, ushering them towards a pair of deep, plastic-upholstered armchairs facing the television. Dalliance sank uncomfortably into his as Phelps asked, 'Can I get you anything? Cup of tea?'

Imagining the milky travesty he was likely to be served, Dalliance declined with an uplifted palm. 'We won't take up much of your time, Mr Phelps.'

'Take as much as you like. I got enough of it.' The man spread his hands in a vague gesture.

'How's that, Mr Phelps?' Riley sat on the edge of his chair, rather than risk its purchaseless depths. He had his notebook poised.

'Took early retirement, didn't I? So I got all the time in the world.'

'And what did you take early retirement from, Mr Phelps?' Dalliance wished he had followed Riley's lead. He could see it was going to be a struggle to extricate himself from the armchair when the time came.

'Driving – coaches. Well, mainly coaches. Changed to vans later.'

'Why did you stop?' Dalliance was only asking out of politeness. A man less like a murderer than Ernie Phelps would be hard to imagine.

'Had an accident.'

'And you were hurt – in the accident?' Riley prompted.

'It wasn't so much I was hurt, more how it affected me, if you know what I mean. Traumatised me. The other people involved – they was hurt. It was horrible.'

'I'm sorry,' Dalliance said. However many blood-spattered bodies you saw, it was always a shock. He could see it affecting Ernie Phelps badly. After a suitable pause, he continued. 'Can we move on to yesterday's cricket match, Mr Phelps? What is your role in the team, if you don't mind my asking? We have you down as number eleven. So presumably you bowl.'

'Not much these days, to be honest. Ted seemed to have lost faith in me. Tended to use me as a last resort, if you know what I mean.'

Dalliance knew exactly what he meant. 'And what do you bowl – spin?'

'How did you guess?' Phelps exclaimed with a wan smile.

How indeed? thought Dalliance, regarding the man's puny frame. Phelps was a representative of a sad tribe of pie-chuckers who occasionally struck lucky and got a wicket. It was the worst humiliation as a batsman to succumb to such rubbish. Dalliance could see Phelps in his mind's eye, sidling apologetically up to the wicket with every fielder cast to the far corners of the boundary, the ball wrapped in his limp fingers.

At that point he stopped the internal film.

'Which hand?' he demanded abruptly.

'What, bowling? I'm a leftie, I am. Left arm round.' He wheeled his left arm in an arc to demonstrate.

'Left arm round,' Dalliance repeated, shooting a glance at Riley.

'And where were you fielding yesterday, when Mr Roper—?'

'Mid-on. Duffers' corner.'

'And you came in – to join in the congratulations?'

'Oh yes. That Mills boy's got a terrible on-drive. Nearly broke my fingers last year.'

Phelps held out his left hand, flexing long, slender, brittle-looking digits. Dalliance noted the absence of rings.

'I was delighted Ted caught him.'

'Can you remember – and I want you to think hard about this – exactly who you ended up next to?'

'What, in the huddle you mean?'

He thought for a moment, then: 'Jez. Yes, it must have been. I remember coming round the back of him. I just got my hand on Ted's shoulder when Rees crashed into us all, running in from cover.'

'Can you remember what happened then – exactly what happened?' Dalliance was fighting the incline of the chair, pulling himself forward by the arms.

'Well, someone else came into us from behind me. That must have been—'

'David Henderson?' Riley prompted.

Dalliance shot him a reproving glance. Don't feed the witness lines.

'Yes, that's right – Dave was at mid-off. And Barney must have come in from gully. And I think Norm was in the covers.'

Norm. How did Standing take to being called 'Norm', Dalliance wondered. But that was village cricket for you. He'd once played in a team with a Nobel-prize-winning astrophysicist and a toilet cleaner. They'd put on nearly a hundred together.

'And on the leg side...?' Dalliance had his notebook open now and was scribbling a rough chart of the fielding positions.

'Well, Des Tucker was at mid-wicket, Steve Royce at square leg – he's got an arm on him, that one. Top of the stumps every time, even from the boundary.'

'And young Daniel was down at fine leg,' Dalliance finished off. 'Well that's everybody accounted for. And they all came in?' Phelps nodded. 'And you didn't see anything suspicious?'

'Didn't see anything at all, once Rees had crashed in – apart from Jez's sleeve. I was more worried about getting my arm out and getting away. It was all getting a bit – you know – a bit matey for me.'

Dalliance looked at him. Yes, not really one of the gang – always on the fringes. By choice – or because he naturally invited exclusion, rejection?

'Okay, Mr Phelps. You've been very helpful. I just have to ask one last question – what were your relations with Mr Roper?'

Something, some trace element of an emotion, flashed across Phelps' eyes – mystification? Or something else?

'I don't know what you mean – I didn't have much to do with him, to be honest. Apart from the cricket, you know.'

'And you weren't a major player in his grand plan?' That was unkind, Dalliance thought, even as he was asking it.

'No, no – not at all,' Phelps agreed with a self-deprecating laugh. 'Some weeks I nearly didn't get a game. But then someone would drop out and I'd get the call on Friday or Saturday night.'

'And you were always available?'

'I didn't have anything else to do, did I?'

Dalliance looked around the living room. No books, no ornaments, not even a magazine or a paper. Just the television set. He gave Phelps a weak smile and started his attempt to struggle out of the chair.

Riley was on his feet in a moment, but a glare from Dalliance made him think twice about offering his hand to pull the boss up.

'You don't murder your captain because he doesn't rate your bowling,' Dalliance said with a sigh as Riley drove them out of the little cul-de-sac.

'He was the most helpful as far as the huddle was concerned.'

'The Huddle of Death,' Dalliance said, pushing his fingers through his hair. The case was beginning to get under his skin, and he'd barely been on it for twenty-four hours. 'Check his accident out.'

'Sir?'

'You heard me. Almost certainly a waste of time, but it won't be much time, and you never know. Left arm round,' he added, as much to himself as to his subordinate.

As long as he doesn't make me stop the car and do another re-enactment by the side of the road, Riley thought, as he changed up a gear.

Des Tucker was a smallish, roundish man with very little hair. He was a busy, confidential man, a natural button-holer, a winker, a nose-tapper; someone who would probably have a very good tip for the four-ten at Wincanton.

'Why here?' Dalliance asked, eyeing the litter box of the lay-by with a sceptical eye.

Des Tucker patted his pockets. Another smoker, Riley thought with a sense of foreboding.

'A bit more – how shall we say – private out here.'

Tucker got his cigarette going. Dalliance stiffened under the provocation. 'We could have done it down at the station if you'd preferred,' he said pointedly.

Tucker laughed. 'Very discreet. Not.' He inhaled again. A car went past.

Any number of people could see them as they drove past, Riley thought.

'I know,' Tucker acknowledged. 'It is a bit out in the open. But—'

'Better than at home?' Dalliance suggested.

'Well, yes. Yes, it is, to be frank with you. You know how it is – 'er indoors. I used to love that programme. Best thing

they ever did, Minder. That would be my Desert Island programme, that would.'

Dalliance refrained from pointing out that Desert Island Discs
did not allow castaways videos – unless, he supposed, they chose
a DVD player as their luxury item. It had been a long day and the
smoke was distracting him. Concentrate, he told himself.

'So, what is it you wouldn't want your wife to hear you
discussing?' Might as well get to the point.

'Oh, nothing really. But...' Tucker lowered his voice,
drawing them in to hear him. 'Look,' he said, glancing from
Riley's face to Dalliance's, 'I know what you're going to
want to talk about, and I just don't want to have to be – you
know, constricted in my answers.'

Everybody seemed to know what they wanted to talk
about, Dalliance thought.

'Okay, so what do we want to talk about?'

'I'm at the heart of things in the Boltons. Taxi service –
and driving instructor.'

'Driving instructor? You didn't say anything about that
yesterday,' Dalliance said.

'Didn't think you'd need one,' Tucker said, 'but seeing as
you get yourself driven around by your sidekick, perhaps you
never took your test. Never too late, you know.'

Dalliance's look was enough.

'Sorry. Anyway, I do give lessons – got the car, and a lifetime's experience. So why not? You gotta maximise the use
of your assets, haven't you?'

'Go on,' Dalliance said, wearily.

'Well, what with the taxi service – and the driving instruction – I'm at the centre of the community. There isn't a bit
of gossip going I don't pick up. And talking of picking up – I
pick up a lot of very interesting people.'

'Such as?' Riley said.

'Perhaps they're not interesting as such – *per se*, as you
might say – but interesting nonetheless.'

He dropped his cigarette and rubbed a suede shoe over it. Dalliance waited until he stood back, then put his own black leather brogue down firmly on the still glowing stub. 'Shall we continue this in the car?' he suggested lugubriously.

'Mine or yours, as the actress said to the bishop?'

With a withering glance at the air-freshener dangling from the Vauxhall's rear-view mirror, Dalliance walked over to the unmarked police car and opened the door.

'As long as you don't have a spurt of enthusiasm and drive me off to the nick,' said Tucker with a slightly false laugh.

'You go in the back with him, Riley,' Dalliance said, heading for the front seat.

Avoiding the smoke fumes, Riley thought as he got in beside Tucker.

Dalliance adjusted the mirror so he could look at the taxi driver without turning his head. Even so, the stale smoke that hung around him was palpable.

'Before we get on to the juicier cuts of local gossip, perhaps we can briefly re-visit yesterday's match. What's your role in the team, Mr Tucker?'

'Des, please. Everybody calls me Des. My role in the team. Apart from licensed clown, you mean? Well, I suppose I'm an all-rounder. Do a bit of this, do a bit of that. I can bowl – a bit; I can bat – a bit; and I can stop the ball and catch – a bit. Bit like those mediocre guys they used to fill the England ODI team with.'

Dalliance nodded his head – in agreement with that assessment, at any rate. 'And where were you fielding?'

'Come on, Inspector; you know the answer to that. You'll have it up on your white board. Des Tucker, mid-wicket. And Phelpsie was to my left, and Roller to my right, and young Danny Boy was all the way down at fine leg. And like everybody else, we charged in, and you're going to ask me if I saw anything suspicious, and I'm going to tell you exactly what I guess everybody else has already said – no, I didn't.'

'But everybody came in?'

'Battened on him like flies on a turd – if you'll excuse my French. Or even if you won't,' he added after registering the unamused silence. 'Because,' Tucker went on, 'that's exactly what he was – a great big steaming turd.'

If he was looking for an effect, he got one. Dalliance scrunched round in his seat and looked into the taxi driver's face. His eyebrows were raised and his lips pursed in a pantomime 'yes-I-really-did-say-that' way.

'Why, if you all hated him so much, did you turn out and play cricket with him every Sunday?'

''Cause he was the captain; he organised it all – and bloody near paid for it all too. Anyway, he may have been a turd, but he was our turd. And he hadn't always been. He was great when he first came to the village. His wife's nice, too – poor woman.'

'Poor woman?'

'Well, I'm not telling tales out of school when I say Ted wasn't exactly faithful to her.'

'And you'd know?' Riley asked.

'Well, everybody knew – including the missus; she just chose to turn a blind eye to keep the marriage going. As they do.'

'But did you have any particular knowledge – of Mr Roper's infidelities?'

'Yes, as a matter of fact. A fair few lovelies slid into my passenger seat over the years – picked up from the station, chauffeured to the airport.'

Dalliance had to repress a smile when the little man tapped his nose with his finger. His self-importance was boundless.

'Like I said, not many secrets in this village I don't know.'

'And how were your relations with Mr Roper?'

'D'you mean what motives might I have had for killing him? Well...' He stretched his eyes owl-wide, then went on.

'You'd probably say he had more reason to kill me – seeing as I knew where all the bodies – all the lovely bodies – were stashed.'

'You never thought to – exploit this knowledge?' Dalliance asked, the distaste clear in his tone.

'What, blackmail him? Like I say – everybody knew, including the lovely Margot. And anyway, you don't grass on your mates. What goes on tour, stays on tour – you know.'

'Mates?' Riley asked. 'That wasn't what you called him a moment ago.'

'I said he was a turd, and he was a turd. But he was a fun turd, a generous turd. He did some bad things to a lot of people; but I wasn't one of them. So why shouldn't I have had a beer with him down the Horseshoes once in a while? He was far better company than most of them down there, I can tell you.'

'And there's nothing else you want to tell us – about your relationship?' Dalliance asked levelly. He had turned back around in his seat now and was looking at Tucker in the mirror. It was a soft question. Did he detect a flicker of relief, a general relaxation?

'He ran me out a couple of Sundays ago. An absolute shocker. Left me stranded halfway down the wicket. I could have murdered him then – but some elaborate plot to stab him in the back with a phial of Ebola or whatever it was? I don't think so. Anyway, even if I had hated him – which I didn't – why kill the golden goose? Ted represented ten percent at least of my turnover. He might not have been a good man, but he was a bloody good customer. I'm going to miss him.' There was a pause. The interview had reached its natural conclusion. Tucker rummaged about in his pocket.

Don't even think about lighting up in here, Riley thought. As though reading his mind, the taxi driver withdrew his hand.

'So, off to see young Rees now, are you?'

Dalliance swivelled round in his seat and met the bright, challenging eyes.

'Your lad's very neat with his schedule.' Riley sheltered his notebook protectively with his hand. 'Too late, sonny. I saw you tick me off, and Rees just happens to be next on the list. He smiled. 'I'd have made a good detective myself, you know. Anyway, good luck with Rees. You won't find him as forthcoming as me, I can promise you that. Still, his girl's easy on the eye. Goodnight, gents.'

With that, the little man climbed out of the car. Riley watched him lighting up as he walked back to his own vehicle, determining to make some very thorough checks on hackney carriage licences and any other damn thing he could think of.

'Don't worry about it,' Dalliance said as Riley slid into the driver's seat. 'He's a wind-up merchant. Little man, big ego. Got to be in your face all the time. But you should watch your notebook. Easy mistake to make, no harm done. On this occasion.'

Riley revved up a little unnecessarily and swung the car out of the lay-by. Des Tucker gave them a cheery wave, before throwing his cigarette over his shoulder and climbing into his own vehicle.

Sanderson Crescent was a soulless array of new build one- and two-bedroom semis. The doorbell of Number 38 chimed with a cheeriness not mirrored in Rees Jones' face as he opened the door.

'Oh, it's you. Suppose you'd better come in.'

They had a much warmer welcome from Hazel, who came out from behind the cupboard dividing the kitchen from the diner-lounge saying, 'Hello again.'

Rees' face darkened. 'What do you mean, "Hello again"?'

'Saw them in the Horseshoes at lunchtime, didn't I, gents?'

Rees grunted disapprovingly. Riley thought he was looking particularly at him.

'Sorry to interrupt your evening. This won't take long.'

'Can I get you anything – tea or coffee?' Hazel asked brightly.

'You're not behind the bar now. Why don't you go upstairs – put the telly on in the bedroom.'

'Okay, honey,' the girl said, adding in a confidential tone before leaving them, 'He's had a long day, poor love, so go easy on him.' Riley willed himself not to look at her trim legs as she left the room, conscious that Rees' eyes would be on him.

'So, what do you want?' Rees said, indicating two chairs on the other side of the dining room table.

'Was your brother wearing his wristbands on Sunday?'

'What?'

Dalliance was pleased to see he'd caught Rees off guard. The in-swinging yorker first up was always a useful delivery.

'His wristbands – was he wearing them on Sunday?' Riley pressed.

'What wristbands? What are you talking about?'

'Those wristbands.' At a motion from Dalliance, Riley had removed the team photo from its envelope and slid it across the table. 'That is your brother Jez, pretending to be Dennis Lillee, isn't it?'

'Course it is. Why do you want to know about his wristbands?'

Dalliance said nothing, fixing him with an unblinking stare.

'Take your time,' he said eventually. 'Though it shouldn't be a difficult question to answer: wristbands – was he wearing them or not?'

God the boss is good, Riley thought.

'Er—'

'Er? Either he was or he wasn't. Which was it?

'Why don't you ask him?'

'Maybe we did. But now we're asking you.'

Riley tilted the photograph so the glass caught the ceiling light. He was enjoying this a lot.

'No.'

'No "er" this time?'

'No, he wasn't wearing wristbands.'

'Why not?'

'I don't know. Ask him. They're his wristbands. Jesus! I thought you wanted to interview me – not talk about Jez.'

Dalliance was right under his skin now, Riley thought. He rather ostentatiously removed the team photograph and put it back in its packaging. Then, with equal ostentation, he brought out his notebook – careful to keep the cover up.

'How would you describe your relations with Ted Roper?' Again, the question seemed to leave Rees floundering. 'Let me put it another way. Did you like him?'

'I didn't kill him, if that's what you mean.'

'Why should I mean that? What possible motive could you have for killing him? I asked you if you liked him?'

Riley noticed a bead of sweat appearing on Rees' forehead.

'Yeah. I suppose so. I mean, we didn't have much in common. Hardly spoke to be honest, except when we were batting together. And then it was just the usual stuff – "he's getting the odd one to move away", "mind the slower ball", you know.'

Dalliance nodded. 'Did you bat together a lot?'

'Quite a bit, I was three and he was five, so unless Norman got going – well, it was down to us really.'

'What was your highest stand, just out of interest?'

'Hundred and fifty-eight.' The answer came without thought. 'I got a ton and Ted made around eighty.'

'Not bad,' Dalliance said admiringly. 'So he was a pretty good bat?'

'Well, he was a bit past it, but you could see he had been good. Not classy, like Norman. But you could rely on him.'

Riley could see he was relaxing. The boss was leading him on, lulling him into a false sense of security.

'Yes, we all get a bit past it – but don't always know it ourselves,' Dalliance mused, as though savouring a deep psychological insight. Then, leaning forward across the table, he suddenly said, 'Tell me, if you were to have discovered, or been told, or perhaps even suspected, that Ted had – how shall I put it? – had an interest in your fiancée...?'

It took Rees a split-second to register that the matey chat about cricket was over. But then he shot out of his chair, and smashed his fist down on the table.

'Who told you that? Was it that little rat, Tucker? I'll wring his bloody neck, I swear I will.'

'I would strongly advise against any such thing, Mr Jones. And for the record, it wasn't Mr Tucker.'

'Who was it then?' Rees was half standing, half leaning on the table, glaring at them.

'Sit down, Mr Jones.'

Glowering, Rees sat down.

'Thank you. Now, can you tell us why you ran off so quickly after Mr Roper collapsed?'

'I was running for my phone.'

'Why?'

'To ring 999 of course.'

'And did you?'

'No.'

'And why was that?'

'Someone already had. In fact, more than one – the Tilsby lot. No point ringing again – the ambulance was on its way.'

'But you still went into the changing room and got your phone?'

There was a pause. Rees went slightly pink.

'Fair enough,' Dalliance said. 'Everybody else phoned home. You were the first, that's all. But you can't have known he was dead at that stage?'

'No,' Rees said, but without conviction. 'It looked pretty serious to me. I could see Barney trying to resuscitate him.'

'So you did know – or think – he probably was dead? And your first response was to ring Hazel.'

A look of pain flashed across Rees' face.

'That's what you've just told us.'

'I ran to get my phone to call for an ambulance.'

'And then, when it became apparent – to you – that Mr Roper was dead, you rang your girlfriend?'

'It wasn't like that. You're making it sound like—'

'Like what, Rees?'

'Like I didn't care.'

'But you didn't care enough to find out what state he was in before fixing up a couple of extra hours with your fiancée.'

There was a silence. Rees glowered at his hands twisting in front of him on the table.

'But perhaps you did know?'

'Know what?'

'What the state of play was – that Mr Roper was dead.'

'What are you saying? That I killed him?'

'Or knew that someone else had – possibly with your assistance.'

'I don't know what you're talking about. You're mad.'

'I'm just following the logic of what you did and what you've told us.'

Dalliance suddenly got up, pushing his chair back.

'Thank you, Mr Jones. You've been most helpful.'

'What's happening? What are you doing?' There was a note of panic tinged with pleading in Rees' voice as he half got to his feet.

'We're leaving.'

'Is that all?'

'Unless there's anything else you'd like to tell us?'

'No...no.' He stood up and showed them to the door.

Back in the car, Riley couldn't suppress his laughter and had difficulty getting the key into the ignition. 'Brilliant, sir. Completely wrong-footed him.'

Dalliance allowed himself a quiet smile.

'What's the expression? Rattle the bars of his cage. That should have done the trick.'

In the house behind them, Rees Jones stood at the bottom of the stairs and shouted above the noise of the television in the bedroom.

'Haze? Hazel? Turn that rubbish off and come down. I want to speak to you. Now!'

The sound went off and the door opened. Hazel stood on the landing looking down at him.

'What's up, hon? That didn't take long.'

She came downstairs slowly. Too slowly for Rees, who went up to meet her, grabbing her arm.

'What is it, babes? What have they done to you? You look all upset.'

'Tell me about Ted,' Rees said, pulling her into the front room.

'Ted?' She turned and looked at him coolly. 'Ted's dead, babes.'

SEVEN

'Dancing Detectives' the headline gloated.

The photographer had obviously climbed into the trees at the bottom end of the ground to get a panoramic view, and must have been close to falling off the branch when he saw what a gift he was being offered – Dalliance and Riley, clutching each other in the middle of the cricket pitch.

The Chief Inspector sat in his glass-walled cubicle, an immovable hulk, like a cast by Rodin. Judging by the deathly quiet in the open-plan office, he'd already exploded once. Riley ran the gauntlet of grins and sat down at his workstation. He fired up his computer. The first thing he was going to do was check every last detail of Des Tucker's life, on and off the road. Passing on a bit of grief wouldn't make him feel much better, but every little helps.

'Riley!' Dalliance's head appeared briefly at the door of his office.

Riley got to his feet. Somebody started to hum a waltz tune very softly and someone else emitted a squeak of suppressed laughter. Riley gave that corner of the room a heart-felt finger and went in to see his boss.

'What those sniggering imbeciles don't seem to have looked at is the front page of this appalling rag.' Dalliance pushed the red-top across his desk.

Riley found himself staring into the face of Rees Jones' fiancée smiling engagingly over the bar of the Horseshoes. Dalliance had been right – it was the smile Hazel had given them when they left the pub yesterday.

'That's what's going to get the whole pack down here – not a slightly amusing snap of two detectives looking silly.'

'Slightly amusing?' Riley didn't dare look through the dividing glass panel to see the craning necks and grinning mouths.

'As I've said before, Riley, being thought stupider than you are is no bad thing. And actually' – he turned the paper's pages till he reached the picture – 'it gives a very good view of the crime scene, and has also given me a new idea as to how the crime was committed. Given that the man probably took a dozen or so, it might be very helpful to have the whole sequence. Could you ask them to send them across?'

Riley checked the boss' face. It seemed a genuine instruction.

'Okay, sir.'

'Thank you, Riley. You might mention to the picture editor that his photographer better not have anything wrong with his car or his paperwork, because if he has, I will take the utmost pleasure in throwing the book at him.'

'Will do, sir.'

Riley went back to his desk, ignoring the hummed dance tunes and someone pretending to quickstep to the photocopier. Bunch of bloody kids, he thought, reaching for the phone.

'Are you threatening me, Officer?' The Scottish voice sounded amused when Riley passed on his message. 'We thought you'd rather like them – showing the police's softer side, an' all that. But joking apart, if they'd be helpful, I'll send 'em across. Any progress? Damien said there was going to be a news conference or something?'

'Didn't happen.'

'We know it didn't happen. Why didn't it happen?'

'Had a lot of people to see.'

'Got a prime suspect yet?'

Only the whole bloody team, Riley thought. 'We're just doing routine interviews to eliminate people from the enquiry.'

'And how many have you eliminated so far?'

Alarm bells were already ringing loudly.

'No comment,' Riley said and put the phone down. He felt he'd been played and dreaded what that seemingly innocuous exchange might turn into by tomorrow's edition. Perhaps if Dalliance actually gave a news conference it would draw the fire. Thinking he'd try to find a good moment to raise the subject, he turned to the box files piled on his desk, and sighed.

Two and a half hours later a discernible drop in the ambient sound levels alerted him to Dalliance's presence in the main work area. He felt his boss' heavy hand drop on his shoulder.

'Come on, let's get some fresh air. You can tell me what you've found in the car.'

In truth, it wasn't much. Ted Roper had had a lot of fingers in a lot of pies – property, at home and abroad: holiday lets in Cornwall, a flat in Camden, three or four terraced houses near the university in Leeds, and a fine-looking timbered building somewhere in rural Germany.

'An interesting portfolio,' Dalliance said. 'Must be worth a bit. Any idea how much equity – ballpark?'

'Not that much, sir. It's all heavily mortgaged – eighty-five percent loan to value, interest only – from before the crash. I mean they're all covering the mortgage repayments and producing a reasonable income; but—'

'So no million-pound get-out-of-jail card there?'

'No way. Some of them I doubt he'd even get his money back.'

'There's some justice then.' Dalliance's views on property speculators were only slightly less vehement than his dislike of footballers and football managers. 'Good work, Riley. Boring but necessary. Simply confirms what Standing said — Roper had more reason to murder him than the other way round. Any idea what Roper Towers is going to fetch? Mrs R. should have enough left to buy something decent, shouldn't she?'

'I should think so,' Riley said.

Dalliance picked up on the hint of doubt. 'Meaning "no"? I thought big houses in the shires were keeping their value? There's always another Russian oligarch with more loot to invest in the UK.'

'Oh, no problem selling it, sir — best estimate from the two high-end estate agents I tried put it in the two/two and a half million bracket.'

'But...?

'Roper had taken a sizeable mortgage out on it.'

'How much?'

'About fifty percent, I'd say. Pretty hefty monthly repayments.'

'H'm.' Dalliance sounded interested. 'So he really did need Standing's latest wheeze to come off?'

'I'd say he was relying on it, sir.'

'Yes. Big windfall, pay off mortgage on the family home. The undoubted benefits outweighed any consideration of the risks.' Dalliance made a noise that sounded like a tut and shook his head in a 'one born every minute' gesture Riley was all too familiar with. 'So suddenly we're looking at financial meltdown.'

'He was on the ropes, sir.'

'Not to mix our metaphors,' Dalliance said, but Riley could see he was pleased with where a morning's routine desk work had got them. 'However, none of that provides a motive to murder him. Suicide, yes; but though we've all heard of murders disguised as suicide, suicide disguised as murder – no. Certainly not in this case. You simply can't puncture yourself in the lower back while embracing your adoring teammates. Drive to the cricket ground.'

Oh no, Riley thought. Not more dancing on the square.

'It's all right, Riley, I know what you're thinking. But you're safe today. Well, relatively.'

What did that mean? Riley wondered as he turned off and bumped up the now familiar lane. The uniform on the gate waved them through. Was that a glint of derision in his eye?

'They've all seen it,' Dalliance said wearily. 'Drive round the boundary to the far end. Stay near the fence. That's the groundsman.' He lifted his hand and drew a grudging wave from the figure chugging slowly up the wicket on the roller. 'Here will do.'

Riley parked a few yards from the sightscreen at the bottom end of the ground.

'Now, time to view the scene from a different perspective,' Dalliance said, leading the way to the boundary fence. 'Here we go.'

The two men eased themselves over the white painted picket, following countless fielders sent into the field to retrieve balls hit straight for six. They approached the copse of trees from which they'd been snapped. What did Dalliance hope to find, Riley wondered. The pap's cigarette butts?

'We should have done this yesterday – before that bloody photographer snuck in,' Dalliance said, looking around him. 'We have assumed – quite understandably – that the poison was pumped into Roper by one of the people on the pitch.'

'How else could it have happened?

'Do you watch natural history programmes, Riley? There must be a moment when there isn't a football match on.'

Riley didn't rise but waited patiently for his boss to elaborate.

'I was watching a fascinating programme about the white rhino not so long ago.'

Give the man a cigarette, Riley thought. There were just too many episodes like this when he seemed to lose the plot entirely.

'Hear me out. The rhino, as I'm sure you know, is an endangered species preyed upon by poachers who kill the poor beasts and cut off their completely useless horns and sell them to the Asian market as completely ineffectual medicines.'

Riley was looking back out over the cricket ground. The roller turned. God, that looked a boring job.

'And to protect the rhino, Riley, the park rangers sometimes pre-empt the poachers by cutting the horns off to save the animals' lives. And they obviously can't do that with the beast fully conscious.'

A gleam of understanding shone in Riley's eye.

'Yes, Riley, not all irrelevant rambling. A long shot, I grant you. But a dart gun could cover that distance, I'm pretty sure.'

Riley measured the distance with his eye. 'But sir, even if someone did shoot Roper like a rhino – what would have happened to the dart?'

'Oh, there'd have to have been two of them, obviously. But in this scenario we'd be looking for someone taking something out of the victim's back, not pushing it in.'

'But – the timing would have to be perfect. Leave aside issues of accuracy.' Riley looked again from the trees to the pitch.

'Highly unlikely, granted. But not impossible. Now, would you kindly shin up that tree and have a shuftie?'

Riley looked at him aghast.

'For goodness sake. I don't need to call in the tree-climbing team, do I? What's the point of all the football training if you can't shin up a tree? That snapper yesterday didn't have any trouble.'

His sergeant looked less than convinced. 'But what if I—?'

'Fall off and break your neck? I'll get the sack for making you do it. So it's a win-win, Riley.'

Dalliance had become positively sadistic since giving up, Riley thought, reluctantly stripping off his jacket, and instinctively transferring his phone to his trouser pocket.

'Good lad. Here, I'll give you a leg up.'

Hoping there might be a remnant of cow shit left on it from yesterday's trip to Ben Cowper's farmyard, Riley planted the sole of his shoe into his superior's cupped palms and pulled himself up on the lowest branch.

Dalliance gave him a shove and watched as he disappeared into the thick leaves.

A minute or so passed. 'All right up there?' he called out impatiently.

Well, I haven't fall off yet, thought Riley, gripping the branch tightly. 'Okay so far, sir,' was all he said.

'What have you got? And don't say vertigo.'

The bastard was enjoying this. Riley inched cautiously forward, when suddenly he felt a stabbing pain in his knee and heard the telltale rip of cloth. Swearing under his breath, he craned round to try to assess the damage. If he'd picked up an injury three weeks before pre-season, he was bloody well going to report Dalliance to the Association.

Suddenly his train of thought flipped onto a different track. Whatever had torn his trousers was sharp. Sharp – as in a snapped-off branch.

'Sir,' he called down. 'I think I've found a broken branch.'

'Excellent. Can you confirm?'

Riley readjusted his position to investigate further. And there it was, on the underside of the branch – which was why he hadn't seen it – a freshly snapped-off shoot, sharp as a spear tip.

'Well?' Dalliance demanded.

'Confirm that, sir. Very recent – and damned dangerous. I've torn my trousers and hurt my leg.'

'You'll live,' Dalliance shouted up. 'Excellent work. Keep talking so I know exactly where you are.'

'Of course, it could have been the photographer, sir.'

'I am well aware of that, Riley,' Dalliance said from more or less directly below him. He could just make out the moving form through the leaves. 'The thing is, Riley, the pap wouldn't have done anything about it. But if our new hypothesis is right, the killer would almost certainly have removed it. Drop something so I can see where it would have landed.'

'Drop what?'

'Anything you like. Car keys?'

Riley made sure of his balance and felt for them. 'Coming down, sir,' he called, dropping them in the hope that they would hit Dalliance on the head.

'Nice try, Riley, but I was ready for you.'

Riley cursed under his breath.

There was nothing from Dalliance for a minute, then: 'No, can't see anything – barely a twig. What can you see? Have you got a clear view of the pitch?'

'Yes, sir.'

'Can you take a photo?'

'A photo, sir? Can't SOCO—'

'Of course they can. They can put up their bloody tent and I can go on national television and announce that there's a suspicious broken branch in a tree behind the sightscreen. Or better still, send you round each of the bloody suspects and tell them personally. Just take a snap on your phone – all right?'

Riley had to admit the sight line was exceptionally good. He wouldn't fancy aiming anything that required both hands, but he managed to get a couple of very clear pictures.

'Let's see,' Dalliance said when Riley reached the ground. 'Good. Well done. And I'm sorry about your trousers.'

'That's all right, sir. I'm more worried about my knee.'

It was clear this was not a concern shared by his boss.

'Car keys, sir?'

'Where you dropped them.' With a nod of his head Dalliance directed him to them. He was right. There was nothing on the ground bigger than a twig. The snapped branch had definitely been moved.

'We're not going to find it, are we, sir?'

'A small, snapped branch – in the middle of the countryside? Of course we're not going to find it, Riley. It's the fact that we won't find it – that it wasn't where it logically should have been – that's significant. If only we'd thought to look in the tree before that damned photographer got up there.'

'We could pull him in, sir – ask him if he broke the branch.'

'Of course we could, Riley; and we probably will. But not just yet. For one thing, I don't want to look as though we're harassing the man. For another, if we start asking about broken branches, we're just going to start a hue-and-cry. We'd have the red-tops talking about aliens with crossbows before we know it.'

'What about sending in SOCO to look for footprints?'

'It's too dry. I've had a good look around while you were re-living your boyhood escapades. Couldn't see a thing. And to be frank, if scenario B is what we're looking at, we're up against a pretty canny shooter, probably professionally trained. Someone who would certainly have covered his tracks – and probably disposed of his footwear into the bargain. Find me an oil drum with the remains of a pair of trainers smouldering in amongst all the other rubbish, and I'll be interested. In the meantime, we're going to talk to our eyes and ears at the scene, our friend Ebby the scorer.'

EIGHT

Ebby the scorer was in his cottage garden. It was hard to see what he was doing exactly, but he took their arrival as an excuse to lean a hoe against the garden shed. He greeted them cordially, waving them to chairs set round a table sheltered from the sun by an arbour of honeysuckle.

'Fancy a cuppa? I'm gasping. Pru!' he shouted. A window opened and his wife smiled out. 'Pot of tea, love, if you wouldn't mind. Now, gents, what can I do for you?'

Once they had sat down, Dalliance opened his notebook at the page showing the fielding positions.

'About right? I mean for the time of the – incident.'

Ebby looked at it carefully.

'To a T, I'd say. Standing started at second slip but moved out half an hour before – at least. Des probably started in ten yards. Likes to get in the batman's eyeline, if you know what I mean. He's a fidgety sort; puts them off. Least that's the theory. As soon as someone bangs the ball past his ear, he's back in the ring. But apart from that I can't think of a single change. Ted isn't – wasn't – the most up-and-at-'em captain, if you know what I mean.'

Dalliance nodded. He didn't have much time for the modern fad of changing the field after every ball.

'Surprised Jez was still bowling after, what, an hour and a half?' he remarked. 'It was a hot day.'

'But he wasn't.'

'He wasn't bowling? But we—'

'No, no – he was bowling – but he hadn't been bowling from the start. Steve opens. He's a bit all over the place but he's bloody quick, if you'll excuse my French. You see the size of his shoulders.' Ebby whistled. 'If he gets it in the right place, he don't half make them jump about. But of course he doesn't have a lot of control – depends on how much he's had in the Horseshoes beforehand to be quite honest with you. If he's not on song, a good bat will take him to the cleaners.'

'How did he bowl on Sunday?'

'Not so bad. Could have got one early on. Chap flashed at it. Went past Barney's nose like a stone from a catapult. Damn lucky it didn't hit him in the face – his hands were still by his knees when it went past.' Ebby laughed, and then half stood up as his wife approached with a tray.

'There we are – an' I brought you some cakes.'

'You shouldn't have gone to the trouble,' Dalliance said.

'No trouble, sir. Left over from the match. A lot of people seemed to have lost their appetites. And no wonder. You will catch 'im, won't you?'

'We will – I can promise you that.'

'And quick, mind. It's already been on the local news, and there's more press down. Not surprising with that picture of Hazel splashed over the front page, giving the photographer her "come hither" look.'

Dalliance and Riley exchanged a glance.

'She's a lovely girl, no doubting that, but I'm not surprised young Rees is so...'

'So...?'

'Well, you know what young men are like. And she is the best-looking girl in the village, so it's not surprising he's a bit possessive.'

'How do you mean?'

'She don't mean nothing,' Ebby said. 'He just don't like other men giving her the eye. And I can't say as I blame him. I was just the same myself all those years ago, wasn't I, pet?'

'You didn't have the temper on that Rees has, love. He's like a powder keg. And if he didn't blow up when he saw that picture – well, I'd be amazed.'

Dalliance looked up at her thoughtfully. 'What time did you get to the ground on Sunday?' he asked.

'Ooh, I was there from the start, wasn't I, Ebby. I mean, I always am when I'm helping with the teas. We drive over together. It would be too long a walk for me, and Ebby has to be there in good time 'cause of the scoring.'

'So you had a bit of time to watch the game?'

'That's right. I don't mind it. Take a bit of knitting, sit in the shade. Of course I can't talk to Ebby, can I dear, 'cause it puts him off, so I have to sit away from the scorebox. But there's other people to talk to. The others on the tea rota, other players' wives. No, the time passes quickly enough.'

'And do you remember anything – anything at all – that struck you as in any way different from normal, any way strange or unusual?' Riley felt he had to butt in before she started talking them through the sandwich fillings.

'No, young man, I don't think I can. Of course I've been through it all with Ebby, but we couldn't think of anything, could we, love? Nothing at all. It was just a normal day, a lovely quiet Sunday in our lovely quiet village, and then...' Her face crumpled slightly at the remembered shock of Ted Roper's death.

'All right,' Dalliance said soothingly. 'Don't upset yourself.'

'Off you go, love. I'll carry on,' Ebby said.

Once they were alone, Dalliance asked the scorer to say in his own words what he saw at the time of the incident.

Ebby shook his head and sighed. 'I know you'd think I was the man to go to, but the fact is, I wasn't looking.'

'You weren't looking?' Riley nearly spat out his mouthful of slightly stale cake.

'You don't know much about cricket, do you, son? Scorers have a job of work to do, and when a wicket falls, that's when they're at their busiest. And of course a catch is worse than a bowled or an LBW, 'cause you've got to write the catcher's name in – and tell your fellow scorer who it was. And their chap's on the deaf side, so I had to show him Ted's name in my scorebook as he didn't seem to hear it when I said it.'

Riley felt his boss' eye on him as he was subjected to this little lecture. He thought wistfully of the day when a case rested on an understanding of the off-side rule.

'So you didn't really see what happened after Ted had taken the catch?'

'Well, I saw them all run in to slap him on the back of course, but after that I was busy writing up the details, noting the score for the Fall of Wicket column, putting a "w" in the bowler's column, making sure Fred got all the details, checking with his book who was coming in next; I don't know how long all of that took, but when I looked up I could see something was wrong.'

'And what did you think had happened? Your first thoughts.'

'I could see somebody down. Didn't know it was Ted at first, but then obviously as people started running about I could see. And then someone shouted to me to ring for an ambulance, so I was scrabbling around in my pocket for my mobile phone and making the call.'

'When you say people started running about, can you remember who exactly was running – and where?' Riley saw Dalliance nod his approval.

Ebby put his hand to his head and pushed his fingers under his cap to scratch his scalp.

'I can't rightly recall, to be honest with you. I mean, most people didn't run at all — just sort of drifted around looking concerned. Barney got Ted over on his back and started doing the kiss of life stuff. And someone ran into the pavilion, though as I was already making call, that wasn't necessary.'

'Who was that?'

The scorer thought for a moment. Then nodded as though to confirm to himself that he could remember accurately.

'Rees. Rees Jones. Shot off like a hare — he's probably the quickest we've got, so it made sense for him to be the one running to the changing room. But like I say, I was already on the line to the emergency lot — and even I'd been beaten to it because one of the chaps who was umpiring had his mobile out there with him. Which he shouldn't have, because it can be distracting if it rings just as someone's coming up to bowl. But you can't tell 'em. And fair play to him, he got the call in first. Not that it made any difference. Ted was dead as a doornail by the time the ambulance arrived. More tea, gentlemen?'

Riley pushed his empty cup across the table. As he waited for it to be refilled, he looked around the garden. A gnome caught his eye, but it seemed at home surrounded by the riot of colour in the beds, and the roses espaliered to the warm stone walls of the cottage. It was peaceful and soothing, making it almost impossible to believe that just two days ago there had been a murder in full public view — and that the kindly, ageing man pushing the cakes across the table towards him had been a witness.

He glanced down at his notebook. Nothing Ebby had said added anything to their knowledge of the sequence of events up to and immediately following the murder — though he supposed it was useful to have their version of the incident confirmed.

Dalliance drained his cup and set it down.

'Nearly done, Ebby. Just a couple of things. First the obvious – any ideas as to who did this? I mean who might have wanted Ted—'

'Dead? H'm. I've been thinking about it – thinking about it damn hard. But...' He shook his head. 'There were – what do they call them nowadays?'

'Issues?' Riley suggested.

'That's right – issues – with one or two of the lads.'

'Such as?'

'Ben Cowper's under pressure with his farm.'

'Roper was throwing him out?'

'Not exactly. I don't know the details, so don't quote me. But let's put it this way, Ben's tenure wasn't as secure as he thought it was. It was probably going to be sorted out, but he felt hard done by. Felt Ted wasn't playing fair – and that they'd had a gentlemen's agreement and Ted was going back on that and going by the letter of the law.'

'And Ben was angry?'

'Yes, you'd have to say so. And I can't say as I blame him entirely. He's worked that farm every hour of every day ever since his dad died. His ma gives him hell, and he's too loyal to her to stick her in a home. Which means he can't do the right thing with Nance.'

'Why not?' Dalliance enquired.

'You don't know Ben's ma.'

Riley thought her one cameo at the bedroom window was enough to be going on with.

'You any idea how two warring women under the same roof can tear a man's peace to shreds? And he's a good man, Ben. Patient. Loyal. All he's ever wanted was to bury his old ma when the time comes, and carry Nance over the threshold as his lawful wedded.'

He'd need all his strength to do that, Riley thought.

'And then Ted comes along and throws the whole thing into doubt. So I don't blame him for getting aerated and mouthing off a bit.'

'What sort of things does he say?' Riley asked.

'Don't you go writing things down in that notebook of yours, young man. If a bloke can't get his feelings off of his chest over a pint on a Friday night, frankly this country ain't worth living in any more.'

Dalliance raised his hand, and Riley let the cover of his notebook fall.

'That's all right, Ebby. Point taken.' Dalliance smiled reassuringly. 'But Ben's not the only one that's come under that sort of pressure from Ted, is he?'

'No, he ain't. If it weren't Ben in one ear, it were young Jez in the other.'

'And what was Jez's beef?'

'Only that Ted was threatening to chuck him out of that old barn he uses as his workshop. Five or six years he's been there now – happy as Larry, just getting on with it. Been the making of him – everyone says.'

'Making of him?'

'Well he used to get into a lot of trouble. Probably below your pay-grade. But if you look through the records – fights, petty thieving, more fights, driving offences…'

Dalliance gave Riley a look. He'd enjoy going through Jez's career of petty crime.

'What sort of violence?'

'Oh, you know – silly Friday night stuff. Young calves bashing their heads together. Mind you, Jez always seemed to come out on top. He's not as easily riled as his brother, but you don't want to get on the wrong side of him, I can tell you that for nothing.'

'How does he get on with his brother?'

'Thick as thieves. Right pair of tearaways in their teens. But then Rees got a bit more savvy. Started taking school a bit more serious. Saw which way the wind was blowing. Went to college and got his bits of paper. He's done well. And when he got Hazel, well that was it. They bought the house together. Going to get married in the autumn – after the cricket season. And I dare say we'll have a new little cricketer in prospect by the end of next year's season.'

Ebby smiled at the prospect.

'And what does Rees do?'

'Don't rightly know. Drives around in a company car contacting clients. Selling them the latest lines. I'm sure someone told me, but...' The scorer shook his head.

'But they're still close, the two brothers – even though he's left Jez behind?'

'Jez don't see it like that. "If Rees wants to go poncing around in an Astra and a cheap suit, let him. Only time I wears a suit's weddings and funerals". No, they're great mates. Really look out for each other.'

Dalliance nodded his head gently, stroking his moustache. 'Anybody else you can think of – that was getting grief from Ted?'

'Steve Royce.'

'Oh, what was his problem?'

'Access to his caravan.'

'Go on.'

'Steve's a good lad, a real good lad, but he's not, how shall I put it, he's not made a great success of life. I blame the army. He saw some shocking stuff out there, you know. That's why he drinks. I'm sure of it.'

'But what about his caravan – and what has Ted Roper got to do with it?'

Ebb sighed, realising he was going to have tell the whole story. 'Steve comes out of the army – invalided out with whatever it is they call it these days—'

'Post-traumatic stress disorder,' Riley suggested.

'That's right, sonny. Shell shock in old money. You couldn't tell he had it to begin with. There he was, back in his usual corner of the bar in the Shoes telling these amazing stories about rolling across the desert in a Jeep in the middle of the night, heading into the biggest firework display you'd ever seen – and making light of it – you know, platoons getting lost in the dark and nearly getting shot up by the Yanks; he made it seem like one big lark. He was just like his old self, only he'd got more to talk about, more stories to tell. But the sad fact was he wasn't his old self. We were all slow on the uptake. First it was his kid going into A&E, and then it was Maureen. It took your boys to put two and two together. And as soon as they did, we all thought, of course – those bruises, the way Maureen crept about like a mouse. She wouldn't let them press charges, but of course he had to leave the house. Ben Cowper had an old caravan he could have. They took it down a lane and parked it up, and Roller's been there ever since.'

'So where does Ted come in?'

'He wants – wanted, I should say – to block the lane with a new road to his fishing lake or whatever it was going to be. "Why can't you just leave my lane coming off your new road?" Roller asked him. But he said no, that wouldn't work. Fact was, he didn't want people seeing Roller's washing hanging up outside a clapped-out old caravan as they drove up for their day's fishing. And you can see his point. But you can also see Roller's point.'

Dalliance gave Riley a 'here-we-go-again' look. 'And Royce was upset by this?'

'He was steaming. The evening he'd had it out with Ted we thought we were going to have to ring for you lot. He was yelling and hollering and saying all the things he was going to do to Ted, and with every round it got worse and worse. But he didn't mean anything by it – not really. I mean, knowing Roller, if he'd wanted to do away with Ted, he'd have broken his neck there and then. It isn't flower-arranging they teach you in the army.'

Dalliance sighed. Had there ever been a murder case when so many suspects had publicly declared their desire to see the victim dead? He wound up with a few questions about people passing by the ground on Sunday afternoon, but what with doing the scorebook and putting the metal plates up on the scorebox, Ebby was kept pretty busy.

'Lots of people go by, you know. Dog-walkers, courting couples. They stay and watch for a bit, then drift off. It's like them Parks they got in Oxford, you know.'

Having played three matches on the Parks, Dalliance did indeed. It was one of the nicest things about university cricket, the way the ground was so open, just a part of the sweeping lawns under the magnificent trees. He got heavily to his feet, concluding the interview with a few easy pleasantries, and the two detectives climbed back into the car.

As he eased out of the tight parking space, Riley wondered aloud, 'Why didn't you ask him—?'

'If he'd seen anyone climbing into the trees behind the sightscreen with an elephant gun? Because, Riley, I think he might have mentioned it, don't you? Sometimes asking questions gives away more than you get back. Christ Almighty. It's looking more and more like a bloody miracle the whole team didn't just beat him to death with their bats like a seal cub.'

'Where to now, sir? Should we go and find Steve Royce in his caravan?'

'I suppose so,' Dalliance said without enthusiasm. 'But you don't honestly think he did it, do you? He'd have torn Roper limb from limb if he was going to kill him. Bloody well wish he had – it would have saved us all a lot of bother.'

Riley always enjoyed these moments of defeatism. Dalliance, he knew, took his work exceptionally seriously, and set far higher standards than anyone else. It was nice to know he felt the strain of that commitment, and not just those working under him.

The lane in question took them across the village once more.

'Close to the Roper's place,' Dalliance observed.

They bumped down another rutted track and splashed through a shallow ford before finding the caravan set like a one-man gypsy camp under a mature ash tree.

It had to be admitted it was not a pretty sight. The caravan was ancient, without any of the charms of antiquity, and as Ebby had warned there was a straggly line of washing – mainly T-shirts, pants and socks – leading from a window to a convenient branch of a tree. Around the door were odd boxes displaying a variety of rubbish, and an oil drum set up on bricks, from which a thin drizzle of smoke appeared like the last breath of a dying dragon.

'There's your oil drum, sir.'

'Find me footwear at the bottom of it, Riley, and the first pint's on me. Doesn't look as though he's in, does it?' He climbed the three steps up to the caravan door and, after banging on it and trying the handle, pushed his face against the grimy glass and peered in. 'No better inside than out. I thought they taught you how to keep yourself neat and tidy in the army.'

'I'm sure they said something about not hurting innocent civilians as well,' Riley said, casting around him for a decent-sized stick. When he found one he went up to the oil drum. 'Phoar! What has he put in there?' he exclaimed, stepping back and turning his head to get cleaner air into his lungs.

'What is it?'

'I think it could be rubber,' Riley said, coughing.

Dalliance approached cautiously. 'Give,' he said, holding his hand out to take the stick. He leant over the drum and thrust the stick in, hauling out a smouldering square of carpet. 'There's your rubber, Riley – carpet backing. But you're right, it's a filthy smell. God knows what it's doing to the ozone layer. If we're still worrying about that. Anyway, no discernible footwear.' He held the carpet up on the end of the stick for a moment. 'I wonder why he decided to burn this.'

'Well, look at it, sir – it's mank.'

'Mank it may be, but it's been that for a very long time.'

'Maybe he's just having a clear-out.'

'Do you see any evidence of an on-rush of tidiness?'

Riley shrugged.

'Look, it's been outside.' Dalliance pointed to some blackened bits of grass sticking to the rubber backing.

Suddenly the square of carpet jolted violently, like a twitched curtain. It took Riley a split-second to realise they were under fire, and when he did, he launched himself at Dalliance, toppling him over behind the oil drum. As the two men rolled in an undignified tangle, Riley felt for his phone.

'What are you doing?' Dalliance said, wiping dust out of his moustache.

'Ringing for an ARU, sir.'

He felt Dalliance's large hand smother his. 'Put it away, Riley, and kindly get off me.'

They heard footsteps crunching down the lane towards them, coming at quite a lick. Before they could quite untangle themselves, they heard the familiar tones of Steve Royce.

'Ah – it was you, Inspector. Sorry about that. Still, gave you two another chance to have a cuddle, didn't it?'

The two detectives made an ungainly effort to get back on their feet, and brushed the dust from their clothes.

'Steven Royce—'

'I am arresting you on a charge of yaddy, yaddy, yaddy. I need not say anything, but anything I do not say when asked—'

'Actually, I wasn't,' Dalliance said. 'I realise that firing an air rifle pellet past my nose was just your way of saying hello, but my sergeant was about to call an Armed Response Unit.'

'Don't worry, son. If I'd 'ave wanted to shoot him, I wouldn't have missed by half a yard. I wasn't the best marksman in 2 Rifles for nothing. Just don't like strangers poking their noses in.' He gave them a surly smile. 'Anyway, my mistake. Here – have a rabbit,' he offered, producing one out of the pocket of his voluminous coat. 'Won't get any fresher than that.'

In confirmation, a fat splash of blood fell on the ground between them.

'No thanks,' Dalliance said. 'And I'd certainly advise you against taking pot-shots at strangers. They might not be as understanding as us.'

Royce shrugged his massive shoulders, and stumped up the three steps to the caravan door. He unlocked it and threw the dead rabbit inside, before settling himself down on the top step. 'So what's so fascinating about an old bit of carpet? That won't help you find out who killed that bugger Roper.'

'It might help us see who's been down here visiting you.'

'I doubt that, I doubt that very much. If you wanted to know who's been down here visiting me, the best thing would be to ask, wouldn't it?'

'You weren't here,' Riley said, still incredulous at Dalliance's forbearance.

'He's sharp, this one, isn't he?' Royce said to Dalliance.

'He'll do,' Dalliance said. 'So, why were you burning that bit of old carpet?'

'Annoying me – getting under my feet in fact. Kept scuffing up.' He looked at the patch at the bottom of the three steps, and then spat for greater emphasis. 'But take it away – waste a bit more of the taxpayers' money on it.'

'I think we just might do that,' Dalliance said. 'Bag it up, Riley. And please don't tell me it's still burning. There's a stream down there.'

Feeling like a child selected for teacherly ridicule, Riley picked up the carpet and plodded twenty yards down the lane.

'So who has been visiting you then?' Dalliance asked.

'Just mates. I still got some, for all the mess I've made of things.'

'And they are?'

'Jez, Ben.'

'No one else?'

Royce thought for a moment.

'No, I ain't got any other friends.'

'So just the two other people who were at the match on Sunday who were also being threatened by Ted Roper.'

'I suppose that's one way of looking at it.'

'You're not denying he was putting each one of you under a lot of pressure?'

'Not denying it all. And we all hated him for it. And speaking for myself, I'm not sorry he's gone. I should think I speak for all three of us.'

'So when were Ben and Jez down here last?'

'Saturday night. Frank chucked us out of the Horseshoes around – well, let's say it was late, but we still had a bit of a thirst on. So we came down here. I got a fire going in the drum, and pulled some tinnies out of the fridge.'

'And what did you talk about?'

'I'd have thought that was bleeding obvious – Ted Roper, and what a bastard he was being.'

'But you didn't plan to kill him?' Dalliance asked.

'D'you know what – we didn't. Might have got around to it in time, but then someone came along and beat us to it.'

'And you have no idea who that might have been?' Riley was back from the stream, the carpet dripping from his hand.

Royce looked steadily at him, then shook his head, though whether in contempt or denial was not immediately apparent.

'Just take your little trophy, sonny – so as not to have had a wasted journey.' He stood up and with a brusque nod went into the caravan and slammed the door behind him.

'Bag that up and let's get out of here,' Dalliance said, moving towards the car.

Riley started looking for an evidence bag in the boot, though it took a while to root one out from under a couple of high-visibility jackets. And then he couldn't find the labels.

'Never mind faffing about with the label. You can do that later. You certainly won't forget where it came from. Let's be off before he changes his mind and pokes a twelve bore out of the caravan window.'

'That,' Dalliance said as they splashed through the ford, 'must be Henderson's – the water Roper was intending to divert for his carp lake. I suppose given what we now know about his finances – thanks to your beavering away this morning – it was a matter of some urgency.'

Riley felt pleased at the acknowledgement. 'Where was he planning to put the lake?'

'Let's go and have a look.'

Margot Roper did not seem surprised by their visit. 'I was expecting a second innings,' she said with a melancholy smile. When told they wanted to see the sight of the pro-posed lake, she readily changed into a pair of stout walking brogues and led the way.

'Was this intended as a commercial venture, Mrs Roper?' Riley asked.

'At first, I'd say no, it wasn't. Ted always liked his fishing. In fact, he liked all sport. That tennis court isn't for show.'

She waved to her left as they walked. Dalliance noted that it looked in very good condition. 'Ted may have put on weight, and I know the cricket team thought he was going downhill. But he could still hold his own with a tennis racket. But as I was saying, he loved to fish, and to begin with, when we were living the rural dream and money really didn't seem an issue, it was just another thing he wanted us to have. And, by extension, all our friends.'

She walked on in silence for a moment or two.

'He was a very generous man – a natural sharer. If he had something, he wanted you to enjoy it too. But of course, that can get you into trouble.'

'Meaning?' Dalliance asked.

'People start to expect things of you – take your generosity for granted – and then take incredible umbrage if, for whatever reason, you can't – or decide not to – keep being quite as generous.'

'Can you give us an example?'

'As you'll have found out if you've been through all his papers, there were people – tenants – whom he couldn't afford to go on being generous to.'

'Ben Cowper and Jez Jones?'

'Among others, yes.'

'And that's because of the general financial situation?'

'That's right. He really did come a cropper with Norman's scheme. That was meant to be the last big gamble – set us up for the rest of our lives – and the kids – and the grandchildren when they came along. It was going to fund the carp lake, and, in answer to your earlier question, yes, more recently, the plan was that the fishing would have had a commercial side to it.'

'So things were getting tight?'

She nodded. 'Ted was always buying more properties, here, there and everywhere. We didn't really need them. Didn't need them at all in fact. They were just another investment. But then the wind changed and they started not to look so good. They still produced a decent rental return, but there was a lot going out as well, to pay the mortgages, and all those other expenses you don't necessarily think about – insurance, repairs – like a bad Community Chest card in Monopoly.'

'And then Mr Standing's scheme hit the rocks and that left you—'

'Right up to here in it, yes, it did, I'm afraid.'

'Do you have any idea how bad it is?'

'A rough idea. As I've already told you, I know I'm going to have to sell the house. Of course, that'll knock the carp lake on the head. Which will please the Hendersons at least.'

'And Steve Royce.'

'Yes. Poor old Steve. I tried to plead for him, but Ted was adamant. Couldn't have clients driving past Steve's combinations hanging out to dry, war hero on hard times or no.'

'And the other people your husband was threatening to evict?' Riley pressed her.

'I think that's a bit harsh. In Ben Cowper's case it was more a question of getting the rent up to somewhere near the current market rate so Ted could sell the farm to an investor. He didn't want Ben to go. As for Jez – well, you can mess about with motorbike engines and lawnmowers pretty much anywhere. Ted reckoned if he could get planning for a house on the site of the barn, it would be worth a lot. Anyway, here we are.'

They had reached something of a summit and were looking down onto a bowl-shaped pasture with a ridge of trees on the far side.

'Beautiful, isn't it? The perfect spot. Only one thing wrong with it – water. A nice healthy stream running from there to there' – she pointed from one side of the field to the other – 'and we'd have had a lovely fishing lake, don't you think?'

Dalliance imagined the anglers bowed over their rods. Ducks and other water fowl would gather among the reeds, occasionally ramping into the skies with a drum roll of wing-beats and a chorus of strained cries. Yes, lovely indeed.

The contemplative moment was of short duration. Both Dalliance and Mrs Roper said 'Oh God' at the same time, and Riley swung round to see a familiar figure cantering down the bridleway towards them.

'She's just come to gloat,' Margot muttered under her breath. 'It is astonishing how some people never fail to live down to your expectations.'

'Hello, Margot,' said Jenny Henderson with rather too much bonhomie as she drew her horse up. 'Inspector, Sergeant. I do hope I didn't spoil your crime scene yesterday – ill met by moonlight, and all that. But when I saw you enacting the closet scene, I really couldn't resist joining in.'

'Just coming to offer Mrs Roper your condolences, Mrs Henderson?' Dalliance asked her pointedly.

'Well, yes, of course. I mean, we've spoken on the phone. I rang on Sunday night, didn't I, Margot dear? It's all too, too gruesome. Well, Poppy needs her exercise, so I must be getting on.'

'Thank you, Inspector,' Margot Roper said with just the flicker of a smile as they watched Jenny Henderson's amply filled jodhpurs disappearing behind a copse of trees. 'But what's all this about you enacting the closet scene?' Then, seeing Dalliance's expression, she hurriedly added, 'Don't tell me if you'd rather not.'

Dalliance raised a hand to indicate the matter was not open for further discussion.

'Fair enough. It's an embarrassment simply being in the same village as her. Actual contact is simply a matter of damage limitation. Come on, let's go back to the house, and I'll make you some tea.'

*   *   *

'So, Inspector, without breaking the Official Secrets Act, can you tell me if you're making any progress?'

Dalliance put his cup down next to an enormous art book, thinking he probably preferred Ebby's wife's builder's brew to Earl Grey.

'Of course we're making progress, but as I'm sure you'll appreciate, it's a slow and painstaking business. Not helped by the fact that he really does seem to have put an awful lot of people's backs up.'

'He knew he was making himself unpopular. He wasn't stupid. But he couldn't explain. That's what made it so awful. I mean, he could hardly go round the village saying "I've just made a mad speculation that's gone horribly wrong and am on the verge of bankruptcy – that's why I'm behaving like a complete and utter bastard", could he?'

'How did you react when he told you, Mrs Roper?'

Margot swung round to look at Riley.

'I was disappointed, of course. I mean, it was worse than I could ever have expected, and, typically, he hadn't told me the full story, so I hadn't known we were gambling the house and a lot else on this one throw of the dice.' Both Dalliance and Riley waited patiently. 'As I've already told you, we had an enormous row, and things were pretty volatile. Telling the children wasn't going to be any fun, and I could see whose job that was going to be.'

'Are they back now?' Dalliance asked solicitously.

'Upstairs, sleeping off long-haul flights. And no, I haven't told them yet. It's enough that their father's been murdered.'

'Coming back to this row you had. Was it violent?'

'I threw something at him,' Margot said. 'A bowl – just what I happened to have in my hands when I was emptying the dishwasher. It didn't hit him. Wasn't meant to. Just letting off steam. I was livid – but it was also panic, I suppose. I mean, we'd had this almost unbelievable run, and now it had all gone smash. We really were looking into the abyss. But I was as much to blame as Ted. Well, if not as much to blame, then certainly to blame. I'd been happy enough to go along with all the other gambles. But I knew more about them. Ted never explained he was borrowing this money from Norman. I'd never have gone along with that. I suppose I should have asked more questions, been a bit more forensic?'

She smiled a wan smile and offered them more tea.

'We would have got through it,' she went on, after topping up their cups. 'I'm sure we would. It would have probably made us stronger. I was getting used to the idea – selling the house, finding something smaller somewhere else. The north-east perhaps. County Durham. I spent some of my childhood up there – bit blowy of course, but you've got space, limitless acres of space. We could have made a new start. And now I'm just going to have to do it on my own.'

There was a slightly awkward silence. Dalliance drained his second cup and set it down in its saucer to bring the visit to an end.

At the front door he said, 'I'm giving a press conference this evening. I won't be saying anything much. It's a holding exercise really; just trying to keep the press at bay.'

'I gather they've already taken quite an interest in the case.'

'Yes,' Dalliance said heavily; 'the joys of living in a country with a free press.'

Margot Roper gave him a sympathetic smile. He wondered who had shown her the paper, which he was sure would not normally have been allowed across the threshold.

* * *

'You didn't find any life insurance stuff in Ted's paperwork did you?'

Riley gave Dalliance an enquiring look as he pulled his seatbelt across his chest. 'You don't think—?'

'It's not for us to think, Riley. At least, not until all the evidence is in. So I'm assuming that's a no.'

'There was a box file for insurance – car, house, the property portfolio. But no life insurance. Anyway, they don't pay out on murder, do they?'

'Depends who murdered whom. Anyway, if he didn't have a policy, it doesn't matter, does it? I suppose like so many people, he assumed he was going to live forever. What time's the press call?'

'Six, sir.' The clock on the dashboard showed it was five-thirty.

'Just drop me back – and then take yourself home. They don't need both of us there. I'll give them the dead bat.'

'Thank you, sir,' Riley said, with genuine relief.

'You've done well today, Riley. Get yourself a good night's sleep, and we'll resume hostilities in the morning.'

Dalliance got through the press conference with reasonable comfort, using the general hilarity at the 'Dancing Detectives' photo as a useful smokescreen.

'Yes, we are exploring the case from every angle – even the foxtrot.' This line brought a good-natured ripple of laughter and perhaps deflected the more penetrating questions. Yes, there was still a murderer at large, but he was confident that this was a crime of personal animosity – whatever the exact motive – so the wider community should not be in danger. Enquiries were on-going and further information would be forthcoming as and when it became available.

After twenty minutes he wrapped it up, gathered his papers and prepared to go home, feeling he'd played a decent innings on a tricky pitch, keeping the journos happy without being bounced into giving out more than he'd intended. He said his goodnights to the duty sergeant, Jenkins, and climbed into his car, anticipating an easy supper from the freezer and a relatively early night.

He might even stay awake to read half a chapter of his current book.

NINE

That, however, was not how things turned out.

The phone on Dalliance's bedside table rang at 23.48. He knew this because the red numbers on his digital alarm clock told him so. So much for his good night's sleep. And also, he suspected, for the comforting thought that the case was to a degree under control.

Pushing Richard Burton's diaries off his pillow, he reached for the phone and listened.

'Are you sure it was the same journo who took the snap of the barmaid?'

'No doubt at all,' Sergeant Jenkins assured him. 'He was staggering around on the side of the road when a passing driver spotted him and dialled 999.'

'How badly hurt is he? I mean, was this an attempt on his life?'

The duty sergeant couldn't tell him.

His mood was black as he kicked his legs into his trousers and fumbled with his shirt buttons. It wasn't just the annoyance of a man disturbed after barely an hour's sleep – it was the thought of the violence lurking just beneath the placid surface of the village. So much for the peaceful idyll of rural life.

The image of Steve Royce marching down the lane towards them with his air rifle under his arm projected itself onto his interior cinema screen. But he wasn't the only one with a proven short fuse and a muscular approach to conflict resolution. A single day's enquiries had revealed a community seething with anger and resentment. It was only going to make his job more difficult if this clear running stream of personal vengeance kept being muddied by cross-currents of village acrimony.

He went downstairs to wait for Riley. As soon as he heard the car draw up he flung open his front door and marched down the garden path.

'What do we know?'

Riley repeated what he had already been told, adding, 'They've taken him straight to hospital.'

'So it's bad?'

'Very bad. They certainly wanted to get the message across.'

'Any ideas as to the culprit?'

'Culprits – though no, he didn't see any of them. Had a sack pulled over his head, then something over his arms to keep them out of the way. They'd obviously thought it through – there was no talking – just fists and boots piling in. There had to be at least two of them, but it might have been three. And when they'd finished, they dropped him in a lay-by three or four miles out of town.'

'H'm. And who do we know with training in targeted violence?'

'Steve Royce, sir. But the obvious suspect would have to be Rees, surely?'

'And the chances also are that he has an alibi for every single second of the entire evening. Still, if we're having a sleepless night, I don't see why he shouldn't.'

'They're already bringing him in – and Jez.'

'We'll see how we get on with the Brothers Kamikaze, but I wouldn't mind betting Royce was involved too –

though he'd probably relish resisting arrest in the middle of the night. First let's go to the hospital and see if the victim can give us any more details.'

'Well, they did a number on you, didn't they, chap?'

If Riley was slightly taken aback by his boss' attempt at a bedside manner, there could be no doubting the accuracy of his diagnosis. The journalist's face was dark with bruising; one eye was swollen shut and the mouth had needed stitches.

'Ho' you haven' co' to gloa'' the man gasped.

'What could possibly have given you that idea, Mr...'

'Peterson, sir,' Riley said, his notebook open.

''Astards. I ho' you ca' the sods. I 'et you know who they are.'

'Lips giving you trouble with the labials? Don't worry; we'll keep this as short as possible, Mr Peterson.'

The journalist looked up through his one functioning eye. It was not, Riley thought, a friendly look.

'You refer to assailants in the plural. I take it you are sure of that?'

'Course I' sure. Leas' two.'

Dalliance raised his hand. In a slightly more kindly tone he said, 'To save you the trouble, Mr Peterson, I'll suggest what I think may have happened, and you can signal whether I'm right or not. How's that?'

Peterson raised his hand.

'So, after the press conference, you returned to your hotel where you received a message suggesting that, if you wanted more information, you could meet your would-be informer at a certain place. And seeing how you'd got precious little out of me, you decided you couldn't pass this up, so off you went. Right so far?'

The hand was raised again and sank back onto the hospital blanket.

'So you arrived at the designated meeting place – I'm thinking isolated, rural, disused farm buildings, perhaps a barn – am I right?'

Again the hand lifted from the bedclothes.

'And then they jumped you from behind, dropped a sack over your head – and got down to business.'

'You 'etter ca' the sods or—'

'You'll write something unpleasant about us in your newspaper. I'm not sure that threatening the officers investigating your assault is entirely sensible. But you'll be pleased to know we have already taken two suspects into custody, and in a minute we'll be on our way down to the station to start grilling them. All I need to know is how the message was conveyed. I'm guessing it was a telephone message taken down by reception at your hotel, and possibly to be found in your jacket pocket?'

Peterson pointed weakly to his jacket on the back of the door. Riley went over and started going through the pockets.

'Gallows Barn, sir – with directions.'

'Out towards the Covings, left at the crossroads by the telephone box. I know it well. A popular spot for various nefarious goings-on over the years. Nice and quiet – not likely to be disturbed, whatever you choose to do. We'll have the SOCO team there at first light. If you'd like, we'll get your car back for you.'

Again the hand signalled assent. Riley retrieved the key from the journalist's fob.

'It says here,' Dalliance said, referring to the notes, 'that you were found on the B1557, so presumably they bundled you into a vehicle when they'd finished with you. Obviously you're not going to be able to give us make or model, but if you can tell us what type of vehicle it was – van, car or pick-up?'

'Van.' Peterson's good eye was closed now. He was clearly exhausted.

'Okay. I'll send Riley round in the morning to see if you can remember anything else that might be useful. We've got more than enough to be going on with at the moment. I hope you don't have too bad a night.'

Outside the room, Dalliance said, 'That was some beating they dished out. Come on, let's spread a bit of misery ourselves.'

'Which one d'you want first?'

'Which would you suggest, Jenkins?' Dalliance asked with a glance at the clock on the wall.

'Well, they're neither of them happy,' the duty sergeant said.

'Let's have the one I'm quite sure didn't do it.'

'That being?'

'Rees.'

'He's in Interview One.'

'And Jez?'

'He's in the cells. Took a swing at the lads who went to pick him up. He's been drinking.'

'What about Rees? Is he fired up too?'

'He's fired up all right, but sober as a judge – in fact soberer than some judges I can think of. Despite claiming to have been in the Horseshoes all night.'

'Ah,' Dalliance said meaningfully. As he'd thought, an alibi for every minute.

Rees Jones looked up from the table in the interview room. 'What's going on? Arresting me in the middle of the night like a bloody police state. You can't hold me like this. What am I charged with? I want a lawyer.'

'Shut up,' Dalliance said, sitting down heavily opposite him.

'I'm entitled to a solicitor.'

'And who would you like to rouse from their slumbers at this hour – and how sympathetic do you think they'd be? Now, calm down and let's get the formalities dealt with.' He pressed the button on the tape recorder and named the three people in the interview room. 'There,' he said, with a tired smile. 'Now we'll be able to check what everyone said.'

'I don't know what I'm doing here. What am I accused of? I don't know what I'm meant to have done.'

'Where were you this evening?'

'The Horseshoes.'

'When?'

'Seven.'

'Till?

'Eleven-thirty-five.'

'Is that the normal chucking-out time on a Tuesday?'

'I wouldn't know.'

'Because you seldom, if ever, go down to the pub on a weekday. On account of your having to get up in the morning, climb into your suit, kiss your very attractive fiancée goodbye and get out on the road to earn the money to pay for your mortgage. Which is why I'm wondering what induced you to spend four hours and thirty-five minutes there this evening. How much did you drink?'

'I don't know. Not much.'

'How did you get home?'

'Drove.'

'Get a uniform in here and breathalyse him.'

'But I told you, I wasn't drinking. I had a lager top, then switched to lime and soda.'

'I'm sorry, Rees, in my experience, when someone spends four hours in a pub, he normally goes over the limit, however little he thinks he's drinking. Anyway, we'll let science decide, shall we?'

The door of the interview room opened and the duty sergeant came in.

'Thanks, Jenkins. Turns out this young man's been sat in a pub all evening and then drove home.'

It took a certain amount of time for the test to be administered; Rees' patience was obviously being stretched further. Even so, he looked nervous when the sergeant was finally ready to declare the result – and relieved when the verdict came.

'Miles off.'

'I told you,' Rees said sulkily.

'You did, and you've also told me a whole lot more besides. Who can vouch for your being in the Horseshoes?'

'Everybody who was in there. Frank behind the bar, for starters. Ebby dropped in. There was Dan and his wife from the post office.'

'And did you go to the Gents at all?'

'Yes.'

'Anyone corroborate that's where you went?'

'As it happens, they can. Owen Unwin.'

'Owen Unwin. Who's he when he's at home? Though of course he wasn't this evening.'

'Neighbour off the close. We'd been talking about going out for a drink. I just said I was going to be in the pub and he said he might pop in. Anyway, we both needed to go at the same time. He was with me all the way.'

'How convenient. And what time would that have been, do you suppose?'

'Nine-forty-five.'

'Nine-forty-five. If only everyone could answer our questions so accurately, eh, Riley?'

Rees looked from one to the other as though he was missing something. 'I still don't know what you've got me in here for.'

'But that didn't stop you rattling off the most rock-solid, unshakeable alibi in recorded history, even and including the time you went to relieve yourself and the name of the guy you manipulated into standing in the next stall to you in the pub toilet.'

Before Rees could respond, Dalliance flashed another question at him. 'Where was Hazel during this epic non-binge of yours?'

'Her mother's.'

'Oh. When did she decide to go and stay at Mum's?'

'Today.'

'After she'd seen the paper – or after you'd seen the paper?'

'It's disgusting. They shouldn't be allowed to—'

'Take snaps of people unawares. No, it is annoying, as DS Riley and I would be the first to agree. But that doesn't mean you can take the law into your own hands.'

'But I couldn't have done it – I was in the Horseshoes all night. Are you stupid?'

'No, I'm not. But I'm afraid you are. What couldn't you have done, Rees?'

'Well, what you said.'

'I didn't say anything.'

'Well,' Rees began to bluster. 'You were talking about me taking the law into my own hands, so I assumed—'

'You assumed what, Rees? You see, you're trying to act like a man who's totally in the dark, and in all probability you are in the dark – as to the precise details. But you know something happened tonight. You were tipped off. Other-wise, why spend the evening in the pub building your cast-iron alibi? Right so far?'

Rees glared at him, but said nothing.

'It's very easy to press your buttons, isn't it, Rees? I mean, if I were to tell you that a couple of press photographers had fol-lowed Hazel to her mother's house and were staking it out—'

Rees knocked his chair over backwards and stood with his fists knotted. Then he looked at Dalliance and saw the truth.

'You – you're just winding me up.'

He sat down, his look even filthier than before.

'You see?' Dalliance smiled at him. 'You're all for saddling up and riding out with a posse of vigilantes to administer a bit of rough justice. But with what justification?'

Rees bit his lower lip, furious with himself for rising to the Chief Inspector's bait. Riley looked on, doing his best to conceal his enjoyment of Dalliance's performance.

'I repeat,' Dalliance said. 'With what justification, Rees? What does rough justice look like? I'll show you what it looks like.' He opened the case file and selected a couple photos, which he passed across the table.

Rees blanched. 'I never did that.'

'We know you didn't, Rees. You couldn't have done it because you were sitting staring moodily into the depths of your orange and lemonade all evening. But someone did. I'm just interested in whether you think they did a good job – exacted appropriate retribution?'

Rees pushed the pictures away, averting his eyes from the bruises and cuts. 'I never asked...'

'Anyone to do that? No perhaps you didn't. But then you didn't need to, did you? It was done for you. The question we're interested in, Rees, is who did it?'

'I don't know. I never knew they would go so far.'

'So you did know someone was going to do something.'

'No – I never said that.'

'I think the record will show you did.'

Rees looked daggers at the tape recorder.

'All the evidence points to the fact that you knew something was going to happen – something criminal and violent. Which is why you were in the pub all evening. What we need to know is how did you know – which means, who told you?'

Rees shifted uneasily in his chair. 'I'm not saying anything,' he said sullenly.

'I wasn't expecting you, to be honest,' Dalliance said. 'Perhaps your mobile phone will be more forthcoming. Could you pass it over to Sergeant Riley please?'

With great reluctance Rees pulled out his phone and slid it across the table.

'Rees Jones has surrendered his mobile phone to Detective Sergeant Riley,' Dalliance declared for the benefit of the tape recorder.

'You have no idea what sort of a hornet's nest you've stirred up. And not just for you – for Hazel, her mother, for the village, for everybody. Not least your brother.'

'Who says Jez had anything to do with it?'

'I'm sure Jez will have just as good an alibi as you. But unlike you, he really did spend the evening on a binge. He's already taken a swing at one of our lads and he's currently cooling off in a cell downstairs. Do you really think it's going to take me all night to get him to compromise himself?'

'You won't get anything out of Jez.'

Rees was trying to sound defiant but Riley could tell he was deflated. Dalliance had outmanoeuvred him at every turn. Played two, lost two.

'Interview ended at – good grief, is that the time?' Dalliance looked up at the clock on the wall. '0245. You best be getting home.'

'Is that it? Rees asked.

'For you, yes; for us, no.'

Rees got up and glared at the two detectives, but Dalliance was flicking through the case file. Without looking up, the detective said, 'Get him a lift home, Riley. And ask the sergeant to wake his brother. Let's hope he's sobered up a bit.'

It was only then that he raised his eyes to Rees. 'A word of advice, Rees. Becoming middle-class means behaving middle-class. If you come out of this with your job and your mortgage and your marriage plans intact, you'll be doing well, lad.'

'You can't prove anything,' Rees said, without conviction.

'Give us time, lad; give us time. There's also the little matter of the murder, for which, may I remind you, you are still a suspect.'

'That went well,' Riley said as they waited for Jez to be brought up from the cells.

Dalliance nodded in acknowledgement. 'What's the betting Jez has as watertight an alibi as his brother?'

Given that Jez too claimed to have been in a pub all evening, it seemed convincing enough. He stank of cider – and cigarette smoke – and although he'd calmed down, his speech was still slightly slurred.

'And which pub were you in, Jez?'

'The Poachers.'

Dalliance laughed. 'Do you know the Poachers, Riley? Never was a pub more aptly named. Up there in the woods, miles from anywhere, surrounded by some of the richest estates in the area. It's a miracle it keeps its licence, it really is.'

'They can't prove nothing, that's why,' came Jez's surly counter.

'Maybe we don't try hard enough, Jez. Maybe we've got better things to investigate. Like assault and battery.'

'What? Who's assaulted who?'

'Well, I'll give you some credit. That's a better shot at surprise than your brother managed.'

'What's 'e on about?' Jez turned to Riley.

'When did you go to the Poachers?'

'I dunno. Half-seven? Eight?'

'Till?'

'You got me there. After twelve. Must have been.'

'And the landlord's got an extension, has he, Jez?'

Jez looked balefully at Dalliance.

'You see, it really wouldn't be hard, would it? But we're not interested in minor infringements of the licensing laws, at least not tonight. We are interested in people taking the law into their own hands. And talking of hands, let's see yours.'

'What do you mean?'

'Put your hands on the table.'

Jez shook his head, but did as he was told. Dalliance and Riley leaned forward. The knuckles of Jez's right hand were grazed, and there was a hint of bruising.

'How did you do that?'

'Trying to get a new blade into that bastard mower of Harry Moore's. Don't know why he don't just sling it. Every year he brings it in and every year I tells him it's knackered, and every year he makes me repair it.'

'And today was the day he brought it in, was it?'

'What's so strange about that? It's what I do. It's my work. And when I've done my work, I likes to relax with a nice, quiet pint. You can ask Sam if you don't believe me.'

'Sam?'

'Hardy. 'E'll vouch for me.'

'I'm sure he will. And who else? Who were you drinking with?'

'Roller.'

'Steve Royce?'

Jez nodded.

'Anyone else?'

'Look, how many do you need? I don't 'ave all their names up there, but Sam'll help you out. You drive up there and ask him.'

'And how did you travel tonight, Jez?'

'Bike out to the pub, lift home from a mate – and then police car into town. And now, if you don't mind, I'd like to get some kip. So either take me back to the cells or let me go home.'

'There's the little matter of your taking a swing at one of our constables, Jez.'

'I never hit him.'

'Resisting arrest—'

'Resisting arrest!' Jez laughed. 'I can do a lot better than that if I put me mind to it, I can tell you. And arrest for what?'

'It's a good point, sir. What can we arrest him for?'

'Not a lot, at the moment; that's why I let him go home.'

The two men sat in the interview room with polystyrene cups of coffee before them on the table. The clock showed 03.40.

'Him and Royce. Quite a team. Hooding, kidnapping, beating – Royce may have had experience of that sort of thing in Iraq.'

'Jez had been drinking, sir. He positively reeked of cider.'

'Doesn't take long to ship a couple of pints or eight. These guys are pros, Riley; they'd drink you and me under the table without thinking about it.'

'So you think they were at the Poachers?'

'Bound to have been. It's just a question of whether they slipped out for a bit.'

'How long would they have needed?'

'Don't know. We'll need to do the timings tomorrow – get a map and work out routes. But the beating we know was handled very efficiently. And presumably pretty rapidly – just jumped him, hooded him and belted him. Then dumped him in the lay-by. Probably only twenty, twenty-five minutes to get back to the Poachers. Throw in slightly less time for the outward journey to Gallows Barn – they could probably have done the whole thing in an hour. And in a pub like the Poachers, it would be perfectly acceptable to ask the others to overlook your absence if anyone came asking.'

Riley nodded, and then yawned.

'You're right. Time to call it a day – or a night,' Dalliance said, thinking moodily of the chore of going back to bed and the steep odds against his getting back to sleep.

Well, at least the Burton diaries made a lively read.

TEN

Five hours later they were back in, poring over a map. Dalliance traced the route with his pen. 'We can time it when we go and get Peterson's car, but I reckon I wasn't far off last night. Ninety minutes at the outside.'

'Less. The meet was at nine, sir. Give it a quarter of an hour in case he was early.'

'Was he?'

'Five minutes. But they were ready for him. He just went into the barn and bang! Bag over the head and then they laid into him.'

Riley referred to his notes.

'And then an indeterminate period in the van,' he went on, 'and another when he was lying in the ditch summoning the strength to get to this feet. He reckons that might have been twenty minutes to half an hour. As the 999 call from the driver who found him was logged at 10.43, that takes us back to ten past ten, say, for the drop—'

'And then drive straight back to the Poachers,' Dalliance concluded. 'Okay, so we'll retrace their steps, look in on Gallows Barn and see if SOCO have found anything. Then you can bring Peterson's car back, and go and see if he's capable of giving us anything new — how big was the van — what did it smell of — if it smelled at all. If there was straw and a smell of animals... I wonder what Cowper drives around in.'

Dalliance thought for a moment.

'And then you'll need to talk to whoever took the message at the hotel reception. Anything they can give us about who dropped the message off. Meanwhile I'll drive over to the Poachers.'

Gallows Barn was aptly named. It was an isolated place down an unwelcoming lane adjacent to a pig farm.

'Perfect place for summary justice,' Dalliance noted. 'Anyone who heard anything would just think it was the pigs.'

The SOCO van was parked close to Peterson's VW. Riley pulled alongside and they got out. Anderson emerged from the barn to meet them.

'Keeping us busy this week, Inspector.'

Us? Riley thought, wondering if that meant Sally. There'd be more twitting about how the case was going if so, but all the same, he hoped she'd be there.

'Got anything for me? Tyre marks would be good,' Dalliance said, looking around him.

Anderson shook his head and indicated the crude concrete track that ran alongside the building. 'That goes round the corner. Hard standing all the way, so you won't get any treads, I'm afraid. Spot of oil, but...' He sighed.

'Anything inside?'

'Again, not much.'

Anderson led the way past the barn door sagging off broken hinges. It was dark and it took them a moment to see the figure kneeling on the floor. Sally Walker got to her feet to say good morning.

'That's where they were waiting.' She indicated a pile of hay bales which had been lugged across the floor to form a hide near the entrance. 'In he comes...'

Riley was taken off guard, and suddenly found himself yet again the central figure in a re-enactment, only this time it was Anderson moving him around the chessboard of a crime scene.

'And out I step with my sack,' said Sally, making a sack-shape in the air around Riley's head.

'Then bind his wrists.' Anderson tugged Riley's hands together behind his back while Sally smiled.

As long as they don't start beating me to a bloody pulp, Riley thought, uncertain whether he should smile back.

'It's all right; I think we've got the picture,' Dalliance intervened.

'I was just beginning to enjoy myself,' Sally said as Anderson released Riley's wrists.

'Well, our vigilantes certainly enjoyed themselves,' Dalliance said sternly. 'Gave him a terrible beating. Vicious. I don't like behaviour like that.' He suddenly punched his fist into his palm to produce a shockingly loud report. 'And then at the end one of them gets the van, then they heave him in the back, and away they go.'

'That's about it,' Anderson nodded. 'They'd thought it all through.'

'So, nothing in here so far?' Dalliance asked.

Anderson shook his head. 'It's been dry, so no boot prints – they scuffed the dust on the barn floor pretty thoroughly. We're going over it with the proverbial fine-toothed comb' – here he nodded towards Sally, who was back on the floor sifting the dust – 'but we're not expecting much to be honest with you.'

Dalliance stroked his chin. 'He was definitely tied with baler twine?'

'Yeah. We've got that bagged up back at the lab. There's a lot of it around.'

Dalliance nodded. 'Well, keep looking. If you happen to find a mobile phone that flew out of a pocket while they were getting stuck in, and then got kicked under a bale… Chewing gum? Cigarette ends?'

'We'll do our best.'

They walked out into the sunshine.

'You'll have done the VW presumably?'

'Oh yes. Covered in prints, of course, but they won't have touched it with a barge-pole. Still, we'll do what we can. Full report by close of play tomorrow.

'Okay, Riley, there you go. Take it back into town, and I'll head on to the Poachers.'

'The Poachers? Rather you than me,' Anderson said, before raising his hand and returning to the gloom of the barn.

It was a drive of a few miles to the Poachers and the country-side seemed to shine in the bright morning sun.

The atmosphere changed when Dalliance took the minor road into the woods. Well-spaced beech trees, with their delicate leaves lit by shafts of sunlight, soon gave way to darker, more densely packed vegetation. Dalliance looked to either side of the car. Rank upon rank of trees, impenetrable, implacable, choking any sign, any memory of the modern world. A sudden shadow flitted on the edge of his peripheral vision – a deer? Probably. But two or three centuries back it could have been a boar. And beyond that, even a wolf.

His front wheel crashed into a pot-hole.

Concentrate, he told himself, cursing the state of the road, wrecked by Land Rovers and the lorries that occasionally removed a consignment of logs.

He drove on, jolting uncomfortably. There was still no sign of the pub. Had he taken the right turn?

But just as he was considering stopping and getting the map out, he saw it through the trees. Surely the most isolated pub in the entire county. It stood in a clearing, which allowed the sun to brighten its aspect. It was a modest building, and with its white walls and low thatched roof it didn't look quite the den of iniquity that Dalliance had painted it in the small hours, and although it undoubtedly merited its reputation, it kept its beer well. He pondered the possibility of half a pint drawn from the wood.

Sam Hardy was new since he'd last been there. A sharp-faced man with a sallow complexion and formidable eyebrows, his greeting extended to no more than a curt nod and a 'What can I get you?' He did not get any friendlier when Dalliance produced his ID.

'Just wanted to ask you about a couple of characters who said they were in here last night.'

'Chances are, if they said they were in here last night, then they were. No law against, is there?'

'Don't you want to know who I want to know about?'

'Not 'specially.'

'Well, I'm going to tell you anyway.'

'Can't stop you,' the man said, taking up a bar cloth and polishing a glass with it.

'Jez Jones and Steve Royce. Said they were in here all evening.'

'Who's saying they weren't?'

'Are you?'

'Wasn't aware I was saying anything.'

Dalliance sighed, and trotted out the old line. 'We can do it here or we can do it back at the station. Now, were they here last night or not?'

'Yes, if that's what you want to hear.'

'What if it isn't?'

Hardy picked up another glass.

'Mr Hardy, do you know either of those men? And give me a straight answer, or I'm ringing for uniforms and you'll be in for a long, boring afternoon. The choice is yours.'

'Yes, I know them.'

'And?'

'They come in from time to time.'

'If I'd wanted to draw teeth I'd have become a dentist, not a detective.'

'What's an interrogation if it's not drawing teeth?'

Touché, Dalliance acknowledged, impressed despite himself at the landlord's cool insolence.

Hardy put the glass down, and picked up another. 'Yes, they were in last night.'

'Thank you,' Dalliance said. 'And what time did they get here?'

Hardy held up the glass and scraped something off the rim with his thumb nail. 'Blessed if I know. Seven-thirty? Eight?'

'And when did they leave?'

'Closing time.'

'Which is?'

'Eleven.'

'Officially.'

'And who's to say it was any later?'

Dalliance raised his hand. 'Okay, let's go with eleven. They were both here at eleven?'

'I just said, haven't I?'

'And did they, at any time, leave the bar during those three or three and a half hours?'

'Yeah.'

'Yes? When?'

'I dunno. I got a job to do – and it's pulling pints, not keeping a bloody timesheet.'

'Okay. But roughly – I mean; if you know they left the bar, you must have some idea of when they went.'

Hardy was working on a new glass. 'Maybe after an hour?'

'So that would be – about eight-thirty?'

'If you like.'

'It's not a question of if I like; it's important.'

'Maybe to you – though I can't think why – but it ain't to me.'

'I need to know in order to pursue my enquiries into a crime.'

'Oh I see, and there I was thinking you were showing an interest in their bladders.'

Dalliance stared at the man.

'Gents is outside round the back.' He put the glass he'd been polishing down and smiled – a thin-lipped, mean-looking smile. 'The amount of cider they were shifting, they went pretty regular; but I don't reckon they'd have had enough time to get up to any mischief.'

Dalliance took it in his stride. 'Is there anyone else who could corroborate what you've told me?' He looked hopefully around the bar. A couple of old-timers were playing dominoes in the corner.

'Jack? Copper here wants to know if Jez and Roller were in here last night.'

'What?'

'THIS COPPER WANTS TO KNOW—'

'All right,' Dalliance said. 'I'll go over.'

The old-timers had gone back to their game by the time he had picked his way through the tables and stools. Jack tapped a domino fiercely on the table to indicate he couldn't go. Dalliance watched in silence as Jack's opponent laid a double three down at the end of a column.

Jack had to rap again. Three moves later, he pushed down his remaining dominoes in disgust.

'What do you want?' he said grumpily to Dalliance.

'Were you in here last night?'

'What sort of a question's that?' his opponent exclaimed in a high-pitched voice. 'Jack's in here every night. I'm not. Can't get home in the dark these days.'

'I'm sorry to hear it. I just wanted to ask you—' he continued, turning back to Jack.

'He's a bit deaf. You'll have to speak up.'

'Thank you,' Dalliance said with a chilly smile.

'What do you want to know?'

'I'm trying to establish whether two people were in here last night.'

'Jack won't help you. He never pays much attention. And his sight's not good. But there's a man who might.'

A large man with a voluminous waxed coat on had just entered the bar. Dalliance caught a glimpse of what looked like the tail feather of a pheasant, but at a glance from Hardy, the man pulled his coat to.

'Jessie Miller, 'is name is. He's in most nights.'

Dalliance got up with a nod of thanks.

'Mr Miller?'

'Whose asking?' the man asked with a raised eyebrow.

He was very large indeed, Dalliance couldn't help noticing as he came up to him. The hand that held his coat closed was richly tattooed with a knot of writhing snakes. Dalliance produced his ID again.

'What can I do for you, Chief Inspector?' Miller rested on a bar stool and looked Dalliance straight in the eye.

'I wonder if you can corroborate what Mr Hardy told me about two men from Lower Bolton, Jez Jones and Steve Royce, drinking here last night.'

'I can corroborate that until the cows come home,' Miller said with a smile.

'And how come you're so sure?'

'I reckon I bought most of what they drank. Which was a lot.'

'Why?'

'Must be my generous nature. No law against standing a man a drink or two is there?'

'No, but there's a law against the man you've bought the drinks for driving home.'

'Which is precisely why I drove them home myself. And before you ask, no, I didn't have a skinful. Which is why I managed to beat them at darts.' He pointed to the dartboard. 'Played till closing time, didn't we, Sam? In fact, you can see the last game up on the blackboard right there.'

Dalliance looked. It had obviously been a short game, the numbers rattling down from 501 in a very short sequence of very high scores.

'Not bad considering the amount they'd had. Mind you, Roller's as deadly with a dart as he is with a gun. And Jez ain't bad either.'

'And you say they were drinking all evening?'

'Drinking for England, they was. Pint after pint after pint.'

'How did they get over here, Mr Hardy?'

'Jez's bike. Which I slung in the back of the pick-up when I took them back to Lower Bolton. Will that be all?'

'And you'd had nothing to drink?'

'Nothing to speak of. Just some good old Jamaican ginger beer.' He indicated the glass that had appeared on the bar. 'I never touch a drop when I'm coming up to a match.'

'And what match would that be?' Dalliance asked, gazing at the waxed coat, as though if he stared hard enough he'd be able to see what it concealed.

'Clay pigeon cup,' came the brusque reply, and then, without touching his drink, Jessie Miller gave a nod to the landlord and stamped out of the bar.

'That was a short visit,' Dalliance said.

'Maybe sharing the bar with a copper put him off his drink,' Hardy said.

'He didn't pay for it,' Dalliance pointed out.

'Didn't need to. He's got a tab. But seeing as you're so concerned about my cash-flow, can I get you something?'

Dalliance hesitated, then shook his head. A silence fell, broken only by the slap of dominoes from the corner – and, Dalliance thought, sounds from a room behind the bar consistent with someone depositing a package on a table before making their exit through a back door.

'Was that a pheasant I saw under Mr Miller's coat? Bit early for pheasants, isn't it?'

'If it was, it would have been roadkill. They're wandering around the lanes like drunks at this time of year. Waste not want not.'

Dalliance nodded. Touché again.

'One last thing,' he said. 'What's this clay pigeon cup he was talking about?'

'Just a local event. All welcome – if you've got a shotgun.'

Dalliance ignored the implicit challenge. 'And he's a contender?'

'He's won it the last five years,' came the reply. 'If you was to balance one of these peanuts' – Hardy shook a bowl on the bar – 'on the tip of your tongue, Jessie would shoot it off from a hundred yards. Best shot you'll ever see. Even better than Stevie Royce, and that's saying something.'

Dalliance left the pub with much to think about. A marksman of the highest quality... Drinking companion of two of the Lower Bolton cricket team... Someone who could hit a tiny target at distance – and Ted Roper wasn't that tiny a target...

'So how did you get on?' Dalliance looked across his desk at Riley.

'Nothing sensational. Peterson's still finding it difficult to talk, but he'ss certainly keen to give us every help he can. Your tip about smell was probably the most useful line in.'

'Well?'

'Nothing in the van – certainly no farm smells. In fact he said it almost smelt clean.'

'Smelt clean?'

'I don't know what he meant exactly either, and obviously he couldn't elaborate. But I suppose a negative can be helpful.'

'Absolutely.'

'Well, here's another. Neither – I say "neither", but he thinks it could have been three – anyway, none of them had been drinking.'

'Was he sure?'

'I really pushed him, sir. But he was adamant.'

'And he couldn't have just missed it because he was in shock?'

Riley shook his head. 'He may be a snoopy little so-and-so but he has got an investigator's instincts. It was obvious he was trying as hard as possible to glean anything – the slightest wisp of evidence. And there's no way, given how close they got to him, that he could have failed to pick up alcohol.'

Dalliance grunted. 'Smoke?'

'Possibly – certainly a whiff of mint.'

'Anything from SOCO?'

Riley shook his head. 'Not yet, sir.'

'What about the message setting up the meeting?'

'Very hurried. Only gave the message once.'

'Male? Female?'

'Female, they thought, but it was a busy time and the girl on reception just scribbled it down and put it in Peterson's cubbyhole without taking a lot of notice.'

They looked at each other glumly.

'You don't suppose Jez and Steve could have held off on the cider till they got back, sir?'

'For an hour? No. And even nursing a token pint would have left a trace on their breath. I think we may have got the wrong vigilantes, Riley.'

'Still, you did discover a shooter who could knock a peanut off your tongue from a hundred yards.'

'And pinging a fat middle-aged man with a dart at half that distance is hardly going to be challenging for a marksman of that calibre. So...' he sighed, swinging round to look at the incident board. He picked up his pointer and jabbed the copse of trees at the bottom of the ground. 'Jessie Miller in there, breaking off that branch – big man – easily done. Waits for his moment. Ted takes his catch. Runs up to meet Jez, who must be in on the plot, as is Steve Royce. Takes his shot, avoiding both Ben and Barney as they close on him. Jez gets him and holds onto him, giving Royce time to come in and yank out the dart before anyone else sees it, and down he goes.'

Dalliance paused.

'Question: How did Steve Royce dispose of the dart? No – how was the dart disposed of? What if Rees is in on it and that's why he hares off to the pavilion. Open mind on who retrieves the dart. Moving on, who saw or heard what? Of course any of them could have seen movement in the tree, but the four most likely observers are Tucker, Phelps, Henderson and Standing.'

He tapped each of the names on the fielding chart.

'And Daniel, sir.'

'Quite right, Riley. Daniel walks down towards the copse at the start of every second over. He then hangs around daydreaming on the fine leg boundary until someone glances the ball and he has to run to retrieve it and throw it in.'

'Could he have heard the branch snap?'

'Riley, we will make a first-class detective out of you yet!'

Dropping his head over his notes to hide his pleasure, Riley said, 'He didn't mention anything though.'

'Of course he didn't, because all the attention, the entire focus of the investigation, was on the business end – Ted Roper collapsing on the pitch. It never occurred to us to put the question into his head. Stand anywhere you like in the countryside, there's a cacophony of noises – birds, cattle, sheep, walkers, dogs, bumblebees. What's a snapped branch amongst that lot?'

'So, we are going to need to interview him properly.'

Dalliance nodded vigorously. 'Have to arrange it with the school. Don't want to embarrass him by barging in on a maths test or something. We could take his kit back if the lab's finished with it. Ring his mum. We can look in on her this evening and find out who we need to speak to at the school. In the meantime, we'd better go round the locals again, asking them about anything they might have seen amongst the trees at the village end.'

ELEVEN

'Who first, sir?'
         'Henderson. If we've got to run the gauntlet, let's get it over with.'

But they were in luck.

'She's in town. Lunch with a friend.'

Dalliance couldn't restrain a glance at his watch.

'It'll be a late one – I don't expect her back till after tea.'

Henderson, Riley couldn't help noticing, seemed much more relaxed in his wife's absence. Rather than seeing them in his office, he had invited them to what he called the Morning Room and bustled about fetching them refreshments.

'Did you get that letter from my solicitor, Inspector?'

'I did, thank you. A long way round the houses to say keep off my land.'

Henderson laughed. 'I'd tried that – and it didn't work. It's like asking people for the money they owe you. Nothing like a solicitor's letter to concentrate the mind. Anyway, as I said on Monday, wholly superfluous now.'

Dalliance raised an eyebrow.

'Margot doesn't want a carp lake in her back garden. It was always Ted's pet project. No Ted, no lake. And yes,

Inspector, that's very convenient for me; but no, not, I think you'd admit, motive enough for me to murder him. But I don't want to pre-empt you. What do you want?'

Henderson threw one leg over the other and took a sip of tea. He was trying his best, Dalliance thought, but there really was no concealing his satisfaction at the way events had unfolded.

'We'd like to take you back to Sunday afternoon, sir,' Riley said, his notebook open on his knee.

'I thought we'd been through all this. Ted caught the catch, he ran up the wicket as though he'd scored the winning goal at Wembley, and the whole team, including myself, mobbed him. I don't know that I can add any more to that.'

'What about before the catch?'

Henderson looked from Riley to Dalliance. 'What about it? It was the most normal afternoon imaginable. We all turned up, Ted lost the toss, we all moaned like hell, and went out to stand in the sun for two and a half hours.'

'And when the bowling was from the top end, you were at mid-off?'

'At both ends, actually. There's a default setting. Everybody has their appointed position – me at mid-off, Phelps at mid-on – which is unfair on me because he never runs for anything. Some people start in one position, then move. We quite often start with two slips and then Norman comes out into the covers. Ted stays – stayed – first slip throughout, even when the bowling was being belted to all parts.'

Dalliance nodded. They knew all this already, but sometimes it did no harm to allow people to warm up.

'So, from the top end, you have a view down the ground to the sightscreen at the bottom?'

'Yes,' Henderson said, his eyes narrowing slightly as though he suspected a trap.

'And there's a footpath round the perimeter of the ground?'

'There is – and a couple of bridleways criss-crossing the fields. I believe Jenny rode over there and found you in the pavilion.'

'She did indeed,' Dalliance confirmed tersely.

'I'm sure she didn't mean—'

Dalliance cut him off with a gesture, then leant forward. 'I'm going to be very frank with you, Mr Henderson, and I would ask for some discretion – especially perhaps with regard to your wife.'

Henderson put his cup down. 'I'm all ears, Inspector.'

'From the start we've assumed that whoever did this was on the field of play – was one of the team. We couldn't see what else it could be other than that.'

Henderson's eyebrows shot up, and he looked as though he were about to speak, but thought better of it.

'Somebody in the team was undoubtedly involved; it couldn't have been done without someone there on the pitch. But we are now considering the possibility of someone else, someone not playing in the match, but working in partnership with someone who was.'

'The grassy knoll,' Henderson murmured. 'Yes, I can see it. From one of the trees in the copse behind the sightscreen. God knows, Ted would have given him an easy enough target. And then his co-plotter pulls the dart or whatever it was out of Ted's back so none of the rest of us see it.' He stopped and looked from one to the other. 'Pure genius. You have been using the little grey cells, haven't you, Inspector?'

'It's only a hypothesis, but you can see the implications.'

'Of course. Instead of just concentrating on those two minutes or whatever it was, it opens the time frame up exponentially.' He whistled silently. 'What put you onto this line of enquiry, Inspector?'

'Sorry, we can't go into that. All we want from you is any detail from earlier in the innings – anyone you noticed walking along the footpath, any movement in the trees –

that didn't seem relevant when we first questioned you, but which now might be.'

'God, it's clever, isn't it?' Henderson said. 'The sightscreen covers the view of the trunks of the trees in the copse, so a good climber could be up into the branches like a squirrel, then work his way along a branch, hidden by the leaves.'

'Exactly.'

'Mind you, he could have been up there a long while waiting for Ted to take a slip catch.'

'Maybe there was a plan B. He'd wait for a while in the hope he would take one, but if he didn't, he'd shoot him anyway, and his partner in crime would just have to make sure he got there first.'

'That would have been Barney—' He broke off and frowned at the implication.

'Let's not jump to conclusions, Mr Henderson. Just try to remember anything that might help us.'

'Obviously I didn't see anything tremendously suspicious or I'd have mentioned it already. But leave it with me and I'll go through the whole match as best I can, and get back to you if I think of anything.'

'However small and seemingly insignificant,' Dalliance said.

'He's right, sir. Barney would be in the frame if we're look-ing for someone taking something out of Roper instead of sticking something in him.'

'Quite difficult giving someone the lifeguard treatment with a lethal dart in your hand, Riley. As I would be very happy to demonstrate.'

'I'll take your word for it, sir,' Riley said hurriedly. He was getting tired of being given the star role in re-enact-ments. The Chief Inspector was the one with the theatrical background after all.

*   *   *

Ernie Phelps seemed anything but pleased to see them. He hovered on the doorstep of his bungalow without inviting them in. When it became obvious that he was going to have to, he reluctantly opened the door and led them down the short hall to the living room with two or three backwards glances.

He was so obviously agitated that Dalliance felt compelled to say, 'Mr Phelps, please relax. We've just got a few more questions to ask you – a slightly new line of enquiry has opened up since Monday, and we're speaking to everyone to get them to think of Sunday afternoon from a different perspective.'

'Oh, I see.' Phelps did seem to relax, and directed them to the two man-eating armchairs, offering them tea and biscuits, which Dalliance declined.

'Thank you, but we really won't keep you very long.'

Phelps continued to hover, not knowing quite what to do with his hands. 'I thought I'd given you all the answers you wanted on Monday. I'm sure I didn't leave anything out. I didn't mean to, if I did.'

'As I said, we're widening our enquiry somewhat.'

'I see, yes. Of course.'

'Sit down, Mr Phelps.'

Phelps perched on the edge of the dining room chair. Dalliance felt the gravitational pull of the armchair and decided to let physics win. He glanced over at Riley, who, as before, was perched on the lip of his.

'Mr Phelps, we'd like you to think back, not just to the moment when Ted Roper caught the ball, but a bit before.'

'How much before?'

'Just to earlier in the game. We think there may have been other parties involved. So what we'd like to ask you to think about is who you saw walking round the perimeter of the ground—'

'Ooh, no one I thought suspicious. Just dog-walkers and the like. There were some boys. They disappeared into the trees behind the sightscreen.'

'Boys?'

'Just kids, you know – mooching around, bored, up to no good because they haven't got anything to do. They'd have been better out on the field playing cricket. Any one of them could have had my place – at least they'd have been able to run to stop the boundaries. But they don't teach them cricket in schools anymore. I noticed that when I was on the buses—'

'You used to drive school buses?'

'Yes.' Mr Phelps looked slightly startled at the question. 'It doesn't matter – not to you – not relevant. It's just that the boys, they were always the rowdy ones. Too much energy, not enough focus, I always said.'

'So what did they do – these boys on Sunday?'

'Nothing much. I wasn't watching them. Nothing to do with me. I was trying to concentrate on my fielding.'

'And when did you see the boys, Mr Phelps?'

'I don't rightly know.' His tone continued defensive.

Dalliance persisted gently. 'Who was bowling – at the time you saw them go into the trees?'

'Ah, I can tell you that. It was Steve. It was the end of Steve's spell. He was tiring. He dropped one short and the chap hit it, right over Des, and I thought, oh no, I'm going to have to run for that, but I didn't because Jez went after it. I was sort of running over, to show willing, and I said "well chased" or something, and he said "Bugger that. It's the last thing I need, a sprint to the boundary, before I come on to bowl." And I'd seen the kids moving round the boundary and into the trees before that.'

Riley wrote in his notebook. Phelps looked at Dalliance. It was almost as though he were pleading to be let off any further questions.

'But you didn't see the boys come out of the copse?'

'No, I didn't. As I say, I was trying to concentrate on the cricket. But I tell you what; they didn't go on round the boundary. I know I didn't see them again, so they must have taken the path back to the village.'

'Did you know any of them?'

'No I didn't – but then I wouldn't. Had enough of kids on the buses, I can tell you.'

'Okay, well, they shouldn't be hard to track down if we need to speak to them. You've been very helpful.' Dalliance began the arduous process of hauling himself out of the depths of the armchair. 'One other thing. You didn't see any movement – in any of the trees?'

'What? Like they climbed up or something? No, I don't think so. But I'm not saying they didn't. I wouldn't put it past them.'

Dalliance suddenly burst free like a whale breaching the ocean's surface.

Back in safety of the car he allowed himself a curse on the manufacturers of such unspeakable items of furniture, while Riley hid his smile by turning his head to look back at the sad little home. He noticed a twitch of the lace curtains and caught a glimpse of Phelps' rabbit-like face watching their departure.

'I suppose we could get SOCO to search that bridlepath,' Riley suggested as they drove off.

Dalliance tugged irritably at his seatbelt. 'Just in case Miller, or whoever it might have been, discarded the wrapping for his dart in the long grass? We can't cordon off the whole bloody village; and anyway, it's far too late now. Goodness knows how many dog-walkers have tramped along it since Sunday, not to mention people trotting along on their bloody horses.'

'Still, Phelps has narrowed the window.'

'You think? The most interesting thing about that interview was how nervous he was about seeing us. Far more jumpy than on Monday.' He finally got his seatbelt fixed.

'It would have been a bit uncomfortable for Miller – or whoever – to be stuck up in a branch with those kids below.'

'Uncomfortable, perhaps; but it doesn't mean he wasn't there. Get some uniforms to track the boys down; we'll have a word.'

'Right, sir. Who next? Tucker?'

'I think we'll postpone that pleasure. He'll probably be buzzing around picking people up from work, or meeting the evening trains. Let's call in on Mrs Pottinger. I feel we should have done that earlier. It's not really what you want, is it, having your son caught up in a murder investigation. A bit of reassurance wouldn't go amiss – and we need to organise a trip over to the school.'

It wasn't long before they were drawing up on a neatly kept gravel driveway in front of a porch wreathed in a climbing rose. A quick ring brought Daniel's mother to the door.

'Come in, Inspector. I was wondering when I might expect a call.'

'We've been busy.'

'Of course, of course. I mean, I'm sure Daniel told you all he could, so why would you need to speak to him again? I suppose I was just curious – like everybody else.' She showed them into an expansive conservatory looking out over a pretty walled garden. The French windows were open and a lazy hum came from invisible bees working their way through the hollyhocks.

'Do sit down. I don't know what the time is exactly, but would a little drink be out of order?'

When she had given Riley an orange juice and prevailed upon Dalliance to accept a very weak gin and tonic, she finally asked, 'So, Inspector, how is it going?'

'We're working through our To-Do list, Mrs Pottinger, though even the most routine enquiry tends to be criss-crossed with distractions and red herrings. And this is emphatically not a routine enquiry.'

'No – I mean it can't be often that a killer disguises himself in a crowd like that. Quite ingenious really.'

'Indeed,' Dalliance said with a finality that signalled an end to that conversational gambit. 'So, tell us a bit about Daniel. I gather he lost his father some years ago.'

'Three years ago – almost to the day.'

'I'm sorry. That must have been hard – for both of you.'

'It was. It is. I still miss him. And I know Daniel does too.'

'He must have been relatively young – your husband. What did he die of?'

'None of the things you might expect. He was perfectly healthy. And, I would have said, perfectly happy. But I was obviously wrong. He killed himself.'

Damn, Dalliance thought. How difficult would it have been to check that before forcing it out of her so tactlessly?

'I'm so sorry. We really haven't come here to rake over the past. Daniel did say he'd lost his father, but not – the circumstances.'

'Fortunately there was enough ambiguity about the circumstances for it to be passed off as an accident. But I knew the truth. I say this in total confidence, Inspector. I can't see there's any need for Daniel to know at this stage. Though of course I will tell him when he's older. It happened while Ian was abroad – he was a marine biologist – and the body was never recovered. We just had a memorial service in the church. The school were incredibly understanding. Said Daniel could stay away as long as he wanted to. But actually he went back pretty soon. He loves it there. I did think about taking him away, but that would have been selfish. I'm sure Ian would have wanted him to stay – it was his old school, and he felt it was right for him. I'm not disparaging the local schools – I think they do a fine job, and Daniel does have some local friends who are all doing well. But somehow boarding suits him. He has some really strong friendships – well, one main one – and he'd miss that and all the camaraderie. Compensation for being an only, I suppose. But I'm sorry, Inspector, I didn't mean to unleash all that on you. Sometimes I don't seem to speak to anybody all day, so when I do, it can all come out in a bit of a splurge.'

'Not at all,' Dalliance said soothingly.

Riley hadn't really been paying attention. The agonies of choice between private and public education were not a matter of much concern. As he watched Mrs Pottinger replenishing her glass – and Dalliance waving away the offer of a refill – it crossed his mind that boarding school might be the better option than staying at home with a grieving mother who had a taste for the gin.

'But what did you want, Inspector?' Mrs Pottinger asked, with what could best be described as a brave face.

'Our enquiries have opened out a little and we've got new questions to ask people.'

'And that includes Daniel? I can't see a problem with that. Do you want me to contact the school?'

'If you wouldn't mind – just to let them know we have your permission. Do stress it's just routine. We'll make an appointment to see him at a convenient moment. And of course he could have a member of staff in with him if you'd like.'

'Oh, there's no need for that. Daniel would hate that and probably just clam up. Just promise me you won't practise your good-cop-bad-cop routine on him!' She smiled with what seemed like genuine amusement.

'Thank you: we would prefer to see him alone. And no "third degree", I promise.'

'I'll ring his housemaster the moment you leave, Inspector.'

'Thank you. Well, we've got some other calls to make, so perhaps we'll be on our way.'

They walked into the hall. There was a school photograph on the wall above a handsome antique table.

'That's Browning House,' Mrs Pottinger said, 'and there's Daniel, and that's his best friend Anthony next to him.'

Dalliance and Riley craned forward politely to peer at the half-dozen rows of neatly blazered boys.

'They're virtually inseparable,' she said over her shoulder as she pulled open the drawer of the table. 'Anthony spends quite a lot of time here because his father's abroad. I love having them; they seem to fill the house with life. Here we are — school number, house number. The housemaster's called Barclay. Very understanding man. I'll ring him now and tell him you'll be in touch.'

'Thank you very much, Mrs Pottinger.'

'Poor woman,' Dalliance murmured once they were back in the car, again regretting he hadn't checked her husband's death.

'I wonder how she knew it was suicide if they never found the body?'

'Let's not intrude on a private grief, Riley. Let bygones be bygones. And let's hope she doesn't rely too heavily on the Gordon's to ease the grieving process.'

A silence fell, though Riley was forced to enquire where they were going next when they came to the crossroads.

'Tucker,' Dalliance said without enthusiasm. 'I'll give him a ring.'

Des Tucker was waiting for them in the market square, but the conversation yielded little.

'Yeah, I saw the kids. They had a bit of banter with Danny and then disappeared behind the sightscreen. I didn't see them after that, so I guess they must have wandered back to the village across the fields.'

Having said he recognised them, he gave names to Riley, making various comments about their home lives and their parents.

'You can't blame people if they ain't brought up proper. If they don't get the guidance, that's where they go wrong in my opinion. And talking of which,' he added, feeling for a cigarette, 'I hear there was some rather shameful behaviour last night?'

'What did you hear?' Riley asked him. All Dalliance's attention seemed to be focused on the smoke rising into the still evening air.

'Oh, come on, it was all round the place by lunchtime. Sounds like they did quite a number on him.'

'Do you have any relevant information you'd like to contribute?' Riley asked.

'What, so I can get my head stuck in a sack and whacked about? Do I look stupid?'

He finished his cigarette in silence, then ground the butt underfoot and walked back to his car.

'How did he know they put a sack over Peterson's head?' Dalliance asked as Riley ran them round the corner to the police station.

Twelve

The school was set in rolling parkland and was approached down a long, tree-lined avenue. The moment Dalliance saw its impressive façade ahead of them, he felt a depressing sense of dread.

His experience of a similar institution had not been a happy one. His right thumb was still weak from the maladroit punch he had delivered to the fourth boy making fun of his name, and continued to give him painful twinges when the weather got cold.

The punch had served its purpose, however, and a compromise whereby he accepted the nickname 'Dally' held through the crucial early years, which, his housemaster liked to say, either broke a boy or made him. As Dalliance had ended up head of house, captain of cricket, star of three school plays, and exhibitioner at Lincoln College, Oxford, he had obviously passed the make-or-break test with flying colours. But he could not honestly say his schooldays had been the happiest days of his life.

Things were very different these days, no doubt.

The first difference was apparent the moment they got out of the car, when a gaggle of smartly dressed young women marched past them with books under their arms bound for their next lesson.

'Riley, we're here to do an interview, not gawp at sixth-formers,' Dalliance said curtly. 'I think reception's this way. And bring Daniel's cricket bag.'

With a last glance Riley joined him and they walked up the well-worn stone steps to a solid-looking oak door.

'Detective Chief Inspector; yes, we're expecting you,' a middle-aged woman greeted them brightly, barely glancing at their ID. 'Come this way.'

Her heels clacked on the parquet and Dalliance again felt uncomfortable as they followed her down the oak-panelled corridor hung with portraits of previous headmasters.

'Here we are. We thought the Founder's Room would be best. No one will disturb you in here.' She showed them into a medium-sized room dominated by the portrait of a Victorian divine who looked down his nose at them disapprovingly from his vantage point opposite the door. There were leather armchairs and a low table offering Country Life and Vintage Cars, as well as a pristine copy of The Daily Telegraph. 'Daniel will be along in a moment. Can I get you some coffee?'

Dalliance was beginning to feel he'd like something stronger, but nodded acceptance to the coffee.

'Weren't you at one of these places?' Riley asked after the door had closed. He spoke quietly, looking around him in awe.

'I was Riley, but before you start getting ideas, in my day public schools were modelled on the POW camp not the holiday camp. The only girls we saw worked in the kitchens, and they were totally off-limits.'

'Still, it was a privilege, wasn't it?'

Dalliance laughed. 'Cold showers, corporal punishment, cross-country runs in the pouring rain, chapel twice a day and an extra-long helping on Sunday – oh yes, Riley, it was a privilege all right, and we were never allowed to forget it.'

The door opened again and the receptionist came in with a tray, on which they could see a battered silver coffee service. Behind her came Daniel. Riley cleared a space on the table for the tray while Dalliance got up and ushered the boy to a seat.

'Thank you,' he said. Dalliance noticed they had only been supplied with two cups, so didn't make the mistake of offering the boy coffee. 'Sorry to break into your morning, Daniel,' he said as the three of them settled into their seats.

'S'all right. I'm only missing economics.'

'And how do you find that?'

'Don't like it much.'

'Why not?'

'Well, it's meant to be a science, but no one can agree about anything. You can't test anything. They're just theories. But everybody believes passionately that their theory is the right one. So it's more like religion in a way.'

Dalliance looked at him. With a response like that to a casual question designed simply to break the ice, the boy would certainly impress an Oxford admissions tutor.

'Before we let you get back to the Thirty Years War between the disciples of Keynes and Hayek, we just need to ask you a few mundane questions about last Sunday. We've brought your bag back by the way.'

'Thank you, sir – but I don't know that I can add anything to what I said at the time.'

'Ah, but we've got some new questions.'

'Oh,' said Daniel. 'What are they?'

'Instead of focusing exclusively on the moment of the catch and immediately following, we're extending the time-frame to the whole innings from the start of the match.'

'Really?' Daniel shot an enquiring glance at Dalliance. 'And why would you do that?'

'Let's just say we're working on a theory – though not one we're prepared to burn people at the stake for.'

The boy nodded. Dalliance felt they certainly had his attention.

'So now you're positing the possibility at least of someone getting the lethal dose into Mr Roper from outside the field of play. I did wonder about that.'

'You did?'

'Not for very long; you seemed so sure that it was – well, one of the cricket team.'

'It would still have to involve one of the team, so anything you can remember about the team huddle, whose hand went where, et cetera, would remain of vital importance.'

'But you'd now be looking at someone removing the dart, or whatever it was, instead of pushing it in. Yes, I see.' He shook his head. 'I'm sorry, I don't think I can help you. Obviously if I'd seen anyone with a dart in their hand, I'd have told you, whether they were pulling it out or pushing it in.'

'We didn't think it likely you'd want to change your account of the huddle. But what we are interested in is whether you saw anything before then – while you were fielding.'

''Cause you were quite close to the boundary at the sightscreen end, weren't you?'

Daniel looked at Riley as if surprised he had spoken. He nodded. 'Fine leg all the way through.'

'So you would have walked back out to the boundary every other over from the start of the innings. What we want you to think about is whether you saw anything, anything at all, which might be suspicious.'

'Suspicious in what way, sir? I mean, there were people walking round the edge of the field on the other side of the fence. But if anybody had tried to take a shot at Ted—'

'No, no,' Dalliance cut in. 'Of course we don't think anyone could have fired at him from there.'

'Oh – how stupid of me. The trees! You think someone climbed into the trees behind the sightscreen and – wow,' he said, nodding his head as the idea sank in.

'It's a hypothesis, as I say,' Dalliance repeated. 'But we're now looking to test it against whatever evidence we can muster.'

'So if you can give us anything from that hour and a half that you wouldn't have mentioned on Sunday because we didn't ask you about it, now would be a helpful time to have it.'

'Yes, I see,' the boy looked at them with a glint of excitement in his eye.

'Did you see anybody suspicious?'

Daniel thought for a moment, then shook his head. 'Not really. There were some boys from the village.'

'We've been told about them. Exchanged a bit of banter with you on the boundary?'

'Who said that? I always thought banter was a light-hearted exchange of slightly barbed pleasantries, not a group of yobs calling you names.'

'Ah, it was like that, was it?'

'I ignored them. They have a very low boredom threshold.'

'Nothing back at all?' Riley enquired.

Daniel looked at him and shook his head slightly. 'You get used to small-minded envy. People think these places are just glorified holiday camps, but they'd be clamouring to go home after a week. Couldn't stand the pressure of the workload. It doesn't bother me. While they're flipping burgers and stacking shelves, I'll be at university – now that really is a glorified holiday camp – or so I'm told.'

There was a slight pause. Daniel looked from one detective to the other.

'Sorry if that sounds elitist, but it's the truth.'

'If in slightly cartoonish mode,' Dalliance said. 'Anyway, from a police perspective, we can only applaud your restraint. You didn't see what the feckless burger-flippers did next?'

'When they got bored with trying to wind me up? No. Well, I didn't see them, but I heard them larking about in the trees behind the sightscreen.'

'How long was that for?' Riley asked.

'Dunno. It's like a road drill. It's there, it's annoying, you live with it; and then suddenly you notice it's stopped, but you can't say exactly when.'

'So, after the road drill, did you hear anything else?'

'Like what? The countryside's full of noises – people shouting at their dogs, sheep, bird calls…'

'Closer to hand – near you. If you could hear the lads mucking around in the trees—'

'Well, you'd have been able to hear that from the square.'

'But what about sounds you couldn't have heard from the square – sounds that only you could have heard?'

Daniel raised a finger, and an intense look of concentration came over his face. 'You're going to think I'm making this up…'

'Try us,' Dalliance said, trying to suppress the excitement he was suddenly feeling.

'I did hear something – something from the trees. After I'd noticed the village boys had left, I suppose I was savouring the quiet, so I'd have been a bit more attentive. Anyway, I definitely heard something – a crack – not very loud or alarming. Normally I'm sure I wouldn't even have registered it. But it was like someone trod on a stick—'

'Or snapped a branch.'

'Yes.' Daniel turned to Riley, his eyes widening slightly in recognition of the possibility. 'Yes, someone climbing, thinking a branch would take their weight. Definitely.'

'And when was this – roughly?'

'It might help if you could remember who was bowling.'

'Right. Well, it was after Steve Royce had come off. He'd started spraying it about. Always happens. He's good for half an hour or so, then he gets tired and his length goes. Trouble is, Ted usually leaves – left – him on that extra over or two, which always costs fifteen or twenty unnecessary runs. Then Jez comes on to tidy up the mess.'

'And Jez was bowling when you heard the crack in the copse behind the sightscreen?'

'Yes.'

A loud, klaxon-like bell blared out around the school.

'Well, that's economics sorted for the day,' Dalliance said, getting up.

'Just one last question,' Riley said, his notebook open. 'Can you give us any idea how long before—?'

'Ted was actually shot – if he was?' The boy stood frowning with thought. 'Twenty minutes? Something like that. I mean, until now I haven't given it a thought.'

'You've been extremely helpful, Daniel. Thank you very much. Don't forget your cricket bag.'

'Thank you, sir. And good luck with your enquiry.'

Dalliance and Riley had reached the door when Daniel joined them with his bag.

'I was wondering, sir – what's happening this Sunday? There was meant to be a match.'

'I don't know is the honest answer to that.'

'It doesn't really matter. I'm coming home anyway. It's just a question of whether to bring my kit.'

'We'll find out for you.'

'Don't start, Riley,'

'I wouldn't know where to, sir.'

'Self-confidence can make people seem unsympathetic at that age,' Dalliance said, noting that they were passing the beech trees on the avenue far faster than they had on their arrival.

'Stuck-up little prick,' Riley said between clenched teeth. 'Well, you know which side of the fence I'm on, sir.'

'Flinging abuse from the sidelines, just like you do from the terraces every Saturday during the football season.'

'Well, he put you in your place about holiday camps, didn't he?'

'He did, Riley, he did. I had overlooked the increased workload they're subjected to these days.'

'While of course our burger-flippers just have to scrawl their name on the top of the exam paper to be fast-tracked through to the nearest McDonalds.'

'I'm not saying it's an ideal system, Riley.'

'Well, we can agree on that, sir.'

They had reached the stone pillars that marked the entrance to the drive. Once on the public highway Riley seemed to relax. 'He did give us some useful information though – I grant you that.'

'Potentially useful information, Riley. Let's not get ahead of ourselves. It's an interesting theory. But that's all it is. Even though we've got a possible shooter – in cahoots with two of the prime suspects – there's still a long way to go. Where did he get the dart gun? Where did they get the poison? Did anybody see Miller in the vicinity of the ground on Sunday afternoon? Where would he say he was if we asked him? Details, details, details. Detective work is—'

'Ninety percent drudgery, ten percent inspiration.' Riley finished the sentence for him, adding the unspoken observation that ninety percent of the drudgery got done by him.

Later in the day, after a great deal more drudgery, he knocked on Dalliance's door.

'Sir?'

'What is it, Riley?'

'That shooting competition—'

'What about it?'

'You'll never guess where it's being held.'

'Do I look like a man who wants to play guessing games, Riley?'

'No, sir. Sorry, sir.'

'Don't waste time apologising – tell me!'

'In the Ropers' woods, sir. For the Roper County Cup. And guess who handed over the Cup last year to our sharp-shooter?'

He passed Dalliance a print-out of an article from the local newspaper.

'Margot Roper presents Jessie Miller with the Roper Cup,' Dalliance read, looking intently at the blurry photograph. He let his hand fall heavily on his desk with the photograph of the two of them smiling at each other over the rim of a large silver cup. 'Come in and shut the door, Riley.'

'It doesn't prove anything.'

'I know it doesn't prove anything – but it gives us a potential narrative, doesn't it?'

'Motive?'

'Beyond the pent up anger and hurt of being betrayed for half a lifetime? Not to say sheer bloody rage at this last gamble, which sent them straight onto the rocks.'

'There's a bit of a gap between throwing a sugar bowl at him and hiring a hit man. I don't see how his death changes anything. I told you, there wasn't any life insurance.'

'None that he'd taken out, no, Riley. But anyone can take out a policy on anyone. I could take one out on you. And a wife can certainly take one out on her husband.'

'Without a medical check-up or anything?'

'That's for you to find out, Riley. And I have every confidence you'll have the answer by close of play.'

While Riley stayed chained to his desk, Dalliance drove into the countryside where he dropped in on Steve Royce. He found the ex-army man no more welcoming than before;

not that he had been expecting much as he'd bobbled down the lane, splashed through the ford, and drawn up outside the caravan.

'Oh. You again,' was all Royce said when he opened the caravan door. He seemed to fill the door frame and, as he didn't step back in welcome, Dalliance had no option but to step back himself. 'Where's your dancing partner?'

'Pen-pushing back at the station. I'll pass on your best wishes.'

Royce scowled.

'And thank you for not shooting me.'

'You've only just got here,' said Royce, rubbing the back of his hand over a very stubbly chin. 'So what do you want?'

'I need to ask you some questions – about Tuesday night.'

'Yeah, I thought you might.' He sat heavily at the top of the steps.

'Well, where were you?'

'You know where I was. At the Poachers. With Jez and Jessie. As everybody's bloody well told you already. Jeez. You're harassing me.'

'There was a very serious offence committed that night.'

'And there'd have been another one if you'd sent the uniform boys round in the small hours, I can tell you.'

'Which is why I didn't. But I still need to ask you about your movements that night.'

'Mainly to and from the dartboard with a couple of fag breaks thrown in. And no, Jez and me didn't jump in Jessie's pick-up, drive over to Gallows Barn and beat the crap out of that journalist. However much he bloody deserved it.'

Dalliance noticed the tattoo on Royce's right bicep was beginning to expand. Perhaps he should have brought Riley along with him after all.

'So why me? Go on, tell me why.'

'Thought I might have detected the hallmarks of a military background. It was all done with what is sometimes referred to as military precision. And I seem to remember seeing pictures of prisoners roped up and hooded.'

Even though he'd been half expecting it, the violence when it came still shocked him. Royce sprang up, his right fist bunched like a sledgehammer. The blow, however, was not aimed at Dalliance, but at the side of the caravan which gave off a low-toned clang.

'So I'm a war criminal too now, am I? You people make me sick. You really do.' He flexed his fingers and stared grimly at Dalliance. 'The only reason I hit the caravan and not you is that I want to see my kids again. And I don't know how long I can keep that up. So if you're going to arrest me, arrest me, and I'll come quietly. Otherwise...' The threat remained unspoken, but it was palpable.

'I'm not going to arrest you,' Dalliance said, beginning to move away, 'and there are other questions I need to ask you – but I don't have to ask them now.' Once back in the car with the engine running, he opened the window. 'Just something you might like to be thinking about – I will want to know how you knew that the incident took place at Gallows Barn.'

Royce lurched down the caravan steps looking like an incensed grizzly bear. Dalliance revved the engine and moved off down the lane, taking the little ford just a little too fast and splashing a mass of water onto his windscreen. He glanced in the mirror. Steve Royce stood impassively with his hands on his hips.

Dalliance could imagine the sneer on his face.

Dalliance sat in his car outside the Poachers waiting for Sam Hardy to open up. The encounter with Steve Royce had shaken him. Maybe he was getting too old for all this?

His phone went. 'Come in, Riley. Over.'

'She did take out life insurance on Roper, sir.'

'Really? When?'

'Few years ago now, sir.'

'H'm. She didn't mention it.'

'To be fair, we didn't ask her.'

'How much will she get?'

'He doesn't know.'

'Who doesn't know – and why not?'

'Norman Standing, sir, and—'

'Norman Standing – he knew? How did he know? And how did you know to ask him in the first place?'

'Her solicitor. He was trying to be helpful but said he probably didn't know everything about the Ropers' affairs, and that Standing might be worth asking. Said he remembered something cropping up – on the rare occasion he spoke to Mrs Roper and not to Ted – and she'd said she'd ask Norman. So I rang him.'

'And?'

'He said he'd advised her to take out a policy – just in case – and anyway, he could get her a good deal which wouldn't be that expensive. If they did it then they wouldn't have to get a medical done or anything. He didn't make it sound a big deal.'

'So does Standing have any idea – ballpark figure? Assuming they accept the claim?'

'Standing doesn't know. He hasn't crunched the numbers. His exact words were' – Dalliance could hear Riley finding the page in his notebook – '"It won't save the house, but it'll help with life post-sale."'

Dalliance held the phone in his hand, staring ahead through the windscreen.

'Sir?'

'I'm still here, Riley.'

'And where's here, sir?'

'Car park of the Poachers – waiting to meet a man who's looking more and more like our prime suspect.'

'Would you like me to join you, sir?'

'D'you know, Riley, I really think I'd appreciate that greatly.'

He had just pocketed his phone when he heard the roar of a large vehicle rocking up the track to the pub. It was a battered Toyota pick-up, and out of it stepped Jessie Miller.

THIRTEEN

He was a big man, but light on his feet. Dalliance could picture him slipping through the woods, making hardly a sound. The pheasants, the deer, the rabbits, they wouldn't stand a chance.

He remembered the sound of shotguns from a brief sojourn in one of the county's more remote villages. Walks on short winter afternoons would be punctuated by what sounded like the slamming of glass-paned doors a mile away across the estate.

The woods around the Poachers were even more remote. Miller clearly had the run of them – probably with the game-keepers' connivance. Why make life difficult for yourself with a man like Miller, who would after all act as a deterrent to other poachers?

That's how the countryside worked – you scratch my back, I'll scratch yours. A bit of unauthorised logging here, the odd tank of pink diesel there. Dalliance didn't mind – provided it didn't get out of hand. But abducting and beating up journalists, leave aside cold-blooded murder, were utterly beyond the pale.

Dalliance set his jaw and climbed out of his car. It must have taken a hell of a lot of guts to be the lone lawman in one of those one-horse towns in the Wild West. He wondered what the life expectancy of the average sheriff was.

'Hello, Inspector. I thought it was you skulking in the car park.' Jessie Miller was sitting on what was obviously 'his' barstool, nursing a glass of ginger beer.

'Get you one?' he asked with apparent friendliness.

'A half,' Dalliance accepted graciously.

Miller nodded and Sam Hardy grabbed a half-pint glass off the shelf.

'Thanks,' Dalliance said as the landlord set it down just hard enough to spill a bit.

'You can never believe two of those would make a pint,' Miller said, looking with amused disdain at the miniature tankard.

Dalliance agreed. It would take some skill to nurse that through a conversation of any length.

Miller pursued his theme. 'Hardly worth driving all the way out here for that, eh, Sam?'

'Expect he wants to more than just wet his whistle,' the landlord said, clanking a few glasses in the basin behind the bar.

'So what can we do you for, Inspector? You're not going to break the lads' alibi for Tuesday night. They were here all evening, till Sam put the towels up. Weren't they, Sam?'

'Course they were,' the landlord growled.

'I'm sure they were,' Dalliance said genially. 'But maybe that's not what I'm asking about right now.'

'I'm all ears,' Miller said.

'Perhaps we could talk over there.'

'Do you hear that, Sam? He doesn't want you ear-wigging.' He laughed and took a pull at his ginger beer. 'And what makes you think I keep secrets from my landlord, Inspector?'

'You may not keep secrets from him, but perhaps I do. Of course, if you'd rather come into the station, I can arrange to see you there.'

Miller seemed to consider this. Suddenly his hand dived into his pocket. For a split-second Dalliance thought he might be about to produce a handgun. As the huge hand re-emerged, he caught a dull metallic glint.

Enjoying his discomfort, Miller slammed the metal box down on the bar and flipped open the lid. Dalliance averted his eyes, becoming strangely interested in a row of dusty Toby jugs on a high shelf. But the smell of the tobacco drew his eye back to Miller's deftly working fingers.

Slotting the perfectly rolled cigarette behind his ear, Miller tidied up the spilt strands of tobacco and packed them back in the box with the cigarette papers. 'Come on then,' he said, and led the way out of the pub to the smokers' lean-to round the side.

'Sorry, Inspector – you seem to be downwind,' he said once he'd got the roll-up alight.

'I'm fine,' Dalliance said, his nose twitching.

'Ah – I see,' said Miller with a laugh. 'Given up, have we? Do you want one? These don't really count.' He produced his tin box. 'I won't tell if you don't.'

Dalliance declined with a shake of the head, but he didn't shift his ground.

'Suit yourself. Now, what's this information you're after?'

'How well do you know Mrs Roper?'

'Mrs Roper? Well, you're full of surprises, Inspector. I didn't think her name would crop up, I really didn't.'

'Well, now it has – how well *do* you know her?'

'She's one of my favourite ladies. We have a hot date once a year. And guess what – it's coming up this Saturday afternoon.'

'Meaning?'

'Meaning I goes out with my twelve bore, shoots a sackful of clays to smithereens, and later on in the afternoon she gives me a big smile and a big cup and next week we have our picture in the paper.'

Dalliance nodded. 'How many years now?'

'Ooh – let me see. This year'll be the sixth. Ted put the cup up eight years back now, and I've won it the last five.'

'Why doesn't – didn't – Ted do the presentation?'

'He was a competitor, wasn't he? What if he'd won? You can't go giving yourself your own cup.'

'Was he likely to win it?'

'Not with me around – but then nobody else is either. He came third one year and made a big fuss of having Margot pin a rosette on his chest.'

'Margot?'

'That's her name, isn't it?'

'It is, but I'm surprised you're on first-name terms.'

'They may be stinking rich, but they're not stuck up. I mean, Ted used to enjoy pretending to be squire, but he knew as well as everybody else that that's all it was – pretending. And Margot – she's a good sort. No airs and graces with that one. None at all.'

'You sound as if you like her.'

'I think the world of her. A top filly in my book. I'd do anything for her.'

He finished his cigarette, and Dalliance watched its flicked parabola.

'Offer still stands, Inspector.'

'I'm all right, but thanks. So, what do you do for her – Mrs Roper? I'm getting the impression you actually see her more than once a year.'

'I do. Rabbits mainly. But also moles. Ruin a lawn, they will. I shoot the rabbits and gas the moles. Oh, and they had rats the other year. Bad. But I sorted it. One-man death machine, I am. Vermin a speciality.'

'And that's it?'

'What do you mean – what else might I do for her?' Miller's smile had gone and his eyes were boring into Dalliance from under beetling brows.

Dalliance ignored the distinct chill in the atmosphere. 'I thought they might be in the market for the odd out-of-season pheasant. Like the brace you brought in for Sam.'

Miller seemed to relax. He laughed. 'Road kill. You always get some – especially this time of year. It'd be a pity to let them go to waste, and I'm not too proud to stop and sling them in the back of the pick-up.'

'And the Ropers?'

'Everyone likes a brace of pheasants from time to time, so yes, why not? And for Margot I'd go the extra mile – for her I'd pluck them. Which is not a pleasant job, as I'm sure you'll appreciate.' He laughed, patted his pocket to check his smoking tin, and started to make for the pub door. At the same time, there was a noise of tyres and Riley's car pulled into the car park. 'Oh look – back-up. I hope he wasn't expecting to find me tearing you limb from limb, Inspector. Couldn't have been more cordial, could it?'

'It couldn't. Just one last thing though. Could you tell me what you were doing on Sunday afternoon?'

'Well, I was in here as usual, playing a nice quiet game of dominoes with Jack. But what's that got to do with anything?'

He looked Riley up and down, and Riley stopped, seeing he'd arrived at a sensitive moment.

'What time did you leave the pub, Mr Miller?'

Hearing such a routine question, Riley advanced to join the pair under the awning. He took out his notebook.

'And,' Dalliance went on imperturbably, 'where did you go next?'

Miller looked from Dalliance to Riley, who was standing with his pen poised.

'Bloody hell, you people take the bloody biscuit, don't you?'

'Mr Miller—?'

But Miller pushed pasted them and slammed back into the pub.

'That seemed to be going well.'

'It had been, Riley.'

'Did I turn up at the wrong time?'

'It wasn't your fault.' Dalliance started heading for the car park.

'Aren't we going to—?'

'Badger him into losing his temper completely? No, Riley, we are not. I've no intention of goading all our suspects into outbreaks of GBH.'

Riley looked disappointed.

'If you want to do something useful, put that cigarette end in a bag.' He pointed to where Miller's butt had landed.

Riley looked questioningly.

'If he throws his butts away we're perfectly entitled to pick them up.'

With a glance at the pub window, Riley squatted down and did as he was instructed.

'Come on,' Dalliance said. 'I'll buy you a drink in a pub where we won't be rubbing shoulders with a prime suspect.'

'So do you think there was something going on – between Miller and Roper's wife?'

'I do not, Riley.' Dalliance looked into the shallow depths of his second half-pint of the evening. 'Not in the sense you mean. But they undoubtedly knew each other quite well. If – and it's a huge, improbable if – she had wanted someone to dispose of Ted, I'm pretty sure Miller would have been the one she'd have asked.'

Riley looked up. 'Really?'

Dalliance nodded, remembering Miller's line about being a one-man killing machine. Of course, it was a long way from rats and moles to errant husbands. But as they were discovering, there was now a discernible motive.

Riley was equally thoughtful. 'You don't think he was just winding you up, sir? '

'No,' the Inspector said. 'He was genuinely put out – he didn't like us prying into his Sunday afternoon.'

'But he can't just refuse to answer questions.'

'He can. They haven't abolished the right to silence yet. But I didn't want to push it. He's hardly going to come out with it and say: "Actually I was up a tree behind the sightscreen at Lower Bolton cricket ground taking pot shots at Ted Roper with a dart gun", is he?'

'No, but if he was doing something perfectly innocent—'

Dalliance looked at him. 'Obviously if he'd had an alibi he'd have told us – however gracelessly. But he doesn't, which doesn't mean he's our man – just that we can't cross him off the list. If he is our man, we've got to do a hell of a lot of work to get him at the scene. And if he was there at Margot Roper's behest, we have to prove that as well.'

'Do you think he was? I really can't see her—'

'Neither can I, Riley, but we can't rule it out. She took out life insurance on Ted; she has plenty of possible motives – the betrayed wife, et cetera. But most importantly, there's the money. If she thought she was going to be left with nothing – nothing for herself, and nothing to pass on to her children. We're potentially in lioness–cub territory here, Riley.'

'So are we going to go back and interview her again, sir?'

'No. At least – not next. Next we're going to go and see Norman Standing.'

'Tonight, sir?'

'Not tonight, Riley. I don't want to spend all evening tracking Standing down through the nightclubs of Knightsbridge – even if you'd like to. No, we'll drive to London in the morning. Ring him when we get back to the office. Say we need to talk to him about possible suspects behind the sightscreen. You don't have to alert him to the fact that we're interested in the life insurance. Though of course, he was the source of the information in the first place, so he's not going to miss the significance of that.'

'But you don't think Standing's in on it? I mean, he sounded pretty relaxed talking about it earlier.'

'It's not something you can hide – a life insurance windfall – is it? There's no point in getting all cloak-and-dagger about it.'

'So you think he could have put her up to it?'

'I don't know, Riley. All I do know is that they were an item at university; Standing has done everything to get the Ropers to where they are today. He even bought a cottage so he could join them in the Boltons. Them – or her?'

'You think he's still holding a torch for her? What about all those other women—?'

'We're living in the twenty-first century, Riley – the age of instant gratification. You can have your heart broken by the love of your life, but you're not expected to ride off into the forest like an Arthurian knight on the grail quest.'

'So Standing might be looking to get her back?'

'The processes of the human heart are complex and unpredictable,' Dalliance said.

'You mean *he* could have had a motive – for murder?' Riley looked questioningly at his boss.

'We haven't ruled it out. He might even have deliberately suckered Roper into this latest sure-fire money-making gamble, intending for it to fail. And then he rides up like the knight in shining armour?'

'I see,' said Riley.

'Anything's possible. Just tell him we're coming to see him in the morning.'

In an empty clearing in the woods, on the stump of a tree, stood a bottle. Resting on top of the bottle was an egg – a small, speckled egg.

The silence of the late afternoon was suddenly broken by a brusque report. The bottle remained intact, but the egg was no longer there.

A moment later the bottle disintegrated.

Fifty yards away, Jessie Miller emerged from the bushes holding a light hunting rifle, a cigarette hanging loosely between his lips.

FOURTEEN

'Welcome, gentlemen. Good drive? I can do it in seventy minutes on a Sunday night. I'm guessing it took you a little longer.'

Norman Standing exuded understated wealth. From his cufflinks to his shoelaces he looked as though he'd stepped from the pages of a top-end menswear catalogue.

'Sit down, please.'

The stylish leather sofas looked inviting. Riley's eye was drawn to the slew of fashion magazines spread across the low glass table. All right for some, he thought.

'I've asked Jan to bring us in some coffee.' Standing sat in an opulent office chair, swinging round from his workstation to smile easily at them. 'I love working from home. Penthouse above; office and reception rooms here; and, by the greatest of good fortune, there's a splendid gym in the basement. I hardly need to leave the premises.'

'But you drive out to the Boltons to play cricket,' Dalliance observed.

'I do. I love the countryside. I love a spin in the car – I hope you found somewhere to park. I'm afraid I've only got the one space.'

Riley had noticed the Aston Martin stuck snugly down an alley off the mews. His own car was two streets away, and he and Dalliance had had to empty their pockets to feed the meter.

Jan, the shapely receptionist, came in with the coffee. Riley made a space on the table, finding himself looking at a simply stunning model in a tasteful swimsuit on the front cover of one of the fashion magazines.

'Page twenty-eight, from memory – I think it's marked,' Standing said, having dismissed Jan with a wave.

There was indeed a marker and Riley flicked through the magazine to find a double-page spread of the same model, posing beside an indoor swimming pool. The headline read: 'Tatiana Takes to London High Life'. Turning the page, Riley found himself looking at a small insert, in which Tatiana was joined by Standing himself.

'She's upstairs, doing something important to her nails,' Standing said with a smile. 'Which, Inspector, is going to help answer one of your questions.'

'Which is?'

'Do I still hold a torch for Margot – and would that torch burn fiercely enough for me to murder her husband?' There was a slight pause. 'Come on Inspector, we're all grown-ups. You're engaged on a murder investigation, and you're finding it damned hard to eliminate anyone from your suspects list. I'm right, aren't I?'

Dalliance granted the point with a brief nod.

'One scenario might run like this: jilted lover waits twenty-five years to bump off rival and scoop up his university flame.'

Riley shot Dalliance a glance – crudely expressed, that was more or less what they had discussed over their drink in the pub the previous evening.

'I adore Margot; I really do. And she did hurt me – very, very badly – when she dumped me for Ted. Which is why we stopped seeing each other. By the time she got back in touch with me – and that was the way round it was – I'd got over her, started being successful, had a lifestyle I was happy with. I went round to have supper with them out of curiosity really. It just went so well – we got back into the groove we'd had as a threesome at Cambridge. They were happy, I was happy; we realised we could resume our friendship, which is exactly what we did.'

Standing leant forward and poured the coffee.

'It all went unbelievably well. I helped make them rich – so rich they could leave London and buy that slightly ridiculous pile in the shires. I found myself going down there more and more, so when Margot heard the cottage was going on the market, she tipped me off and I got in with an offer, and it's been a very good second home ever since. It meant I could go down and not be woken at dawn by Charlie and Fiona, but potter over for lunch and a relaxing afternoon. And of course in the summer the cricket.'

'A bit below your standard, village cricket?'

'I was playing Surrey league on the Saturday in those days. Drive down to the Boltons after the game; nightcap in the Three Horseshoes, and a gentle game of tip-and-run with the locals on Sunday.'

'Slumming it.'

'Village cricket is a great leveller, Dalliance. The village blacksmith is a dying breed; they all watch it on the box, know how to play straight. A big strapping lad who spends his week on a building site will get it round your ears just as rapidly as some Old Etonian opening the bowling for I Zingari. As for the pitches – not exactly roads. And then of course there's the umpires. Back in the day no one in club cricket would ever give you out LBW if you made even half a step forward; not so in the villages. It was like DRS with knobs on. Bat-pad? Forget it. Yes, on a good day – on our pitch – against a weaker side, it was help yourself – and I did

– though I nearly always gave it away in the seventies to give the others a go. But I can tell you, there were other occasions when I felt I was batting for my life. But I'm boring your DS, Inspector. Enough already.'

Riley tore his eye away from the magazine cover and tried hard to think of a question to ask.

Standing went on. 'So, having put the jealous lover exacts revenge after twenty-five years scenario to bed, we move on to the long-time friend and financial adviser helps old flame murder husband for life insurance line.'

'Have you got a figure for us?' Dalliance asked.

'Not an exact one, but it's looking like something in the region of two hundred thousand. That's assuming they accept the claim. Which I do.'

'Can you tell us a little bit more about why Mrs Roper decided to take out the policy?' Riley sipped his coffee. It wasn't the most incisive question he'd ever asked, but at least it showed he was more than just Dalliance's chauffeur.

Standing nodded. 'I can remember very precisely as it happens. It was at the cricket. Margot had come over to watch, and by happy chance, Ted was having one of his good days. I'd got a snorter early on and Ted had to go in and steady the ship. Margot and I went for a walk around the boundary. We didn't say much, but we were obviously thinking along the same lines – how weird life is; how quickly it goes. There was this fat, middle-aged man scything top edges over the slips and running very ponderously up the wicket, and in our minds' eyes we were seeing the young Ted guiding the ball past gully and sprinting up and down to make two. "I do love him," she said, "even though he can be such a shit." It wasn't for me to comment on that of course, so we walked on a bit further. Then Ted actually hit one in the middle. Really caught hold of it. He didn't need to run, but he did that showboating thing, coming half way down the wicket as part of his follow-through. And he suddenly pulled up, mid-pitch, flung his bat down and more or less doubled up. Margot said, "Oh my God, he's had a heart attack", and started to run out to the square. Of course it wasn't a heart attack, it was heartburn brought on by a bloody big roast lunch, too much claret and an unusually long innings. But it gave us pause for thought. I asked if Ted had any life insurance and Margot said she didn't think so. "He thinks he'll live forever," she said; and I said it would be very easy to arrange, and she said he'd never agree to it; and I said it would be very easy to arrange without him knowing. She said okay, and I set it up. I don't suppose she gave it another thought – until last Sunday.'

'But she was thinking about it then?' Dalliance asked.

'Unsurprisingly, given the financial situation. When we spoke on the phone I said I'd find out how much and told her about the process – obviously hugely complicated in the case of murder.'

'And while we're on the "financial situation" – you can confirm that it put your friendship under strain?'

'We've been through all that, Inspector – Chief Inspector. Obviously Ted was bitterly disappointed; obviously he blamed me. Obviously I pointed out that he hadn't had to take the gamble, and that there are not too many bookies who'll lend you your stake out of their own pockets.'

'How big a gamble was it exactly?'

'As I say to all of my clients, don't play with money you can't afford to lose.'

'But that didn't apply to Ted?'

'It did apply to Ted. He shouldn't have made the play. But he wanted the money. He kept badgering me – "Norman, you must have something – what about all those Russian oligarchs – you must have something pretty hot for them". Well, of course I did. But as I pointed out to him, they're rich enough to take the hit.'

'And have they?'

'Absolutely. One guy's down seven million.'

'And how happy is he about that?' Riley asked.

'Un,' Standing replied with a slight sigh. 'But that's my business. I deal with it.'

'And what exactly is your business – what was this speculative venture Ted wanted in on?'

Standing raised his hands. 'How much do you know about futures, derivatives, commodity markets, Inspector? I do have a standard lecture, but I don't think it's relevant. What I do may be high risk, but it's all above board. And anyway, if it wasn't, it would take the Fraud Squad to untangle it.'

'Not a couple of duffers from the sticks.'

Standing gave a deprecating smile. 'I didn't mean it that way. It's just that it's—'

'Complex,' Dalliance finished the sentence for him. 'Getting back to you and Ted.'

'He just kept on and on at me. I tried to put him off, but he wouldn't listen. He was hungry for the money – this fantasy of commercialising the house and its assets – and he begged me to let him in – and lend him the stake. I shouldn't have done it, of course I shouldn't. But I was confident. It really was a beautiful scheme – one of the best. And we all should have made a packet out of it.'

'But...?'

Standing sighed. 'Things went wrong – a bank in Cyprus here, a bad grain harvest there, and suddenly...' He shrugged. 'The perfect storm.'

'So Ted was furious with you?'

'Yes, and we had a blazing row – we've been through all this.'

'And the row – did it turn violent?'

'No way. Ted knows I'm fit as a butcher's dog. Not that hitting people's my style – unlike some people I could mention. This is a pretty pickle, isn't it?' He swung round and picked up a red-top form his desk. Peterson's badly bruised face was splashed across the front page.

'We're working on that,' Dalliance said. 'Let's stick with you and Ted. You had a row. Where was that?'

'It kicked off after the match one Sunday. There'd been a simmering tension all day, and a chance remark about some trivial aspect of the game sparked it off. But we quickly realised that the two senior members of the team tearing into each other was hardly an edifying spectacle, so we stopped. Only to resume hostilities over at the cottage later. We both wanted to keep Margot out of it. He came round and we did some more shouting. And then I sat him down. I went through it all with him – again: what had happened, why it had gone wrong, how we were absolutely stuffed and couldn't get out of it – which meant he couldn't get out of paying me the money he owed me.'

'Did he try – to get out of paying?'

'Every which way – he started by blustering, then tried threats and ended up pleading.'

'What sort of threats?'

'Empty. There was no way he could hurt me, and he knew it.'

'But you – you had ways you could hurt him, if you'd wanted to.'

'That's a big if, Inspector, but yes. I had him on the ropes.'

'And if you'd wanted to knock him out for the count?'

'I certainly wouldn't have staged an elaborate murder in the middle of a cricket match.'

'What would you have done?'

Standing looked squarely at Dalliance. 'There are ways and means, as I'm sure you're aware, Inspector. Life is pretty cheap, I'm afraid. But I didn't want Ted dead, and I didn't kill him.'

'What about Margot ? How did she take it?'

'Livid with Ted, understandably.'

'And with you?'

'She didn't blame me. Well, she wished I hadn't stood banker to him; but she quite understood the pressure he put me under. No, she let me off pretty lightly. It was Ted who took the brunt of her anger.'

'What were things like – between you all, I mean? Before last Sunday.'

'Much as normal, to be honest. We had a pattern, a very pleasant routine, and there seemed no reason to change it. But of course it was there all the time—'

'The financial disaster?'

'Well, it was hardly going to go away, was it? We were all keeping up appearances really, and we knew it.'

'Did you talk to Margot – just the two of you?

'On occasion.'

'And?'

Standing paused, as though debating with himself. 'Okay,' he said, having made up his mind. 'I'm telling you this because it happened, but I don't attach any importance to it, and nor should you.'

'Go on,' Dalliance said, leaning forward slightly.

'The previous Sunday I was over at theirs having lunch as usual, and as usual it was a very good lunch, and Ted had his usual amount to eat – and drink. And then he had another of his turns. It wasn't a bad one, just heartburn again. He left the table and went and lay down in the sitting room, leaving the two of us together to finish the dessert wine.'

Dalliance looked encouragingly at him, his eyebrows raised.

Standing continued, somewhat hesitantly. 'Margot said – and it was really just a throwaway remark – "At least I've got the life insurance to fall back on if he does have a heart attack" – something like that. Totally innocent; just a light-hearted reference to Ted overdoing it – again.'

'She didn't ask about its likely value or anything like that?'

'Good God, no. She wasn't serious. She just smiled wanly, finished her wine and started clearing the table. End of. Hardly worth mentioning.'

There was a natural pause.

'Well, you've been very helpful, Mr Standing,' Dalliance said.

'Not at all. Always happy to spend time persuading people I'm not a cold-blooded assassin.'

Dalliance and Riley got to their feet, and Standing leapt out of his chair.

'There is just one thing, Inspector.'

'Yes?' said Dalliance.

'Have you thought of staging a reconstruction?'

Dalliance stood in the middle of the office. 'Never felt they produced much in the way of results frankly. Everybody's been very clear about what they did, and everybody's corroborated everybody else's story.'

'And you're still left with a cricket team of suspects?'

'We'll get there, Mr Standing; don't worry about that.'

'I'm sure you will. But consider this. We've got another match on Sunday – by some quirk of the fixture list it's also at home. The committee have decided to go ahead with it – Ted would certainly have wanted us to play – and they've also invited me to skipper the side. Which I'm happy to do. The whole team's available again, which makes my life easy – with, of course, the one exception of Ted himself. Now it occurred to me that I might have a natural replacement for whom the experience could be uncommonly interesting.'

Dalliance took a step back. 'No, no – absolutely not.'

'Why ever not, Inspector? You're a cricketer – at least as good as Ted; probably better. If you played, you'd get a sense of things, get a feel for the team, et cetera. It would do everything a reconstruction would do without having to stage it.'

'I hung up my boots five years ago.'

'But you've still got them, I'll bet. And your whites.'

Dalliance shifted uncomfortably. 'Doubt whether I could get into them now. Anyway, I can't commit to a whole afternoon like that in the middle of an investigation.'

'Think about it. I'll get cover for you in case you can't do it – Ted's boy Charlie could play at a pinch, but I don't think he'd want to, and I'm not sure I'd want him anyway. Bit of a prima donna – and not popular with the rest of the team.'

'I'm hardly on everybody's Christmas card list,' Dalliance said with a humourless smile.

'Yes, but they know you're just doing your job. Charlie is genuinely disliked. And would almost certainly want to bat higher than Ted did – and want to bowl his bloody awful off-breaks. No, Inspector, you're the man I'd like, however out of practice.'

Dalliance sighed.

'Come on, DS Riley,' Standing said, 'you try. You can see it could be really worthwhile.'

'Don't start,' Dalliance raised a warning hand. 'I'll think about it, and get back to you. But I won't be any good, you know.'

'Don't worry about that. Ted wasn't much use himself most days. The rest of us were able to carry him. I'm in good nick; Rees is hitting the ball to all parts. Ring me by close of play, and the number five slot's yours.'

'You've got to give it a go, sir,' Riley said after negotiating his way onto the fast-flowing traffic on the Cromwell Road.

Dalliance uttered what could only be described as a 'harrumph'. Riley glanced at him. The parking ticket they had incurred for being four minutes late back to the car was still clenched in his fist.

'Standing's got a point. You'd be there – right in amongst them. They couldn't keep their guard up – not all through an afternoon.'

Dalliance was by no means sure he could keep his own guard up. The thought of being bowled first ball was not an encouraging one. As for taking Roper's place at slip – Christ! He could imagine how fast Jez bowled – not to mention Steve Royce.

'Can you imagine playing in a team, at least one of whom you know has committed murder?'

'But that's the point, sir. We're still no nearer identifying who that is. This would be an amazing opportunity.'

'But they all hate me.'

'I doubt the perpetrators would try it two weeks running. And I'll be there.'

'That's reassuring. If I thought I could teach you the laws of the game by Sunday, I'd insist on your umpiring. But I know you'd just give me out.'

'Seriously, sir – it could be really useful. For a start we could get a man into that tree and see if anyone notices the branches moving. That's the beauty of it not being a reconstruction as such, sir. We can play with it. And if you should happen to take a catch – bingo. Get a couple of cameras on it. I really think it's a goer, sir.'

A goer. Ye gods. Dalliance looked moodily out at the Berkshire countryside as they sped back along the motorway.

As things stood, they had two unsolved crimes on their hands. The murder had obviously been planned to make their job as hard as possible. They just had to be patient, he told himself. But the conspiracy to assault the journalist had been concocted at short notice, and it was disturbing that the alibis of what had seemed the obvious offenders were rock solid. It was also annoying that the key witness supporting Jez, Rees and Steve Royce's alibi was now a prime suspect in the murder. He had no breakthroughs to announce, only the same old anodyne assurance that their enquiries were making progress.

All the public had was the image of Riley putting his arm around his back in the middle of the cricket field – the Dancing Detectives.

The investigation was running out of steam. They needed a step-change to revive it.

'Okay, Riley, time to rattle the bars of a few cages. Send a squad car to bring Miller in. If he's got an alibi, let's have it; if he hasn't, we'll print out a mugshot and have it shown to everybody in the village on the off-chance someone saw him on Sunday afternoon. Next, track down those boys giving Daniel the gip on the boundary; get a uniform to grill them about what they were doing and what they might have seen. And what, if anything, have SOCO got for us from Gallows Barn?'

'Not a lot.'

'But...?'

'There were some boot prints on the edge of the stream that runs behind the barn. Looks as though someone had a pee while they were waiting for Peterson to turn up.'

'Pre-action nerves. That's possible. Good.'

Riley shook his head. 'They're very faint – quite possibly not our villains at all. They couldn't be sure time-wise.'

'Tell them we'll have what they've got. At least that's something I can tell the vultures at the press conference. We are going to have to spread the net on that one. Who else might be prepared to do Rees' dirty work for him?'

'Ben Cowper?' Riley shrugged. 'But no van he drove would smell "clean", would it? Don't even know if he has a van.'

'Well, find out,' Dalliance said shortly. He went on. 'Difficult to imagine Standing or Henderson getting involved in some Hicksville thuggery – and anyway, Standing, like Daniel, wasn't anywhere near the vicinity. Which leaves Des Tucker, the innocuous Ernie Phelps and the affable – and muscular – Barney Grover. You were going to check Phelps' background?'

'Sort of dropped down the priorities list with the life insurance thing coming up, but I can get onto it, sir.'

'Do.' Dalliance drummed on his desk top. 'Talking of the life insurance, I think I'll go over and have a word with Margot.'

'On your own, sir?'

'I think I can manage without a chaperone, thank you, Riley.'

'I'm sorry sir, I didn't mean—'

'I know you didn't. Sometimes a one-to-one can lead to a heart-to-heart.'

'Right, sir. Of course, sir. Look forward to hearing how it goes.'

Dalliance stood under the portico of the Roper mansion, idly wondering what its market value was. When the door opened he took a step back in surprise.

'Can I help you?' a tall young man asked in a supercilious voice.

'You must be Charlie,' Dalliance said.

'And who are you?' the young man asked rudely.

Dalliance was just fishing his ID out when Margot herself appeared beside her son.

'Inspector! Do come in. Charlie, this is Inspector Dalliance. Don't keep him on the doorstep, darling.'

'I thought you said he'd already interviewed you,' Charlie said, moving back grudgingly.

'He has, dear; but perhaps there's something else he needs to ask – or possibly some news?'

'Not that, I'm afraid,' Dalliance said.

'For goodness sake,' Charlie said. 'He was murdered in full view of a dozen or more people – how difficult can it be?'

'Surprisingly difficult,' Dalliance said with asperity. The boy flicked long hair away from his forehead.

'I'm sure the Inspector is doing all he can, Charlie. And I'm also sure he'll want to speak to me on my own. So why don't you go back up to your room and leave us to it. I'm sure it won't take long.'

With a scowl the boy strode across the hall and took the stairs two at a time.

'I'm sorry, Inspector. Can we put it down to jetlag? He could only get a flight back via LA – he had a pretty gruesome journey. Come into the kitchen. I'll make a pot of tea.'

Dalliance followed her into a well-appointed space, noting the substantial Aga, the Welsh dresser, and the well-worn oak table easily capable of seating ten.

'We probably shouldn't run it all the year round,' she said, putting the kettle on the Aga hob. 'It makes the kitchen terribly hot in summer. But I don't care; it's an old friend and I love it.'

She dropped her hand to the metal kitchen-towel rail. Dalliance heard the chink of her wedding ring. Could he really be looking at a woman capable of hiring someone to kill her husband? He profoundly hoped not.

'Earl Grey?' she asked lightly. 'That's what I gave you last time.'

'Could I have something more robust? Bog-standard teabag would do me.'

'Of course, Inspector. Anything you like. Charlie and Fiona are already halfway through a box of Yorkshire. It's the one thing everyone seems to miss when they're abroad. And Marmite, of course.'

'So they're both home now.'

'Yes. Fiona got in at some ungodly hour in the morning. Des Tucker went to get her. Invaluable, that man is. He'd do anything for Ted – and by extension me. So yes, both chicks returned to the nest. Fiona's still in bed actually. It does take it out of you, doesn't it, flying – even though you're just sitting there watching films hour after hour.'

The kettle suddenly whistled causing Dalliance to turn sharply.

'It's all right, Inspector. I'm sorry, it often startles visitors. But once you're used to it, it's rather a comforting sound.' She poured the boiling water into a pot and gave it a brisk stir, before bringing the pot and two mugs to the table where Dalliance had pulled up a chair. She went to the large steel fridge and brought out a jug of milk. 'Now Inspector, what did you want to ask me?'

Dalliance looked into her politely smiling face. He couldn't put it off any longer. He took a fairly deep breath and said, 'Mrs Roper—'

And then his mobile phone rang.

'I'm sorry, I have to take this. Yes?'

Twenty seconds later, his chair scraped over the flagstones.

'My God! Are you sure? ... Is he all right? ... I'll get over there right now. Text me the address.'

Dalliance was already out of his seat and headed for the hall. Margot Roper was hard on his heels but couldn't reach the front door before he did.

'Has something happened, Inspector?' she blurted out.

'Yes. It's serious. I'm sorry, I can't stop.' Dalliance was fumbling with the latch.

'Here, let me do it,' she said, opening the door for him. 'Do come back – when it's convenient,' she called after him. She doubted he heard as he flung himself into his car and sped off down the drive, sending a shower of gravel onto the grass, just as Charlie was coming down the stairs.

'What's going on? Where's he off to in such a tearing hurry?'

'He had a call. Obviously something's come up – something urgent. He didn't say what it was.'

'Looks as if he got an invitation to go on Top Gear.'

'I'm sure we'll find out in due course.'

'What did he want from you?'

'I don't know. He was just about to ask me when his phone went. There's a cup of tea going begging in the kitchen if you want one.'

Charlie followed his mother into the kitchen. She indicated Dalliance's mug. 'It's all right, he didn't touch it.' She rested her hand on the table, and Charlie noticed a strange look on her face.

'Darling, I'm feeling…slightly odd. I think I'll go and lie down for half an hour. Do you mind? I've put the stew in the oven. We can eat a bit later.'

She left her son staring blackly into the depths of the Inspector's abandoned mug of tea.

FIFTEEN

It was a twenty-minute drive to Tilsby. Dalliance took one wrong turn and had to cut back on himself, swearing loudly. But once there the address was easy to find. And he didn't need to waste time looking at house numbers. Outside the house in question were three squad cars and the SOCO van. As he was parking, Riley also drew up.

They ducked under the police tape and a uniform ushered them into the house, where they were met by Anderson. He briefly shook his head in a 'what next?' sort of way, before leading them upstairs. Dalliance was aware of sobbing coming from a room down the hall.

'The wife. She's got a PC with her doing tea and sympathy.'

'And the victim?'

'You've missed him – whisked off in an ambulance a while back.'

'Is he going to make it?'

'Couldn't say. It didn't kill him on the spot like Roper, so I'm guessing there's a good chance.'

'Let's hope so,' Dalliance said, following Anderson into a bedroom off the landing.

'We meet again!' Sally Walker looked up at them from the floor. 'It's all right, it's not a crime scene as such. The criminal never came near the place, so you can walk where you like.'

It was an ordinary bedroom with a big mirror-cupboard opposite the bed open wide. In front of it was a cricket bag, and laid out on the carpet were various pieces of equipment – batting gloves, a box, pads.

'What are we looking at?'

'Those,' Anderson said, indicating a pair of wicketkeeping gloves. 'And "looking" is the operative word. Don't touch.' He crouched down and very gently lifted one of the gloves. Standing up again, he presented it to the detectives. 'There,' he said softly, wagging the middle finger.

Dalliance craned forward.

'About halfway up.'

Dalliance peered closer. Then he saw it. The tiny dark needle sticking out barely a centimetre, like an insect's proboscis. He blew breath through his pursed lips.

'Quite,' said Anderson.

'What happened?' Riley asked.

'He was sorting his kit out for the weekend – and must have pricked himself.'

'If I gall him slightly, it may be death,' Dalliance muttered to himself, not for the first time that week.

'Hopefully not,' said Anderson. 'As I say, it didn't carry him off on the spot, and the medics don't think he got enough to kill him. But it'll be touch and go.'

'But I don't understand,' Riley said, frowning at the lethal glove. 'Why would someone in the Tilsby team have the murder weapon in their bag?'

'Must have been planted,' Dalliance said. 'The perfect hiding place when you think about it. Their kit wouldn't have been under suspicion.'

'But why plant it in the opposition wicketkeeper's glove?'

'Actually…' Anderson picked up the second glove and revealed what was inked inside the gauntlet: 'B. COWPER L BOLTON CC'.

Dalliance whistled through his teeth. 'Well, well. Get him brought into the station, Riley. Now. Even if it is bloody milking time'.

'But we went through his kit,' Riley said after he'd made the call. 'We looked at his gloves.'

'Ah,' sighed Dalliance, as though chiding himself. 'A lot of keepers have two pairs.'

'But he didn't say anything about having another pair.'

'If he'd just stuck it in the opposition changing room because it had a murder weapon sticking out of it, he wouldn't have, would he?'

Riley was fairly sure he heard a suppressed giggle from the figure kneeling over the open cricket bag. Nothing like being made to look a fool by your immediate superior. 'But he must have known he'd be found out – I mean, the glove's got his name on it.'

'You're right, Riley. So what do we deduce from that?'

Riley suddenly felt like a schoolboy put on the spot by the teacher. It didn't help that Sally had sat back on her haunches and was looking at him, as though waiting to see if he'd make a fool of himself.

'That it wasn't Cowper…?' he offered.

'Exactly. It was someone else's bright idea – a spur-of-the-moment thing. Clever, but maybe too clever by half. What have we got inside?' Dalliance asked Anderson.

'Too early to say. I'm not putting my fingers in there. We'll take it back to the lab and then cut our way in – with extreme caution.'

'Have we had the pathology report for Roper?'

'Not yet.'

'So they haven't identified the poison?'

'No. Which means it isn't one of the obvious ones. Something that could be acquired reasonably easily.'

'But will they be able to confirm this is the same stuff – and that that is the murder weapon?'

'Oh yes. Assuming it is.'

'There couldn't be two jokers messing around with poisoned darts on the same cricket team, could there?' Dalliance turned towards the door. 'I think we'd better go and meet the distraught wife.'

'It might be kind,' Anderson said. 'She's desperate to get over to the hospital to be with him.'

'Kids?'

'Two – nine and eleven. They're with her sister round the corner.'

'Okay. We'll be quick. And thanks.'

Dalliance went downstairs to the kitchen. It was a very different place to the one he'd been called away from – small, cramped even, with an array of unwashed pans on the electric stove and a pile of dirty plates in the sink.

'Good evening, Mrs—'

'Williams, sir,' the PC near the door prompted him.

'Mrs Williams. I'm very sorry about your husband, but the medics think he'll pull through.'

'Why would anyone want to hurt my Alan? It's such a shock – after last Sunday, I couldn't believe that, when he came home and said there'd been a murder. And now someone's tried to kill him.'

'I am ninety-nine percent sure that no one has tried to kill your husband, Mrs Williams. He was just unlucky. The killer was looking for somewhere to hide the murder weapon. He rightly worked out that the opposition's kit would be a good way of getting it off the premises.'

'But Alan's not even a wicketkeeper,' wailed Mrs Williams.

'No,' said Dalliance patiently. 'His bag was just chosen at random, and obviously your husband didn't get around to sorting through it until this evening.'

'But it could have killed him! Or the kids. They're always messing around with his kit – looking for balls to play with.' The thought was so disturbing that she started to sob.

At Dalliance's gesture, the young policewoman came forward with a tissue.

'Now, Mrs Williams, we must go I'm afraid. Our team have a little more work to do, and then we'll leave you in peace. If you want to go to the hospital, we can arrange transport. I believe your children are being looked after.'

Mrs Williams looked up through damp eyes. 'I don't know what to do. Nothing like this has ever happened to us.'

'I'm quite sure you and the children are in no danger whatsoever, and there is every reason to believe that your husband will be all right. As I say, if you would like to go to the hospital to see him, we can arrange transport.' With what he hoped was a reassuring smile, he pushed open the kitchen door. Anderson was in the hall.

'This really is the breakthrough we've been waiting for,' Dalliance said in a low voice. 'I want you to tell me everything you can about the needle once you cut it out of the glove.'

'What are we looking for?' Anderson asked.

'I don't know. Anything. Anything that will give a clue as to the delivery.'

'That's pretty obvious,' said Riley at his side.

'No, Riley, it is not. It may look obvious, but I think we'll find that it was made to look that way. And in fact, the murderer may have overplayed his hand.' Then to Anderson he said, 'I'll want to know whether, in your opinion, the needle, whatever it is, could have been fired from distance.'

'A dart of some kind?' Anderson said. 'I had wondered about that.'

'We are still pursuing an active line of enquiry along those lines, even though' – here he looked at Riley – 'the murderer wants us to think it was Cowper giving his captain a friendly pat on the back. At the cost of a very unpleasant experience for the Williams family, the murderer may have given us a very welcome helping hand. I doubt you'll find any other clues in Williams' bag, but check it for prints anyway.'

Sally Walker appeared at the top of the stairs. 'All done, sir,' she said, smiling brightly.

Riley felt uncomfortable craning to look up the steep stairs, and was relieved when Dalliance signalled that they were leaving. Sally gave him a surreptitious wave at chest-height, one he found impossible to respond to beyond an awkward little smile as he followed his boss down the hall-way to the front door.

'You know you went through a red light, sir?'

'Where?'

'Bottom of Castle Street, sir.'

Dalliance groaned. A parking ticket and a traffic offence in one day. 'I was thinking,' he said.

'You know what they say, sir?'

'What, Riley?'

'Don't think and drive.'

Dalliance looked up. 'Riley. We have what may be a long night ahead of us. Please don't make it any longer with piti-ful attempts at humour.'

'Sorry, sir.'

'Let's see what Cowper has to say for himself.'

Not a lot, as it turned out.

'You've taken your time. I've been sitting here for over an hour and a half. I do 'ave a farm to run.'

'And we have a murder investigation to conduct, Mr Cowper. Why didn't you tell us you had two pairs of wicketkeeping gloves?'

'You didn't ask.'

'And you didn't think it might be helpful for us to know?'

'Not my place to think. You're the detectives.'

'So when did you discover that one of your pairs of gloves had gone missing?'

'I didn't.'

'You didn't look in your bag when you got it back from forensics?' Riley asked.

'Why should I? I didn't suppose they'd nicked anything. And they'd packed it all back in so neatly – job done.'

'So it would surprise you to know a pair of your wicketkeeping gloves was found in the bag of one of the members of the visiting team?'

'Which one?'

'Alan Williams,' Riley said. 'Do you know him?'

'I meant which pair of gloves, sonny. The blue ones or the black ones?'

'Which were you wearing on Sunday?'

Cowper looked at him with his head slightly cocked.

'We can check.'

'Course you can. But I'll save you the bother – the black ones. Those are my first pair now; the blue ones are just backup – or for when the other team turn out not to have a pair.'

'Was that the case on Sunday?'

'Nah. Mick Tunley has his own gloves. He's a proper keeper, Mick is – not a stopper like some of them.'

'So can you explain why your blue gloves were found in Alan Williams' cricket bag?'

'Well, I sure didn't put them there. But if you found a ten-pound note in one of the fingers, that's definitely mine. I distinctly remember putting it there for a rainy day.'

Dalliance looked at him across the table in the interview room. 'No; but what it did have sticking through one of the glove fingers was the murder weapon. I'd take this a little more seriously if I were you.'

Cowper smiled back across the table. 'I know I didn't do it. I know you can't pin it on me. If someone stole my gloves and stuck a needle or a dart or whatever it is through one of the fingers – good luck to 'em. But you can't think I'd be so stupid as to put my gloves in someone else's bag – what, and hope nobody'd notice? Remember, Inspector, we had a while between the ambulance taking Ted off and the boys in blue turning up and saying hold on, it's a suspicious death. Why would I do something stupid with the incriminating evidence if I'd had that much time to do something sensible?'

Riley looked at his notebook. 'Did you go into the changing room during that period?'

'Of course I did. So did everybody else. We were all milling around trying to kill time. It wasn't a crime scene then, was it?'

'So why did you go into the changing room?'

'Get my smokes. Maybe check my mobile.'

'Why?'

'Why? You don't know much about farming, do you? Anything can go wrong – at any time. A cricket match is the longest I'm away from the farm in any given week. I just like to check everything's okay—'

'Back at the ranch?' Riley suggested.

'As you say, sonny, back at the ranch.'

'And on this occasion?'

'No sheep got itself tangled up in a barbed wire fence; no bullock got its leg stuck in a rabbit hole; the barn roof hadn't fallen in, and the house wasn't burning down. Now' – he looked meaningfully at the wall clock – 'It's been a pleasure talking to you gents, but talking of the farm has made me come over all homesick. And talking of sick, I do have an elderly mother who'll be creating hell if I don't get back and give her her bedtime cocoa.'

Dalliance looked at him from under hooded eyes. With the briefest of nods he signalled that the interview was over.

Cowper turned at the door. 'Thank you, Inspector – I'm glad you found my second pair of gloves.'

Dalliance was still scowling when Riley came back from escorting Cowper to the front desk. 'He won't be so pleased to see his bloody gloves by the time Anderson's finished with them. No word yet?'

Riley shook his head. 'Are we going to do Miller now? He's not happy, according to the duty sarge.'

'Miller's happiness is not my primary concern.' Dalliance rocked back in his chair. 'He's right, isn't he?'

'Who, sir?'

'Cowper. Cunning as a fox, that one. No way he'd have dumped his gloves in Williams' bag. And anyway, he wasn't even wearing the blue ones. And even if he had been, how do you keep wicket with a poison dart sticking out of your gloves? No, it was a plant, a deliberate attempt to incriminate him.'

There was a knock on the door, and the duty sergeant put his head round it.

'Are you going to see Miller, sir? He's kicking up a bit of a rumpus – saying he's got an important shooting match tomorrow and he needs a decent night's sleep.'

'Don't we all,' Dalliance replied. 'Okay, bring him in.'

Miller seemed even bigger than he had at the Poachers as he loomed in the doorway.

'Come in, Miller. Sit yourself down.'

'You can't send your goons out to drag innocent people in here at all hours of the day and night – I've got an important match tomorrow – as you know. This is harassment.'

'This is a murder investigation, Miller. I'm afraid it out-ranks a clay pigeon match. We've just invited you in to answer a few questions – help us with our enquiries.'

'Yeah, right. You're just trying to screw my chances of keeping the cup.'

'I'd screw them a lot more if I arrested you, wouldn't I?'

Riley watched Miller's shoulders. They looked as though they were expanding. A nerve in his throat started pulsing alarmingly. He was glad the sergeant had taken the precaution of putting a PC in with them.

'On what charge?' Miller asked belligerently.

'Can you tell us where you were on Sunday afternoon?'

'I wasn't anywhere near that bloody cricket ground.'

'The Inspector asked where you were,' Riley prompted.

Miller didn't bother to acknowledge him, continuing to stare across the table at Dalliance. Dalliance looked back at him. Then, just as the tension was getting unbearable, he glanced down at his notebook.

'You say you weren't anywhere near the cricket ground, but we have a witness who saw your pick-up in the village at about two-forty-five.'

'Stand up in court, that, would it? Got the registration?' Miller put both his hands down on the table, continuing to stare defiantly at Dalliance.

'Not the only way of identifying a vehicle, Miller – as you well know. A dark red pick-up with a scratch down the side and a bit of a bump on the nearside rear lights. You really should get that seen to, you know.'

Dalliance paused. Miller sat fuming. The vein in his neck was pulsing even more furiously.

'Yes,' he went on. 'Seen at about two-forty-five.'

'Who told you?'

'The Boltons have a very robust neighbourhood watch – the eyes and ears of the community.'

'If I find out who—'

'You're not proposing to threaten a witness, I hope, Mr Miller? That would be a very foolish thing to do.'

'You may be enjoying yourself, but let me tell you—'

Miller half got to his feet, and Riley and the uniform readied themselves to protect the Chief Inspector, when somebody's mobile rang. Everyone froze as Dalliance coolly picked up his phone.

'What have you got for me?'

There was a pause while Dalliance listened intently.

'And you're sure – absolutely sure? ... Okay, thank you very much.'

Dalliance put his phone back in his pocket.

'You're free to go, Miller.'

The big man stood, nonplussed.

'I thought you had an important shooting match to prepare for?'

Miller looked down at him, the anger draining from his huge face.

'Goodbye,' Dalliance said with the flicker of a smile. 'Oh, and get that rear light fixed. Could be three points if you get pulled over one of these nights. Take him back to the front desk,' he said to the PC, 'and ask the sergeant to arrange a lift home for him.'

As the door closed, Riley let out a sigh of relief. 'You were winding him up a treat, sir. I thought he was going to explode.'

'I'm sure you and PC Sykes would have been up to the task of restraining him.'

'I didn't know about his pick-up being seen. How did you know, sir?'

'As I said, Riley, neighbourhood watch. I put the word out – just on the off-chance.'

'And got a result – brilliant! But why did you let him go, sir?'

'Because whatever else he might have been doing in Lower Bolton on Sunday afternoon, he wasn't shooting poisoned darts into Ted Roper's backside. That was Anderson.' Dalliance indicated his phone.

'And?'

'Cannula. Common or garden, bog-standard NHS cannula that you or I've had stuck in our skin whenever anybody's wanted to draw blood out of us or drip saline into us. Whoever murdered Ted Roper was standing right next to him – not balancing on a branch sixty yards away with an elephant gun.'

Sixteen

On Saturday morning the two detectives sat in the Chief Inspector's office. They had just come from the hastily convened press conference, at which there had been a barrage of questions about the latest poisoning. Dalliance had explained, with increasingly diminishing patience, that he was quite sure the Tilsby player had not been deliberately targeted, that the initial killing was the only one the murderer intended, and that the community at large was completely safe.

'But you're no nearer identifying the murderer?'

'We're pursuing a number of lines of enquiry,' Dalliance had almost sighed in response.

'And what about the assault on Damien Peterson?' shouted a hack from Peterson's own tabloid. 'It's gone a bit quiet on that one, hasn't it?'

Dalliance admitted that it had.

'Are they related?' a voice from the back enquired.

Now Dalliance sat staring glumly into the muddy depths of his coffee. Riley sipped his own, waiting for his boss to break a silence which was becoming oppressive. He looked at the board on which the case was displayed in all its knotted complexity.

'So we can put a line through Miller,' he said eventually.

Dalliance grunted unhappily.

'We had to pursue it, sir.'

'We did indeed, Riley. And I'm still minded to look in on the clay pigeon shoot.'

'Even now Miller's out of the running?'

'It could be interesting. There'll be a lot of people there – we might pick up the odd undercurrent. You never know.' Dalliance took another pull at his coffee. 'How's our unintended victim, by the way?'

'Doing well, sir,' Riley said, noting, not for the first time, how bad his boss was at remembering names.

'And Peterson?'

'Gone home. They've taken him off the story.'

'Good riddance. He certainly kickstarted it all nicely for everyone.'

'It would be good to get the assault cleared up, wouldn't it?'

'It would,' Dalliance conceded.

'If we're sure Jez Jones and Steve Royce are out of the running—'

Dalliance banged his mug down on his desk and looked fiercely at his subordinate. 'We can't change facts, Riley, however inconvenient that may be.'

'So who do you think is in the frame?'

'Wake up at the back! I know it's Saturday morning and you'd rather be lying on the sofa getting the latest transfer news on Sky Sports, but you've got a brain, Riley. Engage it. We've got to look at the other candidates, however unlikely they may seem. What did you get on Phelps, for instance?'

Riley flicked open his notebook, without much enthusiasm.

'The accident was serious. Wasn't his fault. The other driver badly hurt – a broken leg, ribs, et cetera. Passenger on the critical list for a few days but survived.'

'Was Phelps hurt?'

'Nothing much on the physical front – cuts and bruises.'

'But psychologically?'

'Yes. Claimed – and got – fairly high compensation.'

'Which no doubt helped him relocate down here.'

'That's right – about six years ago.'

'And what do we know of his life in the Boltons?'

'Nothing. Living off his windfall and a disability allowance. Just keeps himself to himself.'

'Ever married?'

Riley shook his head. 'Doesn't make him a weirdo.'

'No,' Dalliance said, 'it doesn't.'

'Cricket club's probably the biggest thing in his life.'

'Which might mean he'd be up for handing out a bit of retributive justice to Peterson – to show he was a team man?'

'Seems unlikely, sir.'

'Well, we've got the boot prints from Anderson. Let's go and check his footwear, shall we? We can look in on him before we go to the clay shooting.'

'Did you ring Standing, sir?' Riley asked as he brought the car to a halt at the same lights Dalliance had jumped the night before.

'I did, Riley. You are now addressing Lower Bolton's number five and first slip.'

'Congratulations, sir.' He was pretty sure his boss was secretly pleased to be playing, but he wasn't going to push it.

'You were right, Riley. It is a good idea, even though I doubt I'll get through the afternoon with my dignity intact.'

'You might take a blinding catch, sir. Or hit a six.'

'Of the two, the former is marginally the more likely. And, as I pointed out yesterday, I shall be surrounded by a very hostile group of teammates, some of whom I've had to drag down to the police station for questioning at very unsocial hours.'

'How are you going to play it, sir?'

'With a straight bat, Riley. With a straight bat.'

There was a break in conversation. Riley slowed as they approached the turning down to the valley.

Dalliance resumed his preview of the day to come. 'I've arranged a cameraman. Atkins is going to be there with one of those traffic patrol cameras – so at least now we'll know how fast Steve Royce actually bowls! But I want the filming to be discreet. Actually, I thought we'd use the tree where we now know Miller wasn't waiting for his chance with the non-existent dart gun. There's a pretty good view and, as I say, I'd rather no one knew about it. Can you meet him there – about an hour before the start – and help him get in position?'

'Of course, sir.' Riley concentrated on the road ahead, suppressing thoughts about the comic potential of the match footage, and Dalliance's part in it.

A few minutes later they turned down Ernie Phelps' road.

'What exactly are we after, sir?' Riley asked.

'Results, Riley – however you wish to define that.'

Riley parked outside the drab house and soon they were both standing outside the front door, listening to the underpowered jangle of the doorbell. Phelps appeared and tried to force a smile of greeting, but he was clearly alarmed at their return.

'Mr Phelps. Sorry to bother you, but we'd like to ask you a few more questions if you don't mind.'

'I thought I told you everything you asked me last time,' he said, ushering them once more towards the Venus flytrap armchairs.

'You did, Mr Phelps,' Dalliance said, helping himself to an upright chair at the dining room table.

'But we've got some different questions today,' Riley said, following his boss' example.

'Oh well, of course, I'll do everything I can to help you,' Phelps said without enthusiasm.

'Sit down, Mr Phelps. Please.'

'Can I offer you something to drink – tea?"

'No need, but thank you very much. Now,' said Dalliance briskly. He sounded as though he were calling a meeting to order with a very full agenda to get through. Riley looked on in admiration, knowing that this was the flimsiest of fishing expeditions. 'Let's start with your accident.'

'What's that got to do with anything?'

'Probably nothing at all,' Dalliance conceded. 'But what I am interested in is why you were driving a van in the first place.'

Phelps looked blank. Dalliance raised his eyebrows.

'Well, it was my job.'

'Of course it was,' Dalliance agreed jovially. Phelps seemed to relax. Maybe, his expression seemed to say, if he humoured him, this intimidating detective would go away.

Wrong.

'But why was it your job? Or to put it another way, what was wrong with your previous job – your job driving school buses?'

Bingo! By luck or judgement Dalliance had put his finger on Phelps' weak spot. The man virtually imploded in front of them.

'Oh, not that again. Surely we don't have to go through all that again. It was years ago.'

'Nearly ten,' Dalliance agreed, looking at Riley's notes. 'We're only interested in the past in terms of how it might impact on the present. You have no criminal record, Mr Phelps; no charges were brought,' he said soothingly. 'But' – here he flourished the notes slightly – 'you ended your employment as a coach driver in October – very near the start of the school year. It might be that you fell ill, or changed your mind about the work you wanted to do, or wanted to move somewhere else in the country. But no. Three weeks later you start work as an HGV driver with Stones Transport, based in the same town as your previous employer, Wellington Coaches. That strikes me as curious, Mr Phelps.'

Riley looked across the table at Phelps. All the colour had drained from his face, and he was picking frantically at a shirt button. He looked at Dalliance, his face drawn with panic. Then he closed his eyes, stopped fiddling, and said in a voice barely louder than a whisper, 'All right, I'll tell you.'

There was a long silence. Dalliance waited patiently.

'I liked my job,' Phelps suddenly began. 'I liked the kids. They could be noisy, cheeky; they ragged me a bit. But I liked them, and never had any trouble with them. Nothing serious. Only reported a couple of them in nearly nine years.'

'But then?' Dalliance prompted softly.

Phelps' eyes stayed closed. Riley could see the glint of a tear under the pale lashes.

'They changed my route. Instead of the town they gave me a country route. I didn't mind. Change is as good as a rest. I liked the views out over the moors. I was fine with it. Except—' He broke off, and brushed away the tear. Without taking his eye off Phelps' face, Dalliance signalled to Riley to get a glass of water from the kitchen. Riley poured it as quietly as he could, came back, and set it down on the table.

'Take your time,' Dalliance said, as Phelps opened his eyes and, seeing the water, lifted the glass to his lips.

'It was a longer route – obviously. But I didn't mind that.'

'But there was a problem…?' Dalliance coaxed.

Phelps took another draught of water and nodded. 'Last two stops. Very few kids – just two or three.' Again the narrative ground to a halt.

'Girls?' Dalliance suggested.

Phelps nodded. 'At first I thought they were just larking about – you know, a bit boisterous. But after a while I twigged what they were up to.'

'And what were they up to, Mr Phelps?'

'I suppose they thought it was funny. They'd sit right behind me, giggling and whispering and then bursting out laughing. I should have reported them – straight away. I should have nipped it in the bud. But when I spoke to them they were all apologetic and butter-wouldn't-melt – you know. So I let it go, and they'd be fine for a week or so. But then it would start again – only worse, as though they were egging each other on.'

'There were two of them?'

'Veronica and Stacey. Never forget them. Veronica got off at the penultimate stop, and that left Stacey and an older boy – Jack, he was called. And he was in on it too. He was part of it. Well, they had him round their little fingers, winding him up – showing a lot of leg – asking him whether he thought about them when he went to bed at night – that sort of thing.'

He helped himself to another sip of water.

'On the day it happened, Jack wasn't on the bus. Maybe he was sick, or off on a course, or maybe the girls had told him to miss a day's school. Anyway, it meant that there were just the two girls on the last stretch of the journey, and they were messing about as bad as they'd ever been. Veronica came and sat right up at the front just across the aisle from me, and Stacey took her usual seat behind me. It was obvious they'd planned it, but I didn't know what they had in mind until they started asking questions – leading questions, like was I married? And did I have a girlfriend? Did I like girls? I very nearly stopped the bus, but I thought it would make things worse. Anyway, when we came to the penultimate stop and Veronica was getting up to go – pulling her skirt down and making a lot of her legs, if you know what I mean, she spilt her drink – quite deliberately, I'm sure. Anyway, there was orange or whatever all over the place. I told her to mop it up, and Stacey said something like, "Ooh, isn't she a

naughty girl?" And it must have been then that she did it –
while Veronica was distracting me.'

'What did she do, Mr Phelps?'

Phelps closed his eyes again, and breathed in deeply, then
sighed. Without answering Dalliance's question, he went on
with his story.

'"You look after yourself, Stace," Veronica said when
she'd wiped up the mess. And she said something to me as
well – another wind-up. I just told her to get off my bus
and said I was reporting them both. "We'll see about that,
Mr Phelps," she said, and minced off down the street, leaving me with four miles of Stacey, and wishing I could have
chucked her off the bus as well.'

'What happened?'

Phelps shook his head. 'She came and sat up front where
Veronica had been. And it just went on. Did I like girls? Was
that why I was a schoolbus driver? Did I know that some
girls really liked older men? It was awful. I tried to ignore
her – just concentrate on the road and counted down the
miles to the last stop.'

'And when you got there?'

Phelps ran his hand through his thinning hair. Riley
could see he was close to tears again.

'She got up out of her seat and stood right next to me
and looked down at me. I could see she had undone some of
her buttons and her shirt was untucked. "Well, Mr Phelps,
you are a one, aren't you?" she said, and she reached her
hand out – as though she was going to pat my cheek or
ruffle my hair. I slapped it away and shouted at her to get
off the bus. "Suit yourself," she said, and minced off, just
like her pal Veronica. I was shattered. I wasn't even sure I
could drive back to town, but I knew I couldn't stay there,
so I went back.'

There was a pause. Phelps drained the glass of water.

'And then?'

'They were waiting for me at the depot – your lot. Arrested me on the spot.'

'But it was only her word against yours.'

'It was more than her word,' he said bitterly. 'Vicious little...' He paused, and then almost spat out the word: '...bitch!'

'What had she done?' Dalliance asked gently.

'Only slipped her knickers off and stuffed them down the back of the seat.'

There was another silence.

'Even so,' Dalliance said, 'if there were no forensic evidence...'

'Which of course there wasn't – not a trace,' Phelps said indignantly, looking from Dalliance to Riley as if to compel their acceptance of his story. 'The very idea.'

'Which is why there was no charge, and no stain on your character, Mr Phelps.'

'Yeah, right.' He gave a deflated laugh. 'As the inspector said to me, "You don't need to be found with a black cat and a broomstick to be burnt for a witch."'

'So you quit, even though you were innocent?'

'One of the local papers had already got wind of it. "Paedo Express", they called my coach. They soon stopped that when my solicitor told them how much it was likely to cost them. But I could see which way the wind was blowing. Do you blame me?'

Dalliance shook his head. 'No. I feel very sorry for you.'

'Well, you've made me relive it, but I'm none the wiser as to why.'

Dalliance did not enlighten him. 'So you stayed in the same town, and carried on driving?'

'Long haul. I was away a lot. I didn't want to leave my house. I wasn't going to be driven out of my own home.' He suddenly looked up defiantly.

'But you did leave, didn't you? Why did you come down here?'

'I wanted a change. I wanted a new life. A scandal...well, it doesn't go away. It's always there. No smoke without fire, you know. You get so tired of it. And with the insurance from the accident I had the money to move. I'd done a few deliveries round here. It seemed nice. Thought my luck might change with a change of scenery.'

'And has your luck changed?' Riley asked.

Phelps looked at him in surprise. 'Yes – I should say so. I've been very happy here.'

'Anyone know about your past? Did you tell anyone – what you've told us?'

There was a long pause.

'I think you did,' Dalliance said. Then, leaning across the table, he went on. 'I think you told Ted Roper.'

Phelps closed his eyes again.

'I knew I shouldn't have done. I knew I should have kept my blessed mouth shut. But he was so – he was a nice man, Ted. And I – I don't have many friends. I'm not saying Ted was a friend, I wouldn't presume – but he took an interest – in everyone. Anyway, we were in the pub one evening, and we got talking and – I don't know – he sort of drew it out of me – like you just did. I don't think he meant to do any-thing with the story. In fact, the last thing he said to me was "Mum's the word". And I can remember him putting his finger up to his lips and giving me a broad wink.'

'And he never mentioned it again?' Riley asked.

'Never.'

'But somebody else did?' Dalliance suggested. 'Ted did tell somebody else?'

How does he know that? Riley wondered. Staring at Phelps, it was obvious he was right.

'Why did he tell someone else?'

Phelps sighed. 'Ted wanted to drop me; drop me from the cricket team. I know I'm not much good, but I love play-ing – being part of a team. Anyway, the person he was discussing it with said he should give me another season at least, begged him, really – saying I was lonely, and it really meant a lot to me, and so on, and that I'd hardly been dealt the best hand in life. And Ted said, "You don't know the half of it", and in no time he'd started telling my story.'

Phelps looked a picture of misery, sitting slumped in his chair with his hands limp in his lap.

'And you know that because the other person told you?'

Phelps nodded. Dalliance suddenly stood up.

'Thank you for being so honest with us, Mr Phelps. I'm sorry to have made you revisit the past, but it may be helpful to us.'

'But you won't tell anybody else, will you? If it gets out…'

Phelps let the sentence die out.

'Don't worry, Mr Phelps. Your secret is safe with us.' Dalliance said, getting to his feet. 'Thank you again. You've been very helpful. Come on, Riley. Time for a bit of clay shooting.'

'You didn't push him to say who Roper told his story to.'

'No, I didn't, Riley. Nor did I ask him his shoe size, or what had happened to the pair of boots I'd noticed in his porch last time we called and which weren't there today.'

'But I thought you were after results, sir?'

'I am. But some results are more important than others. We're primarily engaged on a murder case, Riley.'

'You don't think Phelps—'

'Is a suspect? No, I do not. You do not commit murder to avoid being dropped from a cricket team. Well, not at this level at any rate. And nor would a man like Phelps murder to keep the story of his earlier victimisation a secret. Anyway, I am ninety-nine percent certain he only suspected he was in danger of the word getting out *after* Ted Roper's death.'

'But surely it would be helpful to know who it was Roper told, sir?'

'I think we can make an educated guess, Riley. Sometimes it's best to keep one's powder dry, not frighten the horses, if you know what I mean. We know that someone has a hold over Phelps; it is highly probable, though not proven, that the person in question put pressure on Phelps to aid and abet the abduction of Peterson. As you rightly imply, it wouldn't take very much to get Phelps to tell us. But what I am really interested in is whether Phelps could have aided and abetted the same person in the murder of Roper. And the less we rattle the bars of that person's cage at this stage the better – in my judgement.'

Riley nodded, hoping he looked as though he understood Dalliance's thought processes.

Seventeen

'There we go.' Dalliance had spotted a large arrow painted on an oil drum and Riley lurched left up a track into the woods. As they wound further into the trees, they could hear the reports of the shotguns ahead of them. They finally reached a gate manned by a couple of women in waxed jackets and sturdy boots.

Riley lowered his window.

'Five pounds – park up there on the left.'

Riley started to fumble for his ID, before Dalliance muttered, 'Just pay.'

'No point in making a public announcement,' Dalliance explained as they bumped over the rough ground and found a spot in amongst the mud-splashed four-by-fours. Riley wondered how it was going to look on his expenses – five-pound entrance fee for clay shooting competition.

As they got out of the car there was a crescendo of shotbursts in the clearing that opened out through the trees. The shots came in twos, staccato pops in quick succession. In the aftermath there was a round of applause. The score was given out over the PA system, and the next contestant called up to the mark.

There was quite a crowd, corralled behind a rope loosely slung between iron stakes knocked into the ground. On the other side of the grass arena the competitors were similarly grouped. Dalliance noted the clay sling and its two-man team down to the right. Taking centre-stage was the next competitor, positioning himself on the little firing area, littered with empty cartridges. The man loaded his gun, nodded to indicate he was ready, and the clays were launched.

They look like Bakelite ashtrays, Dalliance thought, as his eye followed the dark discs flying against the blue sky. Pop! An explosion of black shards. A second pop! And the same result. Applause while the man reloaded, and then two more shots. The first was a hit, but he was too slow on the second and it sailed unharmed into the undergrowth. There was a slight sigh of sympathy from the crowd, before the man broke his gun and walked back to the competitors' enclosure.

'Bad luck, sir. The one that got away,' crackled the PA. 'And our next competitor, please – Mr Steven Royce.'

There was quite a cheer and Royce gave the crowd a cheery wave as he took his position.

So he did have a shotgun, Dalliance thought. Was he right to have let the incident with the air rifle go the other day? He watched on closely as Royce took out his four clays with time to spare, and walked off to loud applause.

'He'll be among those breathing down Miller's neck for the cup,' Dalliance said to Riley.

'I'm sure you're right, sir. But it would be interesting to know if the gun is his, and if so, whether it's properly registered. And where does he keep it? It won't be properly secure in that caravan of his.'

'Perhaps you could go round and ask him on Monday morning,' Dalliance said dryly. 'Or I could bring it up if I find myself batting with him.'

More competitors followed. The standard of shooting was high, though there was clearly a divide between the very best and the also-rans. One man missed three out of four and retired with the condescending condolences of the announcer ringing out over the PA.

Then Jessie Miller was called. There was a burst of applause and cheering that suddenly hushed as he took his position. He looked, Dalliance thought, like a batsman – a good batsman – standing at the crease: perfectly balanced, watchfully still, relaxed, and above all, confident.

A brace of clays, taken with even greater ease than Royce had displayed; the reload, and then two more – pop, pop – and a second shower of black shards falling on the grass towards the end of the clearing. Miller cocked open his gun, and walked unhurriedly back to the enclosure, merely raising one hand to acknowledge the crowd. He looked every inch the champion.

'Magnificent shot, isn't he, Inspector?'

Dalliance felt an arm thrust through his and found himself looking into the smiling face of Jenny Henderson.

'I didn't know you were interested in "country matters"?' she said, rippling her eyebrows.

Dalliance suppressed a wince, though he noticed that her gaze had turned to follow the retreating figure of Miller.

'I can't see another man to touch him, Inspector,' she said with a light little laugh, and then, releasing his arm, she swung away through the crowd towards the refreshment tent.

'Got off lightly there, sir,' Riley said, watching the shapely figure carving a path through the spectators.

'She seems to have her eye on Miller.'

'Miller?'

'Keep your voice down. There's enough gossip flying around here without us adding to it.'

'So do you think that's why his pick-up was seen in the village on Sunday?'

'Certainly one explanation – while Henderson's otherwise engaged at the cricket.'

'Is that what she meant by "country matters", sir?'

'Shakespeare certainly milks its ambiguity in Hamlet. I tended to downplay it myself.'

Was that a fleeting smirk of self-satisfaction? Riley wondered. But then his attention returned to the shooting area.

'Another familiar face,' Dalliance murmured.

Jez Jones looked anything but relaxed as he took his stance. He snatched at his first shot and missed, but recovered well to score three. Barney Grover followed him and bagged all four of his clays, while Ben Cowper was last to go and ended the round with three.

'Well done, Ben Cowper,' the PA crackled. 'And now, ladies and gentlemen, there will be a short break while the judges confirm those going through to the next round. The finest quality burgers are being served in the refreshment tent, along with tea, coffee and cold drinks. And may I urge you to buy a raffle ticket; first prize – a side of our best local Dexter beef.'

'Not sure I could get a side of beef into my freezer,' Dalliance remarked.

'I've only got a freezer compartment in my fridge, so I'm definitely out of the frame,' Riley said. 'But I could murder a burger.'

'Perhaps not the best choice of words, Riley. But we do seem to have missed a meal, so if you are hungry, there's the place to go.' A lot of people were of the same mind. The refreshment tent was heaving.

'I'd have thought you might have been in the nets, Inspector.'

Dalliance looked to his left to find Norman Standing smiling at him.

'Too late for that I'm afraid – I'd probably pull a muscle or something. No, I just thought we'd look in on the weekend's other main attraction. I see you're taking part.' Standing was dressed in a very smart shooting outfit. 'How did you do? We got here a bit late.'

'Oh, not too bad. I've made the cut for the next round. But it gets tough now.'

'I suppose Jessie Miller's the hot favourite?'

Standing nodded. 'Realistically the rest of us are just competing for the runner-up slot.'

'Well, good luck.'

'Thanks. And see you at the cricket field about two-fifteen tomorrow.'

They had inched towards the burger stall during this conversation, and Riley was peering at the options chalked up on a blackboard. Dalliance was beginning to find the fumes from the barbeque offensive. With a vague hand gesture, he stepped out of the line and edged back towards the opening of the tent in search of fresh air. He had just pushed past the flap when he heard a familiar voice.

'Inspector! What a nice surprise!' It was Margot Roper.

'You've met Charlie, of course,' she said. 'And this is his equally jetlagged sister, Fiona.'

Dalliance nodded at the well turned-out young woman. 'I'm very sorry about your father,' he said.

'Being sorry won't bring him back,' Fiona said tartly. 'I had hoped you might have caught the bastard who did it by the time I got home.'

'Fiona, darling; I'm sure the Inspector is doing all he can.'

'Standing around the refreshment tent at a clay pigeon shoot is hardly cutting-edge detective work,' Charlie muttered, loudly enough for Dalliance to hear.

'Why don't you two go in and get yourselves some food,' Margot said, clearly embarrassed by their hostility. 'I am sorry, Inspector,' she said, watching them shouldering through the crowd towards the food queue. 'I'm afraid they're both taking it rather badly. And they really are exhausted, the pair of them.'

'That's quite all right. These things always seem to take an age, and as we can't exactly post a running commentary of our progress on social media – unlike football players and pop stars – it often looks as though we're not doing anything.'

'I'm sure no one suspects that, Inspector. But have you made any progress?'

Yes, Dalliance thought to himself. We've eliminated you from our enquiries, satisfied that you did not conspire with one J. Miller to assassinate your husband. He sighed, suddenly and surprisingly interested in the trees at the far end of the clearing.

'A little, I think. Things are becoming clearer, let's just put it like that.'

'And that crisis that took you away so suddenly? I didn't see anything in the press about it this morning.'

No, they'd been lucky there; Dalliance hoped that, with the patient recovering strongly, they might keep it off the front pages in the morning. He looked Margot Roper in the eye. 'Crisis over. It was related to Ted's case, and was useful. Very useful, in fact, though I'd rather keep the details quiet for the moment.'

'I do understand, Inspector. Unlike my ungracious offspring, I have complete faith in you.' She smiled warmly at him. Then, as though she'd just remembered it, she said, 'That question you were about to ask me, when you were called away?'

'No longer important,' he said, breaking off eye contact quickly. The embarrassment of suspecting her of initiating her husband's murder was not about to die down any time soon.

'Well, if you do think of anything else you want to ask me, you know where I am. Enjoy the rest of the afternoon.'

Dalliance watched her striding through the crowds, nodding to friends and acquaintances as she went. He was glad the question of the life insurance policy was no longer relevant, and particularly glad her two obnoxious children hadn't got wind of it.

Riley emerged from the catering tent, a burger in hand. 'Delicious,' he said. 'Are you sure you don't want anything? The hotdogs looked pretty good.'

The PA started to announce the names of the competitors going through to the next round.

'You've got ketchup on your chin,' Dalliance said.

The crowds were beginning to return to their vantage point on the rise overlooking the shooting arena, but Dalliance didn't stop once they regained their original position. Instead he marched on through the trees to the parking area.

'Is that it, sir?' Riley asked through a final mouthful of burger.

'Come on, Riley; don't tell me you want to spend the rest of the afternoon watching people blasting crockery to bits. I said I wanted to see Henderson again, and this seems a propitious moment, don't you think?'

Riley wiped his face and hands with the paper napkin provided with his burger and climbed into the driving seat. 'I wonder if he knows his wife's at the shooting?' he said as he edged out from between two giant four-by-fours.

'And I wonder if he cares? Actually, I suspect he's secretly delighted. A lot of marriages only work because one of the parties adopts the blind-eye policy.'

Riley stole a glance to his left and was disconcerted to catch Dalliance's eye.

'In case you're wondering, I found that was not an option.'

Riley nearly hit a tree, so surprised was he at this rare personal confession. He was still trying to formulate some sort of verbal response to it when Dalliance continued.

'Infidelity is very wearing. Some people can put up with. I couldn't.'

On second thoughts, Riley decided, he probably shouldn't say anything. He raised his hand vaguely to the girls on the gate and bumped on down the track to the metalled road that would take them to the Hendersons'.

'Mr Henderson, thank you so much for allowing us to interrupt your peaceful afternoon at home.'

'I don't know about peaceful, Inspector.' They were sitting out on the terrace under a sunshade, well within earshot of the clay pigeon shooting on the other side of the hill.

'It's a lot noisier close up,' Dalliance smiled.

'Did you see Jenny there?'

'We did. Well, she saw us. Seemed to be enjoying herself.'

'She normally does,' Henderson said, pouring himself another tumbler of the Pimm's he'd rustled up after inviting them in. 'So, Inspector, what can I help you with – assuming you haven't come to arrest me?'

'No, Mr Henderson, we haven't come to arrest you.'

'Are you any nearer to arresting anybody else?'

Dalliance looked into the thicket of freshly plucked mint in his glass. 'I wouldn't like to say. Put it this way – some things are becoming clearer. And with your help perhaps they'll become clearer still.'

'Fire away, Inspector. I'll help you if I can.'

'What would you say your relationship with Ernie Phelps was?'

Henderson looked slightly taken aback.

'To be honest with you, I wouldn't think of myself as having a relationship with him – beyond being in the same cricket team together. And even then, we're about as far apart as it's possible to be. And by that I don't just mean I open the batting and he comes in at number eleven.'

'So I don't suppose you spend much time at the crease together?'

'I may have the reputation as the team's Boycott, Inspector, but the days of my carrying my bat are long gone. If I see the shine off and get past twenty I consider I've done my job. If I push on to fifty, it's a red-letter day. We did have one stunning collapse a few seasons back. Ernie joined me with the score on 59 for 9. I think we nudged it up into the nineties. But that's the only time I think I've ever batted with him.'

'And socially?'

Henderson shook his head. 'Don't get me wrong, I enjoy the company of my teammates, and frankly if I didn't, I wouldn't be playing village cricket. Get Ben Cowper going on EU subsidies or Barney on Health and Safety – far more entertaining than a bunch of landscape gardeners, I can tell you. But Ernie – well, he never says anything unless you ask him. One of life's natural wallflowers. And happy to be one, I'd say.'

'But he enjoys being part of the team?'

'Oh, he loves it. To be quite honest, I think it's the highlight of his week.'

'What sort of a bowler is he?' Dalliance asked.

Henderson thought for a moment. 'Deceptive,' he said eventually. 'By which I mean that he looks as though he should go at about twenty an over, but in fact, on a good day, with everyone on their toes in the field and catching their catches, he can be quite effective.'

'Worth his place?'

'I don't know about that. But it's hardly an issue as we're normally scraping round for eleven men who have white trousers and can stand up. And a little bird whispers that you fall into that category, Inspector?'

Dalliance nodded. 'Whether the white trousers are going to survive the experience or not remains to be seen. I've been too cowardly to try them on.'

Henderson laughed sympathetically. 'Any problems, just ring Margot; I'm sure she'd have a pair of Ted's that would fit you.'

'I've heard of dead men's shoes, but I hope it won't come to dead men's trousers,' Dalliance said, looking down at his own trunk. He hadn't put that much weight on, had he? 'Anyway, getting back to Phelps. Is there anybody in the team he seems close to?'

Henderson thought. 'Not really. He's a bit like a dog, really. He just likes being there. And if anybody throws him a conversational bone, he's as happy as Larry.'

'What sort of conversational bone?'

'Oh, you know, a bit of banter about his fielding, or a wicket he's taken. There was one the other week. An absolute pie – full-toss, slow, high, ripe for swatting into the barley. And the chap missed it. Bowled him middle stump. Talk about collapse of stout party – we were in fits. Just couldn't help it. And of course in the pub afterwards, Barney and Rees, I think it was, pushed the tables back and staged a re-enactment. Funniest thing ever.'

'And Phelps didn't mind them taking the Mickey?'

'Absolutely loved it. Never seen him so happy.'

'So if there had been any suggestion of his being dropped from the team...?' Riley suggested.

'Oh, he'd have been devastated. Obviously he can't expect to play forever, but he'd put off hanging his boots up for as long as possible, I'm sure of that.'

'Tell me about Barney,' Dalliance changed the subject. 'Now, he's someone you share a lot of time with at the crease. How does that work?'

'Very well. I keep my end up, and Barney perpetrates carnage at the other end.'

'Aggressive?' Dalliance asked.

'I'll say. He's unbelievably strong. When Barney hits it, it stays hit. I love batting with him. Two fours an over, minimum. All I have to do is nudge a single down to fine leg to get him back on strike and watch the fireworks from the other end. My only worry is him whacking one straight back and pinning me. But there's not much danger of that really – Barney's not the most orthodox – but with an eye like that, it hardly matters.'

'But there must be days when he fails.'

'Of course, and that's when I really earn my keep. Mind you, Rees is a good bat, and Norman – well, Norman's real class. He shouldn't really be playing at this level. But he's good as gold. Never really rubs it in. Gets to fifty, biffs it around a bit and gives it away to let the rest of them bat. Unless, of course, we need him to see it out – and then you really see some skill. Hopefully you'll see him score a few tomorrow. You'll almost certainly bat with him – and that is a joy, I can tell you.'

Dalliance wasn't sure how much of a joy it would be having his rustiness shown up by a class-act in mid-season form, but at least he wouldn't be expected to take the lead. 'Going back to Barney...'

'Pretty much what you see is what you get. Direct, some would say too much so, but I don't agree. It's just his manner. Mind you, he'll fight his corner – and yours, too, if you're on the same team.' Henderson paused. 'I haven't thought about this for ages – almost forgotten it even happened – but there was an instance of that on a tour we went on – oh, many years ago now. It was when Ted still had the energy, the drive, the leadership to make something like that happen. Went down to Devon. Lovely trip – and some good cricket, too. But there was one night – in Barnstaple – must have been the Friday, I think. We were all drinking away in a pub – making a fair bit of noise, I'm sure, but nothing untoward. Anyway, we all lurched out at closing time, and after a while we realised we were being followed. About half a dozen of the locals were of loitering with intent. Big lads too, some of them.'

'What happened?' Dalliance asked.

'Nothing much in the end. But there was an unpleasant moment. We stopped and faced them, and they sort of fanned out. I remember feeling distinctly uncomfortable. Ted opened his mouth and was going to say something, but Barney just put his hand on his shoulder and then walked towards them. I didn't quite hear what he said but it was along the lines of "Who wants it then?" One of their guys stepped out to meet him. Ted called out "Barney", but Barney didn't take any notice. He just stood there with this great hulking fellow towering over him. He didn't strike the first blow; but when the guy swung a haymaker at him, he certainly struck the second. There was no need for a third. Ten minutes later we were all back in the hotel bar getting the pints in – I think Barney bought the first round. And you wouldn't have known it had happened, apart from the bruise on his knuckles.'

'So, a bit of a Bronson figure then?'

'I don't expect you to approve, as a police officer, but I have to say he got us out of a very nasty spot.'

'So if someone's in trouble—'

'He'll be there for you.'

'Even if it means breaking the law?'

'I'm sure if there'd been a bobby on the beat that night in Barnstaple he'd have left it to him – but the fact is there wasn't.'

'Was Steve Royce on that tour?'

'No, no he wasn't. He'd still have been in the army. My word, there'd have been serious trouble if he had been there. I feel sorry for the man; but frankly he's a menace.'

'Dangerous?'

'Extremely. Once he goes, he's gone. No sense of proportion. As I say, if he'd been there that night, there'd have been blood on the cobbles, I can tell you that for a fact. As I say, I feel sorry for him. The army should take more care of their own – they train them up as killers, expose them to the horrors of war, discharge them back into society, and they're damaged – irremediably in some cases.'

'And you'd say Royce is one of those, would you?'

'Look, I'm a landscape gardener not a psychiatrist, but I saw what he did to his wife before she finally saw sense and allowed them to chuck him out. But I shouldn't be sitting here dishing the dirt on my teammates – and yours, come to that. They're a fine bunch taken all in all. They've got their faults, but then haven't we all? I choose to spend my Sunday afternoons in their company and I think loyalty determines that I should talk them up rather than talk them down.'

'Fair enough. But do remember one – or more – of them killed Ted Roper a week ago, and it's our job to bring the guilty to justice.'

There was a sudden crescendo of noise from the other side of the hill – clapping and cheering – signalling the end of the shooting match and the award of the cup to the champion. Riley thought he saw a slight shadow flicker across Henderson's face, but it was instantly replaced by the bland smile of a host at the end of a visit.

'Well, Inspector, I hope my slight indiscretions will prove helpful, though I would thank you to keep this little interview strictly private, and I look forward to seeing you at the cricket ground tomorrow afternoon.'

'Thank you, Mr Henderson.'

'David, please – at least when we're rubbing shoulders in the changing room.'

'David, then,' Dalliance said, getting up slightly stiffly.

He did not, Riley noted, offer his own first name in return.

'Useful, sir?' he asked when they were back in the car.

'Could be,' came the reply. Dalliance was staring out ahead, though Riley suspected he was hardly registering the Hendersons' beautifully landscaped lawns and flowerbeds.

'Where to next, sir?'

'Let's take a look at cricket ground. Perhaps there'll have been a riot of moles on the square enforcing a late cancellation.'

But as they drove onto the field, all they could see was Hancock walking steadily up the wicket with his lawn-mower. Clearly everything in the groundsman's world was as it should be. He broke off to greet them as they approached.

'Good afternoon, Inspector. I hear you're playing for us tomorrow.'

'I'll be here – I can't say I feel very optimistic about my contribution.'

'Ted wasn't a great bat,' Hancock said, glancing meaning-fully up from under his cap. 'Safe pair of hands, but that slip catch was about the only contribution he'd made in a month of Sundays. Poor bugger.' He slipped off his cap, revealing the bevelled indentation across his forehead. 'Any closer to catching the bastard?'

Dalliance shook his head. 'I don't suppose you've got a suspect for me?'

'What with one thing and another, they mostly all had grievances against him. But you don't top a man – and espe-cially your cricket captain – just because he's proving a bit of a bugger as a landlord. I can't make it out. Still, must get on – need to make it as smooth a surface as possible for you tomorrow, Inspector. And I hope you get more than you did last time you played here!'

'Fat chance,' Dalliance muttered as they walked away from the square. As they approached the sightscreen, he pointed to the old oak whose leaves swayed gently in the breeze. 'So, Atkins up there, filming every ball...'

'Have you ever seen yourself bat, sir?' Riley enquired.

'No, and it's far too late to work on my technique now. And don't get any ideas, Riley. I will be keeper of the foot-age, assuming it throws up nothing that can be used in court, so don't get any ideas about slipping clips to your mates in the canteen.'

Riley looked away guiltily. You really didn't get much past him, did you? he thought. Dalliance was looking about him, holding an invisible bat and playing imaginary shots.

'What do you want me to do once I've helped Atkins get set up?'

'Blend with the crowd – not that there'll be a crowd. Just mooch around, I suppose – figure in a landscape kind of thing. This is a low-key operation, Riley. It's going to seem strange enough having the senior officer in the murder enquiry playing in the same team. I don't want to spook them any further. Which is why you'll be the only other officer present.'

'What am I looking for in particular, sir?'

'In particular? Nothing in particular, Riley. Just keep your eyes open. Loiter with intent. I don't know what I'm looking for either. It's just that someone in that team killed Ted Roper, and it's really getting to me that we haven't worked out who.'

'Are you going to stage a reconstruction, sir?'

'Hadn't thought to. I'll suggest we field first – and I'll ask Norman to bowl the same bowlers for roughly the same length of time. But beyond that, just let nature take its course. Obviously it would be wonderful if I got a slip catch – and even more wonderful if I caught it. But if that doesn't happen I might suggest we fake it at the end of the innings. We can watch the footage on Monday morning – assuming I survive in one piece.'

EIGHTEEN

Dalliance felt doubly uncomfortable as he entered the home dressing room at Lower Bolton. Firstly his whites had put up a terrific struggle, and although he had forced them on, it felt as if they could split at any moment. Secondly, he was walking into a room filled with people whose lives he had been making a misery over the previous week.

'Ah, Dalliance, got into your kit, I see!'

Although Norman Standing made a jocular attempt at a greeting, the other faces looking up at him were either indifferent or downright hostile.

'Come over here,' Standing said, making a bit of space on the bench that ran along the wall.

'Thanks,' Dalliance said, dropping his bag on the floor and sitting down to put his cricket boots on. They were tight as well. He was just easing on the second one when there was a commotion at the door.

'If it ain't the Dancing Detective!' Barney Grover made his entry. 'They say lightning never strikes twice, though whether that applies to murder or slip catches I wouldn't like to say.'

Dalliance preferred laughter to the watchful silence. He was obviously going to be the focus of attention, at least until the game started and everyone could concentrate on the cricket. A few jocular barbs wouldn't do him any lasting damage.

'Okay, gentlemen.' Norman Standing raised his arms for quiet, which came, if grudgingly. 'No one's pretending this is just another day at the office. But we're going to try to make it as ordinary a game of cricket as we can. I'm sure you all understand why Inspector Dalliance is here. He is trying to resolve the situation and restore things to normality as quickly as he can. We are going to help him – and the best way we can do that is by behaving as normally as possible—'

'Without bumping anyone off – we'll try.'

'Thank you, Des. While the Inspector is going to help us by standing in for Ted so we have a full team. Which, I see, we don't actually have yet.'

Standing looked round at his team. Dalliance was to his right, then David Henderson, Rees Jones, Barney Grover, Steve Royce nearest the door; and on the other side of the tiny room, Jez Jones, Des Tucker, Ben Cowper and Ernie Phelps.

'Ah, Daniel. Well done. In you come.'

Dalliance looked at the boy trying to take his place as self-effacingly as possible. Like Dalliance he had come ready-changed. He had his bag in his left hand and Dalliance noticed a pink charity bracelet loose about the boy's wrist, setting off the colour of his suntanned arm.

'I've spoken to the Durnley skipper and explained that we need to field first' – there was a suppressed groan – 'because that's what happened last week. But apart from that, we're playing it absolutely straight. This is a proper cricket match, so let's go out there and show them what we're made of. Roller, you'll start from the top end, and Des from the sightscreen end – okay?'

Dalliance got up as gingerly as he had sat down. He'd have to ask for a transfer to another police authority if he split his trousers. He felt his stomach churning. There were nerves, certainly, but just a hint of genuine excitement. He hadn't played in a match for over five years, and that had been just a silly evening knockabout game with half the participants wearing tracksuit bottoms and trainers. This, however, was the real thing, and although he was acutely aware of how far from fitness and any sort of form he was, there was just the most fleeting hope that he might do something useful – a catch or a scratchy twenty minutes at the crease.

'D'you want to check 'em for poison darts?' Ben Cowper held out his wicketkeeping gloves to him, and Dalliance managed a watery smile. 'When am I going to get me second pair back?'

Thinking of the mess Anderson had made of them made Dalliance smile more robustly. He would enjoy returning them when the case was over.

Though goodness knew when that would be.

'I'd give it another yard or two, if I were you. Steve can be a little bit feisty, and I think he's charged up for this one.'

This was Standing, taking his position at second slip. Dalliance stepped back so he was almost alongside him. Beyond Standing, Barney raised a cheerful hand of greeting from gully. 'Good luck! But watch your back if you take a catch!'

The opening batsman was taking his guard from a fellow teammate. Dalliance wished people wouldn't come out in shorts and sandals to umpire, but he knew that was a lost cause.

Meanwhile Steve Royce was marking out his run. It wasn't a very long one, twelve or fifteen paces. Dalliance was briefly reassured, until he saw Royce casually propel the ball to Rees Jones at cover. The ball fairly skipped off the grass.

Dalliance took another step backwards.

'Play!' shouted the umpire.

Watch the edge of the bat, he told himself as he bent down with his hands held loosely in front of him. He was still bent forward when the red blur of the new ball whistled past his left ear. He was dimly aware of a ripple of malicious laughter, and turned to see the ball scudding over the outfield, vainly pursued by Daniel.

'Four wides!' shouted the umpire.

'Come on, Steve, get your line right,' Standing shouted. Then to Dalliance he said, 'I wouldn't watch the edge with Roller. Think Steve Harmison and watch the ball. Sorry, should have warned you.'

The next delivery was straighter and thumped into Cowper's gloves as he took it on the rise.

'Good wheels, Roller!' Barney shouted. The opening batsman looked decidedly uncomfortable.

The next ball released all the pressure, sailing wide down the leg. Cowper got a finger to it, but couldn't stop it, and Daniel ran in and threw it back.

'Good arm, boy – well done,' Des Tucker called out to him.

One bye, and the batsmen changed ends. The new batsman was short, stout and pugnacious. 'Middle!' he almost bellowed at the umpire, and when given his guard started pawing the white line of the crease with his studs.

'Digging your grave then, Alf?' Cowper called out to him.

Alf ignored him and looked up to face Steve Royce. When the ball came, he took a tremendous swipe at it. Fortunately he missed by a mile.

'He's gone fishing!' Barney shouted to Royce.

Much to Dalliance's consternation, he continued in the same vein. Two more heaves resulted in horribly near-misses. When he did finally make contact, it was a meaty top edge that sailed over Norman Standing's head. Rees Jones hared after it but never stood a chance of saving the boundary.

'It gets a little less manic at this end,' Standing said as they walked down the wicket at the end of the over. 'I won't be with you very long – I'll drop out into the covers in a couple of overs. But Des does hurry them through, and there's nothing more annoying than seeing a catch go begging because you haven't got a second slip.'

Dalliance was relieved to see Cowper standing much nearer the stumps, and he and Standing moved up accordingly.

As Des Tucker marked out his ten pace run-up, Dalliance looked down the ground. He thought he caught a glint of the police camera in the leaves above the sightscreen. Near it was a lone figure – Riley, doing his best to blend into the landscape. Unfortunately hovering near the sightscreen was not the way to keep a low profile, and the batsman was soon waving his hand as though despatching a troublesome wasp. The umpire turned and also started wafting crossly. 'Move!' he shouted, and Riley, realising he was the focus of attention, started walking purposefully round the boundary picket.

Can't take him anywhere, Dalliance thought, hoping that no one had recognised him.

With Riley removed, the batsman was prepared to face the first ball of the new over. Everything about him suggested an easy relaxation. And who could blame him? Dalliance thought. I'd certainly aim to be at this end facing Des than Steve Royce's erratic thunderbolts at the other.

Des came in, taking slightly mincing steps, and delivered the ball. The batsman lunged forward – and missed it. Cowper took it and flung it to Standing, rather pointedly missing out Dalliance. It made its way back to Tucker who came in again, and again delivered a decent delivery on a good length.

Dalliance allowed himself a gruff 'Well bowled!' and felt rather self-conscious about it. He rubbed his hands in anticipation. He could be in business if Des kept to what was now known as the corridor of uncertainty. Riley, he was pleased to see, had continued round the perimeter fence and was standing behind Rees Jones at cover.

Tucker's third ball was faster, and induced the edge Dalliance had been waiting for. Unfortunately, it didn't quite carry, squirting along the ground towards him. But at least he got a hand to it and saved himself from the ignominy of letting it through his legs.

'Good stuff, Des,' Barney called out, while Standing murmured encouragingly to Dalliance, 'You never lose it.'

They were the last four words he ever spoke.

'Come on, Des!' Barney called out. Des started his run and trotted up to the stumps to deliver the ball. The batsman raised his bat high, and for a moment Dalliance thought he was going to go for the drive, with the possibility of snicking the ball at catching height into the slips.

Dalliance watched the ball's flight carefully, and the batsman did indeed have a go at it. But it must have moved away at the last minute because it went through to Cowper's gloves without deviating. Cowper let out a shrill expletive to register how close the bat had come to making contact, but Dalliance was surprised to hear what sounded like a sharp appeal from his right. Standing was surely far too classy a cricketer to try to con the umpire into giving a soft dismissal.

But when his fellow slip lurched forward with a terrible moan, he could see he had misread the situation entirely.

Barney got to him first and pointed at the unmistakable dart sticking out of Standing's lower rump.

'Christ!' Dalliance exclaimed, reaching for it and trying to tug it out of the flesh. It was only when he'd wrested it free and flung it onto the grass that he noticed Barney had gone. Looking round, he saw the burly figure sprinting towards the top end of the ground.

'Riley!' he shouted. 'STOP HIM! STOP GROVER!

Riley leapt over the fence and started sprinting across the outfield. He seemed in two minds but Dalliance yelled at him again. 'STOP OUR MAN – NEVER MIND THE SHOOTER!'

A glance at Standing showed that there was scant hope of resuscitation. With a barked order for someone to ring for police and ambulance – and a warning that no one touch the dart – he set off after Barney.

Riley got there first, cutting him off just before the boundary, and made a brave attempt to tackle him, but he was clearly not going to manage on his own.

'Hold him – I'm coming!' Dalliance bellowed, summoning up every last reserve of energy.

Barney had nearly shaken Riley off by the time he reached them.

'Gotcha!' Dalliance sighed as he fell on top of the struggling plumber.

Gotcha? What did he mean? Riley thought as he tightened his grip on Grover's leg. He surely can't have thought Barney responsible?

Barney was obviously thinking along the same lines. 'What are you idiots doing?' he shouted.

'Saving your life,' Dalliance gasped back. 'But don't thank me – it's included in your council tax.'

At that point Barney ceased to struggle. Sitting up and spitting grass out of his mouth, he said, 'He got away. You let him get away.'

'Having only killed one person. The one he came to kill. But he'd have killed you too, if you'd got to him.'

Barney looked at him in disbelief.

'Health and Safety gone mad,' Dalliance said to him. 'Ah, Atkins.'

Riley looked up to see the Atkins sprinting up to them.

'Are you all right, sir?' he gasped.

'Fine, thank you. How much of that did you get?'

'I don't know. I stopped filming after you and the sergeant started to give chase. I have to say, I don't think this is our man.'

'Of course he's not our man. Riley and I were just saving him from becoming another victim.'

Atkins looked nonplussed. 'But I thought the murderer was one of the team?'

'The first murderer, yes. Not the second. Never mind. Go and take charge back there,' Dalliance ordered brusquely. 'Get them away from the body. I pulled the dart out and placed it on the grass. Obviously it's lethal, so don't let anyone touch it. Call SOCO. Anderson and his team can spend another Sunday afternoon looking for evidence, though they won't find much. We can go through the footage at the station.'

Still looking bemused, Atkins turned and headed off to the gaggle of cricketers grouped around the body of Norman Standing. Barney got to his feet and brushed himself down.

'Well, he'll have gone now,' he said, casting a baleful look over the rippling barley beyond the fence. 'I could have caught him, I'm sure I could.'

'Not before he got you.'

'So you say, but I'm pretty handy when it comes to the rough stuff.'

Dalliance shook his head. 'This wasn't a closing time stand-off in a Barnstaple side street, Barney. That was a contract killer, a professional. You'd never have laid a finger on him. And without Riley's commendable intervention, we'd almost certainly have had another corpse on our hands.'

Barney looked doubtfully at Riley, who was no clearer as to what had just happened than he was.

'A contract killer, sir? You seem very sure. Were you expecting this?'

'Of course I wasn't expecting it, Riley! Do you think I'd have been standing next to a man I suspected was going to be shot without doing anything to prevent it?'

'You must have been expecting something to happen if you had a bloke up a tree with a camera,' Barney chipped in.

'Atkins was just getting us some footage to help us get our heads round Ted's murder. I can only repeat, I was not expecting anything untoward to happen today.'

'But when it did—'

'Yes, Riley, when it did, I knew instantly what had happened. I also knew it had nothing whatsoever to do with our case.'

Barney and Riley looked at him, astonished.

'I'm sorry?' Barney said. 'Say that again.'

'Although there was certainly a similarity – a deliberate similarity, I'm guessing – to Ted's killing, the murder of Norman Standing was not related. As I say, it's got nothing to do with our case.'

Barney continued to stare at him in disbelief.

'Detective work's like that. Oh, it's all about taking notes and comparing statements and drawing timelines on the whiteboard. That's ninety percent of it. But the other ten percent – five percent, even – is inspiration, pure and simple. Eureka! You understand something – you get to the answer – before you've necessarily worked it out.'

'And you've just done that with Norman?'

'I think so. Yes – I'd bet my pension on it.'

'What about Ted? You're saying this wasn't related; but have you had a Eureka moment for him?'

'I feel we're getting closer to finishing. But I just need a few more details. Which is why I'd like to have a little chat with you.'

Barney looked at him. 'Fair enough,' he said. 'But two things – one, I badly want a roll-up. It's not many people have their cricket captains murdered beside them two Sundays on the bounce; and two, don't you think we might draw a little less attention to ourselves if you was to give it an hour or so and come round to mine and ask me what you want there?'

Dalliance nodded. 'All right. But now we'd better wrap up the party here.'

Police cars and an ambulance were already approaching down the track as they made their way back to the pitch, where Atkins had efficiently shooed the cricketers away from the scene of the crime.

Dalliance stood and looked at Norman Standing's body, lying face down where he had fallen at second slip. There are worse ways to go, he found himself thinking, wondering if the events of Lower Bolton Cricket Club would find their way into the miscellaneous section of Wisden, the cricketers' bible.

An hour later, after he'd changed, Dalliance sat on the veranda of the empty pavilion flicking through the statements Riley had taken.

'They're all the same, sir, virtually identical.'

'You probably had the best view of it,' Dalliance said, shutting the notebook and handing it back.

'It was all so – well, undramatic. Des came up to bowl, the bloke took a swish at it, Cowper caught it – and Standing took a dive. Took me a moment to realise what had happened. I mean, he might have been doing a special cricketing thing, for all I knew.'

Dalliance gave him a disdainful glance. 'It's footballers who dive, Riley, not cricketers. And the next time you attend a cricket match, don't loiter behind the bowler's arm. It holds play up.'

'Right, sir; sorry sir.'

'Well, go on.'

'It was only when Barney started making a beeline for the fence that it became obvious something major had happened.'

'So you didn't see anything prior to that – no movement in the barley, a gun barrel glinting in the sun?'

Riley shook his head. 'I wasn't looking there, sir. I was trying to watch the cricket.'

Dalliance nodded. 'Well, well done getting to Barney so fast. You almost certainly saved his life.'

'Couldn't believe you were asking me to take him down, to begin with. Then I thought maybe he was our man after all, and was doing a runner.'

Dalliance shook his head. 'No, not Barney. The poison thing was never his style, and I can't think what he'd have had against Standing.' He got stiffly to his feet. 'Come on, there's nothing here for us. Leave Anderson's lot to ruin the barley. Shouldn't think they'll find anything useful. But if they do, it won't be for us.'

Riley looked away to their right where the white boiler-suits were fanning out from the fence. He was still glowing from Sally Walker's coy 'Who's the hero then?' when she'd passed him after Anderson's briefing of the SOCO team.

It had certainly been a more exciting afternoon than he'd expected, and the interview with Barney Grover looked likely to keep the interest level up.

Dalliance had obviously slipped several steps ahead in his grasp on the case.

Nineteen

'Brought your greyhound with you?' Barney said pleasantly, nodding at Riley as he stood in his open doorway. 'Quite a turn of speed, young man.'

'Football training,' Dalliance said.

'Ah,' said Barney. 'Good job anyway. Sorry if I didn't seem so grateful at the time. Anyway, the kettle's on, the missus is putting out the sandwiches I helped myself to from the cricket club tea, and if you'd like to follow me we can have a nice, civilised chat in the back garden.'

Where you can smoke, thought Riley with a glance at his boss. Dalliance's face showed nothing. Riley recognised his famous poker face. He wondered what hand he would see played as the smoke curled up from Barney Grover's nostrils.

The garden was well maintained and longer than might have been expected. There was a sort of arbour at the far end, and that was where Barney led them, carrying a laden tray before him.

The three men sat down at the rustic table. Barney poured tea, then got his cigarette packet out. Dalliance, looked on impassively, before suddenly asking, 'Those knuckles causing you any grief?'

Barney made an infinitesimal movement as though to shield his hand from view. Then he laughed. 'No need of SpecSavers for you, is there? I thought they'd calmed down but you're right,' he said, inspecting them. 'They are still a bit puffy.'

'Tricky bit of pipework, was it?'

'Something like that,' Barney said, narrowing his eyes. Perhaps it was the smoke.

'Easily done,' Dalliance said genially – as though he had been discussing minor industrial injuries with plumbers all his life – before suddenly changing tack. 'Ernie Phelps.'

'What about him?' Barney said, flicking his ash away.

'Friend of yours?'

'Don't know I'd go so far as to describe him as a friend exactly.'

'What then? A teammate?'

'Teammate, definitely. Not exactly Gary Sobers, but that don't matter. He's a good team man.'

'And you like him?'

'I like him for that. Beyond that there isn't much to like or dislike, if I'm honest with you. Keeps himself to himself.'

'So you wouldn't seek him out – for company?'

'I wouldn't say I would, no. But I wouldn't mind spending time with him.'

'But not an evening, or a substantial part of an evening with him?'

Barney shook his head and shrugged, as though mystified at the line the questioning was taking.

'And what do you know of him? Beyond his keeping to himself and all of that. What do you know of his past life – before he came here?'

Barney shook his head, but Riley noticed his eyes darting about anxiously. Dalliance didn't allow him any respite.

'Or to put it slightly more forcefully – how much did Ted Roper tell you about him?'

The light of dawning recognition could be seen in Barney's eyes. He rubbed the stubble on his jaw and then fixed Dalliance with an unwavering eye. 'Ah,' he said. 'So he told you then?'

'No. You have. He told us Ted had spilled the beans. He didn't tell us whom to.'

Barney scowled as though caught out.

'But don't worry. I was nearly certain it was you.'

'And what of it? I didn't blag about it. Never breathed a word to anyone – not even the wife. His secret was safer with me than with Ted.'

Dalliance nodded.

Well, go on then, Riley was thinking. He's there – for the taking. He's about as close to a confession as you're ever going to get.

But Dalliance changed course again. 'What about Des Tucker?'

'What about him?' Barney asked. But with the air of a man miraculously let off the hook.

'He strikes me as a man with fingers in many pies.'

'Too many pies, you could say,' Barney almost laughed.

Dalliance pushed back in his chair, leaving an inviting conversational vacuum. Barney leant forward.

'Look, I wouldn't normally talk about someone else – to the police. But if it's going to help you get the bastard who killed Ted—'

'Even though you had fallen out with him...?' Dalliance prompted softly.

'I was furious with him – really angry. But, come on; I never wanted the old bugger topped. Where's the proportionality in that?'

'So what were you going to say about Des?'

Barney puffed out his cheeks, then made his decision. He was going to talk.

'Des is right in the middle of everything in this village. Knows everybody; knows everybody's business. Always available – doesn't seem to need sleep like normal people. He's so much part of the scenery you don't hardly notice him. But he notices everything. And it's only when you stop to think that you notice things about him.'

'Like?'

Barney puffed his cheeks out again. It was clear this was going against the grain. 'Well...there's a lot of young females slide their bottoms across the seats of that car of his.' Here he gave Riley a piercing look.

'Are you suggesting?' Riley started, only to be cut off.

'I'm not suggesting anything, sonny. Just stating – stating facts. Pretty girls – and women, either as passengers or pupils, and plenty of them.'

'He's got a current DBS.'

Barney curled his lip. 'Half the bloody country's got one of those. All it means is that he's never been charged with an offence. Doesn't mean he's never committed one. Not that I'm saying he has. I don't think he would, to be fair. I'm sure Des wouldn't cross the line. But you couldn't say he didn't have an eye for the girls.'

He stubbed his cigarette out. Dalliance waited. Riley thought of putting in a supplementary question, but an almost imperceptible frown from across the table made him reconsider.

In his own time Barney resumed. 'I can remember when he was giving lessons to Hazel – Rees' girl. Lovely girl, a head-turner if ever there was one. Des was pleased as punch to begin with and used to make her drive all round the village so everyone could see them together. But I think after a while he found the pressure getting to him. He knew if he laid a finger on her—'

'He'd find himself being beaten up through an old sack out at Gallows Barn?'

Barney bridled. 'But you haven't pinned that on Rees, have you? Or Jez?'

'No,' Dalliance said. 'Someone made sure they both had very good alibis.' He helped himself to a sandwich, but beyond putting it on his plate, he didn't seem interested in it. 'Let's stick with Des. What you're saying is he ferried a lot of attractive women around the place and taught some of them to drive. And the suspicion is, if he thought he could have his wicked way with any of them, he would?'

Barney lit another cigarette. His fingers, Riley noticed, had suddenly become slightly clumsy.

'He's got the gift of the gab, Des – chatty, upbeat, but a surprisingly good listener... There's something about those little, round, bald guys... Maybe they just try harder. Look, I'm not saying he did anything he shouldn't have. But I'm not saying he didn't either.'

'And why do you suspect him?' Riley chipped in.

'Things he's said; little nods and winks. You know what it's like in a group of men. Everybody's all for it – provided it isn't with their girl, wife, fiancée. And there were always stunning girls around the Roper house – PAs, au pairs, foreign exchange students – you name it. And as often as not Des would do the driving – back to the station, up to the airport, whatever. He stopped in the pub with one once. Simply stunning – legs like a bloody stepladder, and the shortest skirt you'd ever seen. Des said she wanted some smokes, but she could have got them anywhere. He just wanted to show her off to the lads.'

'And afterwards?' Riley asked.

'I thought I'd got your attention, young man.' Barney smiled at him through wreathes of smoke. 'He never actually said anything, but he didn't go out of his way to stop other people thinking what they wanted.'

He paused to exhale. Then he frowned slightly.

'But you want more than village tittle-tattle, Inspector. And here's the thing – Des and Ted were close. I know Des did the driving for Ted and more than likely knew a few things Ted preferred to keep quiet. But there was something else.'

'What sort of thing?'

'Money, most like.'

'And how did you know?'

'They used to meet in the pub quite regularly at one stage. And it wasn't cricket – often it wasn't even in the cricket season. You'd go into the pub, and there they'd be in a corner, heads together – sometimes looking at some paperwork.'

'And if they saw you?'

'Oh, the friendly wave – Ted would get up and buy you a drink. It was all open and above board. I mean, there they were in the pub – in public. Whereas if it'd been secret, they could have found any number of places to meet. And yet they never told you what they were talking about.'

'And you didn't ask?'

'What makes you think it was money?' Riley added.

'One, what else would it be? Two, it was at the time when Ted was going a bit large. Generous to a fault, you might say, lending money to people, helping them out. It was his heyday as pretend squire, if you like.'

'And you think he helped Des?'

Barney nodded, blowing plumes of smoke from his nostril. 'I'm sure of it. For a start, Des upgraded his motor; in fact, he bought another – a people-carrier for the airport trip; very lucrative that particular line of business.'

'And you're sure that came from Ted? Some sort of personal loan or something?' Dalliance was looking hard at him.

Barney nodded. 'It was something about the way they were – or rather the way Des was – around Ted, I mean. Just little things – a bit more familiar – little references that didn't mean anything to the rest of us.'

'And how long did that last?'

'It ended this summer. No doubt about that. Quite a cooling off. It was when Ted started being a bit of a bastard all round, which is another reason to think it was about money.'

'So a cooling off. Anything more?'

'Yeah, there was actually.'

'Well?' Dalliance pressed.

'I was going up to the big house one evening – about a month ago it must have been. I wanted to talk to Ted about the situation with my mum – you know, man to man. Anyway, I was turning in at the gate at the top of the drive, and I nearly hit Des steaming out onto the road. He must have seen me but he didn't show it. I saw his face – and he looked furious. Never asked him what it was about, and I doubt he'd have told me. Anyway, I had enough on my plate with my own row with Ted.'

'And how did that pan out?'

'Not good. Ted said he didn't want to do it, but he had to, and had I any idea what mum's cottage was worth. And I told him you couldn't put a value on the place someone had called home for nigh on fifty years, and he'd always assured me she'd have it for as long as he wanted. And he said he was sorry, but things had changed and he needed the money. Not that he put it that way – some bollocks about liquidating his assets. I told him where he could put his assets, said he'd be hearing from my solicitor, and stormed out of the house.'

Barney flicked his cigarette angrily.

'If I'd wanted to kill him, Inspector, I'd have done it there and then – with my bare hands. And I think you're intelligent enough to realise that.'

'What do you think will happen about your mother's cottage now?'

'I don't know. Margot's a decent woman, but I don't trust the kids. Fiona's setting herself up as some globetrotting businesswoman. She couldn't begin to understand how anyone would want to spend their lives in one small cottage in one small village. And as for Charlie – he's just a spoilt prick.' He shook his head. 'I'm not holding out any hopes to be honest with you, Inspector...'

'Thank you; you've been very helpful,' Dalliance said, getting up.

'Is that it?' Barney asked, getting up himself.

That seemed a very good question, Riley thought. How close could you get to forcing a confession without pushing home your advantage and nailing it?

But Dalliance seemed perfectly happy with what they had achieved as they made their way back towards the house.

'You can get out through the garage if you like,' Barney said, opening a side door. They eased down the side of the blue van and out into the short drive at the front of the premises.

They climbed back into the car, but if Riley thought Dalliance was going to explain himself, he was disappointed.

'Just drop me at the cricket ground to pick up my car. I'll see you at the station in an hour. We'll work our way through Atkins' footage. Though I doubt there'll be anything useful.'

'And then, sir?'

'And then, I think, another little chat with Des Tucker.'

Dalliance looked more comfortable when they reconvened in his office later. He fell back in one of the two easy chairs across from his desk and said, 'Show me what we've got.'

Riley had downloaded the film onto his laptop, and both men hunched over it. 'You were right, sir, I've only had a quick look, but I can't see he'll have got anything helpful.'

'As I said, I'm not expecting much.'

Riley pressed the play button.

'There you are, sir!' he said. Dalliance was walking out onto the field, deep in conversation with Norman Standing. 'You look every inch the part.'

Dalliance snorted. 'I look like Wally Hammond in 1947 – too old and too fat for purpose.'

But Riley could see him peering intently at the screen. And when it came to Steve Royce's first over, he leaned forward with even more interest.

'My God, he could have killed me!' Dalliance exclaimed when the first ball tore past his left ear.

'I did think you saw it a bit late, sir.'

'A bit late – I never saw it at all!'

'Why not, sir?'

'I was watching the bat, not the ball. You do, at first slip. At least, you do if you can trust the bowler not to take your head off with a wide. Another inch or two and we could have had a death at each end.'

'Do you want to see it again in slow-mo, sir?'

'No, I don't, thank you very much. As it is, I'm going to have nightmares about it.'

'Do you think he did it on purpose?'

'I don't think he had enough control, Riley; but he wouldn't have been exactly heartbroken if he'd got me. Look at that!' he exclaimed as Cowper flung himself despairingly to his left at the wide down the leg side. The camera lurched in a vain attempt to follow the ball and the screen filled with unfocused foliage. It took a moment to reconnect with the game, but there was a nice shot of Daniel flinging the ball to the top of the stumps.

'Beautiful mover, that boy. Lovely arm,' Dalliance said approvingly. At the end of the over he said, 'Well, it's better than nothing, but I think Atkins should keep the day job.'

'Not quite up to Sky Sports,' Riley agreed.

'I wouldn't know,' Dalliance growled. 'Keep going. I wonder if he got anything of the field where the killer was holed up.'

Disappointingly he hadn't. Apart from a fleeting establishing shot, which simply showed the outfield running up to the fence and the barley field beyond, the camera focused determinedly on the game and the cricketers playing it.

Dalliance tutted. 'Well, it wasn't part of the brief to be fair,' he admitted. 'A marksman from the top end was the last thing we were expecting.'

The killing, when it came, was strangely low-key. The ball was delivered, the shot was played, Cowper took the ball. Dalliance noticed that he had half raised his hands at the near-miss. And at the same time Standing simply keeled over. Then there was the flurry of activity, with Dalliance pulling out the dart, before all attention shifted to Barney running towards the boundary, with Riley coming in from the left of the picture to stop him.

'That was a good tackle, Riley,' Dalliance said. 'You should take up rugby.'

'I don't think so, sir. My shoulder's going to ache for a week.'

'You did well – Stop! Stop it there! Can you see?'

They peered into the screen. There was a blur at the top of the picture. It was like an eddy, at the heart of which was a kernel of darker shadow, like the hint of a shark just below the surface.

'That's our man. And that'll be the best shot of him we have. I don't anticipate a high success rate taking that round the village door to door.'

The footage resumed, drawn inevitably to the action on the outfield.

'You arrived just in the nick of time, sir,' Riley said, admiring Dalliance's bear-hug, which was the deciding factor in containing Barney.

'I wish Atkins had stayed up his tree and carried on filming.'

'He didn't know what was going on. I suppose he saw the two of us brawling with Barney and felt he ought to come and help. He'd have looked a bit of a fool if we'd needed him.'

'True,' Dalliance conceded. 'Damned if you do, damned if you don't. Anyway, between us we saved Barney's bacon.'

'You seem very sure he'd have been killed if we hadn't stopped him, sir.'

'I am, Riley. If I'm right, our shooter was a top-of-the-range contract killer. Barney wouldn't have stood a chance.'

'But who would want to take out a contract on Standing? And why go to the trouble of killing him with a dart?'

'Really, Riley? No idea? No idea at all? Think, man. Who else might have been disappointed at the loss of Standing's Midas touch?'

'Other investors?'

'Yes, Riley; other investors, who lost a great deal more than Ted.'

'But the oligarchs could afford to take a hit.'

'That doesn't mean they'd be happy to.'

'Would they really go to the extreme of killing someone?'

'It'll get the message over – we may be mega rich, but don't try to take advantage. They must be surrounded by people – charming, persuasive people – ready to spend their money for them. Norman may just have been the unlucky scapegoat – killed *pour l'encouragement des autres*.'

'But why the dart at a cricket match?'

'Perhaps they're just correcting the perception that Russians are humourless. It's not as though poison is unchartered territory. It was an umbrella last time, you might just remember.'

'So what are we going to do about the killer?'

'What we're told,' Dalliance replied. 'The chances of catching him are minimal. But then it really isn't our problem.'

Riley looked blank.

'I would expect the Met to take over the case tomorrow.' Dalliance leant back in his chair. 'Don't worry, Riley, we've still got the case we started with to put to bed.'

'And are we any closer to doing that, sir?'

'Yes, I think so. I'll tell you in the morning.'

'In the morning? I thought we were going to talk to Des?'

I'm going to talk to Des. Don't look so disappointed. You've had a good day, Riley – a really good day. You get off home and rest that bruised shoulder of yours. There's bound to be a football match somewhere in the world. Have a beer and watch that. It's not often you save a man's life, and if you hadn't got to Barney, I wouldn't have, and there'd now be two corpses in the morgue instead of one. I regard that as successful police work.'

TWENTY

Dalliance was late into the office on Monday morning. There was something about him that seemed different but Riley couldn't place it at first. He seemed fretful, uneasy. Possibly even shifty. It wasn't until he put the mandatory mug of coffee down on the desk in front of him that Riley twigged. The scent was faint, but unmistakable.

He gave Dalliance a sharp glance.

'Don't look at me like that, Riley. It reminds me of my daughter,' the Inspector said. 'Sometimes,' he went on, 'police work requires a sacrifice, and yes, I did join Des in a couple of conspiratorial cigarettes last night.'

Riley's surprise must have shown.

'I know, I know – shameful, weak-minded, pathetic – all of the above. But it yielded results.' Dalliance waved him to a chair. 'It turns out that spat with Ted that Barney told us about was quite a row.'

'What was it about, sir?'

'What do you think? Money, sex and scandal, predictably enough. Barney was right – Tucker did have a special relationship with Roper. In return for being the helpful and discreet taxi service available at a moment's notice, twenty-four hours a day, Roper extended his largesse to Des. Practically a private bank.'

'What, loans to cover new cars?'

'More. Ted got him in on one of Standing's schemes – and lent him the capital to make the initial investment.'

'How much?'

'He didn't tell me. It took every ounce of persuasion I could muster to get him to admit that much.'

'Well, that doesn't give Tucker a motive, does it?'

'No – on the contrary, it made him Roper's staunchest supporter. But Ted didn't like to leave anything to chance.'

'Meaning?'

'Those girls Des got to ferry to and fro for him. Again Barney was right – he did take what perks were on offer.' Dalliance remembered with a shudder huddling next to Des in the backseat of his car, lighting his cigarette off the one the little taxi man offered him – like two boys truanting in the dingiest recesses of the local cinema, back when everyone smoked everywhere all of the time. 'The only trouble was, one of them was under age.'

Riley gave a low whistle. 'And Roper held that over him?' Dalliance nodded.

'But how did you get *that* out of him?'

'Said we'd got Ted's notebooks and records.'

'But we never found anything along those lines.'

'We didn't know we were looking for anything along those lines. Anyway, Des wanted to tell me – tell someone.' Dalliance relived the little man's initial bluster collapsing into abject terror at the possibility of an exposé – and possible prosecution.

'So Roper was threatening him? What for – what did he want?'

'We've ticked off the sex and the scandal, which leaves us—'

'The money.'

'Roper knew he had some – because he'd helped him make it.'

'So it was a straight case of blackmail?'

'No, Roper was a little more subtle than that. He was inviting Des to return the favour, give him a substantial loan. But of course Des had put his windfall into the new people-carrier, the new extension, and a couple of Caribbean holidays to keep Mrs Tucker on side.'

'So the money wasn't there.'

'Not in nice, neat bundles of fifty-pound notes, no,' said Dalliance. 'But Roper pointed out that it could be there if Des would take out a second mortgage. Des said no way could he do that – the wife would kill him, and Roper said, well, she'd probably kill him – only more slowly – if she knew what fun he'd been having in the back seat of his car over the years...'

There was a pause. Riley looked levelly at his boss. 'How many smokes did it take to get all that out of him?'

'Five?' Dalliance suggested. 'You can see why I felt I had to see him on my own?'

Riley nodded. 'You have to put your life on the line in the course of duty, sir.'

Dalliance gave him a tight-lipped smile, and then the phone on his desk rang.

'Dalliance … Okay. Put him through … Good morning, Inspector, I was expecting a call.'

After that he said nothing for what Riley thought must be a record amount of time, during which his face registered little. It was as though he were being told something he either already knew or had suspected all along. Then finally, after a couple of yes's and no's: 'This afternoon? … We look forward to seeing you then, Inspector. Safe journey.'

Dalliance put the phone down. 'The Met.'

Riley raised a questioning eyebrow.

'More or less confirming my suspicions. However rich they are, oligarchs don't like losing money any more than the rest of us. They just have rather more proactive ways of showing it.'

'Meaning?'

'Meaning they not only sent a hit man down to the sticks to take revenge, but they cleared out Standing's pad – absolutely tore it apart and removed anything of any value – aided and abetted, the assumption has to be, by the leggy Tatiana, who may have been a plant from the start.'

'But why kill him here? And by that method?'

Dalliance shrugged. 'At first sight it looks like an attempt to muddy the waters. Same site, same method – therefore same murderer, same motive, or at least part of the same murderous mission. But I don't think they'll expect to fool anyone with that for very long. As I said yesterday, it'll get the message across. Don't mess with us. Don't take our money – or our leggy women, come to that – for granted. What would worry you more as someone who might be contemplating helping themselves to a life-changing bonus at an oligarch's expense? A run-of-the-mill killing, or an elaborate murder like yesterday's, which not only shows they can deliver vengeance, but that they can deliver it in the heart of the victim's private world? If an Englishman's home is his castle, then his cricket pitch must be his hallowed ground, the inviolable sanctuary on which his very being is grounded. I know you don't think that, Riley; but the Russians are a soulful bunch. They probably thought killing Standing on the pitch at Lower Bolton was the equivalent of murdering a man at the altar as he kneels to take communion. Anyway, it shows their ruthlessness, their efficiency and their implacability. As a crime it is distinctive, eye-catching, headline-grabbing' – here he waved a hand at the slew of morning papers on the side of his desk – 'and I suspect it'll be the devil's own job to solve. But happily that now falls to

DI Smethick of the Met, who, as you have just heard, will be with us this afternoon. Or rather, with you.'

'Me, sir?'

Dalliance nodded. 'You can show him around, take him out to the cricket field, introduce him to Anderson – we haven't got the toxicology report yet, have we?'

Riley shook his head.

'Probably take a day or two. I'm guessing it'll show a completely different poison was used from the one that killed Roper. I assume he'll want to go through our case file, but the only conclusion he'll be able to draw is that the two cases are completely unrelated. I don't suppose he'll be pleased.'

'You sound as though you're not going to be here, sir.'

'I'm not.'

'But what are you going to be doing, sir?'

'I'm going to be getting on with our case; spending time going over old ground with a bunch of impatient members of the Met is not the best use of my time. You're my human shield, Riley. Don't worry, they won't hang around long. When they realise the entire case is London-based, they'll disappear down the motorway and leave us in peace. You'll undoubtedly be more polite to them than I would be able to manage, and while the press are going crackers over the second Cricket Ground Slaying, I'll use the smokescreen to carry on quietly with my own investigations. Good luck.'

Dalliance stood up.

'Oh,' he said, pulling something out of his desk drawer. 'Perhaps you could give this to Inspector Smethick to sort out.' It was the parking ticket from their trip to London.

Riley put the ticket in his pocket. He felt Dalliance was pulling a fast one on him. Being dogsbody to a DI from the Met was not going to be any fun at all. 'Are you sure about this, sir? What about upstairs?'

'Riley, I have a case to solve. The Met have a case to solve. The two are not related, so there's no point in us treading on each other's toes going over the same ground. As you know, upstairs is particularly hot on the most effective use of police time. At least, that's how I would explain it to him.'

'You mean, you haven't—?'

'Teamwork, Riley. We work as a team.'

And sometimes you have to take one for the team, Riley thought, not relishing the interview with upstairs one little bit.

Dalliance's expression softened. 'I'm not going for long, Riley. You'll be fine. As I say, they'll soon get bored and leave us in peace. Good luck.'

They met two days later.

'Safe to come out now?' Dalliance texted Riley – much to his astonishment. He rang straight back.

'That's the first text I've ever had from you, sir.'

'It wasn't really from me. I'm staying with my daughter in London.'

'Ah,' Riley said. 'I have been trying to get hold of you, but your phone's been switched off.'

'Libraries, research institutes,' Dalliance said airily.

'But I tried in the evenings as well, sir.'

'Probably forgot to switch it back on. Went to the theatre. With my daughter. I don't suppose I've missed much. So, the all-clear has sounded?'

Riley sighed. The last two days had been a trial, being treated like an office boy by the bloody Met. Dalliance had known what he was doing, slipping out the back like that.

'The Met contingent have cleared off, if that's what you mean. The Chief Constable isn't best pleased with your absence. I had to take an earful this morning. He said it was my job to know where my superior officer was, and could I please tell him when his senior detective was deigning to resume his enquiries into an extremely high-profile murder investigation.'

'I hope you didn't leave him with the impression I had just skived off, Riley?'

'Of course not, sir. But you didn't leave me with much to work with. What were you doing in all those libraries—?'

'Never mind,' Dalliance cut in. 'Look, I'm coming back this afternoon. I'll pop in and placate the Chief Constable. And then we'll be making our way to Lower Bolton.'

'We will, sir?'

'Yes, Riley. There's a meeting at the cricket club to decide the next captain, and I thought we should attend, if only to assure them that the next captain was highly unlikely to be poisoned on the field of play.'

'Have you got any further—?'

But Dalliance had gone. Riley looked at the phone in his palm, and shook his head. But he couldn't stop his face creasing into a smile.

It would be good to have the old bugger back.

'So, how were the Met's finest?'

Riley groaned.

'As bad as that was it?'

'Treated us like serfs.'

Dalliance nodded, looking out over the familiar countryside as they headed out to the Boltons. 'Traditions have to be maintained. They like to think they're the best, and they certainly like everybody else to think so. But as long as you sent them away happy, that's all that matters.'

'I don't know about happy, sir. Anderson didn't have anything for them, so Smethick insisted on another search through the barley field. That didn't go down well with the farmer – but the locals seemed to enjoy it.'

'Find anything?'

'Couple of condoms, empty pack of chewing gum, three bottles of cheap cider, empty, and four cricket balls.'

'Not much to get the detective juices flowing.'

Riley snorted. 'Smethick had them bagged up and took them back to London with him.'

'Even the balls?'

'No – I've got them in the back. But I can't see how any of the other things could be any more help.'

'Got to justify the trip to the sticks. Anything else?'

'Looked at the statements I'd taken. Didn't seem to rate them, though I'm blessed if I know what else I could have asked. I saw it all myself – and there was nothing to see. He went over the camera footage, of course – took a copy – but again, there's nothing to see.'

'As I said – a top-of-the-range contract killer.'

'That's what I said you'd said. And he had to agree, though he wasn't terribly impressed you weren't around.'

'Did you give him the parking ticket?'

Riley nodded. 'Said he'd see what he could do.'

Dalliance gave a wan smile. 'Did he tell you anything about the London end?'

'Beyond the fact that Standing's place had been cleaned out and the lovely Tatiana had cleared off, nothing. He seemed to think he knew who was behind it – said Standing had been playing out of his league for a while and that it was only a matter of time before he came unstuck.'

'Got the gist of that from the Standard. They may think they know who's responsible but they'll have a job proving it.'

'That's why they want the girl,' Riley said, indicating left and dropping off the main road.

'H'm – she'd have been out on the next flight after she'd handed over the keys. I don't imagine she'll be coming back to savour the delights of London high life any time in the near future. Well done, Riley. Mention in despatches and all that. Sorry I rather left you in it, but I have been working on our case, I promise you.'

'Any closer to solving it, sir?'

'I think so.'

Riley left a decent pause, but Dalliance didn't elaborate.

'And this meeting, sir – how did you get wind of it?'

'Oh I've been keeping my nose to the ground. Popped over to the village to see one or two people on my way to London. Nice old boy called Perry is the chairman of the club; said he was calling the meeting – and asked me to come along.'

'And this research you were doing in London, sir?'

'Pretty dull for the most part, as research usually is. But some interesting results. Ah – here we are.'

Riley sighed. Like getting blood out of a stone, he thought as he turned up the familiar lane to the cricket ground. They found themselves behind Barney's van with its cheerful boast: 'No job too small'. Riley glanced to his left, but Dalliance was looking out of his window, refusing to be drawn into further conversation. He did, however, let out a breath of surprise as they swung in through the cricket field gate and caught a glimpse of the damage done to the barley field.

'See what I mean, sir?'

'I do, Riley. Well, they'll have to pay compensation. Good turnout,' he added, looking at the vehicles already parked near the pavilion. 'Come on, in we go. And bring those cricket balls as a peace offering.'

They went into the bar, which was doing a brisk trade. Most of the now familiar faces registered a tight-lipped recognition, but the atmosphere was tense. Des Tucker, Riley noticed, seemed to go out of his way not to catch Dalliance's eye.

'Get us a couple of halves, Riley,' he said, before turning to an elderly man who had been present on the first Sunday afternoon.

Riley found himself at the bar next to Ben Cowper.

'You lot finished, then? Made a fine old mess of Jacko's barley,' the farmer said with a nod of his head. 'Get compensation, will he? Lucky bugger. You can come down and trample my crops anytimes you like. Save me the grief of harvesting them.' He gave a short mirthless laugh and ordered a pint of mild.

Riley ordered two halves. He was served unsmilingly, his change slapped down on the counter. The case had not, he reflected, been a triumph for community policing.

But perhaps, he thought, as he pocketed the loose coins, he was taking it too personally. After all, they hadn't solved the case, so there was still a killer on the loose. Even if, as they assumed, he had finished his business with Ted, it must be unnerving to know that they were still rubbing shoulders with a murderer. Glancing around he could see members of the team looking askance at each other. Mutual trust would not be restored until the perpetrator had been revealed.

When he got back to Dalliance, the elderly man was talking. 'So I'll call the meeting to order, introduce you, you say your bit, and then we'll move on to the business of the evening.'

'Thank you, Mr Perry. That'll be most helpful. Let me introduce my right-hand man, DS Riley. Riley, Mr Perry, Chairman of Lower Bolton Cricket Club.'

Still holding the two beers, Riley couldn't shake hands but did give the chairman a brief smile of acknowledgement.

Dalliance took his half-pint from Riley. 'We're up this end,' he said after he'd taken a sip.

Riley noticed that a table and a few chairs had been placed up against the wall dividing the bar from the changing rooms. In the body of the bar chairs had been drawn up in rows facing the table.

'Right, gentlemen; if you've all got your drinks – thank you,' Perry called out, ushering a man of similar vintage towards the table facing the room. Riley remembered him as another of the spectators waiting at the ground in the wake of Ted Roper's murder. Judging from the leather-bound ledger under his arm, he had to be the club secretary.

Riley and Dalliance joined the club officials at the table, facing the body of the meeting. The front row was left empty, the cricketers cramming into the two rows behind. But they were all there. Riley looked from face to face, once again asking himself which of them was capable of dealing Ted Roper such a subtle and treacherous blow: Henderson, slightly bored; Barney Grover beside him, talking animatedly and using his hands to make a point. Rees Jones was next, still in his suit and looking uncomfortable; Jez to his left was trying to appear relaxed, but only succeeded in making himself look positively shifty. Steve Royce was talking too loudly to Ernie Phelps, who was feigning interest but was clearly lost in thoughts of his own. As for Des Tucker, he was obviously out of his comfort zone, all his usual bonhomie drained from his pudgy features. Ben Cowper sat stolidly staring into the depths of his glass, as though trying to calculate the compensation the lucky owner of the barley field would get. Looking at them all, Riley was none the wiser. Beneath the attempt at normality swirled currents of suspicion.

Riley felt a certain pity for them. He wondered how long it would be before Dalliance put them out of their misery and announced his solution to the crime which continued to cast a shadow over their little community. Perhaps he would do it that evening; he clearly had new information up his sleeve, new information which he was not – yet – prepared to share.

The volume of chatter dropped suddenly, leaving Steve Royce mid-sentence: '...so I told the bastard where he could put his—'

'Thank you, Steve. A time and a place,' Perry said sternly, staring down a titter or two.

'Sorry, Mr Perry.'

Perry raised his hand in acknowledgement. As he did, Riley noticed the door opening and Daniel Pottinger looking in shyly.

'Come in, Daniel, take a seat. It's very good to have you – thanks for coming.'

'Shouldn't he be at school?' Riley whispered.

'Half-term,' Dalliance said, and in response to Riley's frown of confusion added, 'They don't keep to the same timetable as state schools. Holidays tend to be earlier – and longer. One of the actual – as opposed to assumed – privileges of boarding.'

Riley threw his head back in resigned acknowledgment.

Once Daniel had found a seat on the back row, Perry opened the proceedings.

'You all know why we're here. We've suffered two appalling tragedies out on our beloved cricket field on two successive Sundays. We've lost two loyal and stalwart servants of the Lower Bolton Cricket Club, and two men whom we all regarded as friends, colleagues and teammates. We will of course bid them farewell in the appropriate manner, and I also think it would be fitting to observe a minute's silence when the team next take to the field. But this Extraordinary General Meeting has been called for a specific purpose and I would hope to move through proceedings fairly swiftly. But before we get to the business at hand, which is selecting our new captain, I have asked Chief Inspector Dalliance to say a few words about the shocking events which have affected us.' With a nod at Dalliance, Perry sat down.

Dalliance got up and looked at the faces staring back at him.

'I'd like to start by saying that I and my colleagues do appreciate the strain you have all been put under over these last few days. "Murder most foul" Shakespeare called it and, as so often, he hit the nail on the head. To have to witness not one but two in the space of two Sundays is an exceptional exposure to the worst of crimes. In addition to the horror of that experience, I'm afraid being involved in a murder investigation is also stressful. I'm sure you all appreciate that DS Riley and I have only been doing our job, but we in turn appreciate that the questions we have to ask can seem intrusive and prove uncomfortable.'

'You can bloody say that again,' someone muttered, causing a groundswell of murmurings, quickly interrupted by a brisk 'Gentlemen – thank you' from Perry.

Then a lone voice said, 'And after all the bloody questioning, are you any nearer making an arrest?' It was Ben Cowper, who looked belligerently at Dalliance.

'I think we are, Ben,' Dalliance replied. 'But that's not what I'm here to talk about this evening. As you'll be aware, there are now two murder investigations going on – because, despite their similarities, the two murders that you all witnessed out on that square were not related. Norman Standing was almost certainly killed by a contract killer hired by some very rich and powerful people who had allowed Norman to gamble with large amounts of their money. That case began and ends in London and has been taken over by the Metropolitan Police.'

'Why was he killed here?' David Henderson enquired.

'We think it was meant to give a signal to anyone else entrusted with a lot of money. If you can't even be safe standing at second slip on a Sunday afternoon in the middle of rural England, where can you be? Nowhere.'

'And why did you and your young sidekick there stop Barney diving after the hit man? He'd have sorted him out, good and proper.' The question was posed by a middle-aged man with very pronounced sideburns and a flat cap drawn down over his brow.

'Mr Grover has a deserved reputation for resolving issues with a robust physical response' – here Dalliance looked directly at Barney, who found a sudden interest in the palm of his hand – 'but I can assure you that against a trained killer, an unarmed man would have stood no chance. I would not have risked the lives of any of my officers, and I certainly wasn't going to have the death of a civilian on my conscience.' He looked around the bar as if challenging anyone else to throw in a question.

One came: 'How much is Jackson going to get in compensation for his barley?' Ben Cowper wanted to know.

'That I cannot answer, but there is a claims procedure and I'm sure Mr Jackson will be advised on how to avail himself of it. But now I want to finish with what I really came to say: although both killings are still fresh in our memories, I can give absolute assurance there will be no more. Norman Standing's murder I have explained; Ted Roper's killing was a personal matter. That vendetta ended with his death. I give you my word that the next man to assume the captaincy will not be the target of a lethal assault and will, I hope, have a long and successful period in office.'

As Dalliance sat down there was a buzz of conversation, again hushed by Perry.

'Thank you, Chief Inspector – and I'm sure I speak for all at Lower Bolton Cricket Club when I wish you a speedy and successful conclusion to the case. Now, gentlemen, you've heard what the Inspector said. Sadly we have a vacancy for team captain and I am now asking for nominations.'

There was a brief hubbub, with people leaning down the rows to hear what was being said.

'Thank you, gentlemen. Do we have any nominations?'

'Rees Jones.'

'Who proposed?' asked the secretary.

'I did,' said Barney.

'Seconder?'

David Henderson raised his hand.

'Henderson, D. Thank you.'

'Any other proposals?'

'Barney Grover.' It was Rees.

'You can't do that,' Barney said. 'I proposed you first!'

This was met with muted laughter.

'Seconder?' the secretary demanded drily. Steve Royce raised a hand and was duly noted. Perry asked for any more and, when no further names were forthcoming, went on. 'Of course, we need to ask whether you're both willing to stand? Rees?'

'Well, if people want me, I could do it.'

'Barney?'

'Oh, let him do it. He's young. He'll be around longer than me. Provided he lets me stay opener.' There was another ripple of laughter.

'I'm perfectly happy to put it to a vote,' Perry said, but Barney shook his head. 'Anyway,' he said, 'for all we know the Inspector's just about to arrest me!' The laughter that followed had an uneasy edge to it. Dalliance remained inscrutable.

'All right then, Rees Jones for captain it is, unless anyone has another proposal.' Silence fell. 'Carried *nem. con*,' Perry said with obvious satisfaction. 'Congratulations, Rees. If you'd just like to say a few words?'

Rees got up and made his way awkwardly to the table. There was a slight flush to his face but it was obvious he was pleased with his new role.

'Well, I haven't got much to say to be perfectly honest with you. It's shocking what's happened – out there – on our own cricket pitch. But I know Ted and Norman would want us to carry on, and we will. And all I've got to say to you is I'll do the best I can as captain, and if Barney doesn't learn to play a bit straighter, he can drop down and bat with Ernie.'

There was a momentary pause before the joke struck home. Barney reacted to the laughter with a gesture halfway between a presidential wave and an actor taking his bow.

Ernie looked like a rabbit in the headlights. But then as the pleasantry sank in he allowed himself a wary smile.

Perry raised his hand and announced, 'And that, ladies and gentlemen, concludes this extraordinary general meeting. Thank you all for attending.'

As chairs were pushed back and people surged towards the bar, Dalliance and Perry shook hands, and Perry nodded to Riley. Dalliance started moving through the crowd, stopping to congratulate Rees, who managed a tolerable imitation of a smile, though his brother made no attempt to conceal his scowl.

Daniel was standing aloof from them all, fishing out his mobile phone.

'Good evening, Daniel,' Dalliance said to him. 'We can give you a lift if you like. It's on our way – save your mother coming out again.'

'Actually I walked down, which was why I was a bit late. But I was going to ring her for a lift.'

'Well?' Dalliance said.

The boy looked up from his phone. 'All right. Thank you, sir.'

Dalliance led the way to the door, which he held open, and the three of them walked out into the fading light of the summer evening.

TWENTY-ONE

The following morning Dalliance came in later than usual.

'Problem?' he challenged when Riley brought his coffee.

'Upstairs not too happy.'

Dalliance was looking through the papers. 'Double Murder In Idyllic Setting' was now off the front pages, but where the story was still covered there was a distinct sense of impatience. 'Too Busy Dancing To Detect?' asked one headline, above a close-up of the original photo.

'He obviously reads them too,' Riley said. 'He wants a result.'

'We all want a result, but unlike a football manager, I can't be sacked because one doesn't come along right on cue.'

'He somehow thought you were going to make an arrest last night.'

'At a cricket club extraordinary general meeting?'

Riley shrugged. 'I think he thought you'd take the opportunity to – well, wind it all up.'

'Like Poirot at the end of an Agatha Christie!' Dalliance exclaimed. 'Sounds as though he's started on his retirement reading a little early. What did you tell him?'

'Not much.' After a pause, Riley added, 'Well, I haven't got a clue what's going on, have I? He really wants to hear it from you. Are we going to make an arrest?'

'We are,' Dalliance said. 'This very morning. I just thought we could all do with a good night's sleep. Never have liked doing all the paperwork at the end of a long day. If it's not necessary. Which, in this case, it isn't. Let's go. Oh, let's have that team photograph. I meant to take it yesterday but forgot. Did you give those balls back?'

'I don't know about give, sir. No one seemed very receptive. I just left the bag in a corner.'

'Yes, we're not exactly flavour of the month,' Dalliance said as they left his office. 'The natives are getting restless. Time to restore the status quo ante, insofar as that's possible.'

When they got to the car park Riley asked, 'Where are we going?'

'Where you'd expect. Just got one or two loose ends to tie off and then we're done.'

Riley allowed himself a little shake of the head as his boss climbed into the car. He'd been with him almost every step of the way, and then in the home straight he'd done a flit to London for forty-eight hours and suddenly the case was solved. And he's sodding well not going to tell me who it is until the moment he puts the cuffs on him, he thought bitterly.

If Dalliance suspected Riley's thought processes, he gave no sign of it. He looked out at the countryside just coming into its peak of high summer. The hedges loomed, cow parsley reached improbable heights, and there were wisps of hay in the verges. It was a good time of year. He thought he might suggest a few days off – as soon as the case was put to bed.

'Left at the pond,' he instructed Riley as they drove down to the green.

'Where are we going, sir? This is the way to the Pottingers.'

'Well done, Riley – it is exactly the route we took last night dropping Daniel off.'

'Why are we coming back? If there was something you needed to ask him, you could have asked him then.'

'As I said, everybody needed a good night's sleep. Often clarifies things. Here we are. Look at those roses – it really is a lovely garden.'

They waited in the porch, enjoying the warmth of the morning, lulled by the gentle hum of invisible bees. Eventually the door opened. Daniel's mother stood smiling at them, her face lit by the morning sunshine. She was obviously happy to have her boy back for the holiday.

'Oh, Inspector. I wasn't expecting you. What a nice surprise. Come in. And thank you so much for bringing Daniel back last night. Saved me getting the car out. What can I do for you?'

'Is he up? It's just that I need a word with him, if I may.'

'Of course, Inspector. But I haven't heard a dickybird out of him yet – first day home of course. He usually sleeps late. I'll go and give him a shout. Do make yourselves comfortable.' She indicated the chairs in the lounge and went back out into the hall calling, 'Daniel! Daniel! Inspector Dalliance is here. Can you get up, darling? He just wants to ask you a couple of things.'

Dalliance lay back in his armchair, his face impassive. Riley gave up trying to read anything there and instead looked at the photographs arranged on the table. Family pictures, mainly. The usual range of holiday snaps and more formal studio portraits. There was one of a younger Daniel with his father – a good-looking man in early middle-age. Daniel had his arm round him and they looked very easy in each other's company. Another photo showed Daniel and a friend, both in swimming trunks; the location looked exotic – brilliant sunshine, palm trees, a smooth ocean, with little breakers running up a beach of achingly white sand. Presumably the best friend from school, Riley thought, glancing over to Dalliance, who remained utterly still, his eyes fixed unseeingly on a corner of the ceiling.

There was a banging on a door upstairs, and further calls from Mrs Pottinger for Daniel to get up and come downstairs.

'Daniel, please! Come on, now. The Inspector hasn't got all day.'

But Dalliance, to the contrary, showed every sign of having all day. Riley was astonished. Patience was not high on the list of the boss' obvious qualities. After another heavy battering on the door, they could hear the tread of Mrs Pottinger's feet coming down the stairs. She came into the room looking flushed with embarrassment.

'I'm sorry, Inspector; I don't seem to be able to rouse him. It's extremely rude of him, I do apologise. I should never have allowed him to have a lock on his door. But they do want their privacy these days.'

Finally Dalliance roused himself.

'We'll go up.'

With a nod to Riley, he walked heavily out of the lounge and across the hall. Riley followed him. Something was suddenly beginning to feel wrong.

'Daniel,' Dalliance said when he reached the door. He tapped gently. 'Could you please open the door, Daniel. It's important that we speak to you.'

Mrs Pottinger was looking worried now. 'He can't not have heard us,' she said in a stage whisper. Then a note of real anxiety came into her voice. 'There isn't anything the matter, is there, Inspector? What did you want to ask him about?'

'What we need is to get that door open,' Dalliance said in reply.

'Oh my God, you don't think he's done anything stupid, do you?'

Dalliance gave Riley a glance, and after a couple of hefty shoulder barges there was a crack of splintering wood and the door flew open.

'He's not here! What's happened, Inspector? Where's he gone? Oh my God, it's like his father all over again!'

'I don't think you need worry about that, Mrs Pottinger,' Dalliance said, noting all the signs of hurried but careful packing. Suicides didn't usually pack. But they did leave notes. Dalliance saw it first and reached across to the work-station to read it.

'What does it say? What does it say? Oh God, what's happening?'

'It's all right, it's not what you think,' Dalliance said, handing over the folded piece of paper on which Daniel had written simply: 'Sorry Mum, I'll contact you very soon'.

'What does it mean, where's he going? He never said anything about leaving? I can't bear it.'

Dalliance magically produced an ironed, clean handkerchief. 'I think we should go downstairs, Mrs Pottinger, and have a cup of coffee and a chat.' As he steered her towards the stairs, he turned to Riley. 'Make the call – ports, airports, ferries. I suspect he was away before midnight.'

'Photo, sir?'

'Here's one,' Dalliance said, picking up a fairly recent, framed head-and-shoulders shot displayed on the landing table. 'Get the wheels in motion, Riley, and come back here when you're done.'

An hour and a half later Riley returned to find his boss sitting out in the garden with Mrs Pottinger. She was puffy-eyed but had reached the stage of putting a brave face on things. On the low table between them, Riley noted, stood a couple of glasses and a bottle of Gordon's.

'Any news, Riley?'

'One-fifteen flight to Malaga. I'm waiting on a call for information as to his forward journey, sir.'

'Malaga?' Mrs Pottinger half rose from her chair. 'What would he being doing flying to Malaga? '

'Probably the first cheap flight he could get out of the UK. But I'm afraid he hasn't just gone off for a week in the sun.'

Mrs Pottinger sank back into her garden chair. Suddenly her shoulders started to shake, and Riley realised she was trying to control some violent convulsion. It looked as though, whatever Dalliance had been telling her, up to that point she had been in some sort of denial. Now given hard facts about Daniel's actual travel movements, she was having to face up to the awful truth.

Dalliance leaned forward and dropped a splash of gin into her glass. 'Mrs Pottinger?' he said, holding the drink up to her.

She took it with a shaking hand and gulped most of it down at once. Then she shook her head resignedly. 'Oh, what a stupid, stupid boy.'

'But also highly intelligent, Mrs Pottinger. Even if he had hoped he wouldn't have to activate it, he'll have prepared his escape plan well in advance.'

'So you're sure he'll be safe, Inspector?'

'Yes, on balance, I am. We'll let you know the minute we hear anything,' Dalliance assured her, getting up. 'We're going to need to conduct a thorough search of his room. I don't expect to find very much but please don't go in there and touch anything. Nothing can change what has happened, but obviously tampering with or suppressing evidence carries its own risks. You might also consider your own travel plans. As soon as this comes out, which it will this afternoon, you'll find yourself at the centre of another media storm, I'm afraid.'

'Oh God – "Mother of Schoolboy Murderer",' she sighed, burying her face in her hands.

'And I'm sorry, but they'll print any pictures they can get hold of – both of you and Daniel. But,' Dalliance went on in his calm, measured way, 'distance often dulls the tabloid appetite for a hot story. We'd obviously have to know where you were, but if you had somewhere you could go until the feeding frenzy dies down...'

'Yes...yes. There is a place... A friend has a cottage in Wales. Somewhere with a lot of 'l's in Powys. She's always said we could use it any time we liked. I'll ask her.'

'Do it now,' Dalliance said. 'Just ring the details through to me,' he added, fishing out a card from his wallet. 'And if you happen to have a spare key, so we can get into the house...'

Mrs Pottinger took the card, and placed it on the table beside her glass. Then she stood up. Blinking away her tears, she spoke directly to the Chief Inspector.

'This the most terrible thing – even worse, I think, than his father...' Her voice tailed off for a moment. But then she resumed, forcing her face into a watery smile. 'You've been very kind – very understanding. Of all the ways this could have come out, you've chosen the kindest, the most humane way. And I will never forget your generosity, Inspector. Thank you.'

They left her, standing alone in her garden, utterly bereft. Riley felt they were abandoning her, but what more could they do?

Beside him Dalliance muttered, 'Don't look back. No one said this job was easy. We've done what we can. She's on her own now.'

'I'm sorry if you feel I've deliberately left you in the dark, Riley,' Dalliance said once they were back in the car. 'I just felt it had to play out in its own time. And for that it was important that I was the only one in the know.'

'But how long have you known it was Daniel?'

'Known? Not till two days ago. Suspected? A little longer. In a crowded field he was always well to the rear. But then, as the Grand National reminds us every year, you can win a race from virtually position. Especially if the favourites fall.'

'Where are we going, sir?'

'Where indeed? Perhaps back to where we started – the cricket field.'

'And where's Daniel going?'

'South America. Venezuela to begin with – still no extra-dition treaty with the UK. But ultimately, when the heat dies down, Brazil.'

'Brazil? Why Brazil? Who's going to look after him there?'

'Dr Hans Maars – father of his best friend, Anthony Maars, who will already be in the air.'

Riley took the track up to the cricket ground a little fast and was punished with a grating bump.

'Steady,' Dalliance murmured. 'Just concentrate on your driving. I'll explain it all when we're sitting comfortably on the pavilion veranda.'

Once they were just inside the ground, Dalliance motioned for Riley to stop. 'Park here. I want to walk across the square. For what will almost certainly be the last time.'

They passed the spot where they had dragged Barney down. There were a couple of innocuous scuff marks in the grass, as though a fielder had slid across to cut off a hard drive, but nothing to indicate what had been in all likelihood a life-or-death struggle. Thirty metres on they came to the chalk outline of Norman Standing lying spreadeagled on the ground at second slip.

'Lucky he was a good shot, sir. You were pretty close to him.'

'Luck doesn't come into it when you're paying top dollar.'

'Even so, a gust of wind, or a sudden change of position. One bottom must look much like another from fifty metres or so.'

Dalliance didn't rise to that one.

'I still don't really get why they did it that way, sir. I mean, it was surely pretty high-risk?'

'But it was also high-profile, Riley. An umbrella tip to the ankle in a crowded street is efficient but low-key. This has been front page news all week. It sends out a message: "Don't mess with us – or our money".'

'But it's as good as saying "we did it", isn't it sir?'

'Everybody knows who did it; it's a matter of proving it. Which happily now falls to our friend Inspector Smethick. Remember, they only got Capone for tax evasion; doesn't mean they didn't have a pretty good idea of how many people he'd killed.'

They walked on down the square. It really was a remarkably good wicket for a village club, Dalliance thought. He came to a halt at the spot where Roper had been killed, then looked down the ground towards the boundary by the sightscreen. 'Just come in from fine leg, Riley.'

Riley looked aghast.

'It's all right, I'm sure there aren't any paps in the undergrowth, and I'm not proposing any physical contact. But think about it – from down there on the boundary, he had quite a distance to make.'

Riley followed Dalliance's finger.

'He must have sprinted in. But that would have given him momentum. Come on in on that line,' Dalliance said, holding his arms up.

Riley reluctantly did as he was told.

'Yes, the angle's perfect. I've got my hands up here so my lower back is exposed. You come in...' Here he grabbed Riley's right arm and pulled it to his shirt. It was faintly sweaty, Riley noticed with distaste. 'You're last in – because you've run the furthest. But that means no one's taking much notice of you – and you're first out, and because you're a mere boy no one expects anything of you in the crisis of Ted's supposed heart attack. You're virtually invisible. As he was throughout the investigation. Everyone else had a motive, everyone in the team had something to gain from Ted's death.'

'But what was Daniel's motive, sir?' Riley asked, surreptitiously wiping his palm against his trouser leg.

'Revenge. A dish best served cold. But let's go over to the pavilion and I'll explain it all.' He'd taken a couple of steps when he stopped. 'Damn, I've forgotten that team photo again. Go back and fetch it would you?'

As Riley turned on his heel and began to pace back towards the car, Dalliance went and stood where Ted Roper had been when he caught the catch that would sign his death warrant. He half crouched, imagining a fired-up Jez coming down the hill; then the flash of the bat; then the split-second of panic as the ball powered its way towards him, and then the wild elation of realising he'd caught it.

He retraced the twenty paces or so Ted took to meet his death, imagining the adrenalin rush of triumph, the cries of congratulations, the success so hugely farcical, as the poet has it. And then the inexplicable stabbing pain and the almost immediate curtain of darkness.

Not a bad way to go if you've got to be murdered, he thought, noting that Riley was very sensibly driving round to the pavilion and heading off to meet him there.

Riley was waiting for him on the pavilion steps, the team photo in his hands.

'Thanks.' Dalliance took it and indicated the bench. When they were both sitting down looking out over the cricket ground, he began. 'So…why? What reason did young Daniel have for wanting to kill Ted Roper?'

Riley looked expectant. He really had no idea what the answer to that question was.

Dalliance stared out at the square and to the countryside beyond. Insects hummed, a couple of wood pigeons called to each other in the copse to their left. The sun was warm. The setting was as beautiful as it was peaceful. An idyll by the most exacting standards.

He cleared his throat behind an upraised hand and began to talk. 'Ian Pottinger met Hans Maars at Oxford where they were both pursuing their postgraduate studies. They had much in common. They were both biologists, both interested in reining in the effects of global warming and other assaults on the world's ecoytems.'

Dalliance gave another little cough – the legacy of his evening smoking Des Tucker's cigarettes, Riley assumed.

'The two men did what men do – met women they fell in love with, married them, and became fathers – to each a son, Daniel and Anthony. The two families were very close and the two boys were more or less brought up as brothers. The two families went on holidays together and basically formed a small, very tight-knit commune.

'But after several years of seeing each other virtually every day, the career paths of the two men diverged dramatically. Ian had become a marine biologist, Hans found himself drawn to the heart of the rainforest. After his divorce – amicable by all accounts – he decided that, rather than commute between Oxford and the Amazon, he would simply relocate. Ian was away a lot too, but could hardly relocate to a coral reef. These lengthy fieldtrips led to decisions about education which resulted in the two boys being sent first to prep school together, and then public school.

'Absences from the domestic hearth had other consequences, and that's where our story really begins. Mary Pottinger, as I'm sure you'd agree, is a good-looking woman. This fact did not escape a number of male admirers, and that group included – as you'll readily imagine – Ted Roper. Mary Pottinger, as you may also have noticed, has a weakness for the bottle, not a good habit for a woman keen to preserve her honour.

'Roper had been after her for a while – inviting her over to the big house, dropping by at the cottage – exerting what might be described as "heavy charm" in the hope – nay, expectation – that the cumulative pressure would lead to results.

'And so it did. The details are uncertain – all Des could – or would – say, was that he got a late call from Ted and found himself helping a very drunk and distressed Mary Pottinger into – and out of – his taxi in the small hours. Whether Ted had overcome her resistance by force or let the drink do his seducing for him remains unclear, but however it was achieved, he did it. And, when the dreadful truth dawned, Mary was understandably distraught.'

'She could have pressed charges,' Riley said. 'If the woman's too drunk to give consent—'

'I know, Riley, I know. But think that through. It might have damaged Ted, but it would have sunk her. And in a way it did. Because somehow, somewhere along the line, someone got wind of it. Not – thankfully – a natural gossip; but someone dedicated to achieving her own aims, and less than scrupulous as to how she did it.'

'Jenny Henderson? But how did she—?'

'I don't know, Riley. And nor does Des. He swears he never told a soul, and given his complicity in an incident that was shameful at best, and criminal at worst, it certainly wasn't in his interests for anyone to know. But somehow, that Henderson woman got to find out. I suspect Ted may have boasted of his conquest, even as he was rejecting her advances. Anyway, however it happened, she knew.'

'She may be poisonous,' Riley said, 'but surely she wouldn't tell Daniel?'

'No, of course not. But she told his father.'

'What? How do you know that?'

'I don't. Not for sure. But here's my theory: rebuffed by Ted, she went looking for another liaison. Ian Pottinger was a handsome man and, when he came home from his coral reef, must have looked amazing – tanned, well-toned. And he was heroically trying to save the planet into the bargain. A much better catch than Ted all round. The only problem for our Mrs Henderson was that he was utterly devoted to his wife.'

Riley looked at him as the terrible truth dawned. 'So when he rejected her, Jenny told him about Mary – out of spite?'

'It's not an edifying story,' Dalliance said softly.

'And somehow Daniel got wind of it—?'

'Overheard a row between his parents when he was back from school is my guess. Enough to put two and two together and come up with a very clear picture of his own.'

There was a long pause. Riley looked over his shoulder into the home dressing room. To think that a kid should murder a man for what he'd done to his mother – a man of power and standing in the community – and get away with it undetected for so long.

'Yes,' said Dalliance, as though reading his thought. 'It's quite a thing. And if he's lucky with his flights, he'll have got away with it.'

Riley slowly shook his head. 'How much of this did you get from his mother?'

'Ian wanted to go round to confront Roper, but Mary persuaded him that a public row would be disastrous. Her main concern, apart from saving her marriage, was of course protecting Daniel. As Ian's return home had been designed to coincide with the school holidays, this made for a dreadful summer. She doesn't know when Daniel overheard them rowing. They tried to be discreet, but things suddenly blow up, however hard you try to guard against it. She said it was a gruesome six weeks and it was a relief when Ian had to go back to his research. Daniel went back to school and after the worse period of her adult life Mary could wind down and get back to normal. She thought she'd got away with it. Six weeks later, Ian was dead.'

'And was it suicide?'

'Unproven,' Dalliance said. 'It could have been an accident. An atoll in the middle of the Pacific is not the best place to get a definitive answer. But whether he was swept off a rock by a freak wave or decided to end it himself, there was enough in his letters to show that he was very depressed. Either way, Mary felt it was her fault. And the impact on Daniel was equally devastating.'

'Poor kid.'

'I thought you didn't like him?'

'I don't, but I can still sympathise with him. And with what he knew about his mum and Ted Roper...'

'That probably explains the reason he stayed on as a boarder. He didn't want to live with his mother, with that knowledge hanging in the air. He preferred being at school with his best friend Anthony.'

'And you think Anthony was in on it?'

'Undoubtedly. Couldn't have done it without him.'

Dalliance paused. Looking out, unseeing, over the cricket field, he went on.

'It probably just started as a fantasy between the two of them – the sort of thing boys can get engrossed in. How to take revenge on Roper – without getting caught. Which obviously excluded guns, or knives, or the traditional blunt instrument. All too risky. Daniel didn't want to ruin his life at the outset. But he did want to avenge his dad. It was a challenge. Remember, these are bright boys who pride themselves on their cleverness, and they had a lot of time on their hands together.'

Riley nodded, imagining the two boys in their study, batting ideas to and fro. It must have kept them going for months, even if neither thought for a moment they'd actually do anything.

Dalliance went on. 'Time passes. Nothing much happens. And then, after a visit to his father's lab in the heart of the Amazon, Anthony comes back and plants a phial on Daniel's desk. "What's that?" Daniel asks. "What you've been looking for," replies Anthony.'

'And what was it?'

'An incredibly powerful poison Anthony's father's team had got from a recently discovered tribe. They'd been using it as a small-scale nuclear weapon for generations. But it was new to Western science. Which is why the tox report took so long in coming – and was so vague when it did.'

Riley gave a low whistle. 'So this boy stole some from his dad's lab and smuggled it back to school.'

'I know. Doesn't say much about airport security, does it?'

'Or for the security in the lab. How did you find out about it, sir?'

'As part of my research into Anthony. I went onto the website of the foundation his father works for and had a root around. Obviously they didn't declare that they were stockpiling supplies of one of the rarest and most toxic poisons on the planet, but reference to a particular species of toad suggested a line of enquiry. I simply emailed saying had they had any of the stuff go missing recently; they had – six months back.'

'And no one suspected Anthony?'

'Of course not. Why would a teenage boy steal the stuff? Unless he wanted to help his best friend bump off the philanderer indirectly responsible for the death of his father.'

'They still had a long way to go to get it into Ted's bloodstream.'

'I'm sure the idea of the cricket match came much later, once they'd lit on the delivery system. But at least with the nuclear warhead in their possession they had the means of turning the fantasy into reality. You're going off him again, I can see.'

'Cold-blooded little bastard. Why couldn't he have just chosen his moment and – I mean, Roper wouldn't have been suspicious of him.'

'No, he wouldn't – and yes, Daniel could have got him to himself. But then the chances are that someone would have known about that meeting. Whatever people think of us, Riley, they know we're thorough. Anyway, remember these lads think they're very clever. I'm sure part of the plot was to make everybody else, especially us, look very stupid. What could be more spectacular than murdering Ted in full public view – and getting away with it?'

'But how did they come up with the idea in the first place?'

'That came when they stumbled on the means of delivery.'

'And how did they do that?'

'Anthony broke his leg playing rugby – just to confirm your prejudices. When I went to visit the hospital he was treated in, I was surprised to find a supply of cannulae in cellophane sheaths just sticking out of a holder on the wall next to every bed in the ward. There it was, staring me in the face: a nice, long, flexible tube, designed solely for the delivery of liquids into the human bloodstream. The boys just had to help themselves. It made me think of something Daniel said right at the very beginning – the subject he liked most at school was design. They must have had a lot of fun with it.'

'I still don't see how he could have done it without any-one noticing.'

'Part of the answer has been staring us in the face all along.' Dalliance laid the team photograph on his knee. 'You were on the right lines with Jez's wristbands, but when they proved a red herring we lost track of your original insight – because we were chasing non-existent shooters up trees. Look!'

Dalliance pointed to Daniel, standing at the extreme edge on the back row, a year younger, neatly turned out.

'Sleeves, Riley – sleeves.'

Riley nodded slowly. 'But wasn't he wearing a short-sleeve shirt on Sunday, sir?'

'He was, and I noticed – but I didn't make anything of it. He should, of course, have come exactly as he had the week before but he just couldn't bring himself to do it. Anymore than he could resist disposing of the needle in Cowper's second pair of wicketkeeping gloves – and now I know how toxic that stuff is, we're very lucky we didn't have another fatality. That was what made me think that, although our killer was clever, he was in danger of over-elaborating.'

'So,' Riley persisted, 'he comes to the match—'

'Changed, yes, so that he doesn't have to undress in a very small room with a lot of very large men. I took the same line myself. Obviously the cannula tube is taped to his arm, and then there's another attachment which he has in his pocket and can slip on unnoticed while he's on his own down at fine leg. He must have put it on every over – he wouldn't have had time to fit it in the heat of the moment. He and Anthony practise and practise. He can practically do it in his sleep. He has to be pretty adept at it because any mistake could cost him his life.'

'There must have been some sort of cap or nozzle over the needle?'

'Which he pulls off as he runs in, pocketing it so there's nothing for SOCO to find on the outfield. He does the deed in the huddle, then stands by and lets Barney hog centre-stage. And the beauty of it is that it's a medical emergency to begin with – not a murder scene. He's free to drift away – perhaps he lost his cap as he ran in – or left his jumper down by the sightscreen. There'll have been a moment when he'd have been able to divest himself of the delivery system. We know what he did with the needle – stuck it in Cowper's gloves – and I've a horrible suspicion that I gave him permission to take the cannula back to school with him.'

'How do you mean, sir?'

'He wanted his box for a house match – it's a sensitive bit of equipment – not the sort of thing you want to borrow off your mates. Anyway, there it was in its jockstrap. I bet it had the cannula coiled up inside. And I let him take it away from the crime scene.'

Riley looked at him. 'Well, you got there in the end, sir.'

'It's true, I did. But I haven't got my murderer.'

'I was wondering about that, sir. If you knew all that yesterday, why didn't you arrest him last night?'

'Because I'm an old softie, Riley. I was thinking of his mother, poor woman. Given the tsunami of sorrow that was coming her way, what harm could one last night with her boy do? But something made him windy – maybe just the fact that we gave him a lift back last night. Anyway, as I said, he had a plan B. His mother told me he had a generous allowance – bank account, savings account – and a debit card. He was an experienced traveller. Getting to Caracas on his own won't have phased him at all. He'll just have rung Des, sworn him to secrecy and off to Luton for his night flight.'

'And Anthony?'

'He'll be there first. He was meant to be staying with an aunt in London—'

'But?'

'I suspect we'll find he took an earlier flight. Don't look so shocked, Riley. I'm going to get enough grief from On High without you starting. I could hardly have moved on Anthony until I'd got Daniel under arrest. And I explained why I left it overnight.'

Dalliance rested his chin in his hands.

'You know, Riley, in a world where the very rich can have someone killed on a whim, with barely the slightest chance of having to answer for it in a court of law, it's not the worst thing if a bright – however arrogant and coldly calculating, I grant you – schoolboy gets away with an act of personal revenge, is it?'

'Gets off with murder?' Riley looked Dalliance in the eye. 'And does that principle apply to people taking the law into their own hands and beating up journalists, sir?'

'I don't think we have enough evidence to charge anybody – do you?'

'But we know who did it, sir, and if you'd pushed Phelps, you'd have got a confession that would have stood up in court.'

'It might have done, but then a sharp brief might make it look as though I were harassing him, putting words in his mouth, trying to use his past to bully him into a false confession.'

'So Barney's another one who's just going to get away scot-free?'

'Barney is a brave, if brutal man with his heart in the right place. If we hadn't stopped him, he'd have met his death in that barley field trying to catch the killer of a teammate. I respect that. I do not respect his taking up arms on behalf of another teammate's fiancée snapped by the gutter press; nor do I approve of his forcing Phelps to act as his accomplice.'

'Why did he do that?'

'He needed someone to help him – there had to be two people to bag Peterson up. He'd got all the usual suspects establishing their alibis in various drinking holes. I thought Ben Cowper a strong candidate until you told me Peterson said neither of his assailants smelt. Say what you like about Cowper, personal hygiene is not something you can accuse him of. And besides, there are his cows, his girlfriend, his mother. And of course David Henderson and Daniel were non-starters for obvious reasons. Which left Ernie as the best candidate, and the one he had a hold over.'

'Did Ernie really think Barney would leak his story if he didn't go along with it?'

'Almost certainly not. But that might not have been Barney's line. He probably suggested that Peterson might start digging a little deeper, and of course if he got hold of the "Paedo Express"... And he probably wasn't very explicit about how far he was going to go with Peterson either.'

A silence fell. Both men gazed ahead of them over the deserted cricket field. A distant bird sang.

'Peace restored,' Dalliance murmured.

'Two murders and one GBH and we've let all the perpetrators escape?' Riley countered.

'As I said, Riley, I must be getting soft in my old age. Not, I hasten to add, that that's the line I'll be taking this afternoon when I'm called in to explain myself. But perhaps they'll come to that conclusion anyway. Maybe it's time I retired. Meanwhile, it's lunchtime.'

'The Three Horseshoes?'

'I don't think so, Riley. Nor the Poachers. If I'm going to be hauled over the coals this afternoon, it's probably better I don't smell of beer. Just take me back to the canteen.'

Putting the team photograph on the bench beside him, Dalliance got up and led the way back to the car. He had nearly reached it when he was stopped dead in his tracks.

'Inspector – what a pleasant surprise!'

Jenny Henderson was viewing them both from the other side of the boundary fence, against which her horse was rubbing its neck.

'I expect you're off to collar our elusive murderer – "a murderer and a villain" as our sweet prince put it. Is all going to be revealed soon? I do hope so.'

'By the six o clock news at the latest,' Dalliance said.

'How exciting! Do tell me it's David. What a dark horse that would make him.'

Dalliance shook his head. 'No, Mrs Henderson, it's not David.' He paused. Riley assumed he would leave it there, but instead he approached the fence. 'But the House of Henderson is not entirely without involvement.'

'Really, Inspector? How intriguing. Do, please, tell.'

'Do you know the expression "loose words cost lives"?'

'Everyone knows that, Inspector.'

'Yes, but it's surprising how many people fail to remember it.'

'Inspector, this is becoming more and more mysterious.'

'This is not a game, Mrs Henderson. It is deadly serious.'

Riley could see a shadow of anxiety cross the woman's features.

'What can you possibly mean, Inspector? It's almost as though you were accusing me of something.'

'I am. Or at least trying to establish the role – the devastating role – you played in a tragic train of events.'

Mrs Henderson drew herself up in her saddle to her full height. 'I really don't know what you're talking about.'

'Is it not the case that you told Ian Pottinger what had happened between his wife and Ted Roper?'

Riley watched as the haughtiness drained out of Mrs Henderson's face.

'Well? Did you or didn't you?'

'I—'

For a moment Riley thought she was going to come clean. But then her features hardened.

'You can't prove that, Chief Inspector.'

'I can choose whom to believe.'

Jenny Henderson played with the reins and looked as though she were about to turn her horse's head and ride off. Then suddenly she leant forward and in a low but venomous voice hissed, 'You come here, prying into our lives, forking over the past, trying to trap people into incriminating themselves – judging us. Well, I hope it gives you satisfaction, because from where I'm sitting it looks a lot like bullying. Sadistic bullying.'

'You're perfectly entitled to your view, Mrs Henderson. I was simply trying to prepare you. You see, it is my conviction that you played a vital part – in the sequence of events that led to the deaths both of Ian Pottinger and Ted Roper.'

Jenny Henderson's face froze into a mask of loathing, but she said nothing.

Dalliance went on. 'If, as I believe, you did tell Ian Pottinger about the encounter – the sexual encounter – between Ted Roper and Mrs Pottinger – the knock-on effects were ruinous. It seems that it destroyed their previously happy marriage and that Mr Pottinger subsequently committed suicide.'

'It was an accident. Everyone said it was an accident. He was washed off a rock. I was at the memorial service. That's what the vicar said.'

'It is a vicar's job to give comfort. Just as it is my job to find the truth, Mrs Henderson.'

Riley looked up at the woman on the horse. The façade of disdainful indifference was showing cracks.

'Even if that is true, I can't see how it's in any way connected to Ted's murder. You're not suggesting...'

'That Mrs Pottinger was in any way involved? No, I'm not. But there is a third member of the family, isn't there?'

There was a long pause. Jenny Henderson's mouth opened, but no words came.

'Yes,' Dalliance said quietly. 'Daniel. If he overheard a row between his parents and learned the awful truth that you threw in his father's face when the man rejected your advances...'

Jenny Henderson rallied. 'But you can't prove anything. I mean, I can't be held responsible, can I?' She looked down defiantly at the Inspector, her fingers playing impatiently with the reins.

'There will be no charges, Mrs Henderson,' Dalliance said. 'But we each have our own conscience to answer to, don't we?'

Riley noticed a strange look forming on her face. Then, with what appeared to be the glimmer of a smile, she murmured, 'No more, O Hamlet, thou hast cleft my heart in twain.'

Dalliance looked straight back at her before replying, equally quietly. 'Then throw away the worser part of it, and live the purer with the other half.'

With that, he turned and walked towards the car.

Jenny Henderson sat stiffly in her saddle, watching him go, then pulled on the reins and trotted smartly off along the bridlepath, away from the cricket ground.

'So some justice done?' Dalliance said as Riley joined him in the car, before adding, more to himself than to his sergeant, 'My old tutor always said what makes Hamlet so great is its almost universal application. If I'd remembered that at the beginning, the case wouldn't have taken nearly so long to solve.'

Riley waited to see if there was any more. But Dalliance was silent, looking for the last time out over the cricket field and to the ripening fields beyond.

Epilogue

Several months later, on the warm, clean sands of Posto 9, Ipanema Beach, two lithe, tanned young men lay side by side, their well-oiled backs glistening in the morning sun.

Their heads were nearly touching as they peered down at a smart phone, watching a YouTube clip entitled 'Keystone Cops Catch Their Man'. It showed three grown men, two dressed in white, seemingly engaged in a three-way brawl.

They were evidently finding the video hilariously funny, and played it several times over. After a while they switched it off and turned around to sit facing the sea.

'However many times I see it, it never gets old,' said one, casually inspecting the scantily clad bodies stretched out across the surrounding sand. 'Who said policemen didn't have a sense of humour?'

'Bumbling incompetents from start to finish,' remarked the other with a sneer.

'That's not fair, Ant. Dalliance did work it out – in the end.'

'He certainly paid for it,' Anthony said. 'The press crucified him.'

'Well, I can't help that, can I? Come on, let's have some fun.'

They grinned at each other. 'Operation Bodyline?'

Daniel pulled a tennis ball and a child's bat out of their rucksack and watched his friend pacing out a short wicket.

'Play!' Anthony shouted, and lobbed a gentle full toss. Daniel despatched it briskly in the direction of square leg, and stood admiring its parabola.

Just as he'd intended, the ball fell with a sandy explosion in the midst of a group of local girls sunbathing in their bikinis. One of them picked it up and turned around to see where it had come from. Daniel waved and started trotting down the beach towards her.

She looked amazing.

Where would we be without cricket? he thought, allowing his mouth to stretch into what he trusted would be an irresistibly winning smile.

THE END

More quality fiction from
Nine Elms Books

www.bene-factum.co.uk/fiction

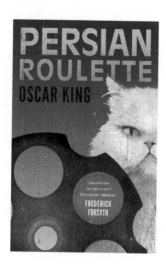

PERSIAN ROULETTE

Oscar King

Nine Elms Books 2015
Paperback and e-book
ISBN: 978-1-910533-00-0
£7.99

The first Harry Linley adventure

In the midst the world's faltering recovery from the economic crisis, listless financier and ex-special forces officer Harry Linley accepts the seemingly innocent task of spending a week cat-sitting for a friend. By the end of the third night, however, two men are dead on the kitchen floor.

A handful of disparate international strangers find themselves subsequently entangled in a web of deceit, sex and murder amongst the glittering towers of Dubai, with a seemingly unstoppable chain of miscommunication threatening to bring them and the world to ruin.

And at the heart of all this chaos – a beautiful, white Persian cat. This hilarious, mile-a-minute thriller provides a sharp-eyed satire of our globalised world, in which those who shout loudest, shoot fastest and spend most always try to come out on top.

THE UNROUND CIRCLE

Pete Bellotte

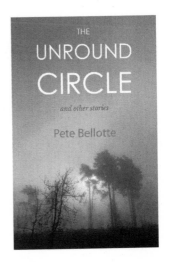

Nine Elms Books 2015
Paperback and e-book
ISBN: 978-1-910533-09-3
£9.99

Just because I made it up, doesn't mean it isn't true.

Master of the written word Pete Bellotte presents twenty-two short stories exploring the limitless range of behaviour that people are capable of.

Amusing, perplexing, dark-minded, or even hilarious, the characters inhabiting this universe have just one thing in common: a determination to challenge expectations and upset the norm. You'll never see them coming.

In their own way, all of them – liars and murderers, heroes and romantics – fight back against the forces, right or wrong, that work against them. They defy convention... Break the bonds... Unround the circle.